FROM PANIC TO PASSION

PLEDGED TO PROTECT SERIES
BOOK 1

VELLA DAY

Erotic Reads Publishing

From Panic to Passion

Pledged to Protect Series

Book 1

Copyright © 2018 by Vella Day

www.velladay.com

velladayauthor@gmail.com

ABOUT THE BOOK

The only thing that separates life from death is trust.

Attorney Susan Chapman thought being a prosecuting attorney was tough. Boy had she'd been wrong. When someone starts killing the jurors in the Caravello trial she'd prosecuted, she believes she'll be next. Sure, it's wonderful the FBI has assigned her a super-hot body-guard, but when she finds how he's connected to the Caravello family, she now fears he's trying to kill her.

When FBI agent Jake Yarnell is asked to protect a woman whose best friend was killed in a bomb meant for her, he's frustrated that the feisty and sexy attorney distrusts him more than the killer. So what is he supposed to do? Answer: keep protecting her until she believes him. Too bad that's easier said than done when at every turn another juror dies and the killers keep finding out where they are located.

CHAPTER ONE

A prickling sensation on the back of Susan Chapman's neck told her that if she answered her front door, her life would change forever.

The doorbell rang again followed by a knock. "It's me, Anne-Marie," her best friend called.

Susan let out a breath. She rushed to pull open the door. Her friend was all bundled up in her pretty pink scarf and wool jacket, looking very cute and professional. "Hey," Susan said with a smile, wondering what Anne-Marie was doing at her door early on a Monday morning.

Her friend's smile evaporated. "You forgot, didn't you?"

Susan stilled. Crap. What had she forgotten? Prosecuting another lowlife had taken over her life for the last few weeks, probably destroying the last of her brain cells. "I'm sorry."

Anne-Marie stepped inside the house, leaned over and planted a kiss on her cheek. "No problem." She stood back and reissued a smile. "I can still borrow your car, right? I really need the Mercedes to impress my mega-big client. He just flew into DC from Los Angeles last night. My rusted out bucket of shit won't cut it."

Ah, yes. The car. She'd promised Anne-Marie she could use it. Duh. A promise was a promise. "Sure."

Anne-Marie dangled her keys and dropped them into Susan's palm. "Enjoy my clunker."

Susan peered over her friend's shoulder to catch a look at her new ride, hoping it wasn't the 2002 SUV. Yup. It was. "I won't break down in the middle of the Beltway will I?"

"Car runs just fine. She just looks bad. I'll let you know how the showing works out."

From the bowl on the table, Susan picked up the keys to her brand new Mercedes and handed them to her. "Here ya go. Just be careful with her."

"I promise." Anne-Marie gave her another hug. "Wish me luck."

"Good luck and drive safely."

"Always do." Her friend blew air kisses. "I love you, sweetie."

"Love you too."

Anne-Marie dashed off toward Susan's prized possession. Before the cold January air sucked all the heat out of the house, she closed the door and had to chuckle. Anne-Marie and her clients. Maybe the car would get her that coveted sale she always talked about.

Susan went into the living room and peered out to make sure her friend didn't have any trouble starting the car in the freezing temperature.

Her friend waved and leaned forward to start the engine. A second later, a loud boom rocked her as a huge ball of fire engulfed the car. Disbelief, panic, and fear squeezed the breath from Susan's lungs, as pieces of metal and glass erupted in the air, imploding her living room window. The incredible force blew her off her feet, and shards of glass cut her arms, her face, and her chest.

A scream ripped from her throat as her head hit the living room's hardwood floor. Then her vision faded to black.

***

"Can you hear me?" The man's deep, rich voice reached deep into her mind and soothed her turbulent thoughts.

Susan could hear him, but her mouth couldn't form a response.

A rough palm covered her hand. "Can you move a finger for me?"

Oh, God. Was that Daddy? He used to hold her hand when she was little, his touch warm, comforting, and so caring. This couldn't be him, though. He'd died two years ago. Or had he come to take her to heaven?

"Mrs. Chapman?"

No, not Daddy. And it was Ms. Chapman now.

What was happening? She blinked. Or at least she thought she had. Why couldn't she see? Panic sizzled up her spine.

What had he asked? To move a finger? Anyone could move a finger. She struggled to lift her pinky, but it refused to budge.

The person nudged her arm gently at first, and then a bit harder. She strained to move her lips, wiggle her tongue, twitch a knee, a foot, a toe—anything. Liquid dripped down the back of her throat, nearly choking her.

"Wake up."

She was awake, wasn't she?

Where was she? In her house? In a hospital?

She must be on drugs. Her inability to move and wake fully was out of her control. Her heart raced, and as much as she wanted to move, she'd have to wait for nature to take its course. She forced her mind to let go of her fears, and her body relaxed.

The next time she became coherent, she succeeded in cracking open her right lid. The picture on the ceiling mounted television flickered above her, the glare stabbing her eye. She could see!

Susan searched the room and glanced toward a darkened window. The strong odor of hospital disinfectant permeated her nostrils, indicating she was in a hospital. The first thing Susan did was wiggle her toes and her fingers. Yes! Air rushed from her lungs at her success. Mouth drier than a sand trap, she swallowed, and then cleared her throat.

"You're awake."

She turned toward the voice. A wave of pain squeezed her chest, rose up, and pounded against her skull. She blinked to clear her vision. Chocolate brown eyes hovered above her. The rest of the man's face and body went in and out of focus, but his warm eyes held her captive.

She licked her lips.

The tall stranger, whose broad shoulders strained against his gray t-shirt, held out a cup of ice chips.

When she raised her arm to take it, a searing pain stabbed her chest. "Th-thank you." Her voice sounded raspy, but she was thrilled she could finally speak.

A whirring noise below her bed startled her, and slowly her back elevated.

He tilted the cup to her lips. "Nice and slow."

He smiled, and she nearly forgot to suck one out.

The cool ice melted against her parched throat. "What happened?"

His smile disappeared. "You don't remember what the doctor told you?"

She'd talked to a doctor? She didn't remember. "No."

"Your car exploded and the flying debris cut you."

She hoped she had imagined the merciless flames bursting from the car window, the glass spewing in every direction, and the unforgettable stench of gasoline and burnt rubber. But apparently not. "Anne-Marie is dead, isn't she?"

Her stomach threatened to revolt as a tear trickled down her cheek. They'd been best friends since second grade.

His gaze dropped. "I'm sorry."

She zeroed in on the gun snuggled in the stranger's shoulder holster, and her heart squeezed tight as she shoved down her panic. "Who are you? Are you with the DC police?"

"I introduced myself after the doctor came in."

Why had her memory failed her now? Her ability to recall even the smallest details about a case set her apart for most other attorneys. "I'm sorry, but I don't remember."

He put the cup back on the side table and dragged the chair closer to her bed. "I'm Special Agent Jake Yarnell. FBI."

"FBI?" Her breath lodged in her throat.

"Yes, ma'am."

"Why are you here?" In her heart she knew, but her mind wasn't ready to accept the reality.

Agent Yarnell sat on the padded chair and leaned forward, his wrists dangling over his knees. "Tell me what you do remember."

Not wanting to relive the horrific event, she turned her head away from him.

"Do you have any idea who would want to harm you?" he asked in the softest voice.

So it was true. Whoever had planted the bomb had intended for her to die—not dear Anne-Marie. Bile raced up her throat and tinged her mouth as her head throbbed. "Every felon I've put behind bars for the last seven years could have wanted to see me dead."

"Does the name John Caravello mean anything to you?"

The name Caravello jolted her from her self-pity. She bolted upright and regretted the quick move. "Yes."

"He was executed three weeks ago."

After sitting on death row for six long years. "I know, and I'm sure the FBI knows I know. I was the prosecuting attorney for the case." She lay back down.

"I wanted to be sure you remembered."

"I understand." He probably wondered if she knew her name.

"You had some brain trauma as a result of the blast, and your memory could have been affected. In fact, the doctors had to induce a coma to let your brain heal."

"A coma?" Dear Lord. Her injuries had been life threatening. Her muscles tensed as her stomach churned. "How long was I out?" She retested her memory regarding her recent cases, the names of her coworkers, the date she paid her mortgage. All seemed in order, unlike moments before.

"Almost two weeks."

The life drained from her. Maybe she had another disability. "Will I be okay?"

"Let me get the doctor. He can tell you."

He jumped up from the chair and raced out of the room, before she could question him further. Was her prognosis so horrible he didn't want to be the bearer of bad news?

Two minutes later, a short, bald man strode in, along with a nurse dressed in teddy bear scrubs. Jake remained standing by the door.

"I'm Doctor Dalton." He didn't smile, but his voice sounded kind.

Agent Yarnell must have relayed her inability to recall his previous visit. She swallowed. "How badly was I injured?"

He stepped next to her bed. "You had a nasty contusion on the back of your head. Once the brain swelling receded, we removed the breathing tube, and here you are." Before she could ask any more questions, he leaned over and flashed a harsh light into her eyes. She blinked and he stood back. "You also received a large gash on your cheek, some glass cuts and small burns on your arms and a rather severe wound on your chest where a piece of glass impaled you. You should be able to be released in a few days." He adjusted his glasses and scribbled something on her chart. "Other than needing some time to heal, you'll make a full recovery."

The doctor turned to Jake. "Don't ask too many questions. She needs to rest."

The agent nodded.

She let out a breath and another tsunami-sized pain tore up her body. Her arms were on fire, and her chest rebelled every time she took a deep breath.

"Everything hurts." She could barely concentrate with her body on fire.

The doctor said something to the nurse. The lady in the brown and green scrubs scanned Susan's wrist band, pushed the touch pads on the IV and did something on a computer. "This should help. You'll feel better shortly."

"Thank you." If only they had medication to help heal the loss of her best friend she might start to heal.

Once the doctor and nurse left, Susan turned back to the agent. She needed to find out who'd killed Anne-Marie more than she needed to rest. Who wanted her dead? "Do you think there's a connection between Caravello's execution and the car bomb?" She gritted her teeth, forcing away the reminder of the blast.

He sat on the chair and kept his gaze to the side. Lines formed around his mouth and eyes. "We're not sure who's to blame, but in the last few weeks, seven of the twelve jurors who helped convict him have turned up dead."

Oh, no! Her pulse skyrocketed. She squeezed her eyes shut, trying to picture those on the jury, and questions stumbled through her brain. The trial had been so many years ago. *"Dead? How?"*

"We didn't put the pieces together until recently. Several of the jurors had moved in the six years since the conviction."

The FBI must believe she was in imminent danger if he was here. "How long have you been at the hospital?"

"About four days. Ever since we realized your life was in danger too."

Goose bumps slid up her spine. Her gaze shot to the door almost expecting the assassin to rush in. "Have my mother or brother been by to see me?" If she didn't remember the doctor coming in or the agent's name, maybe she wasn't awake when Mom and Craig stopped by.

"No." He dragged a hand down his jar.

"That's not possible." They'd be the first to visit.

His gaze shot over her head. "What's important is keeping you safe. The FBI would like to put you into a safe house."

Her heart nearly stopped. Being sequestered from her family might be worse than death. Her head began to throb. "I know the drill. If I stay in a safe house, I won't be able to see my family, take any photos of them, or bring any of my law books with me. My life as I know it will be gone." She locked her gaze with his. "That's unacceptable. My mother needs my help in caring for my brother. Craig's stuck in his wheelchair, which means I can't move away from here."

Every key witness she ever known who'd been placed in the program had suffered from loneliness, loss of control, and depression. Even after the criminals were behind bars, their lives were never the same.

"Someone wants you dead."

"I can't think about that now." She didn't have the strength to deal with a killer, even though she needed to. She looked up at him. "What happens to the Caravello family? They murdered my best friend. Have you arrested anyone?"

Anne-Marie had been the most alive, energetic person she'd known. She didn't deserve to have her life ended so abruptly.

"We don't have absolute proof the family is involved. It's speculation." He looked toward the door, and then the floor.

She wadded the edge of the sheet in her hand. "Yeah, right. We both know that's not true. After Caravello was sentenced, he warned me I'd pay for convicting him. So don't tell me about idle speculation."

"All the more reason to move you."

Could she give up the life she loved? Not easily, but if meant she'd stay alive long enough to see the bastard executed, then yes she could. Not to mention her mother and brother would be in jeopardy if she didn't hide. "Fine, I'll do it your way, but I want to talk to my mom first."

His jaw clenched. "You can't contact her until the killer is caught."

"Like hell." She of all people knew the justice process could be terminally slow.

"For your mother and brother's protection, we informed them you had also died in the explosion."

"You what?" Susan choked on her saliva. Coughing sent her chest into spasms, and pain shredded her body. "You don't understand."

Emotion flicked across his face. "You think I don't know how upset your family is that you're dead? Trust me, I do. I had a brother once."

Sympathy swamped her, but their situations were surely different. "My mom's first defense for anything that upsets her is to drink and take medication to help her forget. She's attempted suicide once before. I couldn't live if I lost her."

He pulled his lips in a thin line. "It's for the best."

Bastard. If he believed he could keep her from her family, he was dead wrong.

***

Jake Yarnell waved a hand toward the new two-story brick safe house as he pulled into the drive and mentally thanked the man in charge of placement. The new housing development was surrounded by horse farms and tree-shaded streets. Not that he'd be there long. As soon as an agency-approved Florida doctor gave her permission to drive, the Bureau would send him back to D.C. With her determination, he'd be gone by the end of the week.

"So how do you like this place?"

Despite sleeping for much of the trip, dark rings shadowed her eyes. If misery had a face, it would be hers.

Susan leaned her head back against the car seat and closed her eyes. "Why did we have to drive all the way to Florida? I don't want to sound ungrateful but couldn't you have found a place in say, North Carolina?"

"I wish we could have placed you some place closer, but we figured the farther you are from Washington, the safer you'll be."

"Did I need to come here because someone broke into my office two days ago?"

"In part."

He'd been in the business long enough to know unless they caught the killer first, the man wouldn't stop until she was dead.

"Agent Yarnell?"

He wished she didn't snarl his name. "Jake. Please. Until this case is solved, we can't have neighbors hear you call me *agent*. It raises questions."

"Jake, then."

Most of the people he'd protected treated him with awe, but not Susan Chapman. Her life had all but collapsed around her, and she must have decided to take out her frustrations on him. He mentally shrugged. It was part of the job.

He cut the engine, slid out, and removed the luggage from the trunk. He followed her up the brick walkway and unlocked the front door. "The sooner you're settled, the less suspicion we'll bring to our doorstep."

She planted herself in front of him and blocked the entrance. "I think I can manage on my own. You don't need to stay."

He raised an eyebrow at her sudden independence. "You know the rules. I don't leave until the doctor clears you." Her injured hand would make doing simple chores like cooking and dressing difficult.

"Do you always follow the rules?"

"I try to." At least when it suited him.

She held his gaze for a moment, rolled her eyes, and then stepped inside. She stopped in the foyer and surveyed the open kitchen and living room. When she stepped into the kitchen and ran her uninjured hand on the shiny granite counter top, her shoulders relaxed. The upscale place seemed to meet with her approval. Good. One less hurdle to jump.

He set down the luggage in the foyer. Jake liked how the sunlight streamed in through the living room window. The large stuffed chairs across from the leather sofa looked comfortable enough to hunker down on and watch sports on the large TV.

She ambled over to the living room and studied the artwork on the wall before turning around. "I understand we didn't fly here because someone could have hacked into the passenger manifest, and I totally get that I can't call my mom because the phone lines aren't secure, but what's wrong with me sending a letter to one of my friends in Ohio to forward to my mother? She needs to know I'm alive." She closed the space between them and looked up at him, her palms held open. "Surely, the FBI doesn't suspect the U.S. Postal service of being corrupt."

He wanted to give in to her to ease her suffering and to see her smile, but regulations prevented him from taking the chance. "As I mentioned before—"

She stepped back and dropped her gaze to the ground. "I know, I know. If my mother knows I'm alive, the person responsible for these deaths might harm her and my brother. Not to mention put one of my friends in danger too."

He was relieved not to have to argue with her. "You nailed it."

Susan shuffled back to the brown leather sofa and plopped down. She grabbed the blue sofa pillow to her chest and drew her knees close. He wanted to tell her things would get better, but the right words wouldn't form.

She looked over at him. "You said the FBI would open a bank account for me since they froze my assets. When will you do that?"

This question was easy to answer. "How does tomorrow sound?"

"Good, I guess."

She still hadn't grasped the magnitude of how events would unfold. "Don't worry about the details. I'll take care of everything. Your hardest job is to remember you are no longer Susan Chapman. She's dead. You are now—"

"I know. Taylor Daniels; a woman without a family, without money, without a job."

Her dejected tone cut him. He knew all about growing up without a family, but now wasn't the time to swap sad stories with her. "It comes with wanting to stay alive."

The usual platitude left a bitter taste in his mouth despite the statement's truth. Having to rip people out of their lives headed his *This-Sucks* list, yet he continued to do it time and again because in the end, it helped keep people safe.

Jake moved over to the comfy looking beige chair opposite the sofa and sat, watching the lines tighten around her eyes. She reminded him of his grandmother's last days. If he could soften the tension rippling up Susan's face, he would. He admired her reputation as a tough prosecutor, but in this new place, she was fragile, so different from the she-wolf he'd expected.

She raised a bandaged arm, immediately squeezed her eyes shut, and lowered her hand to her lap.

Poor woman. Soon she'd be alone, frightened, and unsure of what would happen to her. Susan's, or rather Taylor's life, would never be the same.

She rubbed her chest and winced. "If I can't practice law, what am I supposed to do for a living?"

"I don't think you'll be here that long. We'll get this guy soon. Don't worry." Another platitude he was sure wouldn't fool the savvy woman. He tossed her a confident smile. "Why not relax and try to heal for at least a week? Watch TV or read."

"I have to do something useful with my time, and reading or watching television won't help me regain my life."

"Maybe not."

To give her time to come to grips with creating a new life, he picked up a Tampa Bay magazine from the glass coffee table. The front cover photo was of the Bay and its seven-mile long sidewalk. He flipped though the glossy pages. When he glanced up at her, her eyes were closed, and her breath ragged.

His job was to protect, not soothe, but something inside him lured him into wanting to make her recovery easier. "You want something to drink?"

Her eyes flew open. "No." She swallowed hard as if she were trying to deal with the enormity of her situation. "But, thank you anyway."

He stood, and as soon as he poured a glass of water for himself, his cell rang. He glanced at the caller ID. His boss' name, Stanton Lowry, flashed on the screen. Not good. "Jake."

"We've had another incident," his boss said.

Jake steeled his body, willing his tired muscles to relax from the long drive. He walked over to the open bar, his back to her and lowered his voice. "Hit me."

"Janet Starkey was found murdered this morning. That makes eight jurors dead."

He slid onto one of the stools and shot a glance at Susan. She twisted toward him and pinned him with her probing blue stare.

He dragged a hand down his unshaven chin. "Wasn't she under protection?"

"Yup."

"Which means—"

"No one's safe anymore."

CHAPTER TWO

Jake stashed his phone in his hip pocket and trudged back to his chair. Susan waited for him to tell her about the call, but he stared off into space instead. The way he flexed his fists frightened her. "What was that about?"

"That was my boss." He chugged the rest of his water like a man who hadn't had a drink in months.

"And...?"

His jaw clenched. "Janet Starkey, another juror, who we just put in a safe house was murdered this morning."

A lump formed, and Susan had to swallow before she spoke. "Murdered?"

Every crime scene photo of mutilated bodies she'd shown in court passed across her mind. The victim's cold eyes and the ruthless manner of death etched a notch in her heart. Would she be next? The blood shot to her stomach and her hands shook.

"Mrs. Chapman?"

She forced her analytic and objective mind into action and answered him with a detached tone. "I remember Janet. She was a school teacher. Very sharp."

But Janet was so much more—a woman, a mother, and a caring citizen.

"This is bad. Richard Thomason moved her less than two days ago." Jake straightened. "There shouldn't have been any way to find her."

She pushed aside the fear festering in her belly. "How did she die?"

"Hit and run. Janet was crossing the street and a car came out of nowhere."

Susan's heart dropped to her stomach. "How horrible." She refused to think of herself as a possible victim and grabbed hold of her lawyer self. "Maybe it was a coincidence."

"I don't believe in them."

Neither did she. She needed more information, more facts. "What did the police findings show?" This woman's family and friends would be grieving as much as she was over Anne-Marie's unnecessary death.

"There were two witnesses who both said the man drove straight toward her. Not only did he..." He studied his steepled fingers, acting as if she were some wilting flower. "You really don't want to hear this."

"Tell me."

He clamped his jaw tight and caught her gaze for a long moment as if deciding how much information to spill. "The man hit her once, backed up, and then ran over her again."

The horror slammed into her. "Not a coincidence." Her voice trailed off.

"No."

Her heart pounded in her chest as she shot a glance at the front door and tightened her hold on the pillow. "So how did the Caravellos find her?"

"That's what I'd like to know."

She leaned back against the sofa and checked the clock. "Do we need to move again?" She hated how her voice wobbled. She prided herself on being strong.

Jake's shoulders relaxed. "Not yet. As long as I'm around, you should be safe."

She didn't like the *should be* part.

He jumped up and paced between the living room and the kitchen's open bar. "Let's look around and get you settled."

The avoidance tactic wouldn't work on her, but for now, she wouldn't argue. She needed a bath and a few hour's rest even more than she needed answers.

As she reached up to slip off her bulky, buttoned down sweater, her muscles rebelled and sent a searing pain across her chest. "Crap."

Jake was at her side in an instant. "Let me help you."

"I can do it."

She hated being helpless and relying on others. Her father had taught her the only person she could count on was herself.

He placed his glass on the coffee table. "You don't have to do everything alone, you know. Let me feel somewhat useful."

He'd given her an out. "Thanks."

She turned her back and let him ease the sleeves down her arms. At his tender touch, an involuntary tingle shimmied down her spine. "I can take it from here." She slowly stood and pasted on a smile, hoping the bandage across her cheek hid the heat in her face.

"Pick a room, and I'll bring up your suitcase."

One of the FBI female agents had purchased a few essentials for her. No telling what she'd chosen, but she hoped the clothing would be the easy-on-easy-off type.

Susan hiked up the wooden stairs to the second floor, stopping twice to catch her breath before she entered the first available room. It didn't matter what the rest of the townhouse had to offer; a bedroom was a bedroom. The muted brown and green décor gave off a spa-like atmosphere. Coordinated ocean watercolor pictures hung above the white wrought iron bed, and a set of candles sat atop a pine dresser, their vanilla scent alleviating the smell of fresh paint. To her surprise, there was an attached bath. The combined space was only half the size of her bedroom at home, but the plush carpet and nice accessories would help ease the tension squeezing her into this unwanted situation.

She hadn't stood under a hot shower since the explosion and couldn't wait to get clean, though she wasn't sure how she was going to wash her hair when every time she raised her arms her chest throbbed.

Jake put down her suitcase. "Need anything else?"

Someone to help me, care for me, and be there for me. "Just some quiet time."

"You got it."

Quicker than a blink, he disappeared, and her sense of security plummeted. Before she undressed, she locked the bedroom door and closed the drapes that opened to the wooded backyard.

She hadn't wanted to look at her injuries since the incident, but she couldn't avoid the inevitable any longer. After stepping into the bathroom, the reflection in the mirror startled her. Despite the hospital's attempt to clean her hair, the blonde strands hung in greasy clumps to her shoulders. A large bandage clung to her sunken cheek, and red marks that looked like a bad case of road rash covered her right side. She sucked in a breath. With trembling fingers, she peeled away the bandage.

A wide gouge created a line from her eye to her mouth. "Dear God."

She ran a finger along the raised, ugly welt—a scar that would take years to fade unless she had plastic surgery. Even then, her face would never be hers again.

The nurse told her she needed to change her bandages daily and that she could shower, but afterwards she'd have to keep her wounds covered until the doctor removed the stitches.

Fighting the tears, she removed the rest of the sterile pads and gauze. The many stitches over her breast hurt the worst. It was a miracle she'd survived the blast at all.

She turned on the water to let it get warm before stepping under the relaxing flow. The pulse of water stung her sensitive skin, yet soothed the ache and pushed aside the reality that someone wanted her dead.

Once she towel dried, she entered her bedroom and searched her suitcase for something suitable. Unable to hook her bra, she decided on a heavy shirt and sweatpants. If the situation hadn't been so serious, she would have laughed at her frumpy appearance. In D.C. she never went out without makeup, her hair uncombed, or in an outfit that didn't accentuate her curves. The bastard who blew up her car had stolen her desire to care.

Next she searched her luggage for the bandages the hospital had provided. She pawed through her clothes, twice, in fact, but came up empty-handed. Where were they? Maybe she'd imagined the nurse had given them to her. Whatever. That meant she'd have to go downstairs to see if Jake had seen the care package from the hospital.

As she reached the bottom step, Jake shut off the large screen TV, and his mouth spread into a slow smile. "You look a lot better."

The man was blind. She quickly covered the stitches on her left cheek. "I feel better, but I need to find my bandages. I can't go out in public looking like Frankenstein. I'll scare people." Okay, so some pride still resided in her bones. "The nurse said I needed to keep the wounds covered to avoid infection."

"You're anything but a monster. If you—" His cell rang and he held up a finger. He put the phone to his ear. "Yarnell."

***

"It's me. Peter."

Christ. Jake lowered his voice. "I gotta keep it short. We can't chance a trace."

Jake's gaze shot automatically to Susan. Peter Caravello was the last person he expected to call, especially given the circumstances.

"I'll be right back to help with the bandages," he told her as he headed outside. She didn't need to hear this conversation. Someone in the Caravello family had possibly attempted to murder her and killed her best friend instead.

"I need your help," Peter said. The roar of background traffic on the other end made it difficult to hear his friend's shaky voice.

Jake was about to say FBI agents didn't help people from families who kill young children, but then Jake reconsidered.

He sat on the stoop, hoping the crisp, clean Florida air would relax him. "Tell me what's going on."

"The fucking FBI, no offense to you, came to my house. Good thing I wasn't home. My housekeeper answered. They said they were looking for me. They even had a warrant to go through my things. They mentioned the name Janet Starkey."

"Shit." Jake unclenched his jaw. Sweat beaded on his forehead despite the cool February breeze. "Juror number eight."

"Who?"

"I'm sure you know seven of the twelve people on your father's jury were recently murdered. Janet was number eight."

"Oh, shit. Eight? Christ. They better not try to pin her murder on me—or any of the murders. You know I run a clean business. I'm not my father. You gotta help me."

A car slowed down in front of the townhouse, and Jake stiffened. A man stared hard at him before moving on. According to Richard Thomason, they were one of the first to stay in the newly built complex. As a precaution, he took note of the Georgia license plate number.

"I can make some phone calls, but that's all. I'm on protection detail. If the Bureau ever learns I even know you, I'd get canned."

"They won't hear it from me. Can you dig around to see what they have on me?" A car horn blasted in the background. "Look I have go. I think someone's tailing me. I need to lose 'em."

Before Jake had a chance to ask more questions, Peter disconnected.

The front door creaked opened behind him. He straightened, not needing Susan to see him with his head down. The last thing he wanted was for her to think he couldn't protect her.

"Who was that?"

"You don't want to know." He tossed what he hoped was a look of steely confidence.

***

The sun burned the cut on Susan's face, and she shielded her eyes. "Why don't you come inside and tell me." She hoped her voice came out soft and not demanding.

From the minute she'd opened her eyes in the hospital, she hadn't been kind to Jake. In fact, she couldn't remember if she'd even thanked him for driving all the way to Florida.

"In a minute."

She didn't like how his voice came out cold. "Is it about the case?"

He shrugged. "In a way."

Which meant the call had to do with her. She waited a beat for him to elaborate. Didn't he realize she stood the most to lose in this Caravello revenge scheme? Like her life? Guess she'd have to wait for an answer. She turned and ducked inside. He'd probably tell her in his own way, in his own time.

Unable to sit, she fixed a fragrant cup of Earl Gray tea and doused the steamy liquid with more sugar than necessary. Who'd called Jake? Had another juror died? Was he trying to figure out if they were in immediate danger?

The front door opened, and a strong cross breeze ruffled the magazine she'd been reading on the counter. Shoulders stiff, Jake strode in without glancing her way.

"Want some tea?" She held up her hot cup.

He jerked his head toward her. "A beer would be better."

While on duty? She was better off not bringing up the fact it was hours before dinner and that a drink never helped matters.

Other than large bandages, the FBI had thoroughly stocked the townhouse, but she doubted they'd provided them with alcohol. Just in case, she pulled open the fridge. What do you know? A six-pack of Budweiser sat on the shelf. Amazing. Either every safe house came equipped with something to drink or Jake was psychic.

She ripped a cold bottle from the carton and walked over to the living room. "Here."

"I'm sorry. I should be the one to wait on you." He twisted off the top and took a long draw.

Her stomach somersaulted. The blank look in his eyes sucked all semblance of patience from her. "Tell me what's wrong. My life is on the line here."

When he didn't answer, she grabbed the phone from his hand and pressed two buttons to display the caller's name before he snatched the phone away from her.

Stunned, her legs weakened, and she wobbled back to where she'd been reading. She couldn't believe who'd contacted him.

CHAPTER THREE

Susan's stomach churned as the ramification of the caller struck her. "That scum sucking son called *you*." Unbelievable.

Jake winced. "Yes, but it's not what you think. That's why I didn't want you to know."

She launched off the sofa and leaned forward, pointing an accusing finger at him. "Like you could possibly know what I'm thinking at this moment."

"Calm down."

"Easy for you to say. You get a call from a guy whose father was executed for murder, and I'm supposed to calm down? What if he's the one killing these jurors? What if he's the one trying to kill *me*?"

Her knees gave way again and she dropped back to the sofa, her rear hitting the edge of the seat. Jake jumped up, and she raised a hand. "Don't get near me."

He stopped and then returned to his seat. Jake stabbed a hand through his hair. "Peter is not like his father."

"Like I haven't heard that argument a hundred times before in court." She picked up the blue pillow again and drew the cushion to her chest. "And how do you know what he's like? Are you chummy with him?"

Jake shifted in his seat. "The Bureau is looking at Peter for the murder of Janet Starkey."

Her pulse pounded. Could this nightmare be almost over? She dropped the pillow to her lap. "I knew it!"

"It's possible the Fed's interest is based solely on his genetics."

"You can't really believe that."

Jake leaned forward and balanced his elbows on his knees. "It makes sense. His dad was executed. The Bureau must have concluded no one else would want revenge except for the family."

"Who else could it be if not Peter Caravello?"

"I don't know, but it's possible someone's framing him."

"I repeat. You have no idea how many times I've heard a criminal say that."

"I'm sure, but in this case, I believe someone might be after Peter."

"Because?" Let him wiggle out of this one.

"I need time to think."

"You don't have any facts. Why am I not surprised?" Susan inhaled a deep breath and forced herself to relax. "Why exactly did he call?"

"He wants me to help him."

Her mouth dropped open in disbelief. "A murderer is asking for FBI help?"

"Not the FBI. For *my* help. Like I said, he claims he's innocent." He glared at her. "Shouldn't a lawyer presume he's innocent until proven guilty? I know you've been through a lot, but don't forget the rules of the judicial system."

"I don't need a trial to know a Caravello killed my best friend." She fisted her hands against the cushion. "How long have you been in the judicial system? A week?"

His jaw clenched. "Ten years. I do know most people arrested are guilty but I believe Peter."

She stood, her legs stronger now. "Someone in his family killed Anne-Marie and eight jurors. And now you want to collude with him?"

He narrowed his eyes. "It's hardly collusion to ask a few questions. It's not like I'm leaving you here so I can go off and investigate." He stood too, probably just to be able to look down at her.

"If you help Peter Caravello, I'm sure your boss would consider your activity a conflict of interest." Her lawyer persona resurfaced, pumping her full of adrenaline.

This time he had the decency to lower his gaze. "I know."

She stepped toward him. "Does he even know you're friends with a Caravello?"

His eyes widened. "Hell no. Stanton wouldn't have assigned me to this case if he suspected."

She looked away and studied the photo above the fireplace of two pelicans fighting over a fish. It reminded her of them.

Susan faced him again. "Are you going to call your boss and tell him a Caravello made contact?" She'd believe Jake might be on the up and up if he did.

He glanced toward the ceiling before looking back at her. "No."

His shifting gaze sent alarms off in her head, eating away at the earlier trust she'd placed in him. Dear Lord. Was he going to help the piece of shit murderer escape the law? She rubbed her sweaty palms on her pants. "Then I am."

Susan raced to the wall phone, half surprised he didn't sprint after her. This might be her only opportunity to make contact with anyone. She pulled the receiver off the cradle and dialed 9-1-1.

Shit. The phone was dead. Everything else about the place worked. Why not the phone? She slammed the handset back in its holder.

"Phone doesn't work," Jake said with no remorse in his tone. "We can't do anything that would allow anyone to find us."

She swung around. "Funny. Peter Caravello found *you* pretty easily."

"He has my number." No apology—just a cold, hard statement.

"And now you're going to lead him right to me." Susan blew out a breath as fear drilled a hole in her temple.

She didn't know anything about Jake. He was almost too handsome in a rugged sort of way. She had a lot of experience dealing with criminals who looked good enough to con the habit off a nun.

He'd been assigned to her, but what if he was actually one of the killers? She walked slowly past him toward the stairs before turning back around. "You give your number to all the criminals?" Catty, yes, but she needed an answer.

"Only four people have my cell. My boss, Richard Thomason, a college friend who works at the Bureau, and Peter." He straightened, his mouth set in a grim line.

"Why would a mobster's son have a direct line to an FBI agent?"

"It's a long story. You don't need to know."

"Like hell."

"Peter is not a threat to you. Let's leave it at that."

She turned her mind back to the courtroom, trying to remember who had come to support John Caravello. "If my memory serves me right, Caravello had a younger brother and two sons." One of them could be guilty.

"Nicki is John Caravello's younger brother, and James is the son who now heads the family business, not Peter. Nicki isn't well though. He can't be behind any of this."

She had to admit one of the others could be guilty. Nicki and James had come to trial every day. The third, Peter, had rarely showed.

Her pulse slowed, but something didn't settle with her. "What reason did Peter give for calling you? Aren't you the enemy, so to speak? The FBI testimony was what got his father executed."

He crossed his arms. "I can't talk about it."

She wanted to strangle him. "You can't or you won't."

He finally made eye contact. "Both."

A cold chill raced through her veins. Jake stepped toward her and Susan edged backwards, her feet bumping the bottom step. He might be an FBI agent, but his allegiance seemed to have swung toward the Caravello family.

"I see. Then I'll be in my room." *Away from you.*

With as much poise as she could muster, Susan turned back around and climbed the stairs, wincing as the stitches pulled in her chest.

Footsteps sounded behind her.

Stay calm. Show no fear. Heart pumping hard, she reached for her bedroom doorknob.

A hand planted firmly on the door above her head, preventing her from entering. "I located something you need."

Too close for comfort, she stepped back and looked up at Jake, his brown eyes close to black. When his gaze locked onto hers for a beat too long, her stomach seized up. She cut the connection and stared at his gun wedged beneath his shoulder. "What?" Blood pounded in her ears. A bullet to the head?

"Go see. It's in the bathroom."

She wasn't sure of his game, but if she didn't go along, who knew what he might do. "Sure."

Jake dropped his arm and opened the bedroom door. Susan side-stepped him and strode into the ensuite bathroom.

"It's under the counter," he said with a hint of satisfaction.

It was the one place she didn't look when showering. On the bottom shelf sat a package from the hospital pharmacy. She opened the innocuous looking plastic bag.

"Where did you get these bandages?" They were the ones the nurse had given her.

"From your suitcase."

Her hands flew to her hips. "You looked through my stuff?" Her breath came out ragged.

"Yes."

"That's an invasion of my privacy." How dare he.

"I had to search your bags to make sure you hadn't hidden a cell phone."

Her jaw tightened. "You could have asked."

He chuckled. "I never believe what people tell me. I needed to see for myself."

"When did you have time to put the bandages in my bathroom?" He'd been downstairs after she finished her shower.

"When you were showering."

Blood drained from her body. "You spied on me?"

He held up a hand. "I didn't look. Besides, the place was so filled with steam I couldn't see anything. I knew you wanted the bandages, so I put them away for you. I'm sorry if I caused you any embarrassment."

Likely story. She snatched the bandages to her chest, and with her head held high, ducked around him. Her shoulder brushed his chest. Darn. Being in such a confined space with him sent her senses on high alert. He was too broad shouldered, too tall, too strong.

Heart still in overdrive, Susan hurried across her room and pulled back the door, gesturing for him to get out. Not only might he be involved in the jurors' murders, he had little character if he'd walk into her bathroom without her knowledge.

He strolled past her with an amused look. She had no idea what he thought was funny. Oh shit. Had he lied about not seeing her naked? Bastard. It didn't matter the shower curtain was opaque.

She shut the door, locked it, and plastered her back against the wall until the sound of his footsteps faded and the television switched on. She breathed a sigh of relief, hoping he'd stay downstairs—for good.

With a light tremor in her hands, she reapplied her bandages, thankful her clothes no longer rubbed against her lacerated skin. She purposefully didn't wrap her injured hands since she needed full mobility if she had any chance at escape tonight.

Susan checked the clock. She had a few hours before dinner. Her body ached and her mind raced. A short nap would help her regroup, think, and plan. Fully clothed, she lay on the bed and rested her eyes.

She must have been more exhausted than she realized, because she fell asleep. A loud knock jerked her awake.

"Dinner is ready."

She wet her lips and sat up on the bed, her mind going full speed. "I'm good. I'm not really hungry." She squeezed her eyes shut, hoping he'd buy her story, but the man had a way of seeing through all her lies. Maybe with the door between them, his second sight would falter.

"Mrs. Chapman, you have to eat."

She didn't like being called Mrs. Chapman. The name reminded her of her failed marriage. And why not call her Taylor? She'd have to get used to the name soon enough—unless he was convinced she wouldn't be here long or else she'd be dead soon. Her body trembled. "Please call me Susan." If he felt a connection to her, he might be less likely to harm her.

"All right. Susan, you should eat something to keep up your strength."

"I'm really not hungry. My pain meds took away my appetite." That wasn't true, but lack of appetite was one possible side effect according to her prescription bottle. "I'm going to hit the hay early. I'll see you in the morning." She crossed her fingers in front of her—something her father used to do.

He didn't respond, but the loud pounding of his feet on the stairs as he went back to the living room told her he wasn't happy. Tough.

She raced to the window overlooking the backyard and studied the cement patio below. No way could she jump the ten feet and not injure herself, especially with the metal chairs and glass top table directly below.

Her stomach grumbled, but she ignored the discomfort. Being hungry was better than being with the traitor, Jake Yarnell. She was sure once she explained her situation to the FBI, they would provide her with a different bodyguard.

While she waited for nightfall, she packed a few of her belongings. She left most of the case empty because she needed to fill her suitcase with food. Being on the run would take all of her strength.

Tonight, when Jake was in bed, she'd slip out. With no phone and only the twenty-dollar bill he'd given her, she wasn't sure how far she'd get, but any destination would be better than being locked in with a man in cahoots with a killer. For all she knew, he'd already invited Peter Caravello to their townhouse. She wished she could have listened to their conversation this afternoon. He'd been smart enough to step outside so she couldn't eavesdrop. What did that tell her?

Just as she'd settled into bed, a muffled voice floated through her door. She froze. Was Caravello downstairs? She placed her ear to the wood paneled door. The tone didn't sound like it came from the television. Wait. That was Jake's voice. He was probably on the phone. To his boss? Or to the killer? She peeled open the door and strained to hear the conversation. Suddenly, it turned silent. Damn. He must have hung up.

As she eased the door close, a shiver raced up her spine. There would be no sleeping tonight since she had no idea what was on his agenda.

Susan sat on the bed and waited for her time to escape. Her only entertainment entailed watching the numbers change on the alarm clock.

Around midnight, she heard Jake's door down the hall open and close. At two, she decided he must be asleep. Sneaking into the hall-way, the pressure of the suitcase handle bit into her injured fingers, but she didn't care. Pain could be tolerated if it meant her freedom.

She slipped off her shoes and tiptoed down the stairs, stopping every time the step creaked. With her breath held, she inched her way to the bottom floor, constantly listening for Jake's door to open.

Once in the living room, she let out a breath and placed her suit-case on the kitchen island. The light from the full moon shining in the kitchen window provided sufficient illumination to find what she wanted. Susan grabbed three apples, two oranges, the remaining four power bars, a few slices of bread, and two bottled waters.

Next she put on her shoes. Jake had tossed the car keys on the counter when they'd come in. She patted the cool granite top in a slow manner, careful not to knock anything over. Her fingers touched the keys. Success! With care, she clenched them tight to keep the keys from rattling.

With a last glance over her shoulder, she eased open the front door. The whoosh of cool air pushed the door backwards, causing the hinges to groan. She stilled, her heart beating way too rapidly. She was so close and didn't want to mess up now. When Jake's bedroom door didn't burst open, she stepped outside and inhaled the sweet smell of the damp night.

Moving as fast as she could down the stoop steps, she made for the car parked in the drive. She tested the door handle in case Jake had left the vehicle unlocked.

The latch lifted. Her adrenaline pumped with the thrill of victory. She wrenched open the door and the interior light clicked on.

"Going somewhere?"

Her heart stopped.

CHAPTER FOUR

Jake was torn. He wasn't sure whether to gloat over the fact he'd guessed Susan's next move, or feel bad he'd scared her enough to want to run away. What kind of bodyguard did that make him?

Her mouth dropped open. "How did you...?"

Jake finished her sentence. "Know you'd try to escape? Simple. You think I'm the enemy. I'm not, but you can't be sure. Any rational person would try to run away."

She stood bathed in the glow of the front porch light, shivering in a t-shirt and jeans. They might be in Florida, but the nights turned cold, especially in February. She should have known better. He angled out of the car and slipped off his jacket.

As he came over to her side, she scrambled into the passenger's side. He shook his head and would have laughed had the situation not been serious. With one arm, he grabbed her from behind to pull her out. She tipped backwards, and when her rear snuggled against his crotch, he failed to block the inappropriate lust.

"Let go of me. You can't keep me here." She wiggled her rear right and left to get out of his grasp and swatted her hands behind her, but he held on tight.

"Yes, I can. It's my FBI prime directive. Keep witness safe at all cost."

"That's rich."

He turned her around and placed the jacket over her shoulders. The crisp breeze blew her hair back, and despite the patch on her cheek, the moonlight cast a shadow on her pretty face. He stepped toward her, his lips quivering. He then pulled her toward him and leaned over, his face inches from her.

Shit, he'd almost kissed her. What the hell had he been thinking?

She ripped free of his grasp and bared her teeth. "Don't touch me."

He understood the fear of being touched. As a kid, he'd recoiled from one of his foster father's cruel hands. He wanted to tell her she could relax, but only time would convince her he wasn't the bad guy here.

She tightened her grip on his jacket, and he soaked in the irony of her cuddling in the perceived enemy's clothes. Jake stepped back and held up his hands. "No problem."

When had he decided he wanted to offer her more than FBI protection? The moment she ran?

"I'm serious."

"So am I." He picked up her dropped suitcase. A light turned on across the street in the second floor window, causing his body to shoot to alert. "I think we're being watched." He nodded toward the building.

Susan cast a glance at the townhouse and shivered. "Do you think they know who I am?"

"I can't imagine how they could, but if you continue to make a scene, they might call the cops, and we don't need the notoriety." The light in the apartment clicked off. Good.

"I wasn't shrieking or anything." She rushed past him into the house and slammed the door behind her.

He liked her feisty attitude. She'd need her spirits high for the long months that lay ahead. He just wished he could get her to cooperate instead of doing battle.

Then again, sometimes a challenge spiced up life a bit.

He stepped inside, the warmth comforting his stiff muscles. He expected Susan to be upstairs with her door barred and locked. Instead, she was at the refrigerator scrounging through the items on the shelf.

Her frantic movements stirred his sympathy. "There's left over pepperoni pizza if you're hungry." The meds-take-away-my-appetite claim had apparently been false.

He'd have to remember the saucy lady was a convincing liar.

She whipped around. "You ordered pizza? I love pepperoni."

He swallowed his smile. "The place was stocked with the frozen kind."

"Doesn't matter. I'm starving."

She pulled a container from the fridge and shoved two slices in the microwave.

His cell vibrated and his heart plunged to his stomach. "Jesus." It was two thirty in the morning. He flipped open the cover and relaxed. It was only Tom. "Don't you ever sleep?" Tom Traynor, or T-Squared for short, had been his college roommate for all four years at Virginia Tech and was the current FBI computer guru.

"I'm on the night shift this week. Guess what?"

He respected Tom, but his best friend drove him crazy with his guessing games. "What?"

"Peter Caravello was just brought into custody."

Jake glanced at Susan, but her back was to him. Good. Tom's information was not the news he wanted to hear, and he was sure his face reflected his disappointment.

The Bureau would be recording every call into and out of the FBI office. "That's good news, right?"

"Sure is. Say, if you need to get a hold of me, call me at Joe's Bar."

Code for: call me on my secure line. "Will do. Thanks for the heads up."

"Get some sleep."

He would if people would stop calling him, and if witnesses would stay where they belonged.

He tucked his phone in his top pocket just as Susan turned around, her mouth full. Her brow creased, and she held up a finger.

He answered her unspoken question. "Peter Caravello was arrested tonight."

Her eyes widened and her shoulders relaxed. She swallowed. "Does that mean I can go home?"

"Not yet." He walked over to the kitchen and rested a hip on the stool. "Like I told you, Peter's not our man."

"So you say." She wiped her mouth and tossed the paper towel in the trash. "Now that the world is a safer place, I'm going to bed. Good-night." Her curt announcement confirmed he still headed her bad guy list.

"I'm right behind you."

She narrowed her eyes and pinched her mouth into a small circle. When they reached the top of the stairs, Susan slipped into her room. He followed right behind.

She spun around. "Get out of my room. Now." If she'd been a tiger, she would have extended her claws.

He laughed at her indignity. "Go change." He placed her getaway gear next to the bed.

Her jaw dropped. "I will as soon as you leave." She unclenched her hands grasping his jacket and jerked his coat off her shoulders. She winced. "Is this what you want?"

"No." He didn't care about the jacket. "How do I know you won't try to escape again?"

Her mouthed opened then snapped shut. "You have my word. Now that Caravello is in jail, I have nothing to fear."

Her glance to the side, coupled with her trembling lip, convinced him she was lying. Again.

Jake draped the leather jacket over his shoulder and stepped toward her. She retreated until the backs of her legs hit the bed and dropped down. Susan grabbed a big pillow and clutched it to her chest. As he neared, she scooted backward.

"What are you doing?" she asked.

His gut clenched at the fear in her tone. "Keeping you safe."

He knelt on the bed and straddled her, concentrating on the job at hand and not on the attractive woman beneath him.

His mind lapsed the moment Susan's mouth opened and the tip of her tongue peeked out and caressed her lips. His pulse zipped into overdrive, shocking him at the base urge to taste her mouth.

"What the *hell* are you doing?" She reached up to punch his chest.

Before she made contact, he caught her wrist using the least amount of force as possible. She gasped and he let go. "Look, I'm sorry to have to do this, but I can't chance you'll do something stupid." He didn't say, *again*.

She wrinkled her nose. "What's that supposed to mean?"

Jake whipped out his cuffs from his back pocket, slapped one half on the uninjured wrist and clamped the other to the metal bed. "At least one of us will get a good night's sleep."

He stood back up and headed out the door.

"You can't do this to me," she yelled, as he made his way to his room.

"I just did."

*****

Jake woke up rather refreshed considering he'd spent two hours in the front seat of the car waiting for his escapee and then another two hours tossing in bed. Pleased he'd kept her safe for the night, he showered, shaved and dressed while ignoring the death threats coming from the room next door. Shakespeare's play, *Taming of the Shrew*, kept popping in his head every time she tossed some invective at him. He never liked confining someone, but in Susan's case, it was for her own good. Thank goodness, she only yelled for a few minutes last night before exhaustion took over.

If she had succeeded in tricking him, he'd be looking for a new line of work. And if she'd been harmed on her foray to freedom, he'd never been able to live with himself.

Not to worry. He wouldn't let her out of his sight again.

Keeping an eye on her did come with one danger. If she was by his side for the next week, he might weaken and kiss her before he left. She'd probably slap him, but the stolen touch would be worth the trouble.

He popped into her bedroom. "Good morning, sunshine." He wasn't sure if his cheer this morning was because he avoided catastrophe last night, or if he enjoyed sparring with her.

She narrowed her eyes. "When I get out of here, I'm going to bring you up on charges for holding me hostage."

He did a mock shiver. "The Bureau gives me authority to confine you if need be. I was only thinking of your own good."

She rattled the cuffs. "Bullshit. Now get me out of these chains."

She actually snarled at him. It took all of his control not to laugh. "They're called cuffs." Jake retrieved the key and freed her.

She rubbed her sore wrists. "If you'll excuse me, I need to use the bathroom."

He'd forgotten about her need to go. When he served in Iraq before joining the FBI, he could hold it for days if need be. "I'll have breakfast on the table when you come down."

He backed up, half expecting her to throw something at him. She didn't. Instead she raced to the bathroom and slammed shut the door. Remorse welled inside him. Jake stepped to the closed door. "I didn't have a choice, you know."

"Go to hell."

If she didn't get a grip on her emotions, she might put herself in more danger. "Look, I'm sorry, but your safety comes first."

She banged a few cabinet doors and drawers not answering.

"If you think I want to harm you, you're wrong. No matter how convinced I am that Peter is innocent, I won't let him near you."

"That's because he's in jail."

For now. At least she was listening. "Think about it. With you tied to the bed, I could have killed you. But I didn't. So can we call a truce?"

She said nothing for a good ten seconds. "Maybe."

Her concession was more than he could hope for. "Coffee will be ready when you are."

He left her to do her womanly thing and headed down the stairs, happy he'd conquered at least one of her fears.

***

After her near escape and uncomfortable confinement last night, Jake had insisted what she needed was a day in the Florida sunshine. He claimed some shopping and a walk on the beach would take her mind off her situation.

From the way he kept glancing at her with those sad eyes, she suspected the real reason for this outing was to assuage his guilt at having confined her. Susan begrudgingly admitted he had due cause—but she sure as hell didn't tell him that. Truth be told, she would have tried to escape again. Even though she probably wouldn't have gotten far, her goal had been not only to escape Jake, but to locate a phone to call her mom.

Besides, sitting at home waiting for the next juror to die would have eaten at her nerves. Being in public would give her some sense of security that the killer, whoever he was, wouldn't kill her.

They sauntered on the beach past hotels, condos and a handful of houses. Her chest hurt when she moved suddenly, but the rest of her body was healing nicely.

"If you want to stop for a bite to eat, let me know," he said with a smile that sent a quick shiver of delight down her spine.

Tamping down a smile, she turned toward the beach and pretended to study the squawking seagulls picking up the bits of breads the tourists had tossed them. He was not going to sweet talk her into forgiving him. "Thanks, but we ate a little more than an hour ago. I'm not hungry."

The warm air scented with salt, together with the sand between her toes, had helped to calm her, but the depression over losing her job and basically her life, never lifted, even after a family of dolphins gave a show in the ocean.

"My feet need a rest from the gritty sand," he said.

Liar. It was her tender feet that needed the rest.

He held her hand firmly until they reached the street. Did he actually think she'd try to run away from him—in the middle of a beach town? She'd run track in high school, but she could guess she'd be no match for Jake.

Susan donned the sandals he'd bought her. "Where are we going?"

"There's a shop across the street I think you'll like."

She held in a groan when he marched her toward a bathing suit store. It was the third one they'd been in today, but she'd humored him. After trying on a couple of suits that didn't fit, she gave up. "Please no more suits. Even you said I won't be here that long."

He studied her for what seemed like an eternity. "You didn't have fun shopping? Or walking on the beach?" He raised his brows and turned down the corner of his lips.

She refused to fall for his I-tried-so-hard-to-please-you act. "I will admit the ocean views were fantastic, and the warm sun wrapped me in a sense of security I never expected, but I'm exhausted. Do you mind if we head back?"

He eyed her as if she had a defective gene. "We haven't seen every shop yet."

"Jake, please." She tugged on his arm for effect.

"Sure. Whatever you want. Home it is."

He didn't have to make her feel like a cad. She knew what he was doing—keeping her out of the house for as long as possible to show her life could be good again.

Hold it. Did he have reason to believe staying in the townhouse made them a target? She shivered despite the delicious warm, salty breeze.

He held open the car door and helped her in. Exhausted from the walk and the sea air, she closed her eyes the moment her butt hit the seat.

The driver's side door squeaked open. "You okay?"

He flipped on the heater. The air had turned cool when the sun had set.

"I'm just tired."

At least he refrained from asking her if she trusted him yet. She wasn't sure how she'd answer if he had.

When they returned to the townhouse, she headed straight upstairs.

"Going to bed so soon?" he called after her.

Near the top of the steps, she stopped and faced him. "Today was long. Goodnight." He glanced up at her with sad eyes. She softened. "Thank you for taking me to the beach. I enjoyed it."

No lie. He'd been gentle, considerate, and a good listener.

"Me too." He smiled, looking like the kind of boy a girl dreamed would ask her to the high school prom.

Susan turned around and trudged upstairs, trying to ignore the tug on her heart. He followed behind her but kept his distance. When he stopped at the threshold of her room instead of heading down the hall, a queasy sensation filled her stomach.

"Goodnight again," she said. Though exhausted, she managed to smile.

Jake didn't budge, his intense brown eyes focused on her. Fine. She stepped in the room and closed the door in his face. She'd barely slept last night and in her cranky mood, who knows what she'd say or do if he wanted to have a conversation about his shackling her.

The sand in her toes and the sticky salt on her face demanded another shower. This time, getting undressed didn't cause as much pain. Yay. Maybe her wounds were on the mend.

Her short shower helped relax her. After she dried off, Susan changed into her flannel pajamas. When she stepped into the bedroom, Jake was sitting on her bed, and her pulse raced.

"What are you doing here?"

He stood and waved a hand toward the bed. "Making sure you are safe."

She didn't move as she swallowed the anxiety that tinged her mouth. "Would you mind leaving? I can get to bed by myself."

He dangled the cuffs in front of her and raised his brows.

"You're kidding, right?" How had she misjudged him?

"I'm sorry, but I can't take any chances you'll bolt."

"You don't trust me?"

"Hah. What do you know about trust?"

Very little. She'd trusted her first husband until he turned on her. Cheating bastard.

She glanced right, and then left. There was no way she could race outside without him catching her, so she crawled into bed, hoping her action would show she would cooperate. "I promise I won't try to leave. Besides, Peter Caravello is in jail. All this mess will be over soon, and I'll be back home with my family. I have no reason to escape."

"From the way you shifted your gaze and balled your fists just now, I can see you've come up with a way to blame me again. I would never harm you, but I'm not sure how to convince you. I thought today proved I'm a nice guy."

"Did I say I thought you would hurt me?" *Kill me maybe.* "You're here for my protection. I know that." She shrugged a shoulder and cocked her head to the side, hoping to present an attractive pose.

His mouth sagged. "You didn't believe that fact last night when you tried to escape."

True. She opened her mouth, and then shut it when she couldn't come up with a good comeback. "Fine." She held out her wrist. "But I promise you'll regret this."

"So you've said before."

He stepped over to her, slapped on the cuff, and attached the other end to the bed. He winked and walked out.

"It's not funny," she shouted after him.

He poked his head back in the room. "Never meant for it to be."

Furious Jake would take such aggressive action, she turned off the light by the bed with her free hand and fumed for at least an hour, hoping he'd change his mind and uncuff her.

He never did.

For at least three hours she stared at the glowing numbers on the clock as they changed one by one. Her eyelids eventually drooped as her mind relaxed. Just as she dozed off, her nightmare returned. Flames burst through the picture window, and glass flew everywhere. Her breath lodged in her throat as pain seared her body and blackness met her. She tossed and turned until the images left and were replaced by gentle rolling waves, warm silky sand, and long conversations. Finally, she drifted off to sleep.

Hunger must have awoken her, for she jerked to a near sitting position. Given she couldn't go downstairs for a bite without being freed, she kicked off the sweat soaked covers and turned over. The house was too damned hot. Why did the FBI have to send her to Florida anyway?

She liked the cold, and liked her old, leaky home near D.C. where she slept with lots of comfortable blankets.

Sweat beaded her forehead and arms, forcing her to repositioned the pillows, but she couldn't get comfortable with her arm above her head. Her damn fingers had fallen asleep. Stupid Jake.

Susan had just drifted off once more when a rancid smell poked her subconscious, but her mind wouldn't engage. At first she thought her recurring visions had returned, but nightmares didn't come with the smell of sulfur.

Forcing herself awake, Susan sat up. The wall opposite her bed glowed yellow. Her chest pounded What the...? Hallucinations had taken over her mind.

Heat and light blasted her. She blinked. What kind of dream was this?

When a flame stabbed through the wall, Susan came fully awake. Ohmigod. The house was on fire! She tried to scream, but her throat had closed up. Jake's bedroom was behind hers, away from the fire. He wouldn't realize they were in danger until her bedroom was destroyed.

Her stomach revolted and bile raced up her throat. Had Jake set the fire? Could he really have wanted to kill her that badly? He'd been so nice, so gentle.

Panic nearly locked her muscles as she rattled the chains against the bedpost. Swallowing a few times loosened her vocal chords. "Fire! Help me. Jake?"

Light flickered outside her window. She yanked on her cuffs, trying to get free. The metal scraped her skin as she tugged and pulled. Refusing to give in and burn to death, Susan bucked and kicked, anything to get his attention.

Flames engulfed the far wall, heating the room to near impossible temperatures. Her chest hurt so badly, she gagged and coughed.

"Help me. Jake, help me." Her voice faded.

Placing her feet on the floor, she pulled on the bed to move it closer to the door, but the damn thing wouldn't budge.

Why weren't the smoke alarms sounding? Why didn't Jake wake up? Had someone come in and taken him out first?

Her throat swelled up and her pulse raced as the flames danced across the room toward her. She only had minutes before the flames found the cotton bedspread and incinerated her.

"Jake!"

She couldn't breathe. Susan used all her strength to force air through her mouth. Her pulse raced. Her vision fogged. Oh, God. No one was going to save her.

CHAPTER FIVE

Smoke clogged her lungs, and heat burned her chest. Susan couldn't see, couldn't think. She yanked hard on her hand, hoping the sweat would help free her wrist. Half her palm slipped out and adrenaline pumped through her veins.

"Please God, save me." Susan tugged again, trying to ignore the raw skin.

She kicked the blankets off the bed, and then pulled her legs near her chest, away from the fire.

Pounding feet raced down the hall, and she choked out a sob.

Jake dashed into her bedroom. "Jesus Christ."

Her mouth too dry to talk, she merely moaned. Tears streamed down her cheeks. He'd come. He would save her. Or was Jake here to see his handiwork? She choked on that thought.

"Hold on." When his cry sounded desperate, hope flooded her system.

Through the gray smoke, she could make out Jake fumbling in his pocket. A second later he leaned over her with a key.

He must be Superman, for the cuff attacked to the bed disappeared, and she was instantly in his arms. Not wanting to fall, she wrapped her arms around his neck. Sobs of relief tore through her chest, as she tucked her chin to her neck, squeezing her eyes closed. *Please God, let me live.*

Jake sped out of the bedroom, down the steps, and across the living room. She coughed as tears of joy mixed with the smoke.

"Hold tight," he said.

He grabbed the car keys off the counter with one hand and raced out the front door.

Once in the open, she gulped down the cool, clean air.

The second his feet hit grass, he set her down. Without saying a word, he ran to the car, opened the back door, and was back by her side seconds later.

"Are you okay enough to walk?"

Dazed, she looked up at him.

He gently pinched her.

"Ow."

"Good. Come on, we need to get out of here."

***

Jake paced the hospital waiting room. The doctors had been treating Susan for the last three hours. The attending nurse wouldn't tell him anything other than the physician would be out when he was finished with his examination. Had the smoke done irreparable damage? He'd seen enough fire victims to know inhaling hot air could burn the esophagus lining and cause death. She wasn't unconscious when he found her, but burns could become infected. Too bad Susan didn't remember how much time had elapsed before he'd arrived.

Damn. He should have checked the batteries on the smoke alarm. He should have asked for a key to the neighboring townhouses in case some careless squatter occupied the furnished apartments, but dammit, every time he turned around, someone was calling to tell him another juror had died.

Excuses. Rationalization. He hated them. Bottom line was that Jake had failed Susan. Guilt and anger rippled through him. He should have been more cautious and checked up on her. Maybe he had no right to be a bodyguard.

Jake checked his watch. The fire marshal said he'd have a prelimi-
nary report of what happened by tomorrow morning. Given the Feds
hadn't come up with even a fingerprint around any of the other crime
scenes, he knew the local marshal wouldn't find any incriminating
evidence at the townhouse.

He was no fire expert, but houses did not spontaneously combust.
Someone had found out where they were. Damn it. How?

Jake stabbed a hand through his hair. His stomach grumbled.
Anxiety always fueled his metabolism. The clock might only read six in
the morning, but he needed food. He bet Ms. Hungry did too.

"Mr. Yarnell?"

Jake spun around. "Yes?" He closed the gap between him and
Susan's attending physician. "How is she?"

"Stable. I want to keep her here overnight for observation."

"That's fine. Is she in much pain?"

"She didn't sustain any burns. The smoke damage seemed minimal,
but the full extent of her injury isn't always easy to detect right away.
Given her other injuries, she's in more danger."

"I understand." Infection could work its way into the cuts.

"We'll need to get some information on Mrs. Yarnell."

Mrs. Yarnell? He never thought he'd hear that name. Even if it
wasn't real. When he'd raced in with Susan in his arms, he hadn't been
thinking. Hospital records could be hacked into, and his name was the
first that came to mind.

Jake didn't want anyone to trace credit card records or insurance
claims. "I'm afraid all of our insurance cards and paperwork were at
the townhouse that burned down. Do you take cash?"

The doctor smiled. "Never a problem."

Perfect. He'd stop at an ATM and withdraw the money. Good thing
the FBI had high withdrawal limits.

Jake scrubbed a hand over his jaw and studied the young doctor. He
pulled out his badge. "I'm afraid my wife is part of an ongoing investigation. No information should be released on her condition—to
anyone." He paused to give the doctor time to absorb the information.

"Of course. Whatever you need, Agent Yarnell. We have someone
on staff who can stand watch outside her room."

Jake nodded and returned his badge to his pocket. "I intend to stay by her side also. I'd appreciate it if only medical personnel are allowed in, and then only with an ID." While Jake figured a local cop wouldn't be in cahoots with the killer, Jake wanted to stay in charge.

"I'll inform the hospital."

***

When Susan opened her eyes, it was déjà vu all over again. She was in a hospital bed with Jake by her side.

He smiled. "Welcome to the world of the living."

Despite the gray streaks painted across his cheek, Jake Yarnell was a handsome man.

Her hand flew to her hair. She winced at what she must look like. The strong smoky scent assaulted her nostrils. How could anyone stand to be near her? What she wouldn't do for a shower.

"You look fine," he said, as if he could read her mind.

"I don't feel fine."

His smile disappeared. "What hurts?"

"Nothing more than what was injured in the explosion." She rubbed her chest. "I have a little trouble breathing, but the doctor said that's to be expected."

"I'm sorry I didn't hear you yell sooner. I was conked out."

She looked around the room. "It would have helped if you hadn't chained me to the bed."

"I had no choice."

She could see his point, but that didn't mean she had to like it. "Are we done with tying me up?"

"If you give me your Girl Scout promise you won't try to escape."

She rolled her eyes. "I promise." A wave of pain raced up from her chest. "We don't have time for me to stay in the hospital a few days, do we?"

"Let's wait and see what the fire marshal says. We'll know more tomorrow."

A knock sounded on the door, and Susan's pulse jumped ten beats and she clutched the spread. The man might be wearing a uniform, but anyone could don a costume.

Jake leaned over and clasped her hand. "When I explained the situation, the doctor said he'd have security stand watch."

"Oh, that was nice of you."

"I was hoping you'd see it that way." Jake whistled and glanced to the ceiling.

She shook her head. Talk about asking for a compliment. "You want to know if I still think you're the bad guy, don't you?"

"Maybe. Do you?"

"The jury's out. No pun intended."

His eyes widened. "You're kidding me, I hope. I saved your life, and you think I still want to harm you?" He kept his voice to a whisper. "With Peter in jail, you have to believe he's innocent, so even if you think I'd help him do whatever you think I plan to do with him, he couldn't have set the fire."

The teasing evaporated and reason intruded. "He has enough connections for his men to burn the place down."

Jake shoved back his chair. "I don't get you. I can't win. I'm starving. Bye."

Her hands flew to her stomach. "You're leaving me?"

He spun around. "Isn't that what you want?" His bottom lip hardened.

"Yes." Stupid answer. "No." *Face it; he makes me feel safe.*

"I'm just going downstairs to the hospital cafeteria. When I get back, I hope you can work through your issues."

"My issues?"

"Yes. I understand you're scared. Hell, I've been scared since the moment I saw you in the hospital, but if we don't develop a little trust, I'll never be able to keep you from harm."

He took one step back. As an attorney, she held her ground that the accused was guilty. She never budged, always fighting for what she wanted. But what if she were wrong? Were principles more important than her life?

Her lips trembled into what she hoped was a smile. "I'm starving too and these people won't give me anything until the doctor gives some all-clear order. Can you sneak in something good to eat for me?"

He edged toward her. A slow smile dimpled his cheek. "If I do, can I wear a white hat?"

He wouldn't be flirting with her if he wanted any harm to come to her. He could have pretended to sleep through the fire and let her burn to death. "Okay, fine, but one slip..." She crooked a finger in his direction.

"I'll try to find a juicy steak for you."

"If you can manage that feat, I might imagine you on a white horse."

***

Off to find the perfect steak for the distrustful patient, Jake had just stepped outside the hospital when his cell vibrated. "Christ." He didn't need any more bad news. "Yarnell."

"It's Richard Thomason. How is Susan doing? Loving the warm weather I suspect." The Director of the safe houses often checked up on the witnesses.

"Someone set the townhouse on fire last night—or rather early this morning."

"Holy shit. Is she okay?" Near panic caused his voice to rise.

"We're at the hospital now. No burns, just smoke inhalation."

"Do we have any idea who did this?" Jake could imagine Richard pacing, tugging on his perfectly knotted tie, and rearranging the items on his desk.

"The fire marshall is working it."

"Christ. We don't need this. I'll get right on finding you a new place. Obviously, he's found you."

"At least we know it's not Caravello. I heard he was in jail." Jake reached his car and slid in. He waited to start the engine until their conversations ended.

Thomason didn't answer for a minute. "Who told you?"

Shit. "I don't remember."

Jake turned the key to lower the windows. He needed air. Pissed he'd nearly mentioned Tom's name—the person not privy to some FBI information. Somehow, his friend knew everything.

"Caravello could have pulled the strings."

Relieved Richard didn't press where his knowledge came from, he relaxed in the seat. "Perhaps." He didn't want to be discussing his theory about Peter's guilt with Richard. "I'll take you up on your offer to move." He chuckled, though only for effect.

"Good. I'm afraid I had another reason for calling." The deadly low tone meant the news wasn't good.

"What?" He gripped the wheel tight and sat up straight.

"Juror number nine was killed."

Jake lost his appetite. "When?"

"Sometime before midnight."

Shit. "How?" Sweat beaded his chest.

Papers rustled in the background and phones rang. Richard must be moving across the office. "Gunshot to the head."

Damn. "Who was it? I know Susan will want to know." Because she'd spent close to year on the case, she'd gotten to know the jurors well.

"Travis Simmons."

His hand shook at the ramification. "Thanks."

He'd been about to hang up, when Richard called his name.

"Yeah?"

"I've never seen anything like this. I put two people in a safe house, and now both are dead. I don't know what to do." The man sounded sincerely distraught.

He wanted to say, find the mole, but wasn't sure he'd be wise to voice his opinion. "You'll find a way to stop this guy."

"I hope. I'll call you when I have an exact address for the new safe house."

***

"Where's the girl?" came that horrible voice over the line.

Richard Thomason recognized the blackmailer's voice. He never should have given the blackmailer his cell phone number. "I don't know."

"You're the head of the goddamn relocation program. If you don't know, who does?"

Richard stepped past his secretary into his office, closed his door, and lowered the shades. He could smell his own sweat. Despite the good insulation, he lowered his voice. "They were in Florida, but someone burned down their townhouse last night."

"I know. I ordered the place to be torched. When my men came to retrieve her charred body, she wasn't there. Where did she go?"

Sweat pooled under his arms. Richard loosened his tie. "I called Yarnell a few hours ago, but he didn't answer." Could the guy hear the way his voice wobbled?

"That the FBI guy with her?"

"Yes." Shit. He shouldn't have mentioned Jake's name.

Loud music blasted the background. The man covered the mouthpiece and yelled what sounded like Italian. The annoying music stopped.

"Sorry about that. You've been a good guy. You've told me where all the other jurors are, but this attorney woman is a slippery one."

"What do you want from me? I did what I promised." His guilty conscious ate away at him. If he held on, his family would be safe.

"I want you to find the bitch and tell me where she is."

"I've done enough for you."

The man laughed. "Then I guess you won't mind when your two pretty little girls and your wife disappear for good."

His chin trembled as rage filled his gut. "If you lay a hand on my family—"

"You'll what? Come after me yourself? Ha. I know you can't bring your FBI buddies with you because that would mean you had to tell them you were the mole that got the nine jurors killed. Find the woman." He hung up.

Richard reached for his chair and slid down onto his seat. Tears streamed down his cheeks. He'd put his wife and children in jeopardy, but he'd had no choice. He'd borrowed so much money to give his wife a second chance at life, and now he might lose the one woman he loved.

***

While Jake waited for his early morning take out order, he called the hospital to make sure Susan was okay. Once they assured him no one had entered her room, he dialed T-Squared. His gut churned knowing he'd have to break the news to Susan about Travis Simmons' death. She'd be devastated, and on more than one level.

"Joe's Bar and Grill." His friend used the code they'd established.

"Thank God I got a hold of you."

"I wouldn't have answered if it hadn't been you. You do realize this is when I sleep?"

Jake stepped closer to the restaurant door, not wanting anyone to overhear the conversation. "Sorry."

"No problem. What's up?"

Jake told him about the fire.

"She okay?"

"She will be. Listen, I need you to do me a favor."

"Anything."

The door opened and three kids rushed in, skateboards tucked under their arms. Based on the clientele, Jake hoped the food was good. "I need the names of the remaining three jurors."

T-Squared whistled. "You know that's illegal."

"So is killing people. Think about it. Even after we put those people into our safe houses, someone was able to get to them. You tell me how."

Other than the sound of some construction noise in the background, silence filled the air space.

"You suspect a mole in the Bureau?" Tom said.

A thin girl behind the counter placed an order next to the cash register. "Yarnell?"

Jake held up a finger, and then pulled out cash to pay for his meal.

"You got a name of who you think might be leaking the information?" Tom asked.

Jake maneuvered around two tables and stood at the register. "If I did, I'd be back in D.C. in a heartbeat ready the kill the guy." The cashier's eyes widened. He gave her his best smile and her stance softened. "Look, I need to warn the remaining jurors their location might be compromised."

"That's Thomason's job."

He turned to the side in an attempt to keep the conversation more private. "That might be, but I need to do this on my own. No telling who he blabbed to."

"You think Richard is—"

"I don't know who the mole is."

Jake handed the cashier a twenty and motioned she keep the change. He headed outside.

"You think it's wise to drag Susan around with you?"

He had debated asking the Tampa office to supply her with another bodyguard, but he didn't trust anyone else. "She'll be safer with me than in another supposedly safe house."

Tom groaned. "I'll have to hack into the system to get the information. It's not like they post the addresses on the bulletin board."

A wave of relief hit him. "I owe you one."

Once Jake checked out the parking lot, he jumped in the car and started the engine. The rich aroma of burgers and fries filled the car. They didn't have steak.

"I'd say you owe me about a hundred."

Jake laughed. "And the three times I saved your life doesn't count for anything."

T-Squared cleared his throat. "You know it does. Back at you in a few."

As Jake drove out the entrance, two men in a white sedan glanced his way before looking away.

Shit. He and Susan had to get the hell out of Dodge. Now.

CHAPTER SIX

Susan shifted in the car seat. "I can't wait to shower and put on the new clothes we, or rather you, purchased for me at the mall."

Jake nodded. Thankfully, he didn't wrinkle his nose. Even after doing a sponge bath, she didn't smell the best.

"I wish you had agreed to another day in the hospital to recuperate."

"I didn't trust anyone."

"I understand." Jake adjusted the side view mirror, moved the air slider right, then left, and wiped the dash with his palm.

His obsessive behavior was unnerving her. "What's the matter?"

He twisted his mouth. "Richard Thomason called last night." His hands clutched the wheel so hard the beds of his nails turned white.

"Don't tell me he knew about the fire?" Her pulse rose.

"No. He called because Travis Simmons was shot dead in the head."

Susan gasped, the horror churning her stomach. "Another juror? That makes, what, nine?"

"Yes."

She squeezed her eyes shut, trying to visualize what the juror looked like. Only the image of his stats surfaced. "He was a prominent doctor. That's so unfair." She twisted toward him. "Why did you wait until now to tell me? What was all the talk about trust if you don't share?"

"I didn't want to upset you."

"Like hell. I need to be in the loop and you know it."

"Fine. Next time when you're struggling to survive, I'll be sure to dump more bad news on you." His lips pressed together.

The boring scenery suddenly became interesting with all the scraggly pine trees whizzing by. "Maybe I came across a little harsh, but not telling me the killer is one step closer isn't right."

He waved a hand and glanced at her. "You're smart. I thought you'd figure something was up when I didn't argue much about you leaving the hospital before the doctor was ready to release you."

That's why he'd given in so easily. Two more jurors under FBI protection had been killed. This madman would stop only when all of them were dead—including her.

Sweat slickened her skin from the sun pouring through the car window. Or at least she wanted to believe it was the sun's fault and not fear choking her. She couldn't breathe. Susan pressed the button to lower the window half way, and the cool breeze poured in. She inhaled deeply. The tinge of exhaust mixed with fresh green trees perked her up.

"I can turn on the AC if you'd like," he said. His tone came out so sweet she wondered if he was feeling guilty for withholding information.

"I'm good." She faced forward not wanting to think about poor Travis and his family. "Did you believe the fire marshal when he said the blaze was a result of an overloaded circuit?"

"Yes." He tapped the steering wheel. "What I don't buy is the fact an electrician failed to install all of the fuses properly, especially in an upscale community as the one we stayed in."

Susan kept one eye on the side view mirror, not convinced someone wasn't following them. A gray sedan had appeared and disappeared more than once. She replayed in her mind what the fire marshal had told them.

"Could a lack of fuses actually cause a fire?" Her ex-husband had been the handy man in the family. She didn't know squat how circuits worked.

"No, but a fire will erupt if some worker plugs in a space heater in a socket that isn't rated for that appliance. It was a little chilly last night. Turns out the heater the carpenter brought in clicked on. Without a fuse to stop the overload, the place caught on fire."

She took a sip of water from the thermos Jake has purchased for her. He said she needed to keep hydrated.

"Could overloading the circuit have been done on purpose?"

He glanced up at the rear view mirror, his jaw tense. She didn't like it.

"That would by my guess. It's why I want to head north. But first, I need to shower at the motel." He sniffed the air and scrunched up his nose. "I stink."

The way he skewed up his face made her smile. "Like I don't?"

She guessed it wouldn't hurt to stay in Florida a little while longer if only to get clean.

Susan quickly sobered. "How do you explain the lack of batteries in the smoke detector in our place?"

Jake turned off the main road and entered the motel parking lot. "I can't. That's another problem. You know I don't believe in coincidences. Someone has a way of finding us. I plan to put a stop to that."

"How?"

"Stay where I decide. Tell the Bureau one thing, do another."

She cocked a brow. "I thought you were a big rule follower."

"Not when you could get hurt."

The determination in his tone bolstered her belief he was there to keep her safe. "Thank you."

"Just doing my job."

Oh. Nothing personal. She guessed he didn't want any black marks on his record.

"This place looks nice," she said.

At the motel, Jake drove around the parking lot before stopping, and her good mood evaporated.

"You think someone could have followed us?" she asked.

"Can't be too careful. I thought I noticed someone pull out of the mall right behind us. They kept only a few car lengths behind until I turned in here."

Why was this happening to her? "What should we do?"

"Wait here while I check us in." He jumped out before she had a chance to suggest she go with him.

The three-minute wait seemed to take forever. She half expected someone to pound on the window or come charging at her with a gun.

Jake returned. "All taken care of." He drove across the lot to their first floor room. "Get in the room before anyone sees you. Here's the key. I'll be back in a sec."

Susan was about to argue, but the tight lines around his mouth told her not to put up a fight. She grabbed her purchases and dashed inside the room.

The small room had one bed. Thank goodness they only planned on showering and not spending the night.

She'd just spread out her purchases to organize them when Jake strode in.

He dumped his stuff on the small table in the corner. "I didn't find anyone who looked suspicious."

"Great." Or had he been outside for a quick rendezvous? *Stop it. He saved your life.*

"Why don't you shower first," she said. "I need a few minutes to take off these tags and to figure out what to wear."

He shrugged. "You don't have to tell me twice."

Jake pulled his shirt over his head and dumped it in the trash. Next he unsnapped his jeans.

"What are you doing?" She'd been unable to take her gaze off the strip tease.

"I'm betting the trashcan in the bathroom won't hold my ruined smoky clothes."

He shucked off his shoes and dropped his pants.

"That's not what I meant and you know it."

Part of her wanted to turn her back, while the other half wanted to watch. The good half won and she flipped around.

Jake chuckled.

"What's so funny?"

"I know you were married. You must have seen a man in his underwear before."

"You aren't my husband. Would you mind getting naked in the bathroom?"

"I wasn't going to strip completely."

Heat raced up her face.

Packages rustled, and then his bare feet padded across the carpet before stepping into the bathroom. Susan dropped onto the bed, exhausted from the exchange. She'd never been a prude, but with Jake she didn't know how to react. The last year of her marriage to Carlton had been as lifeless as Travis Simmons' dead body.

Susan sorted through her purchases, deciding what to wear. Whether she looked presentable or not shouldn't matter, but somehow her appearance had become important to her. She hadn't minded wearing a baggy sweatshirt and equally ill-fitting pants back at the townhouse, so what had changed? The day at the beach? The hamburger and fries he'd brought? The nice way he treated her?

Jake stepped out of the bathroom and all thoughts of any outfit disappeared. Man, he cleaned up nice. Dressed in tight jeans and a body fitting t-shirt, her first reaction was that Jake would make a great cover model. She blinked to clear her head.

Her eyes told her to trust him, but the lawyer in her said to hold back judgment.

"Next."

He had the nerve to smile, as if he could read her mind. She wasn't staring that hard, was she?

Head held high, she picked up what she needed and brushed past him into the steamy bathroom. A hint of mint and lemon mixed in with the steam sent her thoughts in the absolute wrong direction. He'd been naked in here—or more exactly—wet and naked. A big, fluffy towel lay wadded on the floor, and for a brief moment she was tempted to pick it up and smell his scent, but the sane side of her said to undress before she became more confused.

Susan locked the door. The last thing she needed was for Jake to accidentally on purpose come looking for something he theoretically left in the bathroom, and she'd be naked with soap clinging to her breasts.

Move. Getting out of the stinky clothes was wonderful, but the sensation didn't compare to the hot shower. While she wanted to spend an hour in the bathroom, they couldn't afford to stay in one place long. She washed her hair as quickly as the pain allowed and dressed in record time.

The moment she stepped out of the bathroom, Jake smiled. Without a brush to pull through her wet tangled hair, she must look like Methuselah.

His eyes widened. "Nice."

She couldn't tell if his comment was sarcastic or not, so she let it slide. "Thanks."

With his feet on the small table, Jake's arms stayed crossed over his chest.

"Can we go now?" she asked.

He jumped up. "Sure. You're the boss."

"As if you believe any part of that statement."

His brows rose and a small smile lifted his lips. At least he helped her out with her suitcase.

Jake scanned the parking lot while she slipped into the car. The man did take his job seriously.

He backed out of the parking space. "While you were in the shower, I called T-Squared."

"Who?"

"A friend of mine who is a whiz at finding anything on the computer."

She appreciated he didn't keep this phone call a secret. "Because?"

"I had asked him to get the names and addresses of the remaining three jurors, which he delivered. I want to warn them to be careful."

"You still think it's a good idea to warn them? The Bureau might not appreciate the interference."

"I don't have a choice." His jaw clenched, which was never a good sign.

Worry rippled up her spine. "Can't the Bureau assign each of them a bodyguard?"

"Contrary to popular belief, we don't have unlimited resources."

She didn't like his answer. "If I hadn't been injured, would I have been on my own?"

His lips thinned. "Mostly likely."

"Which means I'd probably be dead."

"But you're not."

For now.

With the addresses of the remaining jurors in hand, they drove to Lake City, Florida, which took the three hours Jake had predicted. The exit had about fifty restaurants, all clumped near the interstate off ramp. They stopped at a cute cafe with a chicken perched on top, and her meal tasted better than anything she'd ever eaten. Maybe it was the sensation of freedom that gave her back her taste buds.

They didn't dawdle or talk about the case, which was fine by her. Once Jake refueled across the street from the restaurant, he peeled out of the station.

"You know where you're going?" she asked.

He tapped the GPS. "I already programmed Mr. Marcadis' address. It's less than three miles from here."

"Did you call him to let him know you wanted to speak with him? Arriving at his house unannounced and knocking on his door might scare him. He might have learned about the other jurors." He was juror number ten.

"Can't be helped. T-Squared only had the address and not his number."

"Too bad."

She took in the rather rundown surroundings as Jake drove to their destination. Strip malls flanked car dealerships, and there were more mobile homes than site built ones.

When he pulled onto Marcadis' street, police cars and an ambulance sat in front of a yellow wooden house.

Every muscle tensed. She checked she'd locked the door. "What do you think is happening?" She rolled down her window to get a better view.

"I don't like it whatever it is."

Her chest hurt, and not from the stitches, but from the blood knocking around inside. Had Mr. Marcadis been injured? Or was it a neighbor's house? She didn't want to believe he was dead too.

Jake drove on by and circled the block. "I want you to get in the back and lie down on the seat."

His sharp tone sent her on alert. "Why? No one knows me here."

He pulled over to the side of the road and put the car in park. "No one but the killer."

Chills shook her. "Whose place was that?" She had a clue but wanted confirmation.

"That was our juror's house. If the ambulance is there, someone found him before we could warn him. No telling where our attacker is right now." He clicked open the doors.

This time she didn't argue. Susan slipped out the passenger side, hopped in the back seat and laid down, her chest heavy. She prayed the man was still alive and could identify the maniac who was out to get them all.

"Please find out what happened." Her voice shook.

CHAPTER SEVEN

Jake never liked flashing his badge just to gain information, but sometimes the situation called for using his credentials to get what he needed.

A wide-eyed cop stepped closer and examined Jake's badge, his thumbs jammed in his belt. The man whistled. "FBI, huh? Never had one of you guys here before. How can I help, Detective?"

"Does this house belong to Phillip Marcadis?"

"He's a renter. Stan Kranc owns the place."

Two men in white, facing each other, pushed a wheeled cart through the opened screened front door. A black body bag sat on top. Anger and frustration flooded Jake's system. Damn it. They were too late. He swallowed the fear that twisted his gut.

"Watch out, everybody. Coming through," one of the attendants called.

Jake and the two local cops stepped aside.

Jake nodded to the body. "Is that Mr. Marcadis?"

"Afraid so."

He schooled his features. "How did he die?"

The young cop flipped opened his pad. "We can't be sure until the

Medical Examiner takes a look, but apparently he was changing a ceiling fan and forgot to turn off the power."

Electricity seemed to be the culprit again. "You going to treat this as a homicide?"

"Homicide around here?" He chuckled. "No." The young cop sobered. "You think there was foul play? The guy was by himself."

How could he possibly know that? Killers went into homes, murdered the victim, and then left. "Perhaps. How long has Mr. Marcadis lived here?" Jake had the details, but he needed to see if the local police had a clue.

The cop looked to his partner. "You know when, Vern?"

The older man hiked up his pants. "I talked to Dalia Wilson, the neighbor, and she said he only moved in two days ago. Guess he was fixing up the place. It needed it. Ole man Kranc never did give a damn about repairs."

Jake debated telling them about the Caravello trial but decided the FBI needed to do the investigation, not two local cops who probably had never dealt with a homicide. "Mind if I have a look inside?"

The two men exchanged glances. "I don't know why the FBI would be interested, but go ahead." Vern's jaw clenched. "Just don't touch any evidence."

Jake hid his smile. "Promise."

The house smelled of bleach. Given the torn drapes and stains on the carpet, maybe Mr. Marcadis was trying to make the place livable. What was Richard Thomason thinking asking a juror to move into this sty? He better not pull that trick on him in the future or there'd be hell to pay.

Jake studied the scene. A ladder was positioned under a ceiling-mounted junction box, and an old fan lay on the floor. Problem was, there was no new fan kit. Who took down an old fixture without buying a new one first, assuming he wanted to replace the thing?

The chalk outline of the body was off to the side of the ladder. As a kid, Jake often jumped off ladders to the side to see how far he could reach. The force of his foot pressing against the rung usually toppled it. From where the body was positioned, it looked like that's what had happened here, only the ladder was upright. If Marcadis was electrocuted and fell to the side, why hadn't his ladder fallen over, or at least moved? Something didn't add up.

Jake did a walk-through, looking for the new fixture but found none. Maybe Marcadis had been changing the fan for real and the killer threw the power switch to On. Once he was sure the victim was dead, he flipped the power Off. Regardless of the method, Phillip Marcadis was dead. It didn't much matter how.

Having satisfied his curiosity, he pushed open the screen door, stepped onto the porch, and glanced around. Middle class homes filled the middle class neighborhood.

"Find anything?" Vern said, as he climbed the three steps to the sagging wooden deck.

"No. I'd dust the power panel for prints."

Vern puffed out his chest. "Planned to."

"Great. Good luck."

"For?"

"Figuring out how Marcadis died."

"I thought you said—"

"I never said anything."

Using the remote, Jake clicked open the car door, strode down the drive, and jumped in the driver's side.

As he twisted around to back up, he glanced to the backseat. Susan's eyes were closed. She looked as restful as one could be curled up in a tight ball on the seat. He pushed aside the temptation to take her in his arms and give comfort. The poor woman had been through enough, but she'd kill him if he didn't tell her about Phillip Marcadis' death.

He made sure his head wasn't facing the two cops when he spoke. "Let me go around the block before you get up, and I'll tell you what I know."

"He's dead isn't he?" Her voice wavered.

Anger rolled up his throat. "I'm afraid so."

Why was he one step behind this bastard?

"Are you going to call Mr. Thomason and tell him another one of his jurors is dead?"

"When I can find a secure line. Right now, I don't know who I can trust."

"Are you thinking this is an inside job? That someone in the Bureau is killing these people?"

"I doubt directly." He faced front and pulled away from the house. "You arrive at your townhouse, and within a day, the place burns down. Of the five remaining jurors, three are dead within a couple of days of each other. We've never had a leak before. Something is going on."

"And you suspect Mr. Thomason?"

"Could be him. Could be my direct boss, Stanton Lowry, or any number of people. I just don't know what motive they'd have for leaking the addresses."

"There's no one you can count on?"

"Tom Traynor."

Stanton Lowry had come over from a different department two years ago. While his record was impeccable, he and Thomason became instant best buds.

"You going to call your friend Tom?"

"Yes. He'll inform the correct channels."

"Is Caravello still in jail?"

He'd wondered the same thing. "I'll find out."

Once he moved out of sight of the crime scene, he pulled over, and Susan scooted into the front seat.

Jake decided to call T-Squared before they got on the road.

"Joe's Bar and Grill."

"Phillip Marcadis is dead." No use beating around the bush.

"Jesus Christ. How did he die?"

Jake told him about the supposed electrocution.

"It had to be murder."

"Could have been an accident, but I doubt it."

"How could they have found out where Marcadis was staying?"

"You find the answer to that question and we'll be one step closer to finding the killer."

Tom must have placed a hand over the phone for a second as his voice came out muffled. "Sorry about that."

"What about Caravello? Could he have had anything to do with

Marcadis' death?" Jake asked. He held his voice flat. With Susan next
to him, he didn't want give away his concern.

"Lawyers posted bail right away. He walked last night."

"Shit."

If Peter drove straight through the night, he could have made the
twelve-hour drive to Lake City by morning.

***

Joseph Francisco looked at the incoming call and held a finger to his
lips as his grandchildren raced around the room. "Poppy needs you two
to be quiet. Your daddy's on the line."

"Daddy!" the three-year old shrieked and hugged Joseph's leg. He
ran his hand down her blond curls. God they were cute.

Samantha whipped around and raced toward her older brother. "I
get the crayons."

Joseph turned his attention back to the ringing phone. "Hey, Dom.
He dead?"

"Hi, to you too. Yeah. Phillip Marcadis won't be on any jury no
more."

"Good." Joseph cast a glance at Mario playing with his GI Joe
figures. He could remember like it was yesterday when Dom played
with those same plastic toys.

"You'll never guess who showed up at the crime scene," his son
said.

"Who?"

"That FBI guy, Jake Yarnell."

A burst of excitement grabbed him. "No shit. What was he doing
there?"

"Didn't exactly stop and introduce myself. Yarnell flashed his badge
and the local cops acted like he was some god. Then he went into the
house right after the paramedics took the body away."

Sometimes he wondered who'd raised his son. "What were you
doing waiting around a crime scene? Someone could have identified
you."

"Nah, I was careful."

His bravado would be the end of him. "Was the girl with Jake?"

"Not that I could tell."

"Where are you now?"

"I'm about twenty car lengths behind Yarnell."

He'd expected the name of a town, but Dom's proximity to the girl said all was under control. "Good. Follow him. He'll lead you to her."

***

Peter Caravello dragged his lips along Maria Francisco's neck, enjoying her smooth skin and delicious scent, ignoring his vibrating phone.

"Aren't you going to answer that?" she said, as she ran a hand down his belly to his crotch.

"With what you're doing? Not on your life."

She sat back up. "I can't concentrate when someone wants to talk to you. It could be the lawyers saying they caught whoever is killing those jurors."

"All right." He tugged the phone from his pocket. His brow rose. "It's Jake." He punched the talk button. "Yeah, buddy." He ran a hand down Maria's arm.

"Where are you?"

Peter's defenses shot up. Jake's accusation came out harsh. "I'm home. Why?" Had Jake learned he'd been in jail?

"Another juror was killed about an hour ago."

"Where?" He lifted her off his lap and motioned her away. He didn't need her distraction.

"Florida."

Peter let out a laugh. "I've been here all morning." He looked over at Maria and pasted on a smile. She didn't return his apparent happiness. She always could see through him.

"Can anyone vouch for your whereabouts?" Jake's tone had softened, but he acted as though maybe he still believed Peter might be guilty of something.

"Always the cop."

"Answer my question. Please."

The polite request got to him. "I've been with Maria since my release." He motioned he wanted her by his side again now the alert had sounded. She'd have to go back to the hospital soon, and he didn't want to squander their time together.

"Maria, as in Maria Francisco?"

"The one and only, but don't say a word. No one knows we've hooked up."

"Christ, her old man would have a shit fit if he found out." Jake sounded like his old self.

"Don't I know it."

"Oh, I get it now. You were with Maria the night Janet Starkey died, weren't you?"

Smart man. "Yes."

"That's why you said you had no alibi. You didn't want anyone to know about you two."

"Right." He detected a lot of traffic noise. "Where are you? I thought your job was to protect the prosecuting attorney."

"It is. She's with me. We're in North Florida." Jake relayed the story of the fire and how it had nearly killed both of them.

"I'm sorry." Maria returned to her rightful place on his lap and nuzzled his neck.

"Thanks. We got cut off the last time we talked. What did the Bureau have on you that they would arrest you and not James?"

His older brother was the most likely candidate. He had his fingers deep in Dad's counterfeiting practice.

"They found Janet Starkey's wallet at my house, though I don't know how they knew to look there. I had no idea it was there." He held his breath, waiting for the recrimination.

"Who could have planted it there?"

Relief washed over him. Jake believed him. "You tell me."

"James?"

"My brother might not be the most honest person in the world, but there's no way he'd set me up. He has no reason to see me go down."

Maria tapped her watch indicating she had to go soon. He held up a finger.

"You might be right," Jake said.

"Look I gotta go. Keep in touch."

The moment he hung up, he wrapped her arms around her waist and leaned his lips close to her ear, her scent arousing him.

"Does he believe you?" she asked

"I think so."

She leaned back and smiled. "Good. Now where were we?"

She kissed him hard, and he gathered her slim body closer.

Her cell rang and she stiffened. She slipped the phone from her pocket. "It's Dad. I have to answer it."

He knew the routine. "Go ahead. We might as well get all the phone calls out of the way."

She softened her lips and lingered on his mouth before leaning back. "Hi, Dad." She brushed her bangs way from her face. "I can't come now. I'm at the hospital doing rounds." Maria rolled her eyes as she stood again.

He missed her already. Peter mouthed the words *I love you*.

Maria blushed. Cute.

"Stacia is sick and I had to take her shift." She paced in front of him. "Uh, oh. Code Blue. I have to go. Bye." She disconnected and blew out a breath. "I hate lying to him."

"You know the consequences if you don't."

CHAPTER EIGHT

Susan didn't want to leave the motel bathroom. The shower had helped remove the day's grime, and it had also lessened the impact of the newest juror's death. Being cocooned in the tight tiled shower, with the door locked, had given her the sense of security she craved. She wanted to stay there all night.

A tap sounded on the bathroom door. "Susan, you have to come out sometime."

Jake needed to shower, and it was probably way past ten p.m. "I'm coming."

She gathered the clothes she'd neatly folded and left her makeup bag on the counter. Seeing his toothbrush and razor next to her things set off conflicting emotions. After her divorce, she'd sworn off men, but despite her early distrust of Jake, he'd uprooted a deep yearning inside her. Being attracted to him and sleeping next to him though were two different things.

She opened the door. Ohmigod. Jake didn't have a shirt on, and her throat turned dry. His bulging shoulder muscles and amazing abs screamed *touch me*—not what she needed right now.

A band of what looked like barbed wire ran the circumference of his bicep, along with some design poking above the barbs. The tattoo appeared old and distorted, and she wondered why he chose that image to mar his perfectly sculpted body. The last time he'd undressed, she'd been so busy looking at his body that she hadn't noticed the tattoos.

She ripped her gaze away from the enticing view and strode past him, hoping he hadn't caught her staring and her mouth slightly dropping. The steam followed her out.

"You leave any hot water for me?" His voice held too much humor.

She turned and glanced up. His eyes were wide, but in an animated way. "What? You're not into cold showers?"

His gaze ran the length of her. "I might just need one now."

If he hadn't stepped into the bathroom right then, he would have caught the intense heat racing up her face. Maybe she'd asked for that response, or maybe it was exactly what she wanted.

Sometimes Jake pissed her off with his too cocky attitude, but his tender side always wedged a notch in her heart. His strange relationship with Peter Caravello still made her uneasy, but she'd resigned herself that Jake Yarnell meant her no harm.

She willed her body to move once he turned on the shower. She wouldn't think of him naked and soapy. Nope. She wouldn't let his muscular, hard body cross her mind either. That just wasn't going to happen.

Her leg bumped the king-sized bed. It might be large enough for both of them, but there was no way she wanted to be that close, for hours on end, to such a hottie. Besides, she'd never sleep if she had to listen to him breathe and feel the indent of the bed as he rolled over. She'd be wide-awake wondering if he'd accidentally wrap an arm around her and pull her tight.

But how amazing would it be to run her fingers over his rippled abs or have his body pressed against hers?

Dear Lord. How long had it been since she'd lusted after a man? It had been more than the six months since she divorced Carlton. Her ex sure as hell hadn't inspired lust in a long time.

Stop it. Jake was her bodyguard, paid for by the United States government. FBI employees didn't have sex with witnesses, or touch them, or pull them tight against their hard chests.

She scanned the room once more. There wasn't even enough room for a cot, so they'd have to share the bed. At that thought, she shoved aside the thrill that snuck in her belly.

Guess she couldn't control everything in her life.

Poor Jake. Every time she rolled over, she might wake him, and God knows they both needed their sleep.

While he did his thing in the bathroom, she slipped under the covers. Her pajamas were flannel—unattractive and anything but alluring. Good. He'd want to keep his hands to himself.

She ran her fingers along the cool sheets. The clean, crisp cotton made her temporarily forget her dilemma. Fresh linens and a soft bed were better medicine than any pain drugs.

She clicked on the television for background noise and begged her body to relax. Only her mind wouldn't stop the fantasy of the naked man in the shower.

He must have stayed inside the bathroom for a long time, for when she awoke, the lights were off, the television was on mute, and Jake was in the chair by the desk. The picture's glow cast a soft shadow on him. Fully dressed, he was stretched out on the padded chair, much like the first time she'd seen him. He shifted to his other hip, a position that didn't look comfortable.

"Jake?"

He jumped up and looked right, and then left. His frantic movement almost looked comical until his gaze landed on her.

"Are you okay?"

His concern warmed her heart. "Yes. I just wanted to know if you'd rather sleep in the bed."

He took a step forward, but then stopped. "You sure? That chair is rather uncomfortable."

"I'm sure."

He smiled. "My back thanks you."

He took off his shoes before planting himself on top of the spread. What a gentleman. With his arms crossed, his face relaxed. She'd been about to say he could slip under the covers to get more comfortable, but she didn't want to push the boundaries—or test her resolve.

She clicked off the television. "Goodnight."

"Goodnight, Susan." His voice came out as soft as melted chocolate, but she refused to read anything into his tone. He'd just woken up, or so she wanted to believe.

She rolled on her side, her back to him and listened to his deep breaths. He didn't squirm, didn't roll, didn't do much of anything, but she'd bet her twenty bucks he was thinking about her.

Her speeding mind refused to slow. She could tell he hadn't fallen asleep in the minute since he crawled to the bed. "I saw you had a tattoo."

"You did, huh?"

Could he read her mind that she was interested? "I'm curious what's above the barbed wire?" She rolled over to face him.

"A daisy."

She nearly choked. "A daisy?"

"Too feminine for you?" He was teasing her again, and she kind of liked the banter.

"Not on you." And that was the truth. "The flower looked lopsided though."

They were face to face, less than a foot apart, almost close enough to lean over and kiss.

"That's because the flower only has four petals. One at eleven o'clock, one at ten, nine, and again at eight."

She let out a chuckle. She loved playing, *he loves me, he loves me not,* with a flower.

"Why only four petals? Would more have cost too much?" She guessed from the way he admired their first townhouse that he didn't live in luxury.

"Yes, but that's not the reason. I was in four foster homes before I turned eighteen. Hence the four petals."

Every muscle stilled, as sympathy swamped her. "You were in four foster homes?"

"That's what I said."

Guess he didn't want to discuss that aspect of his life. He must understand about loneliness and lack of family then, but she refused to be put off. "What did the daisy stand for?" Odd choice for a flower.

Blood thrummed in her head awaiting his answer. Was it for the one woman who got away?

He sucked on his bottom lip for a moment, clearly trying to decide how much to tell.

"The first foster home I went to was run by nuns. Sister Mary Louise was kind to me, the first person in my life who treated me with respect. She loved daisies."

Her heart nearly burst. "What happened?" To the nun, to the love between them, to the little boy?

"Nothing. When a family offered to take me a few months later, she let me go." Bitterness tainted his words.

He rolled to the other side. Discussion over.

Had he expected a nun to adopt him? How young had he been when he lost his family? He probably wouldn't tell even if she asked. From the way his voice wavered, his past had caused him intense pain.

For a brief moment, she was tempted to ask if she could give him a hug to help fight his demons, but who was she to give comfort? She was barely hanging on herself. If she touched his skin and smelled his scent, would she want more?

Oh, crap. She'd never asked if he had a girlfriend or a wife at home. Given his job took him out of town for unknown periods of time, she doubted any woman who loved him would put up with that schedule. She had assumed he was a loner.

Armed with the new knowledge he'd grown up in foster care, he probably never developed attachments and never would or could. Receiving or even giving comfort would be foreign to him. He was a protector, the one to decide when to care and when to give of himself.

His breaths evened out, and he emitted soft puffs of air. Good. He'd fallen asleep.

She wanted to talk with him about what made him tick, but tonight's explanation of his tattoo might be more than he'd shared with anyone in a while. He would never know how much they did have in common. Her coworkers claimed she was a cold bitch. She'd overheard one attorney say it was no wonder Carlton strayed. She probably sucked in bed.

That wasn't true. She just hadn't found anyone she wanted to give her soul too. Her mom had loved her growing up, but over the years she'd turned to alcohol after her brother's accident. Their family never had been the same after that. Her daddy had doted on her, but again, only when he was home and not working at the office trying to protect the world from criminals. Yet her life was bliss compared to Jake's.

What she wouldn't give to get a hold of his good friend, T-Squared, to find out the lowdown on the enigmatic Jake Yarnell.

He shifted in the bed and a rush of hormones startled her. She was running for her life and had to pay attention to everyone around her—not just Jake. All she could think about lately was him, which was not good for a woman in hiding and now on the run.

She pushed aside the image of the little boy desperate for affection and tried to relax, but sleep didn't come. Her mind bounced between the fire, the dead jurors, and Jake.

She scooted closer. His weight held down the sheet, preventing her from closing in on him too much. His skin smelled of lemons. Without thinking, she reached out to touch his silky hair. Quicker than she could react, his hand grabbed her wrist.

Her heart stopped for a moment and her throat clogged.

"Need something?" he said in a teasing voice.

Had he been waiting for her to make the first move? She could have sworn he'd been asleep a moment ago.

Before she could think, he let go of her wrist, and she cleared her throat. "Just checking you were still there." Very lame.

This time he laughed. "If you want me to get under the covers so we can cuddle, just say the word."

Exactly what she wanted. "No!"

"Thought so. Get some sleep. We'll need it."

Like that would ever happen now. She'd crossed the boundary of propriety this time and wasn't sure if she wanted to step over the line again.

CHAPTER NINE

Jake rose at dawn and went through his bathroom routine before Susan awoke, all the while trying to erase the image of her sweet face holding on to his every word as he let her glimpse what his life had been like after his mom died. Susan didn't judge, didn't criticize, or show signs of pity. She just listened. To him, she acted as if he were the most important person in the room.

He scratched his brain for the last time he'd told anyone about his tattoo. Tom had seen the image but never asked what the flower meant.

He stepped over to the bed and studied her. Susan looked more at peace than he'd ever seen her—prettier, younger, more vulnerable. Something inside him nearly cracked at the connection they'd made last night, but he pushed down his emotions. Even though he'd had several girlfriends, there was something special about her. He liked Susan's assertiveness, her bravery, and her can-do outlook on life. And how she listened.

Even before he shared his story, he'd been interested in her, despite the fact she constantly challenged him, and then rejected him. Add in the fact she didn't completely trust him, and he wondered why he wanted to hold and comfort her.

Then when she'd reached out to touch him last night, his self-control had nearly broken. He was teasing her about getting under the covers and snuggling, but if she'd wanted to, that meant she trusted him. Her willingness to trust might save her life someday.

Her lids fluttered and he stepped back. What if she had agreed to the touching, the cuddling, and maybe even kissing? Would he have followed through? Hell, if he knew. He probably would have jumped out of bed and slept in the chair. Getting involved would cloud his vision, his focus, and his ability to keep her alive.

Not wanting to further address his reaction to the adorable woman, he stepped outside, telling himself he needed to check the parking lot for mysterious men with submachine guns pointed at the door. The air was chillier than he'd expected for a Florida morning.

Only one couple was up and about. He stayed outside for several minutes until he thought he heard Susan call his name.

She wasn't in the bed when he stepped back inside, but the running water told him she'd taken his place in the bathroom. Just as well. He needed to touch base with T-Squared, and it might be better if she didn't hear the conversation. He swiped his cell, the phone becoming like a third arm. He longed for the day when he could talk to his colleagues in person.

"Hiya, Jake."

Tom sounded way too chipper. He must have just gotten home. "How did Stanton, Richard, and the rest of gang react to Marcadis' death?"

"Like you'd expect. The shit hit the fan. Richard looked like he was having a heart attack. I think he was tempted to fly down to North Carolina and protect one of the last two jurors himself. Stanton stayed calm for a while, and then started ordering us to do things. I left, so I don't know what transpired after that."

"What's the Bureau's plan of attack?"

"Thomason insisted we post bodyguards at each of the remaining jurors' places. They're on their way to Atlanta and Brevard right now."

"That's great."

"I almost forgot. Both Stanton and Richard have been trying to get a hold of you, claiming you're not answering. They're worried."

Someone arguing in the parking lot drew his attention. It was nothing to worry about—just a man yelling at his kids.

"I know. I don't want to talk to anyone. Tell them when the house caught on fire, my cell phone burned up. I've called you on a pay phone and don't know when I'll find a replacement."

"Will do." Tom's voice lowered to almost a whisper. "Where are you headed?"

"To Atlanta. Bodyguard or not, I want to warn the next juror."

"Good for you. I'll be in touch if anything comes up."

"Thanks."

They both disconnected, acutely aware long calls were traceable. Jake needed to get a pre-paid phone, one where the FBI couldn't find him.

Just as he returned to the room, Susan popped out of the bathroom, hair washed, cleanly bandaged and sexy as hell in her tight jeans and equally tight top. Quite the change from the baggy sweats.

"What's our plan?" Susan unzipped her suitcase with a slow easy pull, but the strong grip on the zipper told him she was anything but calm.

"We drive to Atlanta."

She glanced up at him. "Who's there?"

"Ashley Wood."

Susan's hands, full of clothes, froze in midair. "She was the young one. I think she was a senior at American when she served on the jury. Her lips turned into a frown. "Sweet girl. She must be so afraid."

"I don't think she knows about the other jurors. We've kept that information as quiet as possible."

Susan shook her head, stuffed her clothes and her toiletries kit into her suitcase, and closed the lid. She swiped a hand over her hair. Gray circles under her eyes appeared more pronounced today. The traveling was wearing on her, but they couldn't afford to sit still. They had to warn the others.

He picked up both her case and his. "Let's boogie."

He kept an eye out for anyone suspicious as he headed to the car. If Phillip Marcadis' place was discovered within a day or two of the witness' arrival, someone had excellent intel—too good in fact. No telling who knew where they were.

Susan climbed in the front seat. Her movements were more fluid today, implying her wounds were on the mend. Eventually, they'd need a doctor to take out her stitches, but for now her injuries wouldn't prevent them from the five-hour drive ahead.

He placed the luggage in the trunk and climbed in the driver's seat. As they exited the lot, a black SUV pulled behind them. Given they were at a motel, it wasn't surprising other guests would leave at this early hour.

He drove slightly under the speed limit thinking anyone willing to drive that slowly would be an obvious tail. Staying in the right lane for about a mile, he drove underneath the interstate in the hopes the black car would hop onto I-75. No such luck.

The number of restaurants thinned, making him question where this guy was going. Jake had debated eating breakfast once they were on the road, but this guy was bugging him. He turned into a car dealership, did a U-turn, and headed back the other way.

"Where are you going?" The tension in Susan's voice cut him deep.

"I won't lie to you. I thought someone was following us, but when I turned around, we lost him." He glanced over at her. "Do you mind if we catch a bite to eat here? I want to make sure this guy doesn't get any ideas."

"Sounds good."

He wanted a place that was fast and with good visibility. Waffle House provided the perfect venue. Unfortunately, the parking lot wrapped around the building, and while he could see all the patrons inside, he wouldn't be able to tell if a black SUV pulled in.

Once inside, the aroma of waffles, grease and bacon permeated the restaurant. Half the booths were full. Jake pointed to a spot near the entrance for a fast getaway.

Susan and he were half way into their meal, when a man in his late thirties, early forties walked in. He glanced around, his gaze lingering on Jake and Susan. The stranger proceeded to take a booth two away from them when three other booths on the far end were vacant. The hairs on Jake's neck rippled.

Something about the short, stocky man looked familiar. He didn't want to frighten Susan, but he thought she might know him.

"Don't look now, but there's a man two booths behind you." He kept his voice to a near whisper. "He's dressed in a nice polo and an expensive jacket. His watch must have set him back five hundred bucks. Would you mind going into the bathroom and waiting a minute before coming out? When you walk back to the booth, take a quick peek at the guy, but be as unobtrusive as possible. Can you do that?"

Her face paled. She drained the rest of her orange juice, acting as if she needed some fortification. She slid out of the booth, her shoulders way too stiff.

The waitress ambled over. "Can I get you anything else, sugar?"

"Just the check," Jake replied.

The drab brunette, who was missing several front teeth, slipped a hand in her pocket and produced the ticket. "Here ya go, hon."

Jake pretended to study the bill. When the bathroom door in front of him opened, he stood and chanced a glance. Susan was returning just as a different waitress was placing a waffle in front of the newcomer.

Jake faced Susan and kept his voice low. "Let me pay and we can go."

Susan's teeth clenched. She followed behind him, her back brushing against his every few steps. He stiffened then forced his body to relax. Since all the waitresses were busy, he placed a twenty on the counter and waved to catch her eye. She held up a finger. Not needing the change, they left.

Wrapping an arm around Susan's waist to make it appear as if they were a couple, instead of a bodyguard and potential witness, he led her outside. Once they were out of sight of the front plate glass walls, he asked if she recognized him.

She bit her bottom lip. "I think I've seen him somewhere, but I can't be certain."

"In that case, I think I'll take some back roads and get on the interstate north of here. It will be harder to tail us on a road not well traveled."

She shivered. "Sounds good."

The pep in her step increased. As they drove out of the lot, Jake glanced inside at the booth where the man had been sitting. It was empty.

Jake's gut clenched. Something wasn't right.

After traveling north for twenty minutes, Jake became lulled into believing no one had followed them. A few fast moving vehicles piled up behind them on the two-lane road. Jake let them pass, but he saw no sign of the black SUV. While he enjoyed the drive on the narrow winding road, the Interstate would be faster, and time was critical. He refused to let what happened to Phillip Marcadis happen to Ashley Wood.

He'd just rounded a curve when someone slammed into the back of his car, jarring him out of his trance. "Jesus Christ."

Susan screamed as her body propelled forward.

He thrust a hand to stop her from smashing into the dash, but her seatbelt luckily held her in place. She gasped.

"Are you okay?" he said.

"Kind of." Her breaths came out fast, and her brows pinched.

He glanced in the rear view mirror. A red pickup truck was about fifty feet behind him but gaining speed quickly. Jake wasn't sure who'd hit him, but he figured it had to have been the truck directly behind him.

Adrenaline pumped through his veins, and he tightened his grip on the wheel. With one eye on the rear view mirror, he sped up, not daring to pull over. If it had been an accidental hit, the person who banged into him would be glad not to get involved in an insurance claim. If the driver had meant to harm them, Jake needed to get the hell away from there.

He pressed his foot to the floor, fishtailing on the road. A cloud blocked the morning sun, casting the ground in shadows. The wind whipped the trees all of a sudden as if a front had descended on them.

Jake took his gaze off the road for a second and one wheel slipped onto the dirt berm, but he managed to bring the car onto the pavement.

"What's going on?" Susan gripped the dashboard. Her voice came out an octave too high.

"I'm not sure." He saw no need to create more fear, especially when he didn't have all the facts.

If he'd been able to do a U-turn without flipping over, he would have.

The red truck was gaining on them. They were the only two cars on the road now. A long bend was up ahead with a large ditch sat to the right. As he held tight around the curve, the truck pulled alongside in the on-coming lane. How had he sped up so fast? Damn his four cylinders.

The truck's tinted windows prevented Jake from seeing who was behind the wheel. He debated slamming on his brakes but decided his best option was to try to keep ahead of this maniac.

Pressing his foot to the floor, his car shimmied as he approached eighty. The bend steepened and his wheels began to slide off the pavement again. The truck's driver kept up with him and bumped into the driver's side, sending the car sideways. Jake held on tight, but the small vehicle wouldn't keep purchase.

Without warning, the truck pulled ahead and turned in front of him, forcing Jake to jerk the wheel to the right to avoid a head on collision. His rental flew off the road. The dirt bit the tires, slowing the car, and rocks pummeled the undercarriage. The vibration shook them hard. His arms wobbled as he tried to keep control of the vehicle.

"Jake?"

Susan's whimper increased his resolve to keep them safe. A large tree stood fifty feet in front of them coming at them fast. He slammed on the brakes and pulled the wheels to the left. As he hit the tree, his head propelled forward, and the airbag deployed. Pain seared his brain. The car bucked and bumped.

Then everything blanked out.

CHAPTER TEN

As Susan's body shot toward the dash, she tried to brace herself. Her left knee hit the dashboard, sending lightning like bolts of pain up her thigh. The seatbelt tore into her body as the airbag stopped her cold.

The engine cut off.

Her mind went numb for a moment. She pushed back in her seat, her breath whooshing out of her. Jake!

His body was crumpled forward over the deflated airbag. Susan squeezed his shoulder, fear and panic gripping her. "Jake?"

Her pulse raced, and her chest throbbed from the pressure of where the seatbelt had bit into her, inches from her previous injury. Her nose hurt from the airbag and her body ached, but at least she was alive—and more importantly alert.

He moaned and she was never so happy to hear that sound. He was alive!

Jake lifted his head an inch then dropped it back onto the deflated bag, his arms limp at his side. Blood coursed down his nose from the head wound.

"Jake?" Her voice shook.

She wanted to shake him hard, to wake him, but if she moved him and he had a concussion, she might do more harm.

She scanned the road to see if anyone was around to help them or if the red truck was hell bent on killing them. No one was around. Why had the other driver taken off? There was little doubt he meant to injure them—or kill them—but why leave before seeing the deed complete?

Jake's bleeding had to take top priority. Then she'd get help, assuming someone would drive by. They'd gone off the road a good hundred feet. Someone from above might not notice them unless she made it up to the ridge and flagged someone down.

She checked the glove box for some tissues, but it was empty. Damn. Her suitcase was in the trunk and the blood had already run down his shirt.

Susan pulled off her lightweight sweater, wadded the material into a ball and pressed the bandage to his forehead.

"This will help stem the blood flow." She wasn't sure if he could hear her, but her own voice comforted her.

His right eye cracked open. "Susan? Ouch."

"Sorry. We were in an accident. You've got blood trickling down your face and shirt."

He moaned again. "You okay?"

"I'm fine. You're the one who needs help." She appreciated how he put her safety above his. How had she ever questioned his need to protect her? She'd been a fool. Maybe being in a coma had messed with her brain function after all.

Jake grabbed the material, leaned back and held the sweater to his forehead. His mouth gaped open as if he were grasping for breath. "Is he gone?"

"If you mean the guy who hit us, yes. We need to get you to a hospital."

"No." Jake winced.

"If my head were cut, wouldn't you insist I get help?"

"Yes, but I'm not you."

Stubborn man.

As he sat up, he sucked in a large breath through clenched teeth. He must have broken a rib. They so didn't need this.

"Did you get the license plate of the red truck?" he asked.

Her mouthed dropped. "You're kidding, right? The whole thing happened in seconds. My heart was pounding so fast, I was lucky to remember to brace myself."

Jake removed the sweater, turned it around and dabbed his forehead again. "You got one of those large bandages in your suitcase I could have?"

"Those I have plenty of." Thankful she was able to help, she pulled the keys from the ignition to unlock the trunk.

As she stepped out onto the grass, her leg buckled, and a king-sized ache squeezed her knee. She dropped to the ground. Jake's door rattled, but apparently he couldn't open it. "Susan?"

"I'm okay. I'm okay. Don't get out."

With effort, she pulled herself up and slowly walked to the trunk, putting most of her weight on her right leg. A moment later, she opened her suitcase and retrieved her toiletry kit with the bandages.

A car whizzed by. She waved, but they didn't even slow down, proof no one could see them from the road.

She came over to the driver's side and yanked on the handle. Crap. The impact had dented the side, preventing her from opening the door. "I need to go to the other side. Hold on."

Once she slid in her side, she reached to take back the bloody sweater.

He held up his hand. "You don't need to be touching my blood." He swiped the sweater across his forehead. "Give me the bandage."

She opened the package and handed it to him. He looked in the rear view mirror, aimed, and pressed it to his head. "Good as new." He smiled, but his lips appeared unsteady.

She didn't like the look of his pasty skin. "How are we going to get out of here?"

"Let me see if I can drive this dented heap. We don't need to open my door."

"Do you have a headache?"

His brow rose. "What do you think?"

"Then I should drive."

"No."

Jake's cell phone had fallen out of his pocket and was on the seat. She picked it up. "I'm calling 9-1-1."

He placed his hand on hers. "No. We can't afford the delay—or have whoever did this learn we lived through the crash."

He did have a point. That horrible person could be monitoring his cell. Somehow the killer had found them. Via Jake's cell made the most sense.

"I'm not letting you drive. You could have a concussion. You were unconscious, at least for a little bit."

"I'm fine."

Men. "If you're behind the wheel and start vomiting, we could be in big trouble."

"You win. I don't have the energy to argue. " He slapped the wheel. "The rental company is going to have a fit. When they see the damages, it might be hard to rent another car from them, and our cash is limited. Cross your fingers this puppy is drivable."

They hadn't hit the tree that hard.

"Don't you have a credit card? We'll need to rent another vehicle, especially since he knows this one."

"Yes, but cards are easy to trace. Someone knows where we've been and where we were staying. Next time they could kill us."

"Which begs the question, why didn't they finish the job?"

He squeezed his eyes shut. "Maybe they wanted to scare us."

"Do you really believe that?"

"No. Someone must have driven by and scared him off."

"If someone drove by, why didn't they stop and help us?"

He opened his eyes and turned his head toward her. "I wish I had the answers to all of your questions, but I don't. What I do know is we need to leave. Now."

"That's the first sensible thing you've said." She twisted toward him.

His jaw lowered. "Susan, you're bleeding."

She looked down at the large, red stain over her breast. Her stitches must have broken. "Damn." She peeked down her top. Blood had caked around her wound. "The impact of the seatbelt must have torn my stitches. I'll be okay."

"If we don't want to cause people to notice us, we both better change."

"Right."

She jumped out again. This time her leg held. She searched through both suitcases for something suitable. She found a new shirt for Jake and a t-shirt and sweatshirt for herself. She still wasn't able to wear a bra and had to cover up the best she could.

She tossed him his shirt. "Here."

He had no problem getting out of his clothes. Once again, Susan was unable to take her eyes off his rippling abs and well-defined pecs.

He glanced over and smiled. "What are you waiting for?"

Jerk. He knew she was staring. While there were only trees on the other side of the car, she didn't want to strip outside, so she climbed into the backseat. With her back to Jake, she took off her shirt and reapplied a clean bandage. Once dressed, she waited for him to get out so she could climb back into the driver's seat. "Let's go find Ashley Woods."

***

During the five-hour drive to Atlanta, Jake had fallen asleep for half of it. His headache hadn't lessened, but it hadn't gotten worse either. He should have forced himself to stay awake. Someone might have followed them, and Susan had no skill to detect a tail.

"Stop worrying," she said the moment he opened his eyes.

"What?"

"I know you think I'm not watching who's behind us, but I am."

The woman was a psychic now? Had she read his mind? Jake studied the rear view mirror as Susan pulled off the Interstate.

"You hungry?" she asked.

"What do you think?"

After they sped through a drive-through, they located Ashley Wood's house, situated a block off a main thoroughfare. No one had followed them—or so he wanted to believe.

"Looks clear. That's the house." He pointed to the small, cozy yellow house with the attached porch. "Park in front." He loved GPS.

Susan wilted once she put the car in gear. Maybe he should have insisted they stop at a motel before coming here. As much as she claimed she was okay, he could tell from the way she kept blinking that she needed to rest.

Once they told Ashley about the impending danger, they'd get a room and relax.

Jake eased out, and then helped Susan out the passenger side door. Having one working door sucked.

Richard did well picking this home for Ashley. It was on a nice street. Even the red and yellow pots next to the white wicker rocking chair oozed Southern charm. He rang the bell and waited.

"How are you going to break the news to her that her life is in immediate danger?" she asked. "Will you make up some story that this place had been compromised?"

"I'll decide when I meet her."

"She's a tough girl. I think she can handle the truth."

He'd been about the knock again when screeching tires and a loud crash tore his attention from the door.

A block down the street at a large intersection, a black SUV had plowed into a blue VW on the driver side, pushing the smaller vehicle across the road.

Adrenaline sped through his veins. "Stay here," he said as he raced down the path to the street, grimacing at the pounding in his head and chest. Maybe he had broken a rib as Susan believed.

Before he reached the accident, the SUV backed up, turned around and drove down the street past him. The dark tinted windows prevented him for identifying anything about the driver, and the vehicle didn't have a license plate. Shit.

Jake's only thought was to help the poor person inside the car once he reached the vehicle.

Another loud crash forced him to stop and look back. The same black SUV had rear-ended the driver's side front bumper of their rental. What the fuck was going on? Susan stood frozen on the porch.

"Get down!" he yelled. The driver might have a gun.

Susan dropped to her haunches and covered her head.

The moment the SUV took off and didn't fire any shots, Jake was torn between going after the guy, helping the victim, and checking on Susan. Since Susan was uninjured and the hit-and-run driver wasn't spewing any bullets, Jake decided the injured person needed him more. The cops could search for the driver.

When he reached the crumpled car, the woman inside was slumped over on the seat, her eyes open, her breath short, appearing to be in shock. Jake patted his pants for his phone to call for help. Damn. He looked up to get Susan's attention. She was at their car with the phone in hand. Smart girl.

He didn't want to move the bloodied victim and saw no reason to touch her. The side window was gone and Jake leaned in. "Help is on the way. Hold on." Her mouth moved, but no sound came out. "Can you tell me your name?"

She blinked, giving him hope she understood.

"Ash..."

Jake's heart nearly stopped. "Are you Ashley Woods?"

Her lips pressed together right before her eyes closed. No answer. While he didn't see any external injuries other than the contusion on her forehead, there might be massive internal injuries. This girl looked like she was hanging on by a thread.

Susan rushed over to his side. "How is she?"

He shook his head. "Unconscious, but alive."

"I called 9-1-1."

"Good."

They stayed by her side to make sure the maniac who'd rammed her didn't return. When he heard the ambulance in the distance, he figured it would be smarter not to become involved. He would call in the description of the car once they were out of sight.

"Come on. We need to leave."

Her brows furrowed, but she thankfully didn't argue. He quickly checked out the damage to the bumper of their rental car. The grill-work was bent, now matching the other side. It was possible the radiator was damaged.

"I hope this sucker runs."

"The bastard rammed us for no apparent reason," she said. "Unless it's the same person who drove the red truck."

"Possibly." The siren neared. "Come on."

Susan hobbled to the door. "I'll drive. You can be the lookout person."

Worked for him. After she slipped in, he got in and kept an eye on the side view mirror.

The car turned over on the third try. "Go, but don't make it look like we're racing away," he said.

She turned and leered at him. "I'm not dumb."

That, he knew. They'd rounded the corner when a light and siren flashed behind them. Shit.

"What should I do?" she said in pure panic mode.

"Pull over. We've got nothing to hide."

She glanced at him, her lips pressed firmly together. Once she stopped, she rolled the window down half way, since the dent in the car prevented it from moving any more.

It took the officer several minutes before he approached them. No doubt he was running the plates, what good that would do him.

"Let me do the talking," Jake said.

"I argue for a living. Maybe I should explain. After all, I'm the one on the run."

"And I'm the one with the FBI badge."

The officer rapped on the window. "May I see your license and registration?"

Her mouth dropped open. She didn't have a license and shouldn't have been driving. They were in a shitload of trouble.

CHAPTER ELEVEN

Only because Jake had flashed his badge had the police been willing to discuss the situation in an office instead of a small, stuffy interrogation room.

He'd waited for close to thirty minutes before Officer Vargas walked in—Hispanic, pock mocked, and thin to the point of anorexic looking.

Jake was hurting, irritated, and had run out of patience. "Where's Mrs. Chapman?"

He was pissed they'd separated them. She didn't need this hassle dumped on her.

"Somewhere safe." Vargas hoisted up his belt, reminding him of the cop in Lake City, only Vargas' pants threatened to slip off his hips if he didn't put another notch in the leather.

Jake had done interrogations and used evasive sarcasm as a way to get the informant to tell the truth. The cop's tactic wouldn't work with him. "I'm not sure what more I can tell you."

He kept his voice non-threatening, hoping Vargas would see his side.

"Other than you went to talk to some witness, and when you were knocking on her door, someone ran into her. You called 9-1-1 and left."

"There's no crime in that."

"It is if you hit the victim and the victim is dead."

A giant claw grabbed his gut. "Ashley Wood didn't make it?"

"I'm afraid not." Any residual sarcasm was replaced with sincerity.

Jake swallowed to keep the bile from rising. "What evidence do you have that my car hit hers?" Once a cop, always a cop, even if he now worked for the FBI.

Vargas skimmed the two-page report. "Your front end is banged up."

Jake had figured that was his only evidence and leaned back in his chair. The sooner he got this bozo to understand the circumstances, the sooner he'd get to take Susan out of here. She needed medical attention.

"I already explained how that happened. Can't you take paint samples and see that my fender was dented by a black car and not a blue one? And the driver's side of my rear bumper was smashed by a red truck."

Only problem was that the test could take weeks. He bet the Atlanta crime lab had more important things to do than test paint chips.

"Your car is being impounded as we speak. Your luck sucks. If I were you, I wouldn't drive for a while."

"Thanks for the advice."

Vargas cleared his throat. "Once we're convinced what you say is true, we'll release your car back to you."

He had to be kidding. "Ashley Wood, as well as Taylor Daniels are both under the protection of the FBI. Call my boss. He'll verify that fact."

Jake debated using Susan's real name, but at this point, no one could be trusted. He didn't like Stanton finding out about this debacle, but Jake didn't see any way out of this dilemma.

"I already contacted the GBI. They're looking into your claim."

A knock sounded on the door and a young woman poked her head in the office. "A detective Brad Carroll, from the GBI is here to see you."

Officer Vargas smiled. "That was fast. We'll get to the bottom of this soon enough."

A tall, beefy man, with a shaved head came in. He flashed a badge and shook Vargas's hand.

He glanced at Jake. "I heard we had a little incident here involving someone in the program."

Jake didn't appreciate his arrogant attitude. "Hardly a little incident. Did you get in contact with Richard Thomason of the FBI in Quantico?" Sometimes it paid to name drop.

"Sure did. He said he never heard of Ashley Wood, Taylor Daniels, or Jake Yarnell."

Every muscle tensed. Jake swallowed his desire to beat the shit out of something or someone. "Do I get my one phone call?" Jake said, his teeth grinding together.

"Of course." Vargas pointed to his phone.

He couldn't count on Stanton backing him, but Tom would cover his back.

He dialed Tom's cell number. Five rings, six rings. *Pick up, dammit.*

***

Tom Traynor and Stanton Lowry burst into Richard's office. From the speed with which they rushed in, and the pissed off look on their faces, Richard knew his grip on things might slip further.

"What's wrong?" Richard painted on his best face of concern.

Stanton stepped forward. "You know damn well what's wrong. Why did you deny knowing Jake?"

He'd already prepared his answer—an answer that held a lot of truth to it. "I wanted to protect him."

Stanton slammed his fist on the desk. "Just tell me how denying you know who Jake is, helps him in any way."

"The Georgia cop told me Ashley Wood was dead, killed in a hit and run. It was the same way juror #8 died. It couldn't have been an accident. I figure the longer I keep Jake and Susan safe in a jail cell, the better."

"That's bullshit." Tom, who was usually quiet, spoke with a wealth of venom.

"Just exactly what do you expect me to do?" He put all acting aside. If these two could figure out a way to get him and Jake out of the mess, he'd be ecstatic. He had to keep his wife and two children safe.

Stanton locked gazes with him. "Call the cops back and tell them to release Jake. Have Jake get back to DC, ASAP. We have to find a better way to protect Mrs. Chapman."

If only Stanton understood why his plan wouldn't work. "If you insist."

Richard would be forced to tell his blackmailer that Mrs. Chapman and Yarnell were on their way back here. Their lives would end too soon. And he liked Jake and wanted to protect him.

He expected the Jake-support team to nod and disappear, only they didn't. Fine. It would be their fault their prize prosecutor died. Not him.

The irony of the situation didn't escape him. His job was to keep people safe and yet he couldn't even protect his own family from blackmailing mobsters. If only his wife wasn't bedridden, he'd put them some place where no one could find them.

Stanton and Tom stepped toward him. He picked up the phone and pushed redial. When he reached the Georgia cop, Richard claimed he wanted to get to a secure line before admitting he knew Jake Yarnell and the girl.

"We have a few more questions for them," the Atlanta cop said. "Then we'll release them."

"Excellent. Do me a favor."

"Sir?"

Richard liked the sound of the respect in the man's voice. "I haven't been able to contact detective Yarnell. Tell him, he's to return to DC, pronto."

"Will do."

Richard swallowed hard and hung up. He stared at Stanton Lowry. "Happy?"

"Tickled pink." Stanton turned his sourpuss ass around and left.

Tom unclenched his fists. "What happened to the bodyguard you sent down to protect Ashley Woods?"

Richard pretended to flip through a file. "He should have been there by now. I'll check that out. "

"You do that." Tom stomped out.

Richard prayed he'd done the right thing.

***

Susan sat alone in a small, windowless room awaiting word about what they were going to do with both of them. No one had come to check on her for three hours. Her butt had nearly fallen asleep from the hard chairs. What could possibly be holding them up? Surely, they weren't going to arrest Jake. She'd been the one driving. Not having a driver's license was bad, but Jake would pay the fine, whatever it was.

A lead ball rattled in the bottom of her belly. Had Jake's brain swelled and he'd shown some signs of disorientation? Had they taken him to the hospital and didn't want to tell her?

Would she be left on her own? Panic sizzled in her stomach. She needed him.

Funny, just a day or two ago, she couldn't wait to get away from him.

Though the room was no more than ten feet by ten feet, she had to pace, had to do something. After she'd sat for those few hours after the accident, her muscles had bunched and tightened. Her knee had swollen, which made walking painful, but sitting was worse.

When she took a step, sharp pains stabbed her chest and her knee, but she was confident she would find some relief if she could just get the blood flowing again.

She tried to do a few exercises to loosen her muscles, but her mind wandered back to Ashley Wood and to who was driving the SUV. Jake had said a black SUV had followed them for a short while in Lake City. There was no way the driver could have known where they would be headed next—unless they had the addresses of the jurors.

That was it. Whoever was killing these people was heading north, picking off the jurors one by one. When the last man was dead, they'd come after her. Though why she wasn't dead already confused her. Why wait to kill her, especially when they had the chance twice now? Was she to play a role somehow?

She leaned on the chair to steady herself from the terrible thoughts. Her stomach grumbled, and she had to go to the bathroom. Bad.

Susan pounded on the door. They couldn't ignore her forever, goddammit.

The door opened about ten minutes later. "Come with me, Mrs. Chapman."

About time. "Can I use the facilities?"

The guard nodded when they reached the bathrooms. "I'll wait outside."

The small bathroom was clean, but the floors were stained with dirt, and the grout needed a good scrubbing. She used the toilet, washed her face and hands and stepped out. In the hours she'd been detained, the sun had set and the sky had turned a purplish blue. Darn. They wouldn't be getting on the road until tomorrow.

When they rounded a corner, Jake was standing, his shoulders tense, and his lips drawn back. The relief forced out a breath. His skin was pale and his head wound was bleeding, but she probably didn't look much better.

When he noticed her, he smiled, transforming his face from tired to handsome, and her heart skipped a beat. For an insane moment, she wanted to throw herself in his arms, but for many reasons, she refrained.

Captain Vargas, or whatever his designation was, turned to her. "You two are free to go. From the impact on Ms. Wood's car, we realized your car couldn't have done the damage. The truck that hit her had a much higher bumper."

Jake narrowed his eyes. "And our car? Will you release it?"

"I'm afraid it can't be driven. You two were lucky you got as far as you did. The front end was crushed into the engine and the axle is nearly cracked. I'm sorry. I'll be happy to have one of my men drive you to a motel."

It was the least they could do. Now they'd have to rent another car, head to another hotel room, all the while using a traceable credit card. Christ. They might as well go on the nightly news and give the killer their room number.

Jake slid next to Susan and slipped an arm around her shoulder, acting as if they were a single unit.

"Fine," he said, but his sharp tone implied losing the vehicle was anything but okay.

As they stepped outside, the cold air slapped her in the face. Even with her sweatshirt on, she shivered. Jake only had on the shirt she'd handed him in the car. Poor man must be freezing, but he didn't act as if the weather affected him.

"What about our luggage we left in the trunk?" she asked. They needed warmer clothes.

"We've got it for you."

She leaned into him. "Can't your people in Virginia have someone deliver another car? Or help us out?"

"I don't think I'm their favorite son. Besides, I think our killer has a direct line to someone in the office."

"Who do you think it is?"

"I wish I knew."

From the rigid set of his jaw, she understood he wouldn't elaborate. Pure speculation wasn't the way he operated.

"I want to stay at the Hyatt in downtown Atlanta. The security will be tighter in a high rise than if we stay in a motel in the suburbs."

"And there's the Marta," she added, having been to Atlanta for a convention two years ago. "We can get anywhere on the rail system."

"True. Our big chore will be to convince another car company to trust us with one of their vehicles."

The Georgia policeman apologized as they pulled to the curb in front of the hotel. "Captain Vargas wanted me to tell you that your boss wants you to call him."

"Thanks."

When they checked in, Jake asked for a room above the tenth floor and with two queens. Susan appreciated his request. She'd never get to sleep if they shared the bed.

Once they arrived in the room, he put her suitcase on the first bed.

Exhausted beyond words, Susan dragged herself over to the bed and sat. "Why did you want the tenth floor or higher?"

"We don't have to worry about anyone shooting out our window."

At first she thought he might be kidding, but from the creases in his brow, he was dead serious. "That's horrible."

"We have to be more cautious from now on." He paced the small room.

The floor choice made sense, but she wasn't convinced they were out of danger even at this height. Susan opened her case and took out her pajamas. "Why can't your friend, T-Squared, contact this last juror? Or have the local police stand watch at his door."

"To address your first question, when a person moves in, they are given a cell phone, but only Richard has the number. Secondly, Richard sent down an FBI agent to protect Gary Cho, our last living juror. The bodyguard may be at the Cho's place now."

"And you don't want to call and ask Richard?" She held up a palm. "I know. He'd wonder why you were asking, and he'd tell you it isn't your job to protect all the witnesses, just me."

"You got it."

She needed a shower, but right now the bed was calling her name. "Where is Mr. Cho staying?"

"Brevard, North Carolina."

Another state, another long drive. "And then where to?" She'd been about to say, what happens when all the jurors are dead, but she figured he'd understand what she was asking.

"We find a place to hunker down and wait for the men in blue to capture the bastard."

CHAPTER TWELVE

Joseph Francisco had finished breakfast when his cell rang. He pulled the phone from his top pocket, and as he checked the caller ID, the maid entered the dining room and removed his plate. She stood next to him waiting patiently for further instructions.

"You may go." He waved her away.

Once she disappeared he answered the call. "Good morning, Dom. I trust you have some news for me." He better not say he'd been arrested. One time when he did an important job, the cops had caught him. It was hell to get the verdict overturned.

"If the pattern holds true, the FBI agent and Mrs. Chapman will be heading to Brevard, and I have the perfect plan."

Don's gloating irritated Joseph, but his son was a Francisco, and Franciscos were born braggarts.

His granddaughter came running in the dining room. "Poppy, Poppy. Look what I drew for you." She held up a picture of him at his desk, and his heart softened.

"This is wonderful, sweetie. Can you put it on my desk for me?"

She nodded and raced away.

Joseph leaned back in his chair, and a sharp pain raced down his leg. Stupid sciatic nerve. "Tell me about this *perfect* plan." He winced and tried to keep the sound of agony out of his voice. If Dom suspected something was wrong with his health, he'd tell Maria, who would insist he go back into physical therapy. He'd rather eat his gun than be subjected to those torturers.

"Cho is the last juror. The Feds put him in some remote cabin. Trees everywhere. It'll be a piece of cake to sneak up on him."

"You've been to his place?"

"Yes. I'm not going to do anything until later though. That's the perfect part." Like always, Dom kept silent after he dropped a bomb.

"Tell me." Dom's excitement about the plan made Joseph curious. Maybe his son had come up with something extraordinary.

"Who is Peter Caravello's good friend?" Dom asked.

An easy question. "Jake Yarnell."

Joseph knew all about how Nicki Caravello had helped raised Yarnell as a kid. Smart man, suggesting his protégé go into law enforcement. Joseph wished he had a cop in his back pocket.

"Wouldn't it piss Peter off if the man trying to protect him is accused of murder?"

His son had misunderstood the whole point of removing the jurors from the face of the earth. "We want the Feds to believe Peter has been killing these jurors, not Jake Yarnell." Idiot.

Dom cleared his throat. "There's a problem with that idea."

Joseph sat up straighter. "You know I hate problems."

"It couldn't be helped. When I was in Florida taking care of one of the jurors, the Feds arrested Peter. He couldn't have gotten released on bail and driven down to Florida in time to kill Marcadis."

"Shit."

"But that's where my plan comes in."

Joseph wanted to spit. His goal was to remove Peter Caravello from society so his precious daughter would look elsewhere for a husband. Now Caravello would be exonerated. His brilliant plan foiled because his son didn't check his facts.

"Tell me." He gulped down the last of his now cool, bitter coffee.

"I've got it all figured out. Don't worry about it."

His son's best trait was the fact he didn't tell him about *how* he accomplished his feats. Only this time he did need to know in case someone better could do the job.

"You're going to be careful, right?"

"I'm thirty seven. I know what to do. I'll call you when it's done."

The line went dead and Joseph squeezed shut his eyes. He'd been so close. But Franciscos didn't leave things to chance. He called his backup man who answered on the first ring.

"Yes, Mr. Francisco?"

"I have work for you."

"Anything, sir."

Now there was a good man.

***

After some haggling with the rental car company and giving them his solemn pledge he wouldn't wreck this car, the company rented Jake a Jeep at a big premium. He signed up for a vehicle with four-wheel drive to handle the North Carolina hills.

"You sure you're okay to drive," Susan asked.

He appreciated the worry in her voice. "You care about me. I like that." He glanced over at her and smiled.

She quickly looked away and rubbed her knee. "I want us to be safe, that's all."

"Bull. I saw the look on your face when you were at the police station. You thought I might not be there when they reunited us. I bet you were worried I had some repercussion from my injury."

"Perhaps."

He waited for a smile to lift her lips, but she schooled her appearance. Just when he thought he was making progress with her trust issues, she turned cold on him—or maybe the pressure was getting to her.

"Don't worry. We'll get this guy."

She crossed her arms over her chest and immediately winced, apparently forgetting her injuries for a moment. She lowered her hands to her lap. "The Feds haven't done a very good job so far."

Too bad she was right, nullifying any comeback.

His cell rang. Keeping one eye on the road, he glanced at the display. "It's Stanton." He ignored the cell.

"You aren't going to answer him?"

"No."

"Don't you think he'll suspect something if you don't?"

The slight panic in her voice made him reconsider, but only for a moment. "Yes, which is why I need to get rid of this thing. I told Tom to tell him my cell burned up in the townhouse fire. I guess he didn't believe him."

"Why did you want to ditch a perfectly good phone?"

"It's got a GPS in it."

Her jaw lowered and her cheeks sagged. "They know where we are?"

"If they're looking."

She dropped her head back against the seat and closed her eyes. "I know you suspect someone in the bureau of leaking information." She sat up and turned toward him. "Do you think they might be telling the killer our exact location?"

Jake gripped the wheel hard. "Yes. We'll get off I-85 at the next exit and get a disposable phone."

He glanced in the rear view mirror for the hundredth time. He'd memorized every vehicle behind him. Everyone seemed to be following them, but he couldn't figure out who.

A mile down the road, he exited and stopped at the gas station on the corner. It was one of those big places that had several fast food restaurants and a fairly complete grocery store. He parked on the side and got out. Susan didn't move. Jake tapped the window and motioned she come inside with him.

She rolled down her window. "I don't need anything. I'll stay here and wait for you."

"I don't want to leave you alone."

She looked around. "I'm safe. There are three people getting gas and lots of people coming and going."

That's what bothered him. Two more cars pulled into the lot and drove up to the pumps. "Please come inside."

"Okay, okay."

He understood that as a prosecuting attorney, Susan was used to calling the shots. Having someone dictate her every move obviously didn't sit well with her, but he had a job to do and couldn't worry about her emotional needs right now.

Liar. He did care about her stability. Maybe too much. He studied her, liking the way she held her own when they discussed their next move, the way her eyes softened when she spoke of her injured brother, and how she moved her hips right then left before she slid out of a car. He prayed his attraction to her wouldn't screw with his logic.

She trudged next him, her limp rather pronounced. He shouldn't make her walk, but mild movement might help ease her pain—or so he wanted to believe.

"As long as I'm here, I might as well use the bathroom."

Jake waited until she disappeared into the restroom before searching for a phone. He picked up some ice for her swollen knee, two cold drinks, and some snacks for the rest of the ride while he kept a close eye on the bathroom door.

After he paid for the phone and the extra goods, he waited for her.

She came out minutes later and looked up at him. "You do take your job seriously, don't you?"

"Yes, I do. When I can't see you, my sixth sense goes into overdrive. I worry something will happen to you." Irrational perhaps. No one knew where they were—or so he hoped. If someone had gotten a lock of their location, they wouldn't anymore. He'd dumped his cell phone in the trash.

He held open the convenience store door for her and checked out the lot. With his hand pressed to the small of her back, he led her to the car.

She looked up at him with a slight smile. "You don't have to hover."

He opened his mouth wide and tapped his chest. Something about flirting with her helped take his mind off the ugliness in the world. "Is that a complaint?"

"I was merely wondering if you were staying close to make me feel safe?"

"Not entirely. I like being cautious when it comes to your safety, that's all."

"Oh."

Once Susan slid into the passenger seat, he walked over to his side, noticing a piece of paper that sat under the wiper blade, flapping in the wind. He hated this kind of advertisement. Most people were probably just passing through. Why waste the ad on a bunch of transients?

He glanced at the cars to either side of them. None had ads on them. Curious, he slipped the paper from the blade and stilled.

Jake must have been staring at the message for too long because Susan opened up her door and came over to his side.

"What is it?"

He debated not telling her, but he decided because her life was in danger, she needed to understand the circumstances. "Seems our mystery man is taunting us."

Jake checked out the cars at the pump and those parked nearby but noticed nothing out of the ordinary. Susan slipped next to him, and he could smell a hint of fresh soap on her.

"Tell me." She grabbed his wrist.

"It says: *Only one more to go, and then you'll be next.*"

Her eyes widened. She leaned back against the car. "He was here?"

"Apparently."

"You think he's still around?" Susan's knees buckled and her body slid down the car. Jake reached out to catch her. Without thinking, he gathered her in his arms. He expected her to pull away. Instead, she wrapped her arms around his waist. He wanted to bring her comfort in the form of dragging a finger down her cheek, touching her, holding her in his arms for a long time, but he didn't dare.

With his chin on her head, he scanned the parking lot for anyone suspicious, but came up empty-handed.

She buried her face in his chest. "I'm so scared."

So was he, but he'd never voice that opinion. He liked being the strong one. Holding her touched something inside him, something fundamental, something he needed. He placed a gentle kiss on the top of her head. She looked up with a mixture of surprise and terror before she broke the connection.

He lifted her chin. "I will do everything in my power to protect you."

She blinked, pressed her lips together and lowered her gaze. A tear streaked down her cheek. "I thought the car explosion was the worst thing to happen to me, but this teasing, this torment by this crazy person is ripping me apart."

Helplessness grabbed him. He was highly trained to deal with psychos, but when it came to dealing with an intelligent, independent woman like Susan Chapman, he was lost.

His agent training kicked into gear. "Get in the car."

Protecting her with his body, he angled her into the passenger side, then jogged to his side, and then climbed in. He started the engine and peeled out of the lot. "We have to warn Mr. Cho. Then we have to hide."

Jake stole quick glances at Susan as they continued to drive north. If the strong jut of her jaw was any indication, she seemed to have a hold of her emotions. Not to mention her lack of tears. His admiration grew.

The drive to western North Carolina took them another ninety minutes. Even though he'd paid extra for the Jeep's upgraded GPS package, the advanced technology couldn't find the remote Sunset Drive where Gary Cho was safely tucked away.

"Maybe we should stop in town and ask for directions," she said.

Jake checked his mirrors. "I'll drive around a little longer."

"You are such a guy."

"It's that I don't like letting the world know we're here."

"Good point, but—"

"But if we don't find Cho soon, my driving around aimlessly could cost the man his life. I get it."

She smiled. "You do read minds, don't you?"

He winked and pulled into the next gas station. No luck. The quaint 1950's style diner proved to be a bust too, as did the used car dealership. No one knew where Sunset drive was—or else no one wanted to tell them where the place was. Small towns were often protective of their members.

"I bet the Sheriff's office will know," she said.

Law enforcement was the last place he wanted to visit. Tell a cop, tell the FBI. "I want to try one more place."

He drove down 64 and headed into Pisgah National Forest. About a mile in, he saw signs to the Ranger Station. "If anyone will know where remote places are, it'll be the ranger."

Around three, they entered the station, the cool crisp air chilling them. The small store had more visitors than he'd expected this time of year.

An older gentleman in a park uniform proudly directed them to the back. Jake knocked on the ranger's open door and stepped in. He was greeted by a friendly smile.

"What can I do for you folks?"

Jake liked the man's open face and handlebar mustache. "We're looking for Sunset Drive."

"You looking for Paul Henley's place?"

Thank God someone knew the location of Sunset drive. Jake flashed his badge and the man merely nodded. "We have someone in protective custody there."

The ranger pulled open his drawer and spread out a map. "Take 276 up to the Blue Ridge Parkway and hang a left at this mile marker." The ranger pointed out a few ways to reach their destination once on the gravel road.

"Appreciate the information."

They shook hands and left. On the way out, Jake did his usual scouting routine. The same number of cars that were there when they arrived were still there, allowing him to let down his guard a bit.

"After we talk to Cho, we'll stop back here and pick up some warmer gear. I saw an outfitter store on the way into the forest."

She nodded. "It's almost over isn't it?"

Far from it. "Let's hope."

The trip up to the Parkway was steep and winding but thankfully free of snow. Once they reached the top and turned left, the clouds began to roll in. Snow clouds. Once that happened, visibility could shoot to zero.

They passed the first scenic overlook, which presented a sparsely filled forest of pines surrounding a large, bald rock. The view of the National park reminded him of T-Squared father's home in West Virginia, where he learned to hunt, relax, and love nature.

"Looks like bad weather's on the way," she said.

"We could get snow."

Susan hugged her knees and leaned against the door. When they made it to a true safe house, he'd build her a large fire so she could get warm.

The last three miles along the gravel road were filled with potholes that jarred his spine. Susan grimaced a few times when a wheel dug deep into a rut, but she kept quiet. She was quite the trooper. Susan had guts and spunk, a combination he found attractive.

The sun set in a matter of minutes and the blackness prevented them up from going much faster than five miles an hour. He made a mental note that a swift entrance and exit would be close to impossible. How anyone could buy food if he were snowed in was a real mystery.

A half-mile later, his headlights captured a gate across one of the crossroads.

"I wonder where that leads," Susan said.

"We've passed a few of them. They're for park officials only, but according to the ranger, this is Sunset."

"Yikes."

His same sentiment. "Wait here."

Jake aimed the car lights on the bar, exited the Jeep, and then swung the gate back. A cowbell attached to the metal pole rang out. Now that was strange.

He couldn't wait to warn Gary and to suggest he find another place to stay. Once he spoke with Mr. Cho, he'd take Susan somewhere safe.

They reached Gary Cho's new residence about three minutes later. One beat up truck sat in the drive. Richard Thomason's budget cutting mindset had struck again. Cheap bastard.

"I love this cabin," Susan said. "It's so warm and cozy." She pointed to the top of the building. "I see smoke coming out of the chimney. He must be home."

He'd never heard such excitement in her voice. If they ever got out of this mess, he might like to see what he could do about bringing her some joy.

Jake pushed open his door. "Stay here while I check out the area."

He'd gotten halfway around the cabin when he heard her door open. Stubborn woman. Jake did an about face and met her along the side of the house. "I told you to stay in the car."

The hands flew to her hips. "I don't like being left alone."

"You didn't have a problem staying snug in the seat when we were at the gas station. What gives now? Are you afraid of being in the woods? Alone?"

"Me? Afraid? Hah. No." She cast her gaze to the ground. "Maybe a little." She looked up and caught his gaze. "Okay, maybe a lot. These woods give me the creeps, especially in the dark. As a matter of fact, I hate the woods at night."

Jake chuckled, grabbed her hand, and walked toward the front. Something caught his attention through the lighted window. He peered in.

"Oh my God."

CHAPTER THIRTEEN

"What is it?" Susan's voice trembled.

Jake wavered. He wanted to protect her from seeing Gary Cho, but, at the same time, he had to bring her inside with him. No telling where the killer might be hiding.

"It's Gary. He's in trouble."

Jake pulled her around to the front. He guessed he'd have to smash the wooden door down, but when he turned the handle, the door swung open.

The moment they stepped inside, Susan choked out a sob. While he wanted to take her in his arms and tell her everything would be fine, he had to take care of the man still dangling at the end of a noose.

Jake righted the dining room chair and stepped up on the seat. The slight Asian man fit snuggly against Jake's chest when he lifted him to release the pressure of the noose.

"Jake!" Susan shouted.

"I think he's still alive."

Her footsteps sounded behind him. "I saw someone peering in the window." Panic laced her tone, but he didn't have time to ask any questions.

"Lock the door."

Saving Mr. Cho had to take priority over looking for some Peeping Tom.

He lifted the rope from around Cho's neck, and the body collapsed in his arms, nearly toppling him. He gently guided Cho's body to the floor. Two brown burn marks, about an inch apart, were on his neck, suggesting the killer had used a stun gun. Bastard.

Susan knelt next to him. "My God. Can you save him?"

"I'm not sure."

He dragged two fingers to the man's throat. A faint pulse beat, though Jake wasn't sure if he was feeling his racing heart or Gary's Cho's barely beating one.

He slipped the pre-paid phone from his pocket and handed the cell to Susan. "Call 9-1-1."

Eyes wide, she stared at him. He understood shock could freeze a person, but Susan was made of sterner stuff. She'd dealt with gruesome photos of real crime scenes. The reality was worse, but she was strong.

A second later, she did as he asked. He didn't give any instructions. She was smart enough to disconnect once she told the operator about Cho.

Cho's mouth opened. "Caravel—," he gasped, and then his body bucked before going limp. Eyes wide open, his head fell to the side.

"Mr. Cho." Jake shook him, even though he knew the man would never speak again.

Jake tilted Cho's head back, pinched his nose and gave him a few breaths. He performed CPR for a few minutes, and then leaned back on his heels.

Still gripping the cell, Susan leaned closer, their shoulders touching. "Is he dead?"

"I think so. I can't find a pulse."

"Was he saying something about Peter Caravello?"

He hoped to hell not. "We may never know."

"Maybe he was identifying the killer. What else could Caravel— mean?"

His gut churned. "He could have meant he was here because of the Caravello trial. That's all." Jake didn't want to discuss what ifs with her. "You said you saw someone peer in the window?"

She blinked a few times. "Yes, when you were trying to get Mr. Cho down." Her voice rose.

"What did he look like?"

Her gaze shot from one side of the room to the other. "I don't know. Something was in front of his face. And it was dark, but I remember a small glowing object in his hand, like a cell phone. He was there one second, gone the next."

"What direction did he go?"

"I don't know. I was rather preoccupied with Mr. Cho's situation."

"I understand." Jake jumped up and sprinted the ten feet to the door. He faced her and pulled open the door. "Keep this locked."

Her body tensed. "You can't leave me here with a dead man."

"I'll be right back. Trust me."

Her mouthed opened but then quickly shut it. As she stood, he jetted out the door. Damn, he needed a flashlight. It was darker than three AM in the middle of the Atlantic Ocean.

Jake raced to the side window where Susan claimed she saw the man and peered right then left. What looked like a path led away from the house. Wind rustled the leaves, a lone plane sped overhead, but nothing else moved. No animal sounds, no voices, no car engines revving, no feet racing through the forest. Where had the guy disappeared? Even after the clouds moved away to expose the half moon, he couldn't see much of anything. Leaving Susan alone, locked door or not, wasn't a smart move. Perhaps when the killer got interrupted, he tried to take advantage of isolating Susan. It was her time. *She's next.*

Not if he could help it.

The cold air froze his nose, ears, and fingers, making a search next to impossible without proper equipment. He'd only been in Florida a few days and had almost forgotten how much he disliked the frigid temperatures.

Who had been at the window? Some kid? A curious local who wanted to check up on the newcomer? Or had it been the person who'd strung up Mr. Cho? If indeed the killer was nearby, he and Susan had to get out of there. Now.

Frustrated, Jake returned to the front of the cabin and knocked. "It's me."

She opened the door, rushed outside, and threw herself in her arms. She buried her face in his chest.

"I don't want to end up like Gary Cho. All the jurors are dead, and that leaves only me."

He rubbed her back. "Shh. He's not going to get you."

She didn't lift her head but remained snuggled in his arms. Jake was tempted to hug her tighter, but he didn't need to complicate their already strained relationship.

"How can you be so sure he won't come after me?"

Jake ran a cold finger down her warm cheek, his finger slipping on her tears. "You'll have to trust that I can protect you."

She stepped back and locked her gaze with him. "I do trust you."

Her admission warmed his heart. "Thank you."

She sniffled. "Maybe we should leave before the ambulance gets here. There's nothing more we can do for Mr. Cho."

"You're right. We don't want a repeat of what happened in Atlanta."

"Amen."

Jake checked out the room once more. Except for the tumbled chair under Mr. Cho's body, everything looked in place. Two bottles of beer sat on the dining room table, making it appear as though Cho knew the assailant. Or had the visitor gone, and Mr. Cho hadn't taken the time to clean up?

After wiping the prints off the door and chair, and making certain they'd left nothing behind to indicate they'd been anywhere near Gary Cho, they returned to the Jeep. The officer part of him told him to stay and report what had happened, but the bodyguard half said to run. The 9-1-1 call would have alerted the ambulance as well as the local police. They would be charging here right now.

Jake had no desire to call the Bureau and report the last juror's death. Richard Thomason dropped to the top of his list the moment he denied knowing Jake in Atlanta.

Once he made up his mind to flee, Jake drove as fast as he could without ejecting them from their seats. When he passed the open gate, something tripped a memory. The cowbell might have been put there to warn whoever was in the cabin that visitors were about to arrive, but how could the killer know he and Susan were on their way? Had the ranger spilled the beans?

It didn't matter. The killer knew they'd been there. He hanged Mr. Cho only moments before their arrival. It was almost as if he wanted Jake to find Cho swinging. But why?

"Hold on." Jake gripped the wheel hard. "This could get rough."

"It already has," Susan said between gritted teeth.

"Sorry."

She took hold of the handle over her head and braced herself against the dash with the other hand. From the fast pace of her breathing, raising her right arm took concentration and a will to push the pain aside.

At the bottom of the long road, Jake came to a rolling stop and glanced left. A stream of colored lights rounded the curve. "They're coming."

Slamming the gas pedal to the floor, he fishtailed out of the dirt road onto the pavement, and small rocks bounced under the carriage. Sirens screamed behind him. He took the next curve too fast and his wheels lost purchase.

"Jake!"

The oncoming car must have witnessed his loss of control. Lights flashed. The car slowed and dipped onto the berm. Jake let up on the gas and eased to his side of the road.

"That was close." He glanced in the rear view mirror and let out a breath. "They turned down the road to Cho's place. No one seems to be following us."

"Do you think they saw you?"

"Most likely, but I don't believe they've put two and two together yet."

"And if they do figure out what happened?"

He wasn't ready to think about the consequences of leaving the crime scene. He might be looking for a different line of work when this mess straightened out. "Let's hope they don't."

Susan leaned her head back against the seat. "Where are we going now?"

"Given it's close to eight, I say we head to Asheville and stay the night. I have an idea where we could go, but I need to check with T-Squared first."

"Maybe it would be safer if they did put us in jail. The killer couldn't get to me there."

He glanced over at her. She was chewing her bottom lip and her arms were crossed over her chest. He needed to come up with a good plan soon if he expected to keep Susan alive.

***

Richard Thomason forced the smile from his lips. He studied his reflection in the men's room mirror. He needed to look upset, worried, and a little out of control. He half unknotted his perfectly tied tie, mussed his hair a bit and left his suit jacket unbuttoned, something he never did.

With the prize winning photo in hand, he strode into the meeting room, precisely three minutes late. Stanton, Tom, William Burroughs, and Nancy Darden were all seated. He needed to convince them his proof against Jake was irrefutable. Once he was brought in, he could report to the bastard that Jake and Mrs. Chapman were in custody. His job would be done, and his wife and children would be safe from harm.

If the blackmailer was able to get to Chapman after her release, fine. Her death wouldn't be on his hands.

As expected, all four of his team stopped talking as soon as he stepped into the conference room and faced him.

"Thank you for giving up a good night's sleep and meeting with me at such short notice." He shoved a hand through his hair for effect. "This was just emailed to me."

He tossed the 8 x 10 glossy photo on the table and waited for their reactions.

Stanton was the first to pick up the photo and study it as the others looked on. He glanced up. "I don't get it. What is Jake doing with Gary Cho?"

Richard took in a deep breath and mentally prepared for his finest acting job. "He was hanging him. The noose is half-way over Cho's head."

"This is impossible," Tom chimed in.

"Pictures don't lie."

Stanton passed the photo to Nancy. "I'm glad to see Mrs. Chapman appears to be alive, but why would Jake harm Mr. Cho?"

Richard had spent time preparing to answer that exact question. "To protect Peter Caravello. To divert attention away from him."

The team searched the faces of the other members. Tom looked more pissed than confused.

Nancy leaned forward. "Why would Jake want to protect a suspect?"

Thanks to one of his blackmailers, he'd extracted a lot of information about Jake Yarnell's upbringing. Richard pulled up the remaining empty chair and sat.

"I think you all know that after Jake's mother died, he was put up for adoption at age seven."

The heads nodded. Richard continued. "Apparently neither his grandmother nor his aunt wanted custody, so he went in the foster care program."

"That's in his file," Tom said.

"What's this have to do with Peter Caravello," William chimed in.

"I'm getting to that. When Jake was nine, he was assigned a Big Brother from the program. You'll never guess who it was."

Stanton's jaw clenched. "Just tell us."

"Nicki Caravello."

All eyes but Tom's widened. Interesting. He must have known about Jake's childhood difficulties. Damn. He'd be a hard sell.

"Shit," Stanton said. "I guess that means he was friends with Peter when they were growing up."

"More than friends. They were like brothers. Peter's mom died of cancer when Peter was twelve and Jake nine. Given Jake was shuffled between four foster homes, he knew what it was like to lose a mom. The two bonded."

Richard waited for them to figure out the connection.

William steepled his fingers. "When we arrested Peter, are you thinking Jake thought that if another juror died while Peter was in custody, we might let Caravello go?"

"That's what happened, wasn't it? We released Mr. Caravello, and shortly thereafter, the juror in north Florida was killed."

Stanton nodded, the bags under his eyes pronounced. He was taking these deaths too personally. He pushed aside his growing guilt.

Richard waited for the next question that someone surely would ask: What should we do next? He tapped his fingers on the table then stilled. He wanted to wring their necks for being so stupid. Did he have a draw them a picture?

"We'll have a put an APB out on Jake and the girl," Stanton said.

Good man, Stanton.

Tom shoved back his chair. "Listen to yourselves. Jake is one of us, not some criminal. Maybe he was taking Mr. Cho down after someone hanged him. Ever think of that? I can see Mrs. Chapman in the background. Now way he would harm Cho with a witness present."

Richard needed to step in, to stop this Jake-is-innocent crap. "I've thought of that, but there were no rope markings on Cho's neck. There would be if Jake had found Cho hanging."

"Where did you get this photo?" Stanton asked.

Richard had expected that question too. "It was sent to my phone."

"From?"

"Number unknown."

Tom slapped the table. "And you didn't question the source?"

"I tried to get a trace, but I couldn't. Besides, what's there to question? This is Jake with a juror in his arms. If you look closely, you can see two burn marks on the neck. I'm betting they came from a stun gun. That's why Cho is limp." He wasn't sure if they would see through his thin evidence, but it might deflect someone drawing any link between him and the crimes.

The group remained silent for a good thirty seconds.

Stanton rubbed his eyes and blew out a long breath. "We have no choice. We have to bring Jake in and ask him to explain."

Perfect. He couldn't have orchestrated the scene any better. "Let's get some rest. I'll see you all in the morning."

No one stopped to discuss Yarnell on the way out. Good. They were all on board. He checked the atomic clock on the wall. It was late and his wife would hopefully be asleep. She always worried when he spent too many hours at work.

At this hour, the usual forty-five minute drive took only twenty-five. He pulled into the garage and headed for the kitchen. He needed a drink.

Once he mixed his scotch, he went to check on the kids. No matter how late he dragged in, he made it a point to kiss them good-night. It didn't matter they rarely remembered the visit in the morning.

He opened Ethan's door. The nightlight next to the bed glowed, but he wasn't in his bed. His youngest son often liked to cuddle with his older sister after Kathleen had her operation. Soon he'd have to insist he stay in his own room, but for now he'd let him have his solace.

Richard stepped down the hall and eased open the door. The bathroom light poured into the pink and lavender room. His heart nearly exploded. It was empty.

Richard raced to the master bedroom. Maybe Kathleen had had a relapse. Heart transplant patients were so unpredictable. He threw open the door. She always left the bedside lamp on for him.

She opened her eyes. "Richard, what's wrong?"

"Oh, God. Where are the children?"

"In bed."

"No they aren't."

Her hand flew to her chest and he ran to her side.

He shouldn't have upset her, but he needed answers. "Are you sure they aren't spending the night with your sister and you forgot?"

"No. Claire is out of town this weekend."

His mind failed to sort through all of the possible scenarios. The phone rang.

He jumped up from the bed. "I'll take it in the kitchen. It might be work."

"Richard, please—"

His hand trembled as he ran out the door, blocking out his wife's pleas.

"Hello?"

"Don't worry. They're safe."

"Who is this?" He tried to keep his voice down to a whisper. He recognized the voice, but he prayed he was wrong.

"You know."

"What do you want?" His legs weakened and he slid down to the kitchen chair.

"I want you to find Jake Yarnell and the girl and eliminate them."

"What the hell do you think I have been doing for the last couple of days?"

"When they are both dead, I will return your children. I'll be in touch."

CHAPTER FOURTEEN

Jake hadn't slept last night, worrying about whether the cops in Brevard had figured out who'd called in Cho's murder. He mentally ran through everything they had touched. Had he or Susan had left any trace evidence or disturbed anything other than the body? Yes, he'd wiped down the doorknob and the chair, but would they think to lift his prints off Cho's neck where he'd taken the man's pulse?

The big question was whether the Transylvania County police department was sophisticated enough to draw any conclusions regarding who'd been there? If the cops did check around town, a few people could attest to fact two strangers were asking where to find Gary Cho's place. Would the department call in a sketch artist and search all the databases for a match? He'd shown his badge to the Pisgah ranger. How much would they learn from him?

Nothing he could do about it now. He thanked the gods he'd gotten an untraceable phone. The 9-1-1 dispatcher would be able to identify the caller as a woman, but since Susan hadn't mentioned her name, they were in the clear on that account.

Even though they'd reserved a room forty miles away under an assumed name, Jake suggested they sleep in their clothes in case the police roused them in the middle of the night. When the authorities never showed up, Jake began to relax, though he'd only slept in short bursts.

Faint light eked through the gap in the curtains. He rose, debating whether or not to wake Susan, since she'd looked too peaceful to disturb. She'd tossed and turned most of the night and had settled down only a few hours ago.

Around three in the morning, he'd been tempted to crawl into her bed next to her and just hold her, to calm her, but getting involved with a client was the fastest road to dismissal. God knows, he might have already lost any chance to keep his job.

Jake checked the time on his cell. T-Squared should be getting home from work about now. Even though he could call his friend on his cell at work, Tom's ability to talk freely diminished when he was on the job.

Jake bundled up and stepped outside, not wanting to wake her with the call. The sun was only now peeking over the horizon, but the brisk breeze shocked his system awake. Several motel guests were piling into their cars, even at this early hour.

After three rings, Tom picked up.

"It's Jake."

"Jesus Christ. Where have you been? I've been calling you for hours."

"I tossed the Bureau phone and bought an untraceable."

"Smart. That's why you didn't answer. Where are you?"

"Asheville."

"The shit hit the fan at work. You gotta hide."

Jake knew that, but how did Tom? "What do you mean?"

"Richard produced a photo of you stringing up Gary Cho."

The anger rippling through his body was the only thing that kept Jake upright. "That's impossible." He told his friend how he'd raced to save Cho. "Susan saw someone in the window. Shit. That's when he must have snapped the picture. I've been set up."

"I told them that. The photo could have been of you taking off the noose rather than putting it on."

"It was. Cho was alive when we got there, so the killer had to be nearby." He turned his shoulder to brace against the wind.

"Is Cho okay?"

"No. He died right after I took him down." No need to mention Gary's last words, or rather the first half of a word. "You said Richard had the photo?"

"Yes. Said someone sent it to him."

"When was this?"

"Around ten last night. He dragged in Stanton, William, and Nancy too. They weren't pleased."

The heavy hitters. "I bet." Jake leaned back against the motel wall. "Then it couldn't have been Richard at the cabin."

"Richard Thomason? What have you been smoking? He's one of the good guys."

"Is he? Think about it. We put five people under protection, and their positions are compromised within a day or two. Only Thomason knew of their locations. He has to be the one leaking the information."

"Or Julie."

Thomason's secretary. "She's nineteen and way too naïve to pull off a crime this sophisticated. With the series of kills, there have to be several different people involved, and I don't see Julie having the brains to coordinate such an effort."

"You might be right." Jake thought Tom chuckled. "Besides, her old man would personally strangle her."

"That's true." Julie's father was third in line to the director.

"What time was Cho killed?"

"Only about two hours before Thomason showed you the photo."

"Brevard's a good day's drive to Virginia, so he couldn't have personally killed Cho."

"He could have paid someone to do it."

"What would be his motive?" Jake had no idea why Tom was protecting Thomason. Neither cared for the man.

"Beats me." The hole in Jake's theory nagged at him, but he didn't need to spend time in idle speculation. Richard appeared to be an honest man, despite his uptight personality. If Jake had had a wife who'd just undergone a heart transplant, he'd be tense and accusatory too. Richard had said the cost nearly bankrupted him. "What else did Richard have to say?"

"You won't like it."

A man slipped out of his motel room four doors down with a small overnight case and headed straight for a black SUV, not even glancing Jake's way. Jake's body shot to alert, nonetheless. The car that had followed them from north Florida had been a black Ford. What was the probability they were the same vehicle? Slim to none.

"Tell me anyway."

"They think *you* killed Cho."

Tension nearly strangled him. "Because of the photo?"

The black SUV pulled out of the lot. The plates were from Georgia. It could have been the same vehicle. Lake City was no more than forty miles from the Georgia border.

"Yes."

"And Thomason suggested they put an APB out on me."

"More or less."

Bastard. Jake's blood nearly burst a vein. "Here I am trying to protect Susan from a killer and my own coworkers think *I'm* the one who's guilty?" This case had been messed up from the start. "Did Stanton agree with Thomason's assessment?" He paced in front of the room, his gut churning up a storm.

"No, but with the evidence right in front of him, he had to do something. Stanton agreed to bring you in for questioning. That's all."

Great. At a time like this, Jake wished he smoked. He needed to use up his nervous energy. Going for a run was out of the question since Susan wasn't in any shape to join him, and he refused to leave her alone.

"Look I need a place to hide until all this mess is figured out."

From the noise in the background, Tom must have been tapping his feet or slapping a hard surface. "Why don't you two stay at Dad's in West Virginia?"

The cabin where Tom and he used to spend every summer. He was hoping Tom would offer the place. "That would be great, but what about your dad? I don't want to put him in jeopardy, nor do I want him arrested for harboring a fugitive."

"He's here with me. He came for my birthday."

Remorse filled him. He and Tom always celebrated their birthdays together. "Hey, sorry I missed it."

"We can party later. You know where the key is, don't you?"

"Couldn't forget."

Jake knew every nook and cranny of the two-bedroom cabin, not to mention all the hiking trails surrounding the remote site. The only problem he might encounter would be convincing Susan to hide in the woods—the dark, scary woods.

***

Maria Francisco slipped out of her nurse's uniform and put on tight jeans along with one of Peter's favorite shirts. She posed in front of him after she took off or put on each new piece.

Peter adjusted his pants. "You look hot. Come here." He wiggled his fingers for her.

He wanted to take her to bed right then and there, but his stepmother had called and asked if they could visit her in the nursing home.

"We can't." Her bottom lip protruded. "Aunt Sophia is expecting us."

"She can wait. Hell, she might not even remember she asked us over." He smiled, hoping to lure her.

"You said she sounded good, right?"

"Yup. Even called me by my right name."

A frown creased her brow. "No telling when she'll have another lapse, and I don't like being with her when she rambles. The last time I went there by myself, she kept calling me Angelica. I couldn't convince her I was Angelica's daughter."

"I know. She often thinks I'm my dad."

Maria settled on his lap and wrapped her arms around him and nuzzled his ear. "Did Aunt Sophia say what was so important that we needed to rush right over?" Her warm breath tickled his cheek.

"No, just that she needed to see both of us."

Sophia Francisco Caravello was the only person on earth Peter had told about his affair with Maria. She would understand because she'd been part of both families. About twenty years ago, she'd married Dad right after Mom died. As a kid, he wanted to believe he had a new mom for good. Then things went south.

Maria jumped up, picked up her purse from the counter and pulled out her lip gloss. She smoothed the shiny stuff on her kissable lips, probably just to torture him. "I'm ready."

He stole a kiss anyway after they were seated in the car. She was silent for most of the ride to the nursing home, and he left her to her thoughts.

When they walked into Sophia's room, the not-so-old woman was sitting with a blanket on her lap, looking out at the lawn. A red and blue awning shielded the bright sun from streaming in.

"Hello, Sophia," he said.

Peter held his breath, wondering if she'd recognize him. Sophia wheeled around and frowned. "James?"

Damn. He and James looked nothing alike. James' hair was jet black, whereas his was a medium brown. Not to mention James was a good three inches shorter and at least thirty pounds heavier. "No, I'm Peter." He wrapped an arm around Maria's waist and pulled her closer to him. "And I brought Maria with me as you asked."

Now she smiled. "Oh, yes. Please sit down. I do so enjoy company."

Maria took the chair across from Sophia while Peter sat on the made bed.

"Has Joseph stopped by lately?" he asked.

"Joseph? You know better than that. My brother and I haven't spoken in years."

He wanted to make sure. Alzheimer's distorted the mind. "You sound good today." She knew who Joseph was, which was a positive sign. "What did you need to talk to us about?" He might as well get to point before Sophia forgot why she wanted to see them.

She dropped her gaze and twisted her fingers together. "I'm getting worse."

"No. You're fine." He saw no harm in keeping the illusion going a little longer.

Her eyes watered and she waved away the assurance. "I know I have my good days and my bad days, and I wanted you both to know something before I forgot my own name." She laughed, but her eyes lacked their usual sparkle.

Peter glanced at Maria whose gaze was locked onto Sophia. "We're listening," he said.

"This is very hard for me to tell you, but do you remember that your mom and I had been good friends?"

"Yes. You two played bridge together. I heard all the stories." Or as many as he could remember.

She smiled. "Your mom was a great card partner, but she refused to follow the conventions."

The number one reason why his dad refused to play with her. "She did like her cards." He hoped Sophia hadn't called them over to reminisce.

Sophia pulled the blanket higher onto her lap. "Did you realize how much she loved your father?"

His parents fought like most married couples, but he assumed they loved each other. "I guess. She never talked about it. It's not something mothers share with their sons. She died when I was only nine."

"I know. Did you know she also loved my brother?"

He jerked as if she'd slapped him. Maria rose, raced next to him, and sat, hip to hip, her eyes wide with fear.

"Aunt Sophia, what are you saying?"

A sweet smile crossed her face. She turned to Maria. "Do you know why I never talk to your father anymore?"

Maria squeezed Peter's hand. "No. Tell me."

"Your father fell in love with my best friend."

The blood drained from his brain to his fast beating heart. He guessed her best friend had been his mom. He didn't want to think how they expressed this love, if indeed Sophia was in her right mind at the moment.

"Aunt Sophia, what are you talking about?" She glanced up at Peter, her brows pinched together.

"I might as well just say it. Maria, your father had an affair with Peter's mother before either of you were born."

Maria slapped a hand over her mouth.

Peter sat up straighter. "How can you be sure? James always told me Mom preached sex after marriage. According to dad, she was a good Catholic. She'd never have an affair."

Sophia reached for a cup next to her and took a sip. "I know it's hard for both of you to believe. We don't want to think of our parents as sinners, but sometimes circumstances bring us together, and we can't help ourselves."

Peter watched for the usual signs of her Alzheimer's but found none. She wasn't staring off into space, and she wasn't rocking in her chair. He wasn't sure what to say. "Did my dad know about this supposed affair?"

She grasped the cup as if it were a lifeline. "Not until John and I married. Your mother made me promise not to tell him either. I didn't for the longest time, but when your father decided he really didn't love me, I wanted to hurt him. So I told him about his perfect wife and how she'd slept with my brother."

He nearly jumped off the bed. "Did he believe you?"

Tears streamed down Maria's cheek. He dragged a knuckle across her cheek. "It's okay."

Maria shook her head.

"How could he not," Sophia said. "Your father had been away on business for a few months setting up one of his restaurants. When he got back home, your mom was pregnant."

His mind raced, but the ramifications were too horrific. Maria slipped her hand from his. "And you know for sure that Maria's father got my mom pregnant?"

"Yes. I'm sorry. But I thought you should know."

"You said it was before I was born. You're not telling me Maria and I have the same father are you?"

Sophia's eyes glazed over. "Do you remember when we went on our honeymoon and you took me out on a sailboat, only you forgot to mention you didn't know how to sail?"

Peter moved over to the window. "Sophia. It's me, Peter."

"I'm sorry I couldn't make you happier. I never did want your money like you always thought."

He wanted to shake her. "We're going, Sophia. Goodbye."

When he turned back to Maria, she was trembling.

Dear God, now what were they going to do?

CHAPTER FIFTEEN

"In the daytime, this place is charming," Susan said, not wanting to spoil Jake's excitement. At night, the woods would be a different story. Dark, creepy, hidden.

A large gust of winter wind swooshed past, and she shivered. Jake stepped behind her and ran his hands up and down her jacketed arms. She inched backwards to bridge the gap between them. If he tilted his head down, she bet his chin would have skimmed the top of her head, and their closeness warmed her.

"Tom and I came up here every summer. It was the best time of my life." Jake dropped his arms and stepped back.

Because of way his voice trailed off, she debated turning around to drink in his expression but decided not to intrude on his privacy.

Instead, she studied Jake's childhood castle. A big picture window took up most of the left side of the single-story log cabin. Underneath the window were two rectangular, wooden boxes that contained only dirt and some unidentifiable dead flowers. When the weather warmed, the flowers would come to life and dress the cabin in color.

She looked up. "It has a chimney!" she said, more excited than she had been in days. "I could use a glowing fire right now."

She'd been in such a rush when they'd gone shopping, she hadn't purchased warm enough clothes for February, and Florida's selection of down jackets was close to zero. To think she had a closet full of ski clothes at her house. What she wouldn't give to sneak back in and grab some warmer gear. Jake had said they'd stop in Brevard and pick up some winter appropriate clothing, but once they found Gary Cho, all thoughts of shopping went out the window.

As Jake searched for the key, she looked down the gravel drive leading to the cabin. Driving on the pebbles had made lots of crunching noises. If someone came up to the cabin, Jake and she were sure to hear him. It was kind of like their own alarm system. She liked that.

"I got it." He waved the key.

Mr. Traynor had hidden it under the lip of a bird feeder. Clever man.

Jake took their suitcases from the trunk and showed her inside.

The fireplace was the centerpiece of the room. "Nice." She could have done without the rifles underneath the mounted deer head though, but refugees couldn't be picky.

He set down their suitcases. "It's small, but the cabin has all the comforts of home."

She liked how the light streamed in through the kitchen window. The view of the forest would be amazing once spring came and the mountain laurels bloomed, though she hoped she wouldn't be here that long. Right now, patches of snow were tucked under some rocks, and only dots of green shot up from the ground. Except for the pines, the trees were stripped bare.

Once the FBI caught the maniac who was killing the jurors, she'd be free to go home and practice law again. A rush of excitement grabbed her until she realized Jake would be off on another assignment, protecting someone else, and she'd never seen him again.

The intense prospective loneliness nearly took her breath away. Strange. When had he turned from being the enemy to a man she wanted to help and care for her?

She kept her back to him as she pretended to study the view, not wanting him to see her chin quiver.

"Pretty nice, here, huh?" he said.

Jake seemed excited to be back in a place that elicited good memories.

"It's much nicer than I imagined." She forced cheeriness into her tone.

Trying to live in the here and now, she passed the kitchen table and checked out the small cooking area. Susan trailed her fingers along the worn countertop. The stove needed a good cleaning, but Tom's dad seemed to have equipped the cabin nicely.

She faced him. "Tom's dad doesn't mind if we stay here?"

"He'll be in Washington for the next week or so. When he comes back, we'll have to find someplace else to stay."

"Too bad. This house is nice." She wrinkled her nose. "Do you think we could open a window for a few minutes? It smells kind of musty."

"Hank probably took a vacation before he visited Tom, but I like the smell. Reminds me of the delicious aroma of those cinnamon buns Mrs. Traynor used to make. Her sour dough bread was amazing. Man could she cook." His eyes shone as he proceeded over to the window behind the kitchen table. "I know this one opens." He lifted the sash.

Cold air rushed in, carrying with it the sweet smell of pine. "Thanks." She waited until he faced her. "I'm feeling a lot better and can manage on my own. If you want to go back to Washington to straighten out this mess about the FBI thinking you harmed Cho, I'm okay with that."

He placed his hands on her shoulders. "You can't get rid of me that easily. I will not leave you until the bastard is caught. We have no idea where he is." He smiled and her insides turned to mush.

Jake tilted her chin upward, and from the dreamy look in his eyes, she knew he was finally going to kiss her. She closed her lids, her heart racing, body waiting. He placed a kiss on her forehead and her stomach caved. Damn.

Her eyes sprang open as she took a step back. "You're right. Absolutely right. The moment you leave here, the guy could find me." Babble, babble. God, this was more embarrassing than when she made the same error of judgment with Timmy. At least she was only ten then and had a good excuse.

Being Jake's friend wasn't what she wanted, but apparently that's how he saw their relationship. Jake was hired to protect her. Nothing more.

She tapped his chest. "I wasn't trying to get rid of you. I didn't want you to feel obligated to stay by my side." Giving him a way out would ease her conscience.

"In case I didn't mention it before, I have a price on my head. I'd like to stay hidden for a little while longer. The Bureau will catch this guy, and then you can move back to Washington and resume your life."

What if I don't want to resume my stressful life? "Great."

"Come on. Let's unpack. We need to discuss what we're going to do for money."

"Money?" Any joy she'd experienced being alone in a cozy cabin with Jake evaporated.

He tapped her nose. "Think about it. I can't use the FBI credit card anymore since the Bureau will know where we are. I only have enough cash to buy about three days' worth of groceries."

She hadn't realized their situation was so dire. "What are we going to do?" Her legs suddenly weakened.

"I'll have to get a job."

She wasn't going to let him support her. "I can wait tables. I got through law school at a diner next to the college."

He picked up her suitcase. "Sounds good. Go pick a bedroom."

For a split second, she wished the place only had one bedroom. She liked knowing Jake was nearby, but she wasn't going to tell him that.

"You said you and Tom came up here every summer. Which room did you stay in?" He'd probably feel more comfortable there.

"Tom and I shared the one on the left."

Sight unseen, she chose the one on the right.

He put her bag in her new room. "Why don't you take a shower, change, and then we can go for a winter stroll," Jake said.

He had to be kidding. "It might get dark before we get back."

"We won't go far. Besides, we have another two hours of light."

Suddenly, she liked the idea of holding his hand, talking freely, and sharing her thoughts. "I'll hurry."

When she emerged from cleaning up, Jake had placed a light blue down jacket, a pretty navy scarf, and matching gloves on her bed.

"Where did these come from?" Her gear wouldn't have kept her warm for long.

"The Traynors are big hikers and hunters. There's a large hidden basement where they keep all sorts of camping gear. I pilfered them from the closet. Tom's mom passed away a few years ago. I guess his dad never got rid of her things."

His gaze slipped to the ground. Not wanting him to dwell on the loss, Susan hurried but struggled to dress. "I'm ready."

The trail heading west behind the house took them past two waterfalls, separated by a large gap.

"I never expected the woods to be so magical. This is really beautiful." Shoulder to shoulder, she looked up at him and smiled.

Jake took her gloved hands in his and pulled her around to face him. "I find there's more beauty right in front of me."

If he hadn't been holding her hands, she would have covered her face. Surely the scars on her cheek made her ugly. He was probably saying nice things to help her relax and forget about being in the woods. Before she could tell him he was out of his mind, Jake leaned over and kissed her, his warm breath fanning her lips. Her eyes seemed to automatically close and her chest move closer. And from the pressure, she'd say friendship wasn't on his mind.

She wanted to open her mouth and invite him in, but she wasn't sure of his intention. Her head swam with possibilities, and the cold air turned warm as her body melted against him. She wanted to take off her gloves and run her hands down his face and under his jacket, but she was too busy tasting his lips. Before she finished exploring the wonders of Jake Yarnell, FBI agent, his hands cupped her face, and then he pulled away.

Bereft of contact, she sagged. He didn't seem to notice she wanted more.

He angled his body toward the waterfall. "Maybe we should get back."

What happened to, *Wow, Susan, that was an amazing kiss; let's not stop?*

When he didn't address what they just shared, she could only mumble, "Sure."

Get real. What had she expected him to say given it was forty degrees outside? That he'd want to strip naked and make mad passionate love on the ground?

If he'd asked, she might have agreed. Oh, well. At least she wouldn't be cold on the walk back to the cabin. His kisses had thoroughly heated her.

***

Jake yawned and fought the urge to turn the Jeep around and head back to the cabin. He'd had absolutely no sleep last night. What had he been thinking kissing Susan?

Call it fatigue, call it fear he'd be falsely accused, call it whatever you wanted, bottom line was, he shouldn't have dropped his defenses.

If she'd slapped him or pulled back, he would have been happy. When she leaned into him and slightly parted her mouth, he nearly died. He wanted to devour her right then and there.

Now he'd have to live with the fact he desired her. He glanced over at Susan. Her head was back against the headrest, her eyes closed. Maybe she too hadn't slept.

He pulled to the curb at the town center and cut the engine.

She yawned and unhooked her seatbelt. "You really think the hardware store will hire you just like that?"

"I'm not planning on working there. I'm looking for some references. Working small jobs makes me more flexible. Besides, I don't want to stay at any one job for long."

"Makes sense."

If he could have worked under an assumed name, he would have, but the town folk of Shepherd Hills knew him as a friend of Hank Traynor's boy. Hiding his identity in this town was impossible.

He had told a small fib to Susan. He did have money to last a week, but staying around the house with nothing to do might have led him to do something stupid. The kiss in the forest had ignited his blood, proving without a shadow of a doubt that he wanted her. Too bad, he understood that no good could come of their relationship.

Asking Susan to come along while he job-searched only added to his desires, but there was no way he would leave her alone.

"Look." She pointed to the Shepherd's diner. "They have a Help Wanted sign."

"We'll check it out as soon as I talk to Mr. Wilkerson, assuming he's still alive. The old coot was a hundred years old the last time I was here."

He and Susan walked side by side to the hardware store. The street hadn't changed much since the last time he was there. He spotted the same antique table and stool set in Art's Collectibles storefront, the same bookstore with the faded posters in the window, and the same empty storefront at the end of the street.

He pushed open the front door of Wilkerson's store, and the familiar ring of the bell sounded. A young man with way too many piercings was behind the counter. Jake scanned the aisles. An old man was placing bags of salt on the shelves, and Jake made a beeline to him.

"Mr. Wilkerson?"

The bent over man in the green apron twisted around and ran his gaze down the length of Jake. "Yes?"

"Do you remember me?" Jake helped Wilkerson to his feet. He hadn't been back in Shepherd Hills in at least five years, but for two summers, he'd worked at the store.

Wilkerson blinked a few times and pushed up his glasses. "Well, I'll be. Jake Yarnell. I hear you and Tom are working together in D.C."

News travelled fast. "Yes, sir. Or at least I was. I quit the force to settle down. This here is my fiancée, Taylor." Before Susan could protest, he wrapped an arm around her waist and squeezed.

"You pregnant?" the old man asked, one brow raised. Jake knew the coot was teasing, but from the way Susan's mouth had dropped, she didn't.

"No," she said, jumping in before he got a chance to answer for her. "We just became engaged. I'm a God fearing woman who believes in marriage first." Her chin notched higher.

His admiration for her picked up. She was a quick study.

"I'm glad to hear it, little lady." Wilkerson turned to Jake. "What can I get for you?"

"I'm looking to do some odd jobs. You know of anyone in need of a handyman?"

The old man scratched his chin. "As a matter of fact I do. Douglas Abernathy, out at Meadow Point, was in here yesterday. He's renovating a room. He and the misses are expecting their first."

He smiled. "You have his number?"

Mr. Wilkerson hobbled back around the counter. "I do, but don't expect much in the way of payment. The wife and he can give you food if you need some. They turned their barn into some kind of organic greenhouse. Even installed a couple of those solar panels."

"That would be great."

"Where are you two staying?"

"At the Traynors for now. We plan to look for a place of our own as soon as Hank gets back from D.C."

"I'll keep an eye out for you." He winked. "Glad you're back."

They said their goodbyes, and Jake escorted Susan out. Once they were out of earshot, she stepped away from him. "Was that wise to tell him where we're staying?"

"If I'd lied, he'd have known."

She chewed on her bottom lip looking way too cute.

"Do you think the whole town will know you're back?"

"I'd give Wilkerson about an hour."

Jake wanted to smooth away the creases in her brow, but given they had to play the role of the happy couple, he might as well make his part convincing. Jake squeezed her hand, leaned over, and kissed her. With real emotion. Her eyes widened this time. He pulled her close to whisper in her ear. "We want the townsfolk to believe we're a couple."

Her grip relaxed. "When I was in front of a jury, I was a great actress, if I do say so myself. Playing your fiancée won't be a stretch."

When she smiled up at him with mischief in her eyes, he knew he'd run smack into trouble.

***

Joseph was hunched over his books when the phone rang. It was Dom again.

"Yes?"

"We're all set."

He assumed that meant the last of the jurors was gone. "Tell me about the secret plan you had."

"I framed Jake Yarnell for the murder of the last juror. It was so sweet."

"Tell me."

After Dom finished, even Joseph admitted the plan was good.

"I called Thomason and sent him the photo showing Yarnell doing the deed."

Joseph stilled. "You what?"

"I said—"

"I heard what you said. Why'd you call him? We don't need him to be able to trace your call."

"I was careful. I used a disposable. How else could I get the picture to him so quickly?"

Dom always claimed he was careful, but he never was. A knock sounded on his door and Joseph spun around.

"Dad, I'm going to pick up the kids from school." His daughter-in-law smiled, and his heart melted.

"Okay."

If he'd told her Dom was on the phone, she would have stiffened, and he hated to see Helena suffer. She was a sweetheart.

Once she closed the door to the den, he returned his attention back to his son. "You know where Yarnell and the woman are?"

"Yeah, I do. When they were parked at the motel, I put a tracer on the car. No problems. They'll be out of your hair soon."

Joseph leaned back in his chair and sighed. "You aren't done until Peter Caravello is six feet under."

"I know. He'll be my reward."

Joseph hung up and dropped his head in his hands. Maybe he was too old for revenge. He should have had Dom kill the son of a bitch. years ago and avoid all the pain of watching Maria fall in love with a stinking Caravello.

CHAPTER SIXTEEN

Dom disconnected. He couldn't wait to see the smile on his father's face the day he announced Peter was dead. He'd worked his whole life to win his father's approval, and he'd be damned if anything got in his way.

Maria on the other hand would never forgive him if she ever learned what he was about to do. He'd be careful, but she'd still be heartbroken. It was for her own good though. Her life with Peter didn't have a chance anyway, not with a father like his.

But first, he had to take care of the attorney and her bodyguard. He checked his GPS, and it indicated they were in West Virginia. Perfect. He'd already driven as far as Virginia. Another few hours and he'd be ready to take them down.

Dom punched in Ronnie's number. While he liked working solo, having backup helped.

"Hey, Dom."

"I got another job for you. Are you interested?"

"How much?"

"Five big ones."

"Where and when?"

That's what he liked about Ronnie. No bullshit. It was all about the money.

The Chapman's Jeep had stopped near the Roanoke airport for an hour. At first Dom thought his two pigeons had flown somewhere, but about half -hour ago, the Jeep headed north. "Can you leave now and meet me?"

"For five grand I can."

They set up to meet halfway between Roanoke and Washington, D.C. Dom checked the dash for the time. "Say nine tonight?" Factoring in for his friend to get lost, that should give Ronnie time to pack and make the trip. "We'll head into West Virginia from there. That's what the GPS locator claims they've gone."

"I'll be there. What are you driving?"

"A red mustang." He liked to rent in style.

"Cool."

Dom leaned back in his seat. Roanoke was a nice town. He had a little philly, Sarah, he used to bang here, but ever since the kids were born, he'd been devoted and hadn't strayed. Damn. Why did he have to be so moral?

He had an hour to kill while Ronnie got his act together. Because he could use a good burger, he stopped in a diner. Turns out, it was a real waste of five bucks. He would have been better off calling Sarah.

Dom pulled out a pad and jotted down some notes and a diagram of how the kill would go down. He liked being prepared. It also helped if he and Ronnie were on the same page. The guy was good with diagrams, not verbal instructions.

Dom waited at the assigned spot for close to half an hour before Ronnie finally showed. The signal on Yarnell and Chapman's Jeep had stopped. Good. Moving targets were harder to deal with. Ronnie pulled alongside him in the parking lot, hopped out, and tapped on Dom's window. He rolled down the pane half way, and the cold air blasted him.

"So what's our plan," Ronnie said, shivering.

Idiot didn't have the sense to wear a jacket. "When we get near to where we're going, we can park your car and we'll go in together. I have it all drawn out for you." Dom shook a finger at him. "Don't lose me."

"I'll stick to you like glue." Ronnie jogged back to his car.

"Wait," Dom called, and his friend spun around. "You rented your car under an assumed name, right?" He nodded toward the Ford Focus.

He froze. "I didn't have time. This is Gina's car."

Dom slammed his palm against the steering wheel. He debated driving off and leaving Ronnie in the parking lot but having backup was more important. "Keep up."

In less than an hour they arrived in West Virginia, five miles from the Jeep's location. Dom pulled into a Wal-Mart since no one would bother Ronnie's car there.

He honked for his friend to get in.

Ronnie sniffed. "I love new car smell. Say, I didn't get a chance to eat before you called. Mind if we grab a bite? I have to keep up my stamina."

Ronnie's need for constant food intake drove Dom crazy. "Sure, but it's got to be a drive-through."

"Fine. How are we going to take them down?"

"We'll have to locate the vehicle first. The GPS isn't exact. The ideal situation would be if they're at a motel. If they are, I'll go in, shoot them both and get out. We can go over the fine details when we get there."

"How are you going to know which room they're in? If you flash that fake FBI badge, the person at the desk is sure to remember you."

He should have thought of that. Dom looked over at Ronnie. Even in the dark, he could tell his eyes were bloodshot. Christ. The last thing he needed was an overtired accomplice.

"It's late. We'll get a room for the night and catch a few hours' sleep. When Yarnell and Chapman come out in the morning, we'll follow them and take them down."

"What if they're staying at a friend's house?"

Dom didn't understand why Ronnie was so nervous. He hadn't had any qualms when he set the townhouse next to Mrs. Chapman's place on fire.

"Don't worry. I have a plan for that too."

"Okay."

The Jeep was parked at a Motel 6. Perfect. He reserved a room under his fake name. As soon as they settled in, Ronnie climbed into his bed.

Dom sat up a little while longer, going over the plan in his head. At midnight, he shut off the light and tried to sleep, but his excitement prevented him from dozing for long. It didn't help that Ronnie snored. To make sure nothing would go wrong, every few hours he crawled out of bed and checked to see if the Jeep was still in the parking lot. It was.

At five, he roused his partner. "Up and at 'em."

Ronnie was slow to move, but after he showered, he was in the car waiting for the couple to get on the road. Dom had photos of both Yarnell and Chapman. Those two should be easy to spot.

When a young black couple with two kids piled into the Jeep, Dom slammed his fist against the dash.

"What are they doing getting into the car?" Ronnie turned toward him. "You sure you got the right vehicle?"

"Yeah. I put the GPS on the bumper myself." Shit. "You know I told you the Jeep sat near the airport for an hour. I bet Yarnell switched cars. Damn it." He wouldn't let his dad know since he couldn't take the put down.

"So now what do we do?"

"Lemme think."

"You think your FBI mole knows where Yarnell and the girl are?"

"My dad said no. If they did, the Feds would have already caught him."

"Caught him?"

He hadn't kept Ronnie in the loop once he set fire to Chapman's townhouse, so he told him about framing Yarnell for Cho's murder."

"Smart."

Dom puffed out his chest. "I thought so."

"So now what?"

"I did some research on Yarnell. He went to school in Virginia. Roomed a guy who works for the guy in charge of the safe house."

"The mole?"

"Yeah. I think I know where they might be hiding." Dom couldn't stop the grin from spreading across his face.

***

Richard paced Stanton's office. "Any idea where Yarnell might be?"

"He could be anywhere." Stanton crossed his arms and glared at him.

"And we don't have any way to trace him?" Richard slapped the desk.

"Calm down. Jake's not dangerous."

"Like hell. He killed at least one juror, maybe more."

"The timeline doesn't fit. He couldn't have killed Janet Starkey for one. Jake and Mrs. Chapman were in Florida at the time."

Richard thought fast. "Or so he said. I only spoke to Jake but never to Mrs. Chapman. He could have lied when he said they were in Florida."

"It's easy enough to verify."

Stanton pulled out his phone and tapped his fingers on the desk. "Tom, Stanton. Would you run me the charges Jake rang up on the credit card from the time he left DC to the time he arrived in Florida?" He held up a finger at Richard.

Smug bastard. He needed Jake to look guilty. Otherwise, he was doomed. Stanton was too smart not to suspect he was guilty of compromising the position of the witnesses.

"Thanks," Stanton said. He swiped off his phone. "Shouldn't take Tom long to check."

Richard sat in the chair opposite Stanton. He didn't enjoy looking up at the man, but the situation was getting more dire. "He could have hired someone to killed Janet and the other witnesses." *Lame, Richard, lame.*

"What do you have against Jake?"

Shit. "Me? Nothing. I'm just drawing conclusions from the facts. Pictures don't lie."

A knock sounded on the door and Richard's secretary came in. She glanced at Stanton and winced.

"It's all right. We're all on the same side. What did you find out?"

"It was too late to contact Jake's college to find out the name of his fraternity." She bit her bottom lip. "I came up with a dead end with his last foster home too. The parents have moved and left no forwarding address. I'm sorry."

From the way she twisted her fingers together, she looked like she expected to get fired for failing to get the information he'd asked for. If her father weren't so high up in the FBI, he'd have canned her ass a long time ago. He wanted to rant, but he stayed calm in front of Stanton.

"No problem. Tomorrow will be fine. I'm sure you'll come up with a list of his friends soon enough."

She half smiled and ducked out.

"What was that about?" Stanton said.

Richard got up. "I'm guessing Jake will want to stay with a friend rather than pay for a motel night after night. Without using credit cards, his funds will run short."

"Jake is resourceful. Now if you'll excuse me, I have work to do."

Dismissed like some probie, Richard straightened his tie and left. Asshole. He'd find Jake if it killed him.

***

Waiting on tables came back naturally to Susan, and best of all, the people of West Virginia were friendly and nice. She couldn't brag they were big tippers, but she was able to eat for free, and for that she was grateful. To her surprise, the owner acted happy she wanted a job. Little did he know how desperate she was for the income.

Working the long hours also helped renew her spirits. She was used to investigating and reading briefs till the early morning, not sitting around helpless.

The switch from mental to physical work didn't bother her as long as she made a few adjustments. She found if she held the tray low enough, the weight didn't tug on her stitches as much, but John Carter, the owner of Shepherd's Diner, insisted she only carry light orders. Poor Rebecca, one of the waitresses who worked the same shift, had to do the heavy lifting for her.

Most of the clientele were kind enough not to ask why part of her face was covered. Jake and she had come up with a good cover story that involved a drunk driver in case they did ask. The hardest part of her job was responding to her new name of Taylor instead of Susan.

She'd only been working two days, but she already missed being with Jake twenty-four seven. He'd begun work this morning at the young couple's house. Of course, if he'd let her have a phone, she might have been able to at least text him.

"Taylor?" Her boss called from behind the counter.

She looked up. He nodded toward the door. Jake stood at the entranceway, a smile on his face, and her heart skipped a beat. Was she psychic or what? Even with paint splatter on his new jeans and bits of white in his hair, he looked handsome.

He sauntered over to her. "Got room for me?"

"Sure. Pick a table." Four of the eight tables sat empty.

"Can you join me?"

She laughed. Actually laughed. "It's noon. I have to work. It's the busiest time of the day, or so I've been told." To punctuate her statement, the door opened bringing with it two more customers.

Jake shrugged and grabbed a booth in the corner, his back to the wall. She figured the strategic position afforded him the best view of what was going on.

Susan gave him a menu. "Can I get you something to drink, sir?"

"Oh, I'm a sir now?" His blue eyes crinkled on the corners. "I like it. Yes, I'd like a cup of coffee. Black."

"Coming up. You want anything else?" She hadn't flirted with a man in years. Somehow it felt right with Jake.

"Nothing I can afford."

His eyes darkened, and heat crept up her face. She wasn't quite sure what he was implying, but it was best if she nabbed the coffee and didn't ask for details. They were supposed to be engaged, so she figured his flirtations were part of the role-playing.

"How about a burger? On the house." She could afford to buy him one.

"Perfect."

She delivered the coffee, and then his meal. When the lunch crowd left, Susan slipped in the booth across from him.

"How are you holding up?" he asked, all flirtation gone.

"I actually enjoy meeting all these people. They're so real and nice. Nothing like the sharks and scum buckets I'm used to dealing with."

Jake smiled as he looked around. "I always had a connection to this place. See that washboard and those bottles on the shelf?"

She nodded.

"They've been there since 1963, according to Hank."

Must be nice to have a place with fond memories.

Since she had a few minutes and Jake appeared to be in a sharing mood, she decided to test the waters. "Where did you grow up?"

A tic caught the corner of his eye. Apparently, his background wasn't a good topic.

"I lived in many different places, from Pennsylvania to Virginia to Washington, DC."

"Was that when you were in foster care?"

"Yes."

She waited a beat for him to elaborate, but instead he stretched his arms back over the Naugahyde upholstered booth. The tension rippling across his neck belied his relaxed pose.

"How did you end up in foster care?"

"My mother died of a drug overdose when I was seven. She was a whore."

Susan sucked in a long breath. "I'm sorry."

"Don't be. Long story short, I went directly into the foster care system. Because I was rather old, I got shuffled from place to place— after I stayed the short stint with the nuns. I went through four families before I turned eighteen."

"Hence the daisy tattoo."

"Yes."

When the lines around his mouth hardened, she had no idea how to respond. "I'm sorry." She had to stop repeating herself.

"Don't be. I turned out all right."

"And here I thought I had it tough with my mother and father always working."

"I did have one family who cared for me." His shoulders relaxed.

"Tom's family?"

"I kind of adopted his family during college, but this was when I was nine. I was assigned a Big Brother from one of those community outreach programs. He taught me everything, from fishing to racing go carts to how to shoot a gun."

She was happy for him. "Do you still keep in touch with this family?"

He locked his gaze with her. "As a matter of fact I do. My *big brother* had a nephew who I grew fond of too. We were like brothers." He leaned forward and took her hands in his. "You want to know the name of this so-called brother."

From the glint in his eye, Susan knew she wouldn't like the answer. Then she recalled the four names on his speed dial. "Don't tell me it was Peter Caravello."

"Yup."

She leaned back and withdrew her hands. "No wonder you wanted to believe he was innocent."

"Turned out I was right. Peter couldn't have committed several of those crimes since he was in custody or in Washington at the time. I think the same person who wanted to frame Peter is trying to frame me."

"Hey, Taylor," her boss called.

Saved by the bell. "Look, I gotta go. Thanks for stopping by." For the sake of image, she debated kissing him, but when Jake chugged the rest of his coffee, she backed away. Too bad he hadn't read her mind.

Jake finished up shortly and waved goodbye. She'd feared he was mad that she rushed away, since it was clear he wanted to talk about Peter with her, but she wasn't ready. Without more evidence, she wouldn't be visiting Peter alone any time soon.

Jake had been gone no more than ten minutes when two men walked in, and her stomach soured for no good reason other than gut instinct. Was it the way they looked at her, or the sharp perusal of the place as if they intended to rob it?

Forget it. Paranoia wasn't a pretty trait, yet the shorter man looked familiar. Too bad she couldn't place him.

CHAPTER SEVENTEEN

By the time Susan's shift ended at the diner, the weather had turned nasty. Rain, mixed with snow, pummeled the large glass storefront windows.

John wiped his hands on his apron and came out from behind the counter. "When Jake comes for you, you go ahead. Rebecca and I can clean up."

She wasn't sure if she should take him up on her offer, but she was too tired to argue. "Thanks. I'm still a little drained from the accident."

"Be careful going home," John said.

By the time Jake pulled in front of the diner, it was past eight. Susan waved to Rebecca who was wiping down the last of the tables. "Thank you!"

Rebecca looked up and smiled. "Have fun on your days off."

She liked having a friend who she could let down her guard around.

Two days off. Hmm. Susan wasn't sure if she wanted to sit in the cabin by herself while Jake worked, but her schedule needed to mesh with the other workers.

Bracing herself against the wind, she lifted her collar and rushed outside. Driving rain soaked her before she reached the passenger's side. She jumped in and slammed the door shut before she dripped water inside the cab.

"Don't you have an umbrella?" Jake asked.

"Obviously not." Damn, she should have been sarcastic, but her feet hurt and her body ached.

"Right."

He pulled out into an empty road. Apparently, no one else was crazy enough to drive in this weather, and they met with little traffic on their trip out of town.

"I'll look to see if the Traynors have something you can borrow." He slid the heater knob to high. "Don't want you to catch cold."

She didn't remember Carlton caring about her health like Jake did, even at the beginning of their short marriage. She needed to shift her thoughts from her problems. "How was your day?"

"Good, but lunch was better." He winked.

Her stomach fluttered. They weren't in public, so there wasn't any need for him to toss out compliments as if they were engaged.

"I enjoyed you stopping by too." God, she sounded like a freshman in high school.

Jake cleared his throat. "How was day two at Shepherd's Diner?"

She nearly laughed at their awkward conversation. "Good until you left." He quirked a brow, and she twisted toward him. "These two creepy men came in that John said weren't from around here."

"Shepherd Hills gets a lot of visitors."

"These didn't act like tourists."

His fingers gripped the wheel tight and his jaw tightened. "What did they look like?"

An oncoming car drove past, illuminating the concern in his eyes. "I didn't pay all that much attention until the shorter guy wouldn't stop staring at me."

"Describe him."

She should have memorized more details. "Caucasian, late thirties, maybe. He had glasses with black rims, wore a plaid shirt, and had dirty boots." Not bad.

"So he wasn't the same as the one at the Lake City Waffle House?"

Her stomach twisted. She wanted to remember. "At first I thought he might be, but because his dress was so different, I couldn't be sure. I'm sorry."

"You did your best." Jake turned left onto a road leading up to mountain cabin. "What did these men sound like? Deep voice, raspy like a smoker, foreign accent, or what?"

She closed her eyes and tried to replay their interaction. "One of the men had a distinctive accent, like someone who lived around New York. The man in the plaid shirt didn't say much. When they finished their meal and left, I made a point of looking at their license plate. They were from Virginia." Pride seeped in.

His brows rose. "Did you get the number?"

She leaned back in the seat. "No. Another car pulled out in front and blocked the back of their red mustang just as I tried to read the plate."

He shook his head. "This town gets a lot of people passing through. The one man who took an interest might have been someone who liked to look at a beautiful woman."

She nearly sputtered. With her scarred face, no one would find her attractive. "If they do stop by again, I'll be sure to ask John or Rebecca to secretly take a picture of them with their camera phone."

"Let's hope they don't come back."

"Amen."

The weather didn't let up the whole ride to the cabin. If anything, the wind had become stronger and the rain more intense. Trees swayed like beggars grabbing for a handout—creepy and disturbing.

Jake cut the engine. "Wait here. I'll get an umbrella for you."

That was dumb. He'd get wet running to the cabin, jogging back to the car, and then rushing inside again. "I can make it. I'm already soaked."

Before Jake could come around to her side, she pushed open the door and hurried to the covered entranceway. She shivered against the cold.

Jake wrapped an arm around her shoulders as he unlocked the cabin door with one hand, and she appreciated his warm body heat.

He ushered her in. Even though they were inside, the walls didn't do a great job of keeping out the winter weather. "It's freezing inside." Chills raced down her back.

"Why don't you take a hot shower and get ready for bed while I light a fire?"

She didn't remember the last time she'd taken the time to enjoy an evening watching flames flicker up a chimney. "Sounds divine."

She wasn't all that sure about walking around in her nightgown, but she did relish the idea of roasting by the fire.

When she finished showering and reapplying her bandages, she pulled on her flannel gown. A little self-conscious, she padded out to the darkened living room and halted. Light from the fire flickered off the walls, giving the room a warm yellow glow.

Jake was lying on pillows he'd taken from the sofa, and two more pillows were next to him. "Come, join me."

She couldn't resist. Given he'd turned off the room lights, her nightgown would provide her a fair amount of modesty. Her back to Jake, she tucked her legs under and admired the flames, letting the heat pour over her.

"Here." He tapped her shoulder and handed her a glass of red wine.

She twisted around. "What's the occasion?"

"Occasion? This may be the first time we've spent more than one night at a place. I'm hoping our days of running are over."

If only. Susan sipped the wine, and the robust liquid soothed her throat. "This is delicious."

"I agree. I'll have to thank Tom's dad."

The flames jumped and shook, mesmerizing her. As she drank and watched the interplay of wood and fire, her body slowly relaxed. Sprawled on the cushion behind her, Jake reached up and twisted her hair in his finger sending shivers of delight along her body. Susan leaned her head back to enjoy his playfulness.

She set her glass down, turned toward him and leaned on her elbow. Shadows danced on his face, and she reached out to touch his bristly cheek.

When he twisted his head and kissed her palm, her soul melted. Maybe it was the stress of not talking to her family, the aftermath of seeing her best friend die, or having to run for her life, but that one act of tenderness did more to give her hope than any words could have done.

"Why don't you move closer?" he said, his voice thick with emotion.

Her logical mind battled with her body. Since her divorce, she'd focused solely on work—meaning long hours that didn't allow her any time for pleasure. She was attracted to Jake—and he to her, she was sure.

But could she afford to get involved? Once the bastard was caught, they'd go back to their old lives.

Stop thinking. Just act.

The crackle of the fire and smell of the pine emboldened her. She scooted forward on the pillows until her lips were inches from his. Somehow her fingers found their way into his still damp, wavy hair. She dragged his face closer and could smell the rain on his skin.

She ran a thumb down his ear. "You should dry off. We don't need you catching cold."

"Trust me, I'm anything but cold." He slid his hand around her waist and pulled her hip to hip. "I've wanted to hold you for so long."

Surprise shook her. He closed his eyes, and she knew her looks didn't matter to him, making her heart soar. Susan's resolve broke, and she let her body and her desires lead the way. Too much thinking and analyzing would just get in the way.

When their lips touched, her mind shut off. Suddenly, her hands found their way to his shoulders, and then over his bulging biceps. She wanted to touch his skin, taste him, and savor everything about him. With fumbling fingers, she unbuttoned his shirt and leaned back to let the light bounce off his magnificent body. A thatch of hair was lightly sprinkled across his upper chest, leaving the bottom half to his navel bare. "You're gorgeous."

He laughed. "I think gorgeous suits you more."

Her face heated. His hands slipped to the end of her nightgown and tugged the cloth upward. Thrill and lust overwhelmed her senses. Living in a dead marriage for so long, she'd forgotten how much excitement could exist between a man and a woman.

"You think we should be doing this?" she said, praying he'd say, oh, yeah.

"You mean exploring each other's bodies with the intent to make love?"

"Yeah that."

His fingers tightened on her back. "I'll stop if you want."

"Never. Now shut up and kiss me."

She didn't have to ask twice, for his lips made her believe in forever after. He rolled her on top of him, his hard erection pressing against her. Would she be able to handle him? He was huge.

A moment later, he'd discarded her nightgown and began sucking on her nipple while he kneaded her other breast. Tender, yet firm, he thoroughly made his way from one breast to the other, while his free hand explored the contours of her neck, her hips, her thighs and her ass. The fire sent out a loud snap and she jerked at the intrusion.

"Shh." He kissed her forehead, and she relaxed.

***

Jake couldn't get enough of her. Susan's long legs made him forget every FBI rule he'd ever learned. He loved her silky hair, soft lips, creamy thighs, and magnificent breasts.

He wanted her. Now. After leaning her onto her back, he straddled her. Without ceremony, he dipped a finger inside her, and she gasped, sending his libido into overdrive. He had to have her, taste her, savor her.

Without asking what she wanted, he slipped down between her thighs and licked her, slow at first, then flicked his tongue fast and furiously as her moans increased. She wove her fingers in his hair and tugged.

"That feels wonderful. Please, don't stop."

He had no intention of doing that. His hands ran up and down the length of her legs, while his mouth explored every fold and nub. When she was thoroughly wet, he fell back on the cushion and pulled her on top of him once more.

"I want you to make love to me," he said. "I'm afraid I might hurt you if I'm on top."

She closed her eyes and smiled. "I don't think you'd ever hurt me."

He wanted to laugh with joy. "Only a few days ago you thought I wanted to kill you."

"That was eons ago."

How true. He'd known her for a short while, yet she let him touch her inner soul. She leaned over and kissed him, tasting like the wine. After a long and thorough exploration, she smiled, and then slid lower. "Time to taste you."

Oh, jeez, he wouldn't last. It didn't matter he could sit still for hours or go without water for two days, the moment Susan touched him, he'd lose it.

Lightly grabbing his dick, she leaned over and dragged her tongue along his length. He had to work hard to swallow the hiss. Jake cupped her shoulder, ready to pull her off should he start to blow.

Between her delicate licks and her slow pumps, the tension nearly ripped him in two. "Kiss me," he begged, though he wasn't sure that would calm him down any more.

"My pleasure."

As she explored his mouth, she lifted her behind and slipped down on his erection. Damn. He nearly came with that first touch.

Hands on her waist, he raised her off him.

"What's wrong?" Her voice cracked.

He pulled a condom out of his wallet and waved the foil packet at her. "I'm the protector, remember?"

Her face relaxed. "Hurry."

Once he sheathed himself, he repositioned her on top once more, and she immediately planted herself on his shaft. Christ. Susan bucked up and down, driving him wild with need.

"Oh, Jake!"

Her fevered cry set his balls on fire. Wanting Susan to be completely fulfilled, he slowed the pace—or rather tried to slow the pace. She lowered her upper body, giving him access to her perfect breasts again. Each nip and lick seemed to take her higher and higher. He wouldn't have stopped except it made his balls tighten further.

He didn't remember how long they made love, but between his hands plying her breasts, and his lips on her, he came the moment her screams of ecstasy reverberated in the room.

Their breaths mingled, and he could almost hear her heart slamming against her chest. With her eyes squeezed shut, she collapsed on top of him. "That was amazing," she panted.

He ran a hand down the curve of her delicate back. "You got that right, baby."

After she didn't move for several minutes, he thought she'd fallen asleep on him. As the fire spit and hissed, he continued to stroke her soft skin.

"Mmm." She snuggled on his chest. "I'm so comfortable."

"You don't have to move."

She rolled off and cuddled against him. Nice. The logs had burned down to a few glowing embers and a chill filled the air.

"Maybe we should move to the bedroom."

She glanced up at him. "Your place or mine?"

***

"I think the bitch poisoned me." Ronnie leaned over the commode and retched.

Dom plastered a hand against the bathroom doorjamb. "She had no idea who we are. She didn't poison you." *Idiot.*

Ronnie swiped a hand across his mouth. "Didn't you see the way she looked at you? I think she might have recognized you."

Dom worried about that. "All the more reason to end this run around as soon as we can."

Ronnie vomited again. "I can't help you tonight. We got to wait until tomorrow."

Dom slapped the door edge. "You better be ready first thing in the morning. I want the bitch dead, so I can go back to my life."

If he didn't accomplish his goal, he worried his father would make good on his threat to take James Caravello into the business. And that would happen only over his dead body.

CHAPTER EIGHTEEN

Sunlight streamed into the bedroom window forcing Jake to crack open an eye. He squinted against the brightness pouring through the sheer curtains. Finally, it was going to be a nice day.

He rolled over and came face to face with a sleeping beauty. Lips slightly parted, face relaxed, Susan's arm was draped over his waist. He closed his eyes for a moment to savor his memory of their passionate lovemaking.

Susan Chapman was one hell of a woman, but he'd crossed the line last night. Until now, he'd never gotten close to anyone he'd protected, but Susan had wormed her way under his skin. She'd touched his soul in a way no other woman had, and he'd thrown all caution aside. Stupid. After years of not feeling connected to anyone, other than Tom and Peter, Susan had filled a void in his life.

He waited for remorse to come crashing down on him, half expecting some voice from above to shout down and say he should set her free—that she didn't need to be with a wanted man—but the lonely part of him blocked out his moral obligation to find her another bodyguard.

He rationalized that not knowing who to trust in his department gave him reason to stay by her side. Pure rationalization, but he was good with that for the moment.

Jake pulled the blanket over her bare shoulder and slipped out of her grasp. He wanted to shower and pack for their surprise date, an idea he'd conjured up in the middle of the night. A nice picnic by the waterfall might help boost her spirits and ease his guilt.

Between the rain and love making, he'd forgotten to mention Nancy and Doug Abernathy had decided to visit Nancy's sick mom today, which gave him the day off.

His bare feet hit the cold, wood floor and a quick chill snaked up his legs. How did the pioneers enjoy life day in and day out in the harsh winter? Maybe they had the right equipment—like wool, flannel, and long underwear. His cotton briefs didn't cut it.

Jake jogged to the bathroom and turned on the shower. Hank had installed a tankless water heater that provided instant heat. As much as he would have enjoyed a long shower, he had a meal to prepare. After he finished washing and shaving, he tiptoed back into his bedroom and grabbed some clothes.

Once dressed, he left Susan sleeping and entered the living room. He kicked aside the rug in the middle of the room to expose the trap door that led to the secret basement containing all of the camping supplies.

He eased open the creaky lid and left the door open in case she awoke and wondered where he might be.

A blast of cold, damp air rushed up to meet him. The steps were steep, but the shaky wooden handrail gave some sense of security. Half way down, he tugged on a hanging string to turn on the light.

Dust and the stench of dried animal blood nearly choked him, but he focused on the task at hand. Off the main room was a smaller area where Tom and his dad prepared their game. Hank must have recently been hunting if the red stains on the butcher table were any indication.

The main room contained shelves where the Traynors kept backpacks, sleeping bags, boots, rifles, and boxes of clothes. Only because he was Tom's best friend did Tom show him the secret passageway that led five hundred feet to the outside. According to Tom's father, this basement had been used as part of the Underground Railroad to transport slaves.

Knowing how easily chilled Susan became, he pawed through three boxes until he came across some ski pants, a pair of extra thick mittens and a wool blanket. On the shelf, he found a large picnic basket, but decided a backpack would be easier to carry their romantic getaway meal.

Once he collected the needed gear, he brought the essentials upstairs. The shower was going full blast, and Jake smiled. He looked forward to kissing her silly this morning.

Before she finished, he placed the extra clothes on her bed, and then prepared sandwiches for their special date.

"What's all this?" she said as she stepped into the kitchen, dragging the towel over her wet hair.

"I don't have to work today, and I thought it might be nice if we went on a little trip. The view from the top of Cedar Rock is fantastic, and a nice picnic lunch is just what the doctor ordered."

She smiled. "Sounds wonderful."

"I left some warm clothes in your bedroom."

Rubbing her head with the towel, she disappeared to the back. Jake had finished making the sandwiches when a noise alerted him to possible danger. He stilled. The sound of gravel clinking together implied they had a visitor.

"Susan?"

"Yes?" she called from the bedroom.

"Grab your clothes and come here." He hadn't meant to shout, but he couldn't be too careful.

Jake raced to his bedroom and snatched his gun and jacket. She had her jacket and gloves in hand when he met her in the hallway. "Someone's coming."

Her face paled. "You don't think it's a friend of the Traynors?"

"I don't know."

Her arm firmly clasped in his hand, he led her into the living room and to the open door in the floor. "Get below and stay there until I come down."

"Shouldn't we see who's here first?" Her gaze flicked to the dark pit and shivered.

He picked up the two sandwiches and handed her the food. "Go."

Her fingers dug into his arm. "I'm afraid of the dark."

Shit. "There a light switch halfway down the stairs." She wouldn't be safe staying in the living room. "You need to hide. And dress for the cold."

Once she descended, he closed the lid and replaced the rug. No one would ever know she was there. Gun in hand, he raced to the window and peered out.

A white Ford Focus crept up the drive and stopped behind his car. Jake's shoulders relaxed when a tall, gawky blond man, dressed in a blue uniform, eased out of the front seat. Jake couldn't make out the letters on the man's nametag, but if he had to guess, the logo might say the name of a garage or that of a landscaping company.

Hank must have forgotten an appointment. Not wanting to incite trouble, Jake slipped his Glock into the coffee table drawer.

Before the man had a chance to knock, Jake opened the door.

"Howdy." The man's smile implied he hadn't visited a dentist in the last several years.

Jake shot a look outside to make sure this guy was alone. "How can I help you?"

"Hank Traynor around?"

A hint of a Bronx accent surfaced, and Jake's mind raced to Susan's description of the two men at the diner, but he dismissed his concern. If the man knew Tom's father's name, he must be on the up and up.

"No. He's visiting his son."

"You alone then?"

Odd question. "Yes."

"Mind if I come in?" The man stepped into the entranceway before Jake answered.

"As a matter of fact I do mind. Why don't you come back in about two weeks? Hank should be here by then."

The man's pleasant smile disappeared as he shoved past him. Jake stepped back, his mind racing as to how much force he wanted to use to make this guy leave.

The second the sunlight glinted off the steel blade of the man's knife, Jake's body shot to red alert. Blondie waved the weapon in front of Jake's face.

"Where's the woman?"

"What woman?"

"Susan Chapman. Don't lie to me. She's staying here."

Jake inched back toward the coffee table and drew on his FBI training to keep the man talking. "Who told you that?"

"A little birdie at the local diner."

Diner, knife. "You harm Rebecca?"

"The redhead?"

"Yes."

Jake lunged toward the man and pushed him backward until Blondie's back slammed against the wall. As Jake reached up to grab the man's hand wielding the weapon, the goon wrenched his arm downward and smashed the side of Jake's neck with an elbow.

Shit. Pain stunned him for a moment, and he teetered backward. The man sprang toward him and swung his knife hand in a low arc, contacting Jake's thigh. A sharp ache sizzled up his hip. Jake ignored the searing injury, cocked back his arm, and threw an upper cut, knocking Blondie on his butt.

Jake glanced at the blood racing out of his thigh. Shit. With the cut on his leg, he needed his weapon. Jake turned, raced toward the coffee table and whipped open the drawer. His fingers were inches from the weapon, when the man wrapped two arms around Jake's waist and jerked him backwards.

Jake elbowed his attacker in the gut and stomped on the man's foot.

"Fuck."

Jake twisted around. Eyes glazed, Blondie swayed. Jake smashed the man's nose and followed up with a one-two punch to his attacker's stomach.

The bastard wouldn't go down. Instead he attacked, swinging the knife high. Jake ducked the attack but not before the blade sliced open his cheek.

Jake grunted.

Drawing on his reserve, he threw himself at Blondie. Outweighing the man by at least thirty pounds, the two tumbled to the wood floor. His attacker's head sent out a loud crack as his skull smashed against the floor.

Jake's breath whooshed out, but he managed to push up and place a knee in the middle of the man's chest. "Who are you?"

Blood dripped from Blondie's nose. The man's eyes glazed over before rolling back in his head.

"Damn it."

Jake rose and staggered over to the table where he retrieved his weapon. He cocked the gun and pointed the Glock at the still man. His pulse throbbed in his head as blood leaked into his mouth.

"Move and you die." He wiped the blood running down his cheek.

Jake waited for the man to respond, but he remained still. Susan told him two men had showed up to the diner. If this was one of them, where was this man in the plaid shirt? Well, he wasn't going to wait around for him to show.

Assuming the accomplice was nearby, Jake needed to make sure Susan remained safe. Halfway to the cellar door, he spotted the trail of blood behind him. His leg was gushing red.

He clasped a hand over the gash and searched the kitchen for something to stem the flow of blood. He took a handful of towels, grabbed his jacket, and then raced to find Susan.

He expected her to cry out when he opened the door, but she remained quiet. In fact, no light appeared downstairs, and his admiration hitched up again. She was hiding—in the dark—facing her worst fears.

He'd just replaced the carpet over the trap door and closed the lid, when a shout sounded outside.

He threw the bolt to lock the entry from above, and then edged his way down the steps. The accomplice had arrived.

"Susan?" Jake whispered.

No answer. At the bottom of the steps, as he reached up to tug on the light cord, his leg gave way, and Jake stumbled down the last step and collapsed.

***

"Jake?"

Susan couldn't see anything since the room was entombed in darkness. The loud thud ten feet from her had scared her. Jake had called her name, so why wasn't he answering? And what was that thud?

She inched toward the stairs. Feet pounded above and she stilled. Her voice came out raspy. "Jake?"

Holding her breath, she waited for him to answer. A low moan came from a few feet in front of her. On her next step, her foot hit something hard. She knelt and patted the air in front of her. A hand grabbed her wrist and her heart nearly stopped.

"Shh," Jake said.

He let go of her and pushed up to a stand.

"Are you okay?" Something wasn't right.

More footsteps sounded above them. Jake tugged on her upper arm and led her to the far corner. She tripped over the jacket she'd left on the floor, but he steadied her.

He leaned over. "Stay here." His breath rippled down her cheek. "I need to turn on the light. We have... to get out of here."

The pain in his voice shot adrenaline through her system. "You're hurt." She reached out to touch him, but he slipped out of her grasp.

He slapped a foot on the first step. "I'm, ah, fine." The bulb above the stairs came to life.

Relief washed over her until he turned around. "Oh my God." His left eye was swollen half shut, a gash cut across his cheek, and his chin sported a purple bruise. "What happened?" Dumb question. He'd been in a fight. She hoped he'd be able to tell her who he'd battled.

"Someone wanted to find you."

"Me?" She'd thought the Feds had come to arrest him.

"He asked for you by name."

Her stomach churned. Jake lifted a cloth from his leg. A six-inch circle of blood pooled on the white material.

"Jeez." She leaned forward to examine his wound, but the light wasn't sufficient to see his injury. "Were you shot?" She hadn't heard a gun go off.

"No. Asshole stabbed me."

He hobbled to the back room and returned a moment later with duct tape. "Can you wrap this around the towel to keep it in place?"

"I need to clean the wound and take you to a hospital."

He snorted. "What we need to do is get the hell out of here."

As if to punctuate his comment, someone stomped on the trap door. "Where the hell are they?"

Blood pounded in her temples, and she clutched Jake's arm. He held a finger to his lips and limped to the back room. A moment later, he dragged in two backpacks and a walking stick. "Put this on."

"What about fixing up your leg?" Susan strapped on the pack.

"We'll deal with it later. Come on."

"You want us to go upstairs?" The blood loss must be messing with his mind.

"No." He headed to a bookcase and leaned the stick against the wall. "Give me a hand. There's a tunnel behind here. They'll never find us."

CHAPTER NINETEEN

Dom paced the living room pissed as hell Ronnie hadn't been able to take down the chick and her bodyguard. He stood over his moaning partner who was groaning like a girl, rocking on the floor.

Dom's patience was running thin. "Get up." He was tempted to kick his ass, but he needed Ronnie's help.

Ronnie would probably be okay with a day's rest, but Dom didn't have the time to let those two get a head start, nor did he want to wait around for Hank Traynor to come waltzing back home and find them holed up in his place.

Dom bent over at the waist. "What the hell happened?"

His useless hired hand hefted himself onto his elbows. "I stuck him with a knife and sliced him up real good, but he jabbed me with an upper cut. Next thing I know, you come in." He looked around. "Where are they?"

"They didn't come out the front door, that's for sure. I would have seen them. I'll look around. Stay here." Not that the crybaby would get up any sooner than he had to.

The room check took all of one minute. No door led to the outside and all windows were locked from the inside. Dom strode out. "They aren't here."

He was half way across the living room when he spotted two red blood drops illuminated by the sun. Dom knelt and swiped a finger across the wet goo. "Unless this is your mess, Yarnell's cut all right."

"A ghost didn't knock me out. He was here, trust me."

Part of the rug's binding was bent under, exposing a separation in the wood. Dom peeled back the edge. "I'll be damned. A trap door."

Ronnie sat up. "They got to be down there."

Dom tugged on the latch, but the door remained closed. "He must have locked the damn thing from below."

He smashed his foot on the wood, but the cover didn't bend. Dom pulled out his gun and shot holes in the trap door, enough to weaken the structure. He then kicked the slats hard until the cover splintered.

Ronnie chuckled. "That's one way to skin a cat."

Smart ass. If Ronnie weren't such a sharp shooter, he'd put him out of his misery.

Taking care not to cut himself, Dom reached in and pulled back the latch. Clever people to hide the entrance to the cellar under the rug, but not so clever they'd escape him. Those two were sitting ducks in the basement.

Dom slipped another magazine into his gun and headed down the steep steps. The overhead light glared, giving him a good view of the fifteen by ten foot dirt packed room. He stopped every time the wood creaked. Not that they wouldn't figure he was on his way down, but no use giving away his exact position.

Gun held high, he searched the empty room. Besides the shelves lining the wall and a few tools on the floor, they weren't in sight. Where the hell were they? The place stunk worse than the urine ridden back alleys of D.C. Christ. How could they stay down here?

Dom edged his way into the second room. All that graced the ten by ten foot room was a large table in the middle of the room and a freezer against the wall. He lifted the lid to the cooler. The thing was stuffed with white paper packets but no bodies. Damn.

No windows, no doors, and no way to escape, yet the Fed and the woman had done the best magic trick in town and disappeared.

Shit. They had to have escaped to the outside somehow.

He raced up the steps. "They're gone."

Ronnie rose to his knees, swayed a bit, and then pulled himself up. "What the fuck do you mean they're gone? Is there a door to the outside down there?"

"No."

"Then where are they?"

"Hell if I know. But they aren't there."

"Then let's go get 'em."

Ronnie would only slow him down. "You sure you're okay to hike in the woods? I don't think this is a two man job."

"No you don't. You hired me to do a job, and I plan to do it." Ronnie straightened. "I got a bitch of a headache, but nothing is going to stop me from chasing after those two."

Dom smiled at Ronnie's feisty attitude. "You okay to shoot?"

"You can have all my sharp shooting medals if I don't nail that son of a bitch from a hundred yards."

"You're on."

Dom snagged a couple of power bars from kitchen and shoved them in his pockets.

Ronnie picked up his blood-streaked knife and waved it like a trophy. "Yarnell won't be going far with his injuries."

Dom pointed to the floor. "Clean up that mess in case someone comes looking for them. We don't want anyone to think they're running for their lives and go after them to help."

Ronnie's shoulders slumped, but he didn't argue. While his partner did as he asked, Dom filled two bottles full of water.

Within minutes they left, leaving the place almost like new. He hoped the owner didn't have any need to go into the basement and discover his broken door.

The wind whistled through the trees, and Dom tugged his jacket closer to his chest. He opened the trunk, extracted the rifle with the scope and handed his baby to Ronnie. "Let's go hunting."

***

The cold, creepy tunnel closed in on Susan. "Are you sure whoever is after us can't tell there's a tunnel behind the bookcase?"

"No. Even if he figured out we went behind the shelves, he wouldn't know there's a lever that slides the case to the side."

"That makes me feel somewhat more secure."

"I'm glad." She thought she heard a chuckle in his tone.

She tripped on a rock but caught herself on the wall. Being in the pitch black, with the ceiling no more than three inches from her head, sucked.

"How much farther?" She hadn't meant to complain, but the uneven ground and the spider webs slapping her in the arms and face had undone her composure.

Jake stopped, his breath ragged. He braced a hand on the wall over her head. "The tunnel is five hundred feet long. Hold on. We'll be in the open soon."

Susan took two long breaths, hoping the deep breathing would cut through her nerves. "Okay."

She didn't know how one and half football fields could be so long. They'd already travelled a good ten minutes, or so it seemed.

As the walls narrowed, she ran a hand on the side to keep her balance. *Stay strong for Jake.*

"There's a flashlight in the pack if you need one," he said. "But we might want to use it later. I didn't throw in any extra batteries."

From his worried tone she could tell he didn't want to waste the precious resource. "No problem. Seeing is highly overrated." She swallowed her fear of the dark.

The path curved to the right and she ran into a wall. Susan ran her hands up and down the solid surface, needing to find some way out. "It's a dead end." She nearly choked on the fluid clogging her throat.

"It means we're close." Jake took a few steps to the right and pushed hard on the wall, forcing chunks of dirt to fall outward.

Scant light peeked in, and her shoulders sagged. "You found the exit. Thank God." Had the ceiling been taller, she would have literally jumped for joy.

Susan helped peel away the earth wall. Soon, the only obstacle was the dense underbrush blocking their exit. He pried the leaves and branches apart, providing enough space from them to crawl through.

Jake held up a hand. "Let me go first to see if it's safe."

This time she wasn't going to argue.

Jake retrieved his walking stick he'd set against the wall and forced his way through the small opening. He returned in less than a minute.

"I don't see anyone. Come on."

He stuck out a hand to help her through the narrow portal. Once in the fresh air, Susan took a deep breath. The heavy scent of pine and oxygen bolstered her spirit. The cold air did not.

"Jake, you're bleeding again." Or else she hadn't remembered the stain on his pants leg being so large.

He looked down at his wound. "It's stopped. I'm fine."

His bravado had its limit. "The cut could become infected. Stuff the towel down your leg and I'll wrap the whole area with tape to secure it. Dirt has a way of worming its way into small places."

"I didn't know they taught medicine in law school."

"I'll have you know—"

"Shh. We need to keep our voices down. Sound travels far in the woods."

"Fine," she whispered. "Now stuff."

Jake did as she asked, and she then attended to his injury as fast as she could. "That's the best I can do."

While the cut on his cheek had scabbed over and his eye had swollen shut, she didn't have any other first aid equipment to tend to those injuries.

"Those gunshots we heard means there are at least two of them. We need to hurry," he said.

He didn't need to prod her anymore.

Twigs cracked behind them and Jake spun around, his weapon pointed in the direction of the noise. Susan froze. Most of the trees were bare, but a large amount of underbrush, fallen logs and tangled branches provided places to hide.

After scouring the area for a minute, Jake lowered his weapon. He motioned his head away from the house and toward a path. When he didn't move, she guessed he wanted her to lead.

Every step she took made noise. Either the leaves crunched or sticks broke. If the killer was out there, how could he not find them?

They were sitting ducks in the open and making more noise than kids at play.

Adjusting her backpack, she plowed ahead, determined to get away from the maniacs. Worried when his pace turned labored, she checked Jake every few minutes to make sure his leg was okay.

They'd trekked about ten minutes when Jake stumbled. She twisted around. Oh, no. He was on his knee, hand to head. She closed the gap between them and leaned in close.

"What can I do?"

"Nothing. Give me a sec. The leg just gave out."

Susan plucked Jake's cell phone from his jacket pocket and punched the On button. "We need to get help."

She expected him to stop her. If getting a phone was as easy as taking his, she could have contacted her family days ago. She glanced down at the display. "No Service."

"Unless we get on top of a mountain, you won't get any around here. There aren't enough towers."

No wonder he didn't freak when she grabbed his lifeline.

Jake eased up to a standing position. There was no way he'd be able to continue for long. He wiggled his fingers for the phone.

She handed the useless lifeline back to him. "You have to rest."

"I will when we get to the highway."

Highway? Is that where they were headed? "How far is this road?"

"Maybe fifteen miles."

"Fifteen miles?" Her voice rose and she stiffened. She had to stay calm.

"We don't have a choice. The guy isn't going to let us get away." He dug the walking stick into the ground, pushed off, and moved forward. "Was the man at the restaurant a tall, thin blond man?"

Her stomach twisted. "Yes."

"Then we need to move extra fast."

***

Peter had tried to reach Jake on his cell several times, but the man wasn't answering. Just as well. He needed to stop procrastinating and face his brother to ask James about the story Sophia had told him and Maria. Did James know about the rumor that Joseph Francisco had had an affair with Mom? That James might really be Francisco's son? He did the math and figured Sophia wasn't talking about him being the byproduct of their union. Or had her speech come from her imagination?

Jake's question about who would want to frame Peter nagged at him. He denied James would ever harm him, but now he wasn't so sure.

Peter pulled up the drive of the ten thousand square foot mansion. The fountain wasn't running, but the up-lighting illuminated the imaginary water.

His heart pressing against his chest, he jumped out of his car, rushed up the door, and knocked. A moment later, James answered, a drink in his hand.

"Well, well, lookie who showed up."

Peter wanted to wipe the smirk off his brother's face but getting nasty wouldn't give him any answers. "May I come in?"

James swept a hand. "You don't need permission to enter. It's been what, a year since you've come? You should see the renovations I've done."

"Later. We need to talk."

"You going to lecture me on how I'm running Daddy's business?"

Peter knew all about the counterfeiting scheme, but he'd never turn in his own brother. Peter just wanted to live his life within the law.

"No. I drove by the restaurant the other day and the lot was packed."

The place was a front for laundering the counterfeit money, or so he surmised. The prosecuting attorney tried to prove Dad dabbled in human trafficking, but he didn't want to believe his father's dishonesty would reach as far as stealing women and selling them into prostitution. It had been hard enough to believe his own father had murdered an entire family, including their two young children.

"Can I get you a drink?"

"Yes." He needed fortification for the discussion.

Peter followed his brother into the modern living room. Blacks, whites, and reds created a stark atmosphere. Even the paintings on the wall that looked like someone had spattered paint on the canvas in a drunken stupor, held little warmth.

James poured a drink from a cut glass decanter and handed him a scotch.

"Here. So tell me what's stuck in your craw?"

James dropped on a plush leather chair, black of course, and Peter sat across from him. "I'll get to the point. I visited Sophia."

His brother cocked a brow, but no worry lines creased his forehead. "How is the crazy old lady?"

"She has her days. She told me a story about Mom and Joseph Francisco being lovers."

Peter watched his brother's eyes for shock, but none came. "So Dad claimed."

"Dad told you?"

"We had no secrets."

Peter refused to acknowledge the lump in his stomach was jealousy. Nerves always did a number of his gut. "When?"

"The night before he was executed." James lips turned up slightly.

"He never mentioned anything about the affair when I was there."

James downed the contents of his glass. "Don't you remember how you got caught in traffic? Dad and I had a little chat before you got there."

"There was a hurricane warning out and traffic was a bitch." Actually, he delayed going, not knowing if he wanted to say goodbye to his father.

"I know."

"What did Dad say?"

"He told me I wasn't his son, but that he forgave me for not being his blood."

At least James was the bastard son and not him. The possibility he and Maria might have been related had nearly given him ulcers.

James' fingers tightened around the empty glass, as lines formed around his brother's mouth. His eyes hardened, but the small smile on his lips remained, contradicting what must be going through his mind.

"Are you okay with that?" Peter asked. A sudden wash of sympathy filled him. "Shit, if I found out Mom and Dad weren't who they claimed to be my whole life, I'd have freaked."

"That's one difference between us. I don't give a fuck who screwed Mom." He leaned back in the seat as casual as could be. "Look on the bright side. At least *my* dad is still alive."

Bastard. "Our father was the only dad you ever knew." Peter polished off his glass and set it down. "Have you been in contact with your biological father?"

"Now, why would I do that?"

"Maybe to get a piece of his pie too. You add his human trafficking to yours, and you'd have a monopoly in Tampa." Peter had no idea if his information about what illegal activities his brother was into was correct, but understanding James' motivations would help him figure out if his brother was behind the frame job.

"Peter, Peter, how little you think of me. No, I am not, nor will I ever be a Francisco. And I don't deal in human trafficking. I don't know where you get your ideas."

"Could be because the courts claimed Dad did."

"That was your father. I only run the restaurant."

Liar. Peter pulled out his phone to check the time. "I have to go."

James stood. "You need to rush back to Maria?"

The blood drained from his brain. He couldn't know. But somehow he did.

CHAPTER TWENTY

Richard smiled at the information his secretary had unearthed. How had he missed that Tom Traynor and Jake Yarnell went to school together? Tom's former suitemate told Julie that Jake spent every summer with Tom and his family in a cabin in West Virginia.

Julie clutched a Manila folder to her chest. "Before Tom left, he told me he and his dad were going out to dinner tonight in Old Alexandria to celebrate his birthday."

The dots suddenly connected. That meant the cabin would be empty for a few days. Perfect. Richard wouldn't be surprised if Jake and Susan Chapman were holed up there. Once he found them, he'd get his children back and bring his wife home from the hospital. The stress of the kidnapping nearly sent her into cardiac arrest.

"Thank you, Julie. You've been a big help."

He understood that his wife would hate him once she learned what he'd done, but at least Ethan and Courtney would be safe. That's all that mattered.

He followed Julie back to her desk, and then headed to Stanton's office.

He calculated the next leg of the journey. The drive from Washington to Shepherd's Hill would take a good three hours. If he found nothing, he'd be back by dinner, in time to visit with Kathleen before she fell asleep.

Richard tapped the doorframe to get Stanton's attention, and then marched in when the man at the desk didn't react. "I think I know where Jake might be hiding out."

Stanton's fingers froze on the keyboard. He looked up. "Where?"

"Did you know Tom and Jake were roommates in college?"

He hesitated before he spoke. "I heard them mention that fact once or twice. Why?"

"The Traynor's have a cabin about three hours from here. I'm going to check it out."

"Why not ask Tom to do it?"

The man was denser than concrete. "So he can tip off his best bud?"

Stanton's mouth twisted into a frown. "Fine, but I'm going with you."

He didn't want the company, but if he had to take out Jake or Susan, it might be better to have Stanton along as a witness. He'd make sure it looked like an accident. "Come on, then."

Stanton gathered his laptop, made two quick phones calls, and then clicked off his office lights. On the way out of town, Richard called the hospital to hear his wife's voice and to tell her he loved her, but she was having some tests run and wasn't available to talk. Damn. He might never get the chance to hold his wife in his arms again.

His stomach soured. His hole was so deep there was nothing he could do to rectify his situation other than to do whatever it took to keep his kids safe.

"Did you get an address of this cabin?" Stanton asked, jarring him out of his reverie.

"General directions, but when we stop in town, I'm sure I can get a better idea of where to find them."

Sure enough, the second restaurant they stopped at in Shepherd's Hills provided the needed intel. A tall, shapely girl, with bright red hair, was sporting a large bruise on her cheek. She seemed eager to share the information once he flashed his badge along with Susan/Taylor's and Jake's photos.

"Taylor works here, but it's her day off," Rebecca said.

"She's staying at the Traynor cabin, right?" Richard asked.

Her eyes widen. "Yes."

Her fidgety hands alerted him something was quite right. "Something wrong?"

"You're the second person to ask about her."

Shit. "Who else did?"

"The person who did this to me." She pointed to the bruise on her face.

"Does he have a name?"

"None he was willing to share. He and a friend came to the restaurant last night, but I'd never seen them before."

"What did you tell them?"

She cast a gaze downward and pressed her lips together.

Stanton stepped forward. "Miss, we're the Federal Bureau of Investigation. We're the ones trying to keep Taylor safe. Can you tell us where to find her? We think her life might be in danger."

Her hand flew to her chest. "I knew her story about being hit by a drunk driver was fishy. Is Jake her bodyguard or something?"

"Jake works for me," Stanton said. "We sent him here to protect Taylor."

She smiled. "I knew it. He kept telling everyone they were engaged."

Richard didn't have time to discuss her crush-of-the-day. "Did you tell this guy what he wanted to know?"

"Yes. He would have killed me if I hadn't." She scrunched up the hem of her apron.

"Did you tell the Sheriff what happened?" He wanted to see if the cops had checked out the cabin.

She touched her cheek. "No. He said he'd burn down the diner if I told anyone. You'll make sure that doesn't happen, right?"

"Don't worry. We'll arrest him before he has a chance to do any more harm." Richard couldn't keep his nice guy attitude going much longer. "Can you give us directions?"

"Sure." She took a napkin and drew a map. "It's only about five miles from here."

He grabbed the paper. "Thanks."

The directions were simple enough. Take the only road out of town four miles south, turn right at the red mailbox. Great.

"You're going to stop that man, aren't you?" The waitress' brows creased so deeply, he thought she might create permanent frown lines.

"That's our plan."

To his surprise, her instructions were dead on.

"I see the red mailbox," Stanton announced without any emotion.

A red mustang was parked half on, half off the road, ten feet beyond the mailbox. "This must be the place."

"You sure," Stanton said. "Jake wouldn't drive this kind of car."

Too impractical for Tom Traynor's dad too. "Let's check it out anyway."

He turned up the drive. The car bounced on the rough gravel road as they climbed the mountain, and dust billowed behind them.

"This must be a bitch in the winter when it snows," Stanton said, hanging onto the overhead handle for dear life. "I sure as hell wouldn't want to live here."

As the road narrowed, a cabin came into view. Two cars were parked there, one behind the other.

"Someone has company," Stanton said.

Richard cut the engine, slipped the weapon from his shoulder holster and eased open the car door. The wind slapped him in the face, but he kept his focus on the living room window. He motioned for Stanton to check out the back.

Once his partner, if he could call him that, disappeared around the side, Richard pressed against the front door and peered through the window. No one was in sight. He tested the doorknob and found it unlocked.

With his gun ready, he burst in and scanned the living room. Nothing. A hallway led to the back. Walking as softly as he could, he inched down the hall and checked both rooms.

"Damn." They were both empty.

Richard returned to the front just as Stanton past the kitchen window. "Stanton." He waved him inside.

He ran in a little out of breath. "Nothing out back."

"They were here. Susan's stuff is on the bed."

"You think they're spending the night in the woods?"

Given it was close to five and getting dark, he didn't know what else to conclude. "With two cars here and one by the entrance, I can guess that was the plan. I imagine one of the cars is Jake's rental, but who owns the other two cars?"

"Let me see if I can run down the owner of the car up here."

Stanton dashed outside and returned ten minutes later. "The Jeep is registered to Jake. The other one is registered to a Gina Stenoff from Arlington, Virginia. I had the office find her number. I called and she said her husband, Ronnie, took off in her the car."

"Does she know he came here?"

"No. She said she didn't know when he'd be home either."

Richard paced in front of the sofa. "Doesn't give us much to go on. I wonder if Peter Caravello hired this Ronnie guy."

"To kill Susan?"

"Yes. I'm sure he won't stop at Susan either." Now wasn't the time to push the Jake-is-guilty claim. Richard decided to toss the proverbial ball to Stanton's court. "How do you think we should proceed?"

"We'll need some gear if we want to go after them."

"Shouldn't be a problem. We went passed a hiking store on the way in. The place might still be open."

"I hope they have a map of the woods."

Richard wondered how far Stanton would make it in the forest, given he sat at a desk all day and his middle was spreading. Wouldn't it be a shame if he slipped off a mountain and died?

His own life meant little. Ending up in a jail cell for the rest of his life wasn't on his to-do list. He'd take them all down, and then disappear. Who better equipped at creating a new identity than him?

***

Susan had wrapped Jake's leg twice now, but the damn thing kept seeping blood. If they didn't rest, he'd be useless to her.

Jake spotted an indent in the side of a hill, partially covered by an outcropping of rock. "It looks like we might get a little snow. I think we should call it a night and hunker down here."

If he didn't insist he needed the rest, Susan would want to keep moving. From the way she was favoring her right leg, she had blisters on her feet, which, if they became infected, could cause a lot of trouble.

"We can't stop now, not when someone is chasing us."

"Without the proper gear, they won't last the night out here. We need our strength for the big push tomorrow. It's nearly dark. I think we're pretty safe from capture for a while. Besides, we took about four forks."

"That makes me feel a little better." After climbing the rather steep embankment, she dropped her pack when they reached a flat area. "Ouch."

"You okay?" He stepped next to her.

"The backpack straps rubbed against my injured chest."

Damn it. He should have been more considerate. "I can carry both for us."

"Don't be silly. Your leg is worse off than my injuries."

They didn't need to waste the energy arguing over who was more debilitated. He should have seen Blondie's arm swing low and moved out of the way. He was slipping and that fact was eating away at him.

She sat on her pack and leaned against a tree. "Not to complain, but how must farther do we have tomorrow?"

He was glad they were onto future plans. "Probably six or seven miles. And before you ask, at about one mile per hour, it will take us most of tomorrow to reach the highway."

She faced him, the scant light defining the drawn lines on her face. "We can move faster than that. When I power walk, I can go a good four miles an hour."

"Not when we're going up and down mountains. Besides, your feet are hurting and my leg isn't at full strength."

"Sorry." She hugged her middle and dropped her chin into the top of her jacket for warmth. "Do we have a tent or something? Or do you expect us to sleep sitting up? I was the only girl in my town who flunked girl scouts."

He chuckled. He doubted she failed at anything. "I don't know what's in the gear bags. I never had time to look, but Tom was always Mr. Ready. He'll have some kind of protection against the elements."

He dumped out the contents of his pack and fumbled through the gear until he found a flashlight. He clicked it on.

"Wow, that's bright," she said.

"Our eyes have gotten used to the darkness. Help me look through your stuff."

She stood and tilted the bag upside down. He found a nylon tarp that would keep out the snow but not any wandering animals, two sleeping bags, a water purifier, a collapsible shovel and a cook set.

"Wow. Score one for Tom, but no stove?" Her mouth formed a big O and her eyes widened.

"Can't pack everything. We don't need to cook sandwiches or power bars."

"Good point."

As if they'd worked together for a lifetime, they set up the tarp by stringing the covering between four trees. The overhang would help keep the rain or snow at bay from the east.

"We'll be warmer," he said, "if we zip the two bags together."

Her brow rose. "Take your mind out of the gutter. I'm not getting naked."

He closed the space between them and lifted her chin. "While I'd like nothing more than to make love with you in the woods, I don't think my leg could handle the stress."

"I'm sorry. I forgot."

They didn't need to dwell on more negatives. He broke the connection. "Let's split the sandwich. Afterwards, I want to safeguard our little camp."

"How?"

"You'll see."

When they finished their meal, Jake dug out his pocketknife. "I need you to collect sticks, maybe half-inch in diameter and ten inches long."

"How many do you need?"

"Maybe twenty."

"I better hurry."

He appreciated her not wasting time to question his request.

Keeping one ear for the sounds of her footsteps as she gathered the wood, he picked up the shovel and headed back down the path. The ground would be too hard to dig, except near the stream.

When he located the perfect spot, he scratched the dirt with the tip. He picked, stabbed, and cursed until he managed to cut a small trench two feet wide and one foot deep. Sweat beaded off his forehead from the exertion and his thigh rebelled when he squatted, but the manual labor took his mind off their situation. At least he was being proactive and not the victim.

As Jake trekked back to their small camp, he met Susan coming from the opposite direction.

"Here." She handed him a pile of perfect sticks.

"Great. Now we need to whittle the ends into spikes."

She slapped her hands on her hips. "Why?"

"You'll see." He handed her a knife. "There's another knife in one of the packs. Be right back."

Susan found a log to sit on while he scrounged through the side pockets for the extra Leatherman. When he returned, he sat opposite her, and they carved away. In less than a half hour, all of the sticks were seriously sharp.

"Now what?" she asked with less agitation in her voice. "These look really dangerous."

"They are. But we're dealing with killers. Follow me."

They hiked back the two hundred yards to the stream. Jake knelt down and stabbed the non-pointed ends of the sticks into the hole. Some were horizontal to the ground, others straight up.

Susan's eyes had widened every time he glanced up at her. "Gather some leaves to cover the pit, will ya?"

She raced off. With her sharp mind, she seemed to understand how this trap worked.

After a few trips, the hole was completely camouflaged.

"You sure this will work? Someone could step over this trap."

He'd expected the question. "The person will probably jump across the two-foot wide stream. I dug the hole one step past the river's edge.

He can't step right or left since the trench is the width of the path. He'll step in the hole. Trust me. The sudden drop will either break his ankle and/or cut him severely either going in or pulling it out."

"Where did you learn to make this kind of thing?"

He snickered. "Actually, Nick Caravello taught me."

"Figures."

"'Uncle' Nicki isn't a bad person. He served in Nam. He told me the Army instructed them to dip the sticks in animal dung. When the enemy landed in the hole, the sticks would break the skin's surface and the feces would get into the bloodstream. Death followed shortly thereafter."

"Nice."

"Come on. Let's finish setting up camp."

They put the sleeping bags together and shoved them under the tarp.

"I guess we can't have a fire, huh?" she asked.

"Ah, no. We might as well have a loud speaker announcing where we are."

"Too bad."

He would have liked one too. Nothing was more romantic that a hot fire, but tonight wasn't for love. It was for survival.

She took a sip of her water and crawled into bed. "Should we take turns staying awake?"

"Sure. I'll take first watch." Jake placed his weapon on the ground behind them. "You ever shoot a gun before?"

"As a matter of fact, I took lessons after my father was killed by someone he prosecuted."

"Christ. And you still wanted to practice law?" The woman had less sense than he did.

"Now you sound like my mother, brother and ex-husband, except he liked the paycheck too much to complain a lot."

Her bitter tone sent his body on alert. "What was he like?"

He couldn't tell if her eyes were open or closed because she'd laid her arm across her forehead.

"There's not much to tell. He turned out to be a deadbeat and a cheat. I left him after he turned violent."

He swallowed hard, the pain rolling off her. His fists balled at his side. The image of anyone hurting her tore at his gut. Jake needed to find out if she was vulnerable with regards to her ex-husband, so he leaned closer. "Do you still love him?"

"No! He used me." She flipped over to face him again. "Could you love someone who cheated on you? Or hit you?"

"Absolutely not."

She sat up and bumped her head on the nylon overhang. A rustling in the woods echoed down the path. "Shh." He wanted to learn more about her, her disappointments, her dreams, but that priority dropped when the noise filtered into his conscious.

"What is it?" she whispered.

Jake snatched up the gun and slithered out of the bag. "Wait here."

CHAPTER TWENTY-ONE

Using his years of hunting experience in this forest, Jake crept through the woods without making a sound. From the moans and curses coming from the direction of the river, he figured he'd trapped someone and prayed that person wasn't an innocent bystander who'd been at the wrong place at the wrong time.

Instead of following the path directly to the spot, Jake climbed a small hill and cut along the ridge careful not give to away his position.

Looking down from above, he spotted a man in a beige jacket struggling to free himself from the trap. Moonbeams reflected off his blond hair. Bingo. He appeared to be the man with the knife. One down, one to go.

After Jake sliced off a few sapling branches with which to tie up the man should he try to escape, he headed toward the river, his weapon fixed on the man's head. With the moon behind him, he bet the man wouldn't recognize him right away.

"Need help?" Jake said, trying to gauge the seriousness of the injury.

The man fell back onto his elbows. "Oh, thank God. I thought I'd never see another human being again. I broke my ankle." His breaths came out rapid. "It hurts like a son of a bitch."

Jake spotted the man's sniper rifle next to him. "You out hunting at night?" Though no hunter would use such a weapon.

Blondie looked up, pain creasing his forehead. "It's you."

Before the captive could reach his gun, Jake raced toward him and kicked the rifle away. "Yeah, it's me."

"Yarnell, you got to help me. I'll die out here." His voice didn't ring true. His partner in the plaid shirt had to be near.

"Pity. You planned on me dying out here."

The man had the decency to look away. "What do you want for your help?"

"Some answers."

"Fine." His mouth dropped open, and he squeezed his eyes shut for a moment. "What do you want to know?"

"Who hired you?"

Blondie tugged again on his leg, and his foot lifted out of the hole. Jake backed up, cocked his gun, and then lowered his arm when he saw the foot at an odd angle to the leg. It was definitely broken. The guy wasn't going anywhere.

Blondie took several breaths, his lips in a grimace. "Dom hired me."

"Dom who?"

"Francisco."

Jake's body stiffened at the familiar name. "Why would Francisco want me dead?"

"Not you. The girl."

The girl was a woman, but he didn't need to point out that fact. "Why does he want her dead?"

The Caravellos and Francisco's were sworn enemies like two pit bulls fighting for the same bone, or rather the same humans. Revenge for Caravellos' death wasn't a motive. Joseph Francisco probably threw a party the day his archenemy was executed.

"She's a lose end."

"How?"

Before he got his answer, a muffled scream came from the direction of the campground. Susan! Jake snatched Blondie's rifle and ran the best he could back toward the camp.

"You can't leave me here, Yarnell. Come back. I'll tell you more."

Jake disregarded Blondie's pleas. Susan was in trouble, and she needed him.

Leaves rustled, indicating a struggle. He dashed up the incline to the camp, ignoring the searing pain stabbing his wound. He'd failed to save his mother when she needed him. He wouldn't lose Susan too. Blood trickled down his leg from the cut.

When he reached the rocky overhang, the tent was empty, and so was the camp. Shit. He stilled, willing his heart to slow so he could hear the sounds of the forest.

Susan let out another sound, softer and more muffled than before. Adrenaline fueled him. He had to get to her before the bastard harmed her, or worse, killed her.

There! Susan and her captor were high on the ridge above their campsite. Jake pictured the nearby fork on the path below and how it wound back to the other side of the ridge. Instead of taking the direct route upwards, he charged down the ridge and headed away from the river.

He hoped to attack from the far side, surprising whoever had Susan. If Blondie could be trusted, that someone was Dominick Francisco, one mean son of a bitch.

He was halfway around the bend when all noise stopped, and Jake stilled. Leaves blew in the wind but little else. With care, he moved onward, hoping Dominick was distracted by his captive to notice his approach.

Jake neared the incline but waited to get an exact location before he continued his pursuit. He tucked the Glock into his jacket, deciding to use the rifle instead. At night, the red sniper beam would illuminate his mark. When he'd served in Desert Storm, he'd used the same kind of gear. Luckily, he knew the weapon by touch.

"Don't move." The command came from fifty feet above to his right.

Jake's muscles locked.

"What are you going to do with me?" His heart broke at the panic in Susan's voice, but he thrilled she was alive.

Like a cat stalking its prey, Jake moved forward a step or two, halted, and then continued, stopping and starting. He hoped the random noise wouldn't alert the killer to his presence.

"Where is he?" Dom whispered, his voice floating down the hill.

"I don't know." Susan sounded convincing. Good.

What followed sounded like gunfire to his heart, but the impact was more of a slap than a shot. She didn't whimper or beg after the hard facial strike, and his pride bloomed.

Inch by inch Jake moved toward them. The clouds separated, casting Francisco in moonlight.

The moment Jake was high enough to take aim, Susan jerked her head toward him. Crap. He lifted his finger to his lips, hoping she could see he needed her to be silent.

Dom twisted around, his gun raised.

"Yarnell, that you?"

So much for stealth. Before Jake could decide how to answer, Dom fired a shot. On instinct, Jake fired back—right after the red dot found its sniper mark.

Francisco stumbled backward, and then collapsed after taking a bullet to the chest.

Susan let out a small scream and he raced toward her, thankful Francisco's aim was off. His leg buckled as he reached her.

"Oh, God. Jake, are you hit?"

"I'm okay. I'm okay." He stood and grabbed her shoulders. "What about you?"

"I'm fine, now that you're here."

Brave woman. He pulled his Leatherman from his pocket and cut the rope binding her hands. The moment he freed her, she wrapped her arms around his neck. Nothing ever felt so good. He kissed her forehead, and then her salty lips. He thanked God he'd reached her in time.

"Where did he hurt you?" he asked.

"Just my face, but I'll live." She looked in Francisco's direction. "Is he dead?"

Jake stepped over to the man. The whites of his eyes glowed. "He ought to be. I shot him in the heart." To make sure, he nudged him with his foot, but his prey didn't move. Knowing two of the pursuers were out of commission boosted his flagging energy.

"What about the other man?" She clung to Jake's arm.

"He's injured. He won't be going anywhere."

"Do we know who they are or who they work for?"

"This fellow," Jake said, nodding his head toward the dead man, "is Dominick Francisco."

She sucked in a breath. "Joseph Francisco's son?"

He was surprised she knew the name, but one of her colleagues probably had tried the SOB at one time. "The one and only."

"Why would he try to harm me?"

"That's the mystery of the day."

"And the other man? Who was he?"

"I never did ask his name, but he said Dominick, here, hired him to take you down. You screamed before I was able to extract any more information. When I knew you were in danger, I ran."

She dragged a hand down his shoulder. "My hero."

"I like the sound of that, but a true hero wouldn't have gotten you into this mess in the first place."

She leaned her head against his chest. "You didn't do anything to cause this mess."

He rubbed her back, trying not to get sucked into believing she'd be willing to stay in his arms. "I should have anticipated someone would figure out I used to stay at the Traynor's house every summer."

"Don't worry about it." She stepped out of his embrace. "What are we going to do now?"

Jake had wondered about their next move. "We can't count on there only being two men. Francisco might have called for backup. As to what we're going to do? Get the hell out of here."

"Are we going back to the cabin?"

"No. It's shorter to go to the highway than hike back. Let's head to our campsite."

"I don't think I can sleep knowing that crazy person is by the water."

Ever the sympathetic. "I meant, we need to collect our gear and head out."

"Oh. Are you going to leave that man out in the woods alone?"

"No. Even if he did try to kill me, I couldn't willingly let him freeze to death. That's part of the reason why we need to leave now and get help. I'll wrap him in one of our sleeping bags to tie him over."

"Don't you need to rest?" she asked.

"I'd like a week vacation on the beach, but that will have to wait." He tugged on her waist. "Come on."

***

Richard stilled. "Was that a shot I heard?"

Stanton clutched his weapon. "Sounded like two back-to-back rounds to me. One from a rifle."

At least the man proved useful for something. Had they not brought flashlights, Richard didn't think Stanton would have made it this far. The man kept stumbling over roots and rocks. It became quite clear that Stanton had never been in the woods before.

"Can we slow down?" Stanton asked, clutching his chest.

"Jake might be in trouble. You can wait here, but I'm going ahead." Richard hoped the let's-save-Jake card would work.

"I'm coming with you."

Figured.

"How far away do you think the shot was?" Stanton asked.

"Hard to tell in the woods. Could be a mile or two."

"Okay."

They hiked in silence. Richard listened for voices, footsteps, and anything out of the ordinary. They came to a fork in the road—the third so far—and stopped.

He turned around to Stanton who was clutching the limb of a tree. Sorry sap. "You want to take a guess the direction of the shot?"

If he was wrong, they'd miss Yarnell and the woman.

Stanton came alongside him, his breath ragged. "I think the shot came from over there." He pointed to the right branch.

He thought so too. Richard took three steps and halted. "I think I hear someone."

Without getting confirmation from his partner, he took off at a faster pace. Less than a quarter of a mile later, he spotted a man down in the path, but waited for Stanton to catch up before he approached. It could be some kind of trap.

"You see something?" Stanton whispered.

Richard nodded and pointed to a large rock for his partner to crouch behind. He didn't want him to muck things up.

With gun ready, Richard eased his way across the stream. The man in the path didn't move, so Richard gave him a small kick to see if he was alive.

The downed man groaned, and then moved his fingers.

"You need help?" He wanted to appear friendly should this person not be related to their case. The FBI to the rescue and such.

The seemingly comatose man rolled onto his back and shielded his eyes from the flashlight. "Thank God. I didn't think you'd come until tomorrow."

His comment made no sense. "We heard two gunshots. What happened?"

Richard didn't recognize the guy. For a split second he'd prayed it was Peter Caravello. He might have accidentally shot him in the head if he had been.

The man pointed up the trail to the left. "I heard them too. Up on the ridge. Don't know what happened." He grabbed his leg.

Richard wasn't interested in this man's problems. Rather, he needed to locate Yarnell and Chapman. He turned around. "Stanton. Want to see what we can do for this guy?"

Stanton turned on his light and made his way over to the river. "My phone doesn't work here. I'll have to go back and get help."

"Your ankle broken?" Richard asked.

"Yes. The bastard set a trap for me." When he lifted the sleeping bag, the extent of the man's injuries became apparent.

"Christ." The man seemed to know his trapper. "You know who did this?"

"Guy's name was Yarnell. At least he gave me this sleeping bag once he saw I was out of commission."

Richard couldn't believe his luck. "Was Yarnell with a woman?"

"No."

Damn. "Which way did he go?"

"Up the path. But that was about half an hour ago." He pulled the bag closer to his body. "You got anything to drink?"

Richard flashed the light on the man again. His lips were cracked and pale. If he hadn't had the bag to keep him warm, Richard bet he'd be dead by now.

Stanton handed him his bottle of water. "Here."

"Thanks."

While those two played nice, Richard wanted to investigate the man's claim that Yarnell was near. Things couldn't have worked out better if he'd planned it. With Stanton not on his tail, Richard might find a way for the two of them to eat a bullet. He'd never killed anyone in cold blood before, but with the twelve jurors deaths on his head, he might as well try to do what he could to lessen the chance he'd be found.

The image of his wife and children burst to the surface, and he wanted to protect them at all costs. Never did he conceive the threat against their life would push him to the dark side.

"I'll catch up with you later," Richard said. "I want to see where the gunshot came from. Maybe it has something to do with the attorney."

He didn't wait for Stanton to respond before he took off.

A few hundred feet away, his flashlight caught site of some rope hanging from a few trees high on the ridge. Richard climbed up the incline, slipping repeatedly on the wet leaves. He never should have let Stanton talk him into getting cheap boots.

He found a blood stained towel, freshly used. Had Jake been shot? Or the attorney? He routed around the area, looking for the injured party, but found no one. Damn it.

Given he was no tracker, he headed down the slope until he met the path. If Jake had taken a shot, he couldn't be too far ahead.

CHAPTER TWENTY-TWO

Jake shone the light on the eight-foot wide stream. "We'll cross over there on the logs. The mold makes the wood slippery, so hold onto the handrail."

Jake crossed first and aimed the beam at Susan's feet to help guide her. Halfway across, she glanced up at him for a moment, and her foot slipped off the log into the frigid water. Shit. The rippling current toppled over the edge of her boot and down her foot. The impact of the freezing water took her breath away. Before she could let out a scream, a strong hand lifted her up.

"You okay?"

"It's only a wet foot. A really cold, wet foot." She hadn't meant to sound bitchy, but every muscle ached, and she was tired of running.

"We're pushing too hard," Jake said. "You need to rest."

She wasn't going to let exhaustion stop her from moving toward the highway. "I can make it. You said we'll reach the road in another five or six hours."

"Then let *me* rest for a moment."

He grabbed her hand and led her down the side of the hill, stopping at a five-foot tall boulder.

"You're just saying that so I'll slow down, right?" She gently removed the light from his hand and shone the beam onto Jake's leg. His pant leg was crusted in blood, but the wound hadn't reopened.

He retrieved the light from her and clicked off the beam. "Susan. Listen. Those voices we heard when we were on the ridge?"

"Yes."

"I recognized one of them. It was Richard Thomason's."

She latched onto his arm. "That's a good thing, right? At least it's not another assassin."

"Don't forget what T-squared said. The FBI still wants to bring me in."

"Talk to him. Tell him you had nothing to do with the murder."

Jake took her both of her hands in her. "Richard is as straight as they come. When he received that picture of me with my hands on Cho, he had no choice but to suggest they bring me in. He's following protocol. Nothing I can say will persuade him to let me go."

"The FBI can't be that by-the-book. Surely, your record will speak for itself."

"Not in this case."

She leaned against the slab of granite. "We'd be safe if they escort us back to D.C."

He dropped his backpack. "If I'm in jail, or being questioned, who would look after you?"

She didn't want to think about being on her own. "Can't they assign me someone new?"

If she still had the light to shine on his face, she bet he winced. She wanted to tell him she felt safe with him but didn't want to burden him with guilt at needing to put her safety above his.

"They might replace me, or since they think they have their murderer—as in me—in custody, they'll believe you'll be safe without protection. We both know that's not true. Besides, you can take care of yourself now, and as far as the FBI is concerned, their job is done."

Physically she might be able to cook and drive, but she still jumped at every noise. Susan doubted she'd ever be able to walk down the street without looking over her shoulder.

A crisp breeze rustled the trees, and the noise unsettled her. If a storm hit, they'd never get out of there alive.

"Susan." He leaned in closer. "Are you okay?"

"Yes. I'm a little on edge, that's all." She let out a long breath, her mind jumping over one hurdle, and then another. "Hold on a minute." She placed her gloved hands on his broad shoulders. "If they come across the man you snared, they'll find out that you had nothing to do with the murders."

"We can't be sure he'll admit to anything. If he tells them an FBI agent attacked him, they'll be more convinced than ever I'm guilty."

"Damn." She slumped down onto the ground, and the heat drained from her body. "I guess we have to keep going then."

"We can rest a little. We've taken enough different paths that we're probably safe for the night. We don't even know anyone is after us."

"You don't believe that. You said yourself Richard Thomason will bring you in at all costs."

"Right."

He nudged her. "Take your pack off so we can sit on them. Then lean against this rock and we'll wrap ourselves in the remaining sleeping bag."

"You don't want to put up the tarp?"

"I don't think we'll be sleeping for long."

Damn. She glanced around. No one could see them from the path. Their hiding place appeared safe. "Sure."

She wanted to absorb the safety of his arms but getting too close would mean more heartbreak. Their flight was nearly at an end.

"Take your boot off," he said.

"Why?" Her foot was cold enough. Exposing it to the thirty-degree temperature would give her frostbite.

"You need to dry your foot after you stepped in the river. You don't need to get trench foot."

"Eww."

She couldn't tell if he was being serious but getting dry sounded divine. She dug through the pack. "There aren't any extra clothes, and definitely no socks."

"Tom and Hank weren't expecting a woman to use the pack. Here, let me help you. Sit on the pack and let Dr. Yarnell do his magic."

She liked the levity. "Yes, sir."

He untied her laces, slipped off the boot and sock and placed the bottom of her frozen foot on his bare belly. He jumped the second her skin hit his, but he pressed her sole firmly against his stomach.

"That feels wonderful," she moaned.

He chuckled. "For you it might."

He vigorously rubbed her calves and massages her aching feet.

"Please don't stop."

He smiled. "I'm only doing this so I don't have to drag your sorry ass out of here." He tapped the end of her nose. "Why don't you wring the water from your sock?

"You expect me to put this cold thing back on?"

"It won't be cold once you place it on your warm skin."

"You're kidding, right?"

"Do I sound like I'm kidding?" His voice came out deep and serious, but she could tell he wasn't trying to be mean.

"All right."

"Seriously, the heat from your body will help dry the sock in about, oh, ten hours."

"Super." Despite the extra chill, Susan didn't mind the discomfort. His tender care helped heal the ache in her heart.

After the circulation returned to her foot, she slipped on the still wet, but now warmish sock. "Thanks." He helped her with the boot.

"Now, what say we share some body heat?" he asked.

"Sounds good to me."

They arranged their packs next to each other. She twisted her back to his chest, leaned her head against the rock, balancing on her wool cap while trying not to slip off the lumpy backpack.

Once they reached their destination, wherever that place was, Jake would leave to work on saving his own life. Her stomach twisted at the thought.

She turned around, her mind refusing to relax. "All I can think about is finally making it out of this forest only to face a line of wailing cars waiting for us."

He smoothed a hand down her cheek. "There are a lot of exits. I can't see the Bureau spending the resource power to cover all of them. Besides, they can't be sure we're in the woods."

"Unless Thomason contacted them first." Cold drilled through her jacket and she shivered. "I wish we still had both sleeping bags."

"Sorry about that, but I didn't want to be responsible for that man dying, even if he tried to kill me." The moon reflected off his smile. He wrapped an arm around her. "All the more reason to snuggle." Once Jake tucked the sleeping bag around her, he pulled her close and her heart melted.

Susan squeezed her eyes shut and let the warm tear dribble down frozen cheek. Her nose clogged. Great. Could this get any worse? Yes, she could have a gun to her head with that terrible man threatening to kill her. *Don't go there.*

"Susan."

Daddy was kneeling next to her bed, rubbing her shoulder. Warmth spread through her at his kindness. "Daddy?"

"Wake up." The voice came out a whisper.

She lifted her lids, her face inches from his chest. "Jake?"

He placed a finger on her lips and her body shot to alert. As she jerked to attention, her stiff joints rebelled.

"Someone's coming."

"Is it Richard Thomason?"

"Possibly."

A shout came from the west. "Yarnell?"

"Shit," Jake said. "It's him."

"Are you going to let him know you're here?"

"So he can drag me in? No way. I'll go back to DC on my own. If I let him take me in, I won't be able to investigate or protect you. Stay here."

She clasped his arm. "What are you going to do?"

"Slow him down. I don't want him in front of us."

Jake lifted the sleeping bag to get out and icy air attacked her. She pulled the bag closer once he moved away. He handed her the flashlight, and then dug a hand into the backpack. He pulled out what looked like a small rope.

"Be careful," she said, not happy he was going out on his own.

He leaned over and kissed her, his warm lips shooting her thoughts in a different and more dangerous direction.

***

Jake ran through a few scenarios as he headed back down the path. Richard shouted again. Once he had a fix on the man's location, Jake went down the steep embankment below the level of the path to wait for Richard to pass by.

His superior sounded like a heard of horses. His feet must have stepped on every stick. As Richard approached, Jake eased his way up the side of the hill until he was within ten feet of the path. He lay on his belly, his breath ragged. Harming a fellow officer was illegal, but Susan's safety had to come first.

The moment Richard passed by, Jake counted to twenty before crawling up to the path. The crunching continued and Jake stood. His wound rebelled and nearly toppled him. Damn leg. The image of Susan scared to death behind the rock propelled him forward.

Matching his cadence with Richard's, Jake took longer strides until he was close behind him.

Jake went down on his knee. "Help me."

Richard whipped around, his gun ready in his hand. "Jake? That you?" The flashlight clicked to life and nearly blinded him.

"You know me?" That sounded lame, but he didn't want Richard to think he'd been following him.

"It's Richard Thomason."

Jake waited for Richard to put away his gun, but he didn't. "Thank God you're here. You've got to help me. I've been stabbed." He placed his hand over his wound hoping to get some fresh blood on his palm to prove his claim.

Richard lowered his arm and stood over Jake. A light flashed on his leg. "Let me see."

Jake uncovered the wound. "I think it's clotting, but it hurts." God, he hated acting like a wimp.

"We need to get you help." Richard looked around. "Where's Susan Chapman?"

"Dominick Francisco killed her." He hadn't meant to tell that tale, but if the FBI thought she was dead maybe whoever was after her would believe the story too.

His mind fogged when the real pain crept up his leg.

Richard bent down and helped Jake to his feet. "We need to get you out of here."

Jake was surprised at the concern in Richard's tone, but Susan and he couldn't have Richard tag along.

Jake looped an arm over Richard's shoulder and leaned heavily on him. Richard shoved his gun in his holster and slung an arm around Jake's waist. He could take Richard down now but wanted the man to drop his guard.

"What the hell are *you* doing out here anyway," Jake asked with genuine interest. What he really wanted to know was how the hell had his location been compromised so quickly? The most logical explanation was the most painful. Tom had sold him out.

"To be honest, Stanton figured you might be staying at Tom's father's place. I'm ashamed to admit that we got some intel that showed you hanging Gary Cho."

Jake stepped away from Richard. "Me? You're shitting me, right? You think I killed Cho?" He tapped his chest, carrying his acting skills to a new level.

"I didn't want to believe it, but I saw a picture of you with one hand on the rope and Cho limp in your arms."

He lowered his head as if to ponder the event. "How the hell did you get that picture?" Even Tom hadn't known the source.

"Someone sent it to me on my phone, but I couldn't trace the call. I wish to hell I knew who was right outside the cabin photographing you with Cho."

That was the same story Tom relayed to him. Maybe it was true that Richard believed Jake was responsible for Cho's death.

He faced Richard. "Did you come all the way to Shepherds Hill to bring me in?" He tried to sound more taken aback than pissed.

"I wanted to hear your side of the story."

Bullshit. "You come alone?"

"No. Stanton is with the man you trapped. He's getting him help."

"I didn't kill Cho, you know. I found him swinging and took him down."

Richard's shoulders slumped. "I know that now."

"You do?" Richard sincerity had a ring of truth to it.

"We found Ronnie Stenoff. He told us what happened."

"Who?"

"The blonde guy who attacked you in the cabin. The one you trapped. He confessed. Said he'd been hired by Dominick Francisco to kill Susan Chapman. You happened to be in the way."

Jake wished he could see Richard's eyes. "Did Stenoff tell you he and Dominick were the ones responsible for killing the jurors?"

"He told me Francisco killed Cho."

"So why come after me now if you know I had nothing to do with the hanging?"

"To tell you don't need to run anymore." He latched onto Jake's arm a little too aggressively. "Come on back to the cabin. We'll drive you to a hospital."

How the hell had he known he was running? Richard wouldn't have known he knew the FBI was after him unless Tom blabbed he'd relayed the Cho hanging to him.

"Sounds good to me." Jake pretended to stumble as they turned around. "Can you find me a stick or two to lean on?" He'd left his walking pole back with Susan.

"Sure."

Jake limped over to a tree and leaned against the rough bark. Richard's light scoured the forest floor allowing Jake to follow the man's every moment. A small animal darted across the path and Jake's pulse skyrocket. He needed to get a grip.

"Here ya go." Richard handed Jake two four-foot long sticks.

"Perfect." Jake motioned Richard ahead.

The moment Richard's back was turned, Jake lifted the stick and swung, knocking Richard to the ground. "Sorry."

Richard grabbed his neck and tried to get up. Before the agent could get to his feet, Jake hogged tied his feet and pulled Richard's hands behind his back to secure them.

"What the hell are you doing?" Richard said, panic evident in his quick words.

"I know you still think I had something to do with those murders, but I didn't."

"No. No. I know someone tried to frame you. You've got to believe me." From the way his voice wavered, Jake was tempted to see it his way.

"As soon as I get out of here, I'll send help for you." Jake took Richard's gun. "I promise."

Richard rolled on his back. "You know you'll lose your job over this."

"Better than losing my life."

"You can't leave me here."

"Watch me."

Jake trotted off toward Susan, his leg suddenly in better shape with his newfound freedom.

Given Richard was out of commission for a few hours, he chanced using the light once he was out of sight. He shone the beam down the slope to his right looking for their large rock, while ignoring Richard's screams for help.

For a moment, Jake questioned if he'd misjudged the man. It was possible, but he couldn't take the chance.

He spotted the rock where he'd left Susan, and half slid, half strode down the side of the hill. When he reached their hiding place, his backpack was against the rock, but Susan was nowhere in sight.

CHAPTER TWENTY-THREE

Jake's heart cracked. He swept the light around for a clue where Susan might have gone. Pine scented the blowing wind and icy cold air jammed down his throat. She was too bright to attempt to find her way out of the forest on her own. She didn't know the paths, the forks, the cutoffs, or the direction of the highway. Without a map, she'd get hopelessly lost. Add in her fear of the dark, and he expected her to be balled up in the fetal position waiting for his return.

Wait a minute. Had she thought Richard had captured him, and her only hope of survival was to flee on her own? Or had she believed he and Richard were in cahoots to take her down? Surely, she trusted him more than that.

She must have had a good reason to leave.

His body shook as other images of abandonment assaulted him. He could still see his mother lying with man after man. The vision then switched to her dead body collapsed on the floor of their small apartment. Finally, he could see the faces of both his aunt and grandmother as they refused to take him in.

People were false. He grew up not being able to count on anyone or anything other than his gut instinct. When Richard showed up, he'd even wondered if Tom had betrayed him. How else had they found them?

Enough. Susan wasn't like them. They had a connection. She wouldn't have made love to him in the cabin if she didn't trust or believe in him. She was missing, and he wouldn't abandon her, even if he'd just broken the law by hog-tying an FBI agent.

With her backpack missing, he assumed she'd taken off on her own. No way would someone else be out here looking for her. He doubted Richard had notified the locals to keep a watch out for Susan or him. Even if he had, the sheriff would have been smart enough to hike in from the highway entrance. Is that what happened? Had Sheriff Stukes found Susan and escorted her out?

No. The good sheriff wouldn't have believed the word of an FBI agent unless he checked with Tom or Hank Traynor first. Jake was like a local to the people of Shepherds Hills.

He chanced a call, loud enough for her to hear, assuming she was nearby, but not so loud Richard would realize Susan was still alive. "Susan?"

He stilled, listening for some kind of movement. The trees creaked in the wind and blocked out most sound. Where the hell was she?

Twigs cracked in front and to his right of him. Jake froze. He pointed the beam toward the copse of trees hoping to capture the animal in the light. From behind a large oak, Susan stepped into the open and shielded her eyes.

His relief nearly dropped him to the ground. "Susan, it's Jake." He lowered the light's ray to the ground.

"Jake?" She raced up to meet him and threw her arms around his neck. "I was so worried."

"Where were you?" He hugged her tight. "You left our rock."

"I had to take a pee. Tell me what happened with Thomason."

He debated how much to tell her, not wanting her to be involved in his crime. "Let's just say Richard Thomason won't be bothering us."

"You killed him?" She pushed away.

Her action stung. "No. I merely incapacitated him. Don't worry. Stanton's nearby."

"Where?"

"Shh. He might hear us."

"You left him to freeze to death?"

Ever the prosecutor. "No. When Richard doesn't return with my head, Stanton will go looking for him. When that happens, they're sure to come searching for us."

"Did they still plan on taking you in?"

"Richard claimed he believed I had nothing to do with Cho's death. The blonde fellow who attacked me said Francisco killed Cho."

"Did Richard believe him?"

"He said he did, but I don't know how much I can trust him."

She planted her hands on her hips in her usual *Susan* pose. "Now we have to avoid not only the FBI and the Caravello family, but also the Francisco family?"

"I'm afraid so." He dragged a hand down her smooth cheek. "As soon as we get back to Washington, I'll find some answers, and we'll sort all of this out. Are you ready for the hike?"

She groaned. "Remind me never to go on a picnic with you again."

He inwardly chuckled at her attempt at levity.

The next six hours were hell. His leg throbbed, and from the way she favored one leg and then the other, her feet were bothering her, but she didn't complain. To keep from focusing on their injuries or what awaited them in the *real* world, they talked about the home comforts they missed the most, as well as their best and worst cases. He enjoyed seeing another side of Susan Chapman, lawyer extraordinaire.

Headlights flashed in the distance and he changed his normal tone. "We're getting close."

"I can't believe we're going to make it. My legs are rubber and my muscles need a good massage."

He'd been about to say he'd do the honors of rubbing her down, but talking about their feelings or any future plans wasn't appropriate, especially since their emotions were still so raw from all the deaths.

They finally emerged from the forest and tromped down the wooden steps to the side of the road.

"Are we going to hitchhike?" she asked.

He smiled down at her. "You have a better idea?"

"No." She slapped his arm, and he hid his smile.

The sun was peeking over the horizon. He wanted to find a ride before they became sitting ducks for any law enforcement agency.

"We need to head east," he said more to himself than to inform Susan.

A truck passed them and they stuck out their thumbs. The man slowed, and then an arm waved them on.

"Say goodbye to the forest," he said.

"Good riddance."

He laughed, falling a little more in love with her.

***

The phone call rattled Joseph out of a deep sleep. He glanced at the caller ID but didn't recognize the number.

"Francisco."

"Mr. Francisco. This is Gina Stenoff."

"Who?"

"My husband, Ronnie, works for your son."

Joseph pulled himself up to a sitting position and turned on the bedside lamp. "Oh, Ronnie, yes."

What the hell was she calling for at seven in the morning?

"Ronnie called me from North Carolina. He's in jail."

Shit. "And my son?"

"I'm so sorry."

Joseph's hand clutched the phone tight. "Sorry about what? Calling so early?"

"Ronnie isn't quite sure what happened, but he said Jake Yarnell shot and killed Dominick. The FBI found the body in the woods."

Joseph dropped the phone, her words echoing in his head.

Dominick was dead. His son had always been a screw up, but he was his screw up. He loved his son and his son loved him. He'd spent his life trying to build a safe world for him and Maria. And now Jake Yarnell had taken that life from him.

He wiped the tear brimming on his lid. The woman's voice came through the line again, but he disconnected. He didn't want her sympathy or to deal with her husband's problems. God knows, he had enough of his own.

He let the self-pity twist into rage. Now more than ever, he wanted revenge.

Richard Thomason was his only hope. The bastard better take down Yarnell or the punk would never see his kids again. Joseph never planned to harm the young things after he took the children, but that was before he'd learned his only son was gone.

His pulse raced. That wasn't true. James was his own flesh and blood. The man had been willing to frame his own half-brother for a piece of the Francisco pie. He bet he'd be willing to do one last deed.

With renewed hope, he called James.

***

"Sorry about the cramped space," the mountain man said.

Jake had been hesitant to hitch a ride in a car with two large dogs caged in back, but a ride was a ride. Fugitives couldn't be picky. He slid in first since he didn't want Susan to have to sit next to Mr. Snaggle-tooth. Unfortunately, they had to go without their seatbelts since the front seat was designed for two.

She might be slim hipped, but she had to sit slightly sideways to even fit. Without asking, he lifted her left leg and placed it over his right to give them more room. She smiled and he dropped his head back against the seat.

"We're you going to?" the driver asked.

"As far as you can take us. We're heading to the DC area." No need to give specifics.

"I'm not going that far, but I can take you as far as Moorefield."

He had no idea where that was, but east was east. "Perfect."

After fifteen minutes, Susan's body began to relax. She dropped her head on his shoulders, and for the first time in a long time, he allowed his bunched muscles to release their grip.

When the dogs barked in the back at the passing traffic, the driver knuckled the window separating the cab from the back.

"Sorry about that. They can't wait to go hunting."

"Ah."

Jake figured the less he said the better. He didn't want the driver to remember much more than he picked up two hitchhikers—one with a bloodied leg and a large gash in his cheek.

Snaggletooth clicked on the radio. Country Western. No surprise. Jake closed his eyes and let his mind drift until the music ended and a man's voice droned the news.

"...Jake Yarnell and Taylor Daniels are wanted in the connection of the murder of an FBI witness."

Jake shot straight up, reached over, and turned down the radio. "I've been thinking about getting me some huntin' dawgs. What's the best breed?"

The man sat up taller in the seat and started yammering about his animals. Susan must have heard the radio announcement for her hand gripped his.

She straightened and leaned forward. "Sir?"

"Call me Randy."

"Randy, I'm sorry to ask, but we've been hiking for several hours. Is there any way we could stop since—?"

"If you gotta take a leak, just say so, little lady. I'm not in a big hurry. Only the dogs are."

She smiled. "Thank you."

Snaggletooth leaned over and turned up the volume. Shit.

"The man is thirty three, six foot two with short cropped hair. The woman is—"

"How much further?" Susan asked, loud enough to cover the radio voice.

"I can stop by the side of the road if that would help?"

The alert ended.

"I can wait. Thanks."

She glanced over at Jake and motioned with her eyes they needed to find a way out. Before Jake could formulate a clear plan, a gas station came into view.

The mountain man turned left and pulled up to the pump. "I gotta get gas anyway."

After Susan opened the creaky door and stepped out, Jake scouted over. His boot hit the pavement and his knee buckled, but he caught himself on the door.

"You okay, mister?"

"Just stiff from a lot of hiking."

Jake stepped to the back to retrieve his backpack, and both dogs snarled. "Easy fellas."

"They won't hurt you. Especially since they're caged." The man chuckled. He tapped the cage. "You boys hungry?"

Both dogs barked and seemed to lose interest in protecting their territory.

Jake lifted their packs and handed Susan hers.

"You can leave them here. I'll watch them."

"My money's inside," Jake said.

Susan chimed in. "I need mine for, ah, female reasons."

It was hard to tell in the morning light, but underneath the beard, Jake could have sworn the guy blushed.

As they headed toward the small store inside, Jake threaded his arms through the straps on his pack. Their strides were slow and even to avoid looking like they were trying to run away.

He leaned over to her. "If you need to go to the bathroom, make it quick. I need to find a way out back."

"I'm good."

"Then grab some food. We might be on our own for a while." He took off his pack and dug his hand in the side pocket. "Here's the last of the cash. Use it wisely."

She raced off. Her focus and her ability to understand the ramifications of his requests drew him more to her. Susan was an amazing woman.

The back entrance was easy to find. The door was next to the bathrooms. Perfect.

He stepped back into the main store area and glanced out the windows. Snaggletooth had finished filling up.

"Susan." He attempted to keep the urgency from his tone, not wanting to alarm anyone else in the store.

She held up a finger to indicate she'd heard, grabbed her change, and hurried toward him with her purchases in hand. He motored toward the back, presumably to use the bathroom.

He pushed open the back door and the cold air blasted him. Just as he'd warmed up, they were on the run again. Damn.

Behind the store was a copse of trees, and beyond the small forest were a few farmhouses. As if he was in the Army again, he waved her away from the building. He wouldn't be surprised if their driver came looking for them so they needed to move fast. Jake would be the hold up with his bum leg.

With teeth clenched, he led the way. This time there was no neat path maintained by the forest service. Downed limbs, prickly weeds, and basic scrub brush blocked their path every few feet. The going was tough, but Susan didn't say a word. She tripped and went down on her knees once but then managed to keep going.

Shouts sounded from the direction of the gas station. He prayed Snaggletooth would assume he'd done something offensive to drive them off or that his passengers were two crazy people hell bent on a new adventure.

In less than ten minutes, they'd fought their way through the woods. About six houses, all fenced in, sat on one hundred acres.

They halted. Susan dropped her hands on her knees, her breaths coming out too rapidly. "Now what?"

He spotted an old truck behind a barn. "Wait here."

She straightened. "What are you going to do?"

"Pretend you don't see me."

He took off, leaving Susan by the side of a dirt road. She didn't need to be an accomplice in what he was about to do. He'd grown up on the streets. Hot-wiring a car was standard fare. He'd stolen a few vehicles in his time to go joy riding when he wasn't old enough to legally drive, but he always returned what he took—unharmed. He hoped he could do the same with this truck.

His lucky day the passenger side door was unlocked. He climbed in, withdrew his knife from his pack and went to work. In less than sixty seconds, the engine roared to life.

He tossed his pack in the back, slid back into the driver's seat and picked up Susan.

"This is illegal," she said. Her brows furrowed.

Her disapproval bit into him. "My other choice was to turn us in—or rather turn myself in."

She reached over, clasped his arm and squeezed. "You did what you had to do."

Wow. Her understanding meant the world to him. "We aren't out of the woods yet. No pun intended."

"Once we get to Virginia, where do you plan to hole up?"

"We can't go to my place or yours. The department will have both of our homes watched."

"Then where?"

"The last place on earth they'll think of looking."

CHAPTER TWENTY-FOUR

Jake stopped the truck on the side of the street. Every house would qualify for HGTV's beautiful homes series. Mansions—every one of them.

"Who lives here?" Susan asked.

"Wait here."

Jake crawled out of the driver's seat. Damn him. Every time he didn't answer her questions directly, the shit hit the fan.

She must have looked really pissed off for he reopened her door and leaned in. "You're safe. I promise. I won't be long."

He'd promised her she'd be safe when they reached the Florida townhouse and again when they left the woods. Each time someone found them. Maybe someone had implanted a chip under his skin to act as a homing device—or else she had one.

She rubbed her wound where the glass had impaled her. No way a whole team of doctors could have been bribed to put one of those invasive devices in her body. When this was over, she'd get a full body scan.

Susan pushed aside the horrible thought and slid down in the seat to avoid detection. This beat up farm truck would surely draw attention in this fancy neighborhood. The security guards were probably out patrolling the streets right now, trying to prevent people like them from casing the place.

She lifted her head and peeked out her side, and her breath fogged the window. The wet snow fell in light delicate flakes, creating magic on the trees. The driver's side door eased open, and she shot her hand to her pounding chest.

"Jake, you scared me."

"Sorry. Come on."

"Who lives here?"

He raced to her side and helped her out. He led her down the street and up a front walkway.

She looked back over her shoulder. "What about our gear?"

"No one would steal those packs."

That was probably true.

While she couldn't smell herself, she could feel the dirt and grime rub against her skin when she moved. Maybe whoever lived here would be willing to let her shower. But could she really put on these stinky clothes afterwards? Maybe not.

Jake rang the front doorbell that was in the shape of a snake. What did that tell her about the occupant?

An old Asian woman, dressed in a black and white maid's outfit that seemed miles too big, answered the door. Her hand flew to her mouth. "Mr. Jake? That really you?" She sent him a toothless grin.

"Yes, Mai, it's me. I'd give you a hug, but I don't think you'd want to get near me."

"Come. Come. Mr. Nicki will be so happy to see you. He don't get many visitors these days."

Nicki? Susan tugged on Jake's arm. "There is no way I'm going to stay in a Caravello house."

"We don't have a choice." He leaned in closer and whispered, "I thought about seeing if Peter could put us up, but I'm sure the cops have his place covered too."

"What about T-Squared?"

His jaw tightened. "His house is probably being watched also. Besides, I'm hoping Uncle Nicki will let us stay in his vacation home on the bay."

A tall, thin black man, who looked no more than twenty-five, pushed a very old Nicki Caravello down the hall. He'd aged badly in the six years since the trial.

Nicki smiled. "Jake. It's so good to see you." He slid his glance over to her and his cheer evaporated. "What's *she* doing here?"

Susan didn't have the energy to absorb his insults. "I'll wait for you in the car."

Before she took a step, Jake swept an arm around her waist and pulled her to his side. "She's not the enemy, Uncle Nicki. The Francisco's have ordered a hit on her head. I've been hired to protect her."

His brow arched. "Is that so?" He looked over at her. "And what did you do to piss off that family, my dear?"

Suddenly, she was the favored child. "I have no idea. To be honest, I thought your family was responsible for the deaths of the jurors, but from my up close and personal meeting of Dominick Francisco, I know I was mistaken." She shot a glance at Jake to gauge his reaction, but he was closely watching Mr. Caravello.

The old man relaxed his grip on the wheelchair. "I'm glad to see we aren't the bad guys anymore. And Dominick? How did he fare in the exchange?"

"He won't be bothering anyone anymore. Ever," Jake said.

"He's dead?"

"Yes."

The old man slapped the arm of his wheelchair. "Excellent."

Jake dropped his arm from around her waist and stepped forward. The loss of his protection sharpened her nerves.

"Uncle Nicki. We need a place to hide. The FBI thinks I'm responsible for the deaths of some of the jurors. They came after me, forcing me to put one of them out of commission for a few hours. I'm not safe at work, home, or much of anywhere else."

"For you, anything." He turned around. "Henry?" A second later, the young black man appeared. "Would you please get me my keys?"

"Yes, sir."

A moment later he returned and handed the keys to his boss. The old man handed the chain to Jake. "Take off these two keys. This one is for the front door of my house in Maryland. You remember the place, don't you?"

"Fondly."

"I'm betting you'll need different transportation too."

"I had to steal an old farm truck. It kind of sticks out in this neighborhood."

He smiled. "I'm glad my lessons helped. Here." He handed him a car key. "Henry can show you to the Navigator. Wait here."

Nicki wheeled himself down the hall and through the second door on the left. He returned with a metal box. Using the smallest key on the chain, he unlocked the box and withdrew a stack of bills. You'll need cash to stay out of trouble."

"I can't take your money."

"Nonsense. I insist. Buy yourselves some new clothes. You two look a mess. No, wait." He craned his neck to the side. "Henry, could you get me Mai."

She had no idea what he was up to, but the way Mr. Caravello embraced Jake impressed her.

"Yes, Mr. Nicki?"

"Would you run to the store and..." He crooked a finger for her to bend near. The rest was lost in a whisper.

"Now?"

"Yes, now. And hurry."

Mai edged over to them. "Mr. Nicki thinks you need a makeover. Both of you. Nobody will recognize you when I finish. What size you wear?"

Oh, boy. She hadn't thought of a disguise, but she liked the idea. The facial scars would be hard to cover up, but from the excited tone, Mai would come up with something clever.

The maid handed them a pad and pencil and they each wrote down every size from underwear to shoes.

"I get color for hair too."

Instinctively, Susan touched her limp strands. "I've always wanted to be a redhead with blond highlights."

She nodded in apparent approval and moved away.

Nicki wheeled toward them. "How about a drink?"

Jake pulled her close. "That I could use."

***

Henry was the one who suggested Jake shave his head but leave the two-day old beard. The clothes weren't what Jake normally wore, but that was the point. Pressed slacks and a buttoned down shirt were not his style either, but the new look might make him blend in.

Mai had performed a miracle on Susan. While Jake liked her elegant blond hair when it was up in a twist, the short spiky red hairdo gave her a wild look. And sexy as hell.

Susan spun around for him and posed. "You like?"

He whistled.

Mai handed Susan a black see-through scarf. "Wear on head. If you tie under chin, you can hide cheek."

The clever woman had managed the impossible. He bet Susan's own mother would take a moment before recognizing her.

"Thank you." Susan gave Mai a hug and stepped over to Jake. She ran a hand over his bald head. "You better get a hat. You'll catch cold."

He scrubbed a hand over his chin, fishing for a compliment. "But what do you think? Is it me or what?"

"Definitely not you."

"Perfect."

He laughed, believing for a moment that they could move around unnoticed for a while.

Nicki's wheels squeaked on the tile floor as he came toward them. "Let me take a look at you two."

He and Susan stood side by side. "I wouldn't recognize either of you without further study. Now you better get a move on it before someone figures out you might have stopped here."

She stepped next to his chair, leaned over, and kissed him on his paper-thin cheek. "Thank you for all your help."

He grabbed her hand. "Just make sure you take care of Jake."

"No problem." That brought a smile to her lips.

Nicki turned back to Jake. "Go before the neighbors spot that truck of yours and call the cops."

Jake leaned over and gave Nicki a hug. "Thanks old man."

"Don't you old man me."

Jake squeezed the key chain in his fingers. "Any way Henry can do me a favor?"

"Name it."

He told them where he'd grabbed the truck. "I'd like to see it returned." He faced Henry. "You think you can hotwire that puppy?"

Henry stole a glance at his employer. "Not a problem, sir."

"Dump the backpacks somewhere too."

Henry nodded.

After a few more goodbyes, they grabbed the suitcases Mai had purchased, stuffed with at least a week's worth of clothes and toiletries, and left the Caravello sanctuary.

With the scarf securely tied under her chin, she braved the weather with a smile. The light snow tickled her nose, and the air seemed sweeter and fresher. Even the thin layer of snow on the lawns lay undisturbed, signaling a fresh start. Like them.

With more pep in her step than she remembered having in a while, she waited for Jake to unlock the door of their very nice ride.

Using the GPS as a guide, they took back roads to the Maryland shore. As they drove through St. Michaels, she admired the majestic homes.

"When was the last time you visited Uncle Nicki's place?" she asked.

"Oh, gosh. Maybe ten years ago? He used to bring Peter, James, and me here during the summer. As a kid, I couldn't get enough of the place. Especially the fishing."

Her family had had a boat, but Dad was often too busy to take them out on the water. "I remember we'd fish for flounder for hours on end."

"You had a nice childhood, I take it?" he asked.

"When my father was home." Her tone came out too wistful. She hadn't planned to bring up her issues. If she were honest, her life had been quite good before Carlton entered it and before Craig was in his car accident—and before Mom became depressed. Susan had tried to hold the family together after Dad died, but all she'd held dear was gone when he passed.

Jake must have sensed she didn't want to talk about those times and kept quiet. They made a quick stop at a fast food restaurant before picking up some food supplies at a local market. They didn't talk about anything they didn't want the world to hear.

Less than twenty minutes later they pulled into the drive of a two story, Craftsman style home. Not as big as she expected, but quaint and cozy nonetheless.

He cut the engine and slipped out. This was déjà vu all over again, only this time, the weather wasn't balmy and her wounds weren't making her body scream.

He slipped the suitcases out of the trunk while she shuffled up the walkway with her head down, careful not to slip on the snow. She shielded her face with one hand to avoid anyone identifying her.

Once on the porch, she stomped her boots on the straw mat to rid them of the slush and waited for Jake to unlock the front door. No one had driven by on the brick street since their arrival. Maybe they had escaped unnoticed.

They entered without a problem. She expected the furniture to be covered in white sheets and the inside air temperature to be cold and damp, but someone must have come in recently and freshened up the place.

"Nice." While not as down-to-earth as the Traynor's cabin, this house oozed an elegant comfort, decorated in polished cotton prints and antique furniture. Uncle Nicki must have had a decorator. She didn't see him the kind to pick out the feminine style.

Jake set the suitcases down and marched around the house, checking the window locks before closing all the blinds. "We don't want anyone snooping." He waved a hand. "Look around, pick a bedroom, and then relax."

Pick a bedroom? They'd spent the last few nights next to each other, and she liked the security. She debated telling him she wanted to sleep by his side, but he was back into the I-am-the-protector-role now. "Sure, as soon as I put away the groceries."

Once she emptied the food into the fridge, she carried her suitcase upstairs. After checking out each of the three bedrooms, she picked the one with the attached shower. Not knowing how long they'd be here, she decided it was best not to unpack.

Voices from television floated upstairs. With all chores completed, she went downstairs to see what Jake was up to.

She stepped into the living room and found him asleep on the sofa. His face looked relaxed for the first time in many days, and she itched to touch him but held back. They had to stay alert, even if they were hidden away in a small town on the ocean.

Susan debated waking him to suggest he climb into bed, but given he hadn't slept in who knows how long, she let him be. So much for them having a meaningful conversation before she went to bed. She mentally shrugged. It was close to bedtime anyway, so she tiptoed upstairs. Susan sat on top of the comforter, leaned against the padded headboard and clicked on the TV, her mind not ready to rest.

She watched the weather channel for a few minutes where more snow was predicted for tomorrow. Wonderful. Just what they didn't need. Of course, if they became snowed in, no one would be out looking for them.

Next, she flipped to the local Maryland news. Instantly, her body shot to alert. "There has to be a mistake," she mumbled.

The screen showed a photo of her brother in his wheelchair, bound and tied. Every muscle tensed. She upped the volume.

"Craig?" Her throat clogged and her pulse raced.

CHAPTER TWENTY-FIVE

Palms sweating, Susan flipped through the channels, trying to find more information about her brother's kidnapping. How was this possible? Dominick Francisco was dead. Wasn't he the one behind all the murders?

All of the channels showed the same image but with little information. Shit.

Susan jumped off the bed and paced. She stabbed a hand through her spiked hair, forgetting for a moment there was little to play with.

Mom. My God, she'd be beside herself. First her mother was told her daughter was dead and now her son had been kidnapped. With no one to calm her, there was not telling what kinds of pills her mother would ingest.

Susan pulled back the curtains to check the weather outside—snowy, dark, and windy. *Think*. It was a little after nine, and Arlington was only ninety miles away. If the storm took a turn for the worse, it might take her two to three hours to reach her mother, but she would arrive before her mom went to bed. Susan had to see her and tell her everything would be okay.

Jake. Dammit. He'd never let her waltz out of the house and drive by herself, and he sure as hell wouldn't come with her. It didn't matter the person who was after her no longer was alive. He'd argue someone was trying to get her attention.

Her gaze shot around the room. Climbing out of the window wouldn't work. She was on the second floor, and Jake had the keys to the car.

A phone sat next to the bed. Dare she hoped it work? Walking softly across the plush carpet so as not to disturb Jake below, she picked up the phone and listened for a dial tone.

She pumped a fist at the sound. Wait a minute. Given the age of the house, the walls were probably not insulated.

In order to lessen the chance he'd overhear her conversation, she turned on the shower full blast and dragged the phone into the bathroom. The cord to the landline barely reached so she sat on the cold floor and dialed her mom's number.

The phone rang and rang. "Pick up, Mom."

The answering machine came on and she dropped her head against the tiled wall. Her fingers trembled and her throat nearly closed. Susan cleared her throat when the beep sounded.

"Mom. Don't freak. It's Susan. I'm alive. Are you there? Please pick up."

Seconds went by—and then her mother answered. "Susan?" Her voice cracked. "Is that really you?"

She sounded drunk, tired, and depressed.

"Mom, I'm okay. The FBI lied to you and Craig. I wasn't in the car when it blew up." She didn't have time for a long discussion. "I can only talk for a minute. What happened to Craig?"

"You heard?"

Isn't that what she just said? "Yes."

"I came home from work and Craig wasn't here. I thought maybe Doug had picked him up, but when I called, he said no. Then I received a phone call from someone who said they'd release Craig if you came to the warehouse. I told him you could never come because you were dead. I didn't understand what he wanted me to do."

Her mother must have mixed up the information. "Who called and what did he say?"

"I just told you." Her tone came out scolding, like it did when she was ten.

"Did he give you a name, a number, the location of the warehouse?"

"A number." The mom rattled off a Virginia number.

"Let me get something to write with. Hold on." She set the phone down, opened the bathroom door and pawed through the side table drawer next to the bed. She came up with a pen but nothing to write on.

Her hand. She'd write the number on her hand. "Give it to me."

Once her mother told her the number, Susan knew what she had to do. "Mom, I love you, and I'll talk to you soon."

"When can I see—"

Susan disconnected, her blood pressure drilling a hole in her temples. The number on her hand mocked her. Dare she call this person? He'd tell her where she could retrieve her brother, and then she and Jake would figure out a plan of attack.

With her heart beating slower, she dialed.

An electronically altered voice answered. "Hello."

Did she want to talk to this robot? "This is Susan Chapman."

"Tomorrow at 8AM, meet me at the warehouse on Richter and Arlington if you want to see your brother again."

"Can I—"

The dial tone didn't answer back. Stunned, she dropped the phone back onto the receiver. Was Craig even alive? Would this villain kill both of them once he lured her to the site?

In need of a warm shower to help her sort through the tangled emotions before she broke the news to Jake, she stripped and jumped into the stall.

The hot water poured down her face and her body, and the steam helped settle her mind. As she lathered the minty soap, she came to a decision. They would do what the man asked. If Craig died because she stood by safe and sound, she'd never be able to live with herself.

"Were you on the phone a minute ago?"

She jerked, nearly slipping on the wet tile. She must not have heard Jake knock, if he had at all, but she was thankful the steam had misted the glass shower door when he stepped in.

Shit. She didn't have to see the expression on his face to know he was beyond pissed. "Maybe."

"We need to talk."

She didn't do commands well. "When I'm done showering, I'll be happy to discuss the length of the stick up your butt." She dropped her head and sagged. "I'm sorry. That was rude."

"Water off. Now." He waited a beat before he added the magic word, "Please."

She shut off the water, reached outside the shower for the towel and wrapped the fresh smelling cloth around her body. She stepped out with shoulders straight, ready to do battle.

His eyes widened perceptibly, but his wide stance told her the rest of the night wouldn't go well. Her father always taught her to go on the offensive.

"My brother was kidnapped, and I spoke to his captor. There. Happy?"

"I wondered if you'd seen the report. Apparently, you had." He stepped toward her and she battled fear, lust, and need at the same time.

"Yes."

"You want a hug?"

Those were the sweetest words she'd ever heard. All she could do was nod and step into his waiting arms. He cradled her, rocked her, and kissed her, and then stepped back.

"Now tell me everything."

***

Without help, Jake realized he could never protect Susan. Stubborn woman wouldn't take no for an answer. She wanted to leave right then and go to her mother.

That was out of the question. Whoever had Craig would no doubt have the mom's place under surveillance. If he still had his cuffs, he'd chain her to the bed again since this running had to stop.

"I want to get the bastard as much as you do," he said, wanting to make sure she understood he was on her side.

"Thank you." She ran a hand down his arm.

"Whoever orchestrated this kidnapping has to know we'll bring reinforcements, unless this person believes I'm persona non grata."

"Which you might be," she said.

"True." His mind spun with different possibilities. "It's possible Joseph Francisco found out Dominick is dead and wants revenge."

"How would he know that? Would your boss have called him?"

"I don't even know."

She sat on the bed. The towel dipped, revealing most of her breasts. He didn't need to be lusting after her. They had a plan to conceive.

He cleared his throat. "How about you change and meet me downstairs?"

She glanced down and turned a pretty pink shade. "Sure."

"I'm going to call Tom."

"I thought you believed he was the one who leaked our location at his dad's cabin."

"I did, until I realize lots of people in the office knew I used to stay there every summer."

"Then by all means call him. I'm up for all the help we can get."

Jake spun on his heels and raced downstairs, wondering if he could trust Tom, or should he call Stanton instead? If only he understood how the Francisco's were tied into the murders, he might make a more informed decision.

He understood Dominick wanted Susan dead. According to the partner, Ronnie Stenoff, Dominick had killed Cho. But why? The Francisco's hated the Caravellos. The logic made no sense to him.

Not wanting anyone to trace the call, he used his disposable cell, which was in a dire need of recharging. Jake dialed Tom, who picked up on the first ring.

"It's Jake."

"Where the hell are you?" Tom asked.

"Hello to you too."

"Jesus. I thought you were dead. Richard said you were seriously injured. When I didn't hear from you, I thought the worst."

Most of his muscles relaxed. Tom hadn't betrayed him. "I'm fine.

Or at least I will be with a little rest." His thigh ached, but his leg functioned just fine.

"Is Susan dead?" Tom's voice cracked. "I heard Dominick Francisco killed her."

"No. I told Richard that's what happened. I figured he might let it leak she was dead and whoever else was after her would believe it too."

He regaled his friend with what happened and how he'd killed Francisco.

"Where did you go afterwards?"

"You won't believe it. We hitched a ride out of the area and ended up visiting Nicki Caravello."

"No shit. How is the old guy?"

"Good. I know he'd love for you stop by."

Susan came downstairs and stood next to him, her brows furrowed. "Ah, I called because Susan's brother was kidnapped today."

"The guy in the wheelchair?"

"That's him. I need backup. I can't go in alone. I know I tied down Richard and broke just about every rule in the book by doing so, but—"

"You didn't hear?"

"Hear what?"

"Richard confessed everything to Stanton. Told him how he was being blackmailed into giving the addresses of the jurors. When the guy took his kids, he went ballistic. Richard was told to kill both you and Susan. Only he believed Francisco had taken care of Susan for him."

"Jesus. Does he know who the guy was?"

"No, and we'll never find out. Richard ate a bullet this morning."

Jake's muscles weakened. "I thought he'd gone off the deep end, but I couldn't be sure he was our mole."

Susan waved her hands and mouthed, "Who?"

He placed a hand over the receiver. "Thomason."

Her eyes widened, and she nodded as if she might have guessed.

"What do you want us to do?" Tom said. "You'll get the full cooperation of the department. You know that, right?"

He hadn't five minutes ago. "I have a plan I want to pass by you."

"Let's hear it."

***

She wasn't happy they had to leave this nice house, but she understood her phone call to her mom had put them in jeopardy. Would the sick bastard have put a bug on her mother's phone now too? If he'd ripped her brother right out the house, he probably did have some kind of surveillance in the house.

Whatever. Tom said he'd give the local PD a call and ask them to watch over Caravellos' Maryland house in case anyone tried to break in. He also put a detail at her mom's place too.

Right now, they were on their way toward DC in a badass snow-storm—to Tom's house. The speedometer rarely reached forty and cars were piled up on the side of the road, either broken down or waiting out the storm. Good luck to them. She bet the snowplows wouldn't be able to keep up with this massive dumping.

Best case scenario, if they didn't run out of gas or get in an accident, they would make it to the meeting a little after midnight. Tom had assured them, via Stanton's instruction, that the team would have everything under control by the time they reached Virginia.

She appreciated their effort to plan a strategy, but she didn't need a bunch of agents plotting what might be her last moments on earth without any input from her.

Jake stifled a yawn as he wiped the frosty windshield with his palm. "There's one thing we can be sure of."

"What's that?"

"No one would chance attacking Fort Traynor with a gazillion agents inside."

"You do have a point, but I for one will not be sleeping even if I know I'll be safe. I'll be worrying all night about what they might have done to my poor brother."

"Or what they might do to you if you walk in there alone?"

She knew Jake's opinion on her decision to follow the man's instructions. "I don't care what you big agents say, I'm going in."

"We'll see."

An hour after they planned to arrive at Tom's place, they finally rolled in. From the number of black sedans lining the road, half the FBI was there.

"We'll have to park at least a block away. I'm sorry."

"I can walk a block," she said. The trek to Tom's front door would be easier than what she would have to do in seven hours.

Tom met them at the door and gave Jake a hug. "You must be Susan."

"You guessed it."

Tom sent Jake a how-did-you-get-so-lucky look, and Susan's face heated up. No makeup, bloodshot eyes, and about a ten pound weight loss made her less than attractive, but she was happy she hadn't scared them with her appearance.

"Come on in. We've tweaked your plan a little."

Tom introduced her to the other five agents, four of whose names she couldn't remember. Stanton's name she recognized. He was older than she expected, and not in the best of shape, but he had an honest look about him.

The rest of the men all had short haircuts, were about six feet, well built, and looked between the ages of thirty and forty. Short life span for an agent, she guessed.

Tom spread out a large pad on the coffee table with a diagram of the building.

Stanton leaned over the map. "We debated sending in a trained FBI agent in your place, Mrs. Chapman, but if you were familiar to any of them we—"

"No substitute. I'm going in. I don't want to give whoever is doing this a reason to shoot Craig. And, before you ask, I won't wear a wire. They'll find it and kill me and Craig."

All six men nodded, including Stanton, who was clearly the lead. "We agree. No wire, but we'll give you a cell phone with GPS on it."

She leaned back against the seat, but the thick tension in the air kept her alert. "Fine. Then what?"

"You'll take one of our cars to the site. We'll be...around. No one will know we're there."

This kidnapper seemed sharp and knew she was under the protection of the FBI. He'd suspect the agents would be strategically placed but out of sight, which meant they must have concocted some kind of escape route for her.

"And Jake? Where will he be?"

Jake took a hold of her hand and squeezed. "The less you know, the better."

She swallowed, not liking the way he wouldn't look at her, but she didn't argue. Jake would do what he thought best for both her and Craig.

Stanton hadn't factored in one thing. "What happens to my mother during this whole plan? I don't want anyone to go after her."

The tallest of the group raised his forefinger. "We've got that covered, ma'am. She'll be safe. No one will get to her."

Good. Her pulse slowed knowing someone was looking out for her.

Tom chugged the rest of his drink. "We all know what we're going to do. Let's get some shut eye and be back here by 0600 ready to rock and roll."

*   *   *

Despite cranking the heat to full blast in the unfamiliar sedan, her bones refused to warm up. Her fingers were stiff despite sweat dripping down the back of her neck. Nothing was working right. Not her mind, not her heart, nothing. She'd never been this scared in her life.

Take that back. Almost being burned to death came close, and then having a gun pointed at her chest certainly hadn't lowered her blood pressure any. Knowing she could turn back at any moment had her doubting her decision to be here until Craig's face entered her mind. He'd always been her baby brother. When he lost use of his legs after the accident, she'd been the one to hold him and care for him. She'd promised she'd take care of him no matter what.

The FBI agent's voice on the other end of her headset startled her. "Take your next right."

Even with the Bureau spread around the warehouse, Susan's nerves took a beating. She glanced at her hand gripping the wheel. The kidnapper's number hadn't washed off the skin, reminding her she could die today.

Jake's voice flashed in her head. What would her death do to him? Would he pine over her loss before moving on? Or would he fall apart? Like she'd do if he took a fatal bullet.

"You're almost there," the annoying, yet somehow comforting voice announced.

Tom had put a trace on the phone number she'd given them but had found nothing. He said the man probably tossed the pre-paid cell in the trash. It didn't matter now. She was here, ready to confront the bastard.

The large red brick warehouse loomed before her. Alone for the first time in days, or was it weeks, her vulnerability index shot through the roof. Could she leave the safety of the car and enter a building filled with men with submachine guns aimed at her? Was she willing to die today? Would her actions save her brother?

She prayed the answer was yes—to the second questions, not, God forbid, to the first.

"I'm turning off the phone now."

"Good luck, Mrs. Chapman."

She wanted to ask if she could speak with Jake, but in case the kidnappers were monitoring what she said, the team thought it better to restrict conversation.

If she had spoken to him, what would she have said? Be careful? Don't do anything foolish? Or would she have told him what was on her mind? That she loved him.

Better not to tell him that last bit. He had enough to think about. The next time she held him in her arms and ran her hands down his chest, she'd let him know how much he'd grown on her, how much he meant to her.

She wiped the moisture threatening to spill from her lids and pushed open the door. The morning sky was bright blue, clear and cold —innocuous and inviting but certainly not calming. The wind was nearly still, the ground white and pure. Some broken equipment lay buried under the winter blanket giving the area a look of abandonment.

She studied the pristine landscape. Some might call this moment of reflection something akin to procrastination, but that wasn't entirely true. She wanted to memorize the details in case she needed to escape later.

Bullshit.

Okay. Okay. She wanted to know how the kidnappers had entered the building? There weren't any tire tracks. Anywhere. Had they spent the night inside before the snow fell in earnest? If so, where were their cars? And how had they brought Craig inside?

Stop asking questions.

No doubt, someone was watching her. She didn't dare look up to the rooftops where she would hopefully find a hundred agents with guns trained on all the windows since she didn't want to give anything away.

Susan had promised she'd come alone. No cops. No friends. No one. He'd made sure to say, no Jake Yarnell. To her, his threat implied that's all the man wanted. Jake.

She believed she'd be facing daddy Francisco, a man who wanted revenge. Not for putting away his arch enemy, but for Jake killing his only son.

She had yet to figure out why he wanted the jurors dead in the first place, but she had more immediate issues to attend to.

Taking a large breath, she plowed ahead, her heart beating against her ribs, much too fast to provide her with a sense of calm. Who was she kidding? Not even her pinky had an ounce of calm. Her legs were leaden, her breath shallow, and her mind told her to run.

But she wouldn't. Couldn't. Too many lives—hers, Craig's, her mother's and Jake's—depended on her doing as the man instructed.

She reached the front of the building. The windowless front door was made of heavy metal, all rusty and paint chipped. She tugged on the handle and the door eased open. The temperature warmed slightly once she stepped inside. She wiped her nose—one bad effect of winter.

The dark interior corridor was lit with one small bulb so she waited a moment to allow her eyes to adjust to the darkness.

"Hello, Susan. I'm glad you came."

CHAPTER TWENTY-SIX

Susan shielded her eyes against the glare of the flashlight pointed at her face. Heart blasting, her feet stayed rooted to the floor. Her throat was too dry to talk, so she waited for further instructions, expecting at any moment to feel the piercing of a bullet.

"Come, come. I know you want to see your brother." He sounded friendly and encouraging, but she knew he was far from the grandfatherly type.

The flashlight swung about and hit the worn hardwood floors. The man holding the light had stooped shoulders and white hair, but he walked with a strong stride. They'd guessed right. He must be Joseph Francisco.

In her heart, she knew her brother's kidnapping wasn't about her. The fact he wanted Jake made her step slower and her heart sink a little further into her stomach. If she turned back now, they would kill her brother just for her act of defiance.

Go.

Putting one foot in front of the other, she followed behind the man of death. As soon as he turned left at the end of the hall and out of sight, the instinct to flee grabbed hold.

Don't give in. See that Craig is okay first.

Slow and steady, she studied the bare walls as she moved down the hall, hoping to learn something about why he'd picked this building. Not that it mattered, but examining the environment gave her something to do for the next few seconds until she learned her fate.

When she rounded the corner, she halted. Craig was in his own wheelchair, arms bound, mouth gagged, and eyes blindfolded. She nearly sank to her knees. She wanted to run to him and comfort him, but when one of his men took a step forward with his gun aimed at her chest, she remained by the entrance, mentally sending support to Craig.

"Craig?" Her voice came out sounding too thin—scared, weak, and helpless—when she wanted to be strong for him.

He grunted something through the dirty looking rag.

"What did you say?" She dragged her wet palms down her hips and turned an ear toward him.

He mumbled again. Had he recognized her voice? Did he think his mind was playing tricks on him? To him, she was dead.

She swallowed to get her tongue to work. "I'm alive, Craig. I hope they didn't hurt you."

Stupid thing to say, but the words she was usually good at formulating into eloquent sentences had evaporated.

Of course, he couldn't answer. All he could do was wiggle, shake, and grunt. From the motion of his head, he wanted her to run.

No way. "I'm going to help free you."

Three men, with semi-automatics, not big Uzi's as she'd expected, stepped closer in unison, as if some silent signal had been given.

"Check her," Francisco said. This time the steel in his voice would have crushed the hardest diamond.

She shifted her weight to her right leg and tilted her head, trying to act bored, praying they wouldn't see the need to search her. She held up her palms. "I'm not wired, guys, and I don't have a gun or any kind of weapon." She spread her arms wide as they approached. "I did exactly as you asked." True, the wonder phone was clipped to the belt at the small of her back, but maybe they wouldn't consider it a threat.

Her ploy didn't work. The fat one with the pimples must have drawn the long straw, for he patted her down, making sure to rub against her at every opportunity. He smelled of body odor, sharp and pungent. When he swiped his hand to her butt, he retrieved the phone.

"Got something."

"It's called a phone, dumbass." Crap. She hadn't meant to let the sarcastic retort slip out, but her sleep-deprived brain wasn't functioning very well.

The guard reared up and slapped her. Hard. She cried out, and then clamped her mouth shut, not wanting to give Mr. Francisco the satisfaction his man had hurt her. Bastard. Why did men have to hit her on her most vulnerable side? Blood trickled down her cheek, but she didn't attempt to wipe it away.

Craig struggled against his restraints. If he'd been able to walk, he would have done something heroic. Poor Craig.

"I'm fine, Craig."

Francisco waved his men to the other end of the hallway. "Let's go."

The fat, pimply man grabbed her by the arm and dragged her away from her brother.

"Craig, it's okay," she yelled behind her. Not that he could see her, but the clicking of her boot heels on the hardwood floor would clue him into her movement—away from him.

The harder she dug in her heels, the more pimple face tugged. She lost the battle. "Mr. Francisco, please." Oh, shit. She shouldn't have said his name. Now he'd have to kill her for knowing his identity.

The older man turned around and smiled, benevolent like, though she knew he was debating whether to order the hit right then.

"You have a request, Ms. Chapman?"

"Will you let my brother go? I did as you asked."

"Of course, just as soon as we get out of here."

Like she believed him.

Mr. Francisco gave one nod to her jailer. Something prinked her arm, and then her knees weakening a second before her body collapsed.

***

Jake checked the time on his cell five more times. Still nothing. No shots, no explosions, no Craig wheeling out of the building. Where the hell was Susan? Had they harmed her? He wanted to rush in and save the day but he understood the need to follow procedure.

He tapped his earpiece. "Anyone see anything?"

"The brother is in the middle of the room. Looks like he's alone." This must have come from one of the snipers on top of the roof across from the building.

"And Susan? Do you still see her?"

"No, sir. I did see her, but she's no longer in the main room."

Shit.

"Stanton, we have to go in." Jake's voice cracked, and his muscles bunched.

He pounded the steering wheel. The team had insisted he remain a block away. Dan Pritchard, some newbie punk agent, was in the car behind him—for his own protection Stanton had said.

"Don't do anything stupid, Jake. Hold on. We'll go in shortly. Without you. You hear?" His boss' tone came out demanding.

Fine. "Clear."

The windshield fogged and he turned down the heater. He wanted the cold to chill his body, to numb the flesh to the point where he had no sensation. If he lost Susan, he'd lose everything he wanted. She'd been difficult to handle at first, but once they worked together, the battling turned to banter, which turned to trust.

That was it. He trusted her to never leave him. Only now she had.

"Got the boy." Stanton's voice came in loud and clear.

Jake held his breath, waiting for word of Susan.

"Stanton?"

No answer.

"Stanton, what about Susan?" His heart rattled against his ribs, and the air sucked from his chest.

He opened his door, hoping to get a better feel for what was going on and to draw in some air.

"Jake. They're gone," Stanton finally reported. The clinical statement nearly froze him to the spot.

"I'm coming in."

He jumped out of the car without waiting for the go ahead. The probie behind him must not have gotten the word, for he took off after Jake. Jake looked over his shoulder and slowed, his leg not ready to work overtime. He shouted at the man gaining speed. "I've been given the all clear to enter."

The man looked doubtful as he slowed. It would only take a minute for the kid to learn he wasn't lying.

Once Jake reached the door, he drew his weapon in case it was a trap. He eased inside and waited for the kid to join him. Jake held a finger to his lips the moment Pritchard entered.

Jake led the way down the long corridor. Seconds later he rounded the corner and saw five agents surrounding the boy in the wheelchair. He scoured the large room but Susan was nowhere in sight.

He raced up to Stanton and grabbed his arm. "Where are they?"

"We don't know. They didn't climb out the windows, and we've checked every exit."

"They have to be somewhere."

Stanton crouched in front of Craig. "Did you see where your sister went?"

"That was really her?" His eyes widened as his mouth lifted into a smile.

"Yes. Susan is alive."

He wiped a tear from his cheek. "I can't believe it. They blind-folded me, so I can't be sure. One minute they're standing around me, and the next, they hightailed away from me. Then you guys barged in about two minutes later. I thought I was a goner."

Jake didn't need to hear anymore. He raced to the back of the room. The only door there led to a large closet with no egress. Where the hell had were they?

The Traynor's cellar flashed in his mind. There had to be a hidden door and a hidden tunnel to somewhere. He placed his palms on the walls, hoping to find a switch. He pressed, pounded and pushed. No luck.

"Damn it."

Stanton called from the other room. "You find something in there?"

Jake stepped out of the closet. "No. I was hoping for some kind of hidden door. There has to be something we can't see."

Stanton flipped a switch on his phone. "Chuck, do a perimeter search for any exit doors." He pressed a different number on the walkie-talkie. "Bill?"

"I'm here."

"Search any cars leaving the area."

"Will do."

Jake appreciated his boss' forward thinking, but he needed an activity to focus on. "You going to dust the place for prints?"

"Already called Trip. He and his team will be here shortly but don't get your hopes up. I'll call Tom and ask him to pull up the construction plans of the area to see if there's a tunnel going somewhere." Stanton took one step and knelt down. "Looks like blood."

Craig wheeled around. "Some jerk slapped her pretty hard."

Stanton nodded. "She had a cut on her face. Maybe the hit made her bleed. We'll check it out."

Jake stepped closer to his boss and kept his voice low. "You know this kidnapping might have nothing to do with the jurors' deaths and everything to do with the fact I killed Francisco's son."

"It's possible, but we don't know Francisco is behind this mess."

"Think about it. Francisco's son killed at least one juror, and probably more. I don't think Dominick was bright enough to orchestrate these kills. He had to have help."

"Good point."

His heart lightened. "Do you now believe that Peter Caravello had nothing to do with any of the jurors' deaths?" He wanted his friend to be innocent. The betrayal might kill him.

Stanton stared at Jake for a split second too long. "Probably not, but what was he doing with Janet Starkey's wallet in his house?"

"He was framed."

Stanton cocked one eye. "By whom? And why?"

The tumblers in his mind clicked into place, but he didn't want to toss out his theory just yet. "Couldn't say." He shuffled his feet. "You need me to do anything?"

"No. Go home and rest."

He'd go but rest wouldn't be on his mind.

Half way to the door, Stanton called after him. "Jake?"

He glanced over his shoulder. "Yeah?"

"If anyone calls you, don't play hero. Let us handle the details."

He held Stanton's stare. "I won't do anything stupid."

"Cross the line and it'll be your job."

Jake's fist clenched. He wanted to flip his boss the bird. Instead, he strode away, his blood pounding in his head.

***

Throbbing pain thudded in Susan's head. Where was she? She couldn't see anything, but one thing she knew. It was cold as a bitch. Her eyes felt as if she'd fallen face first into a sand pit, and her body ached even worse than after the explosion. Her muscles were leaden and her throat raw and dry.

How had she gotten here? And when?

She searched her memory. Craig had been held captive, guns had been pointed at her, and then she'd be given a needle in her neck.

She'd been drugged. Francisco's cruel face and pimple face's pawing made her skin crawl. Susan blinked, trying to see something. Why was it so dark? Her breath came out fast and her heart beat even harder. Bile shot up her throat and goose bumps spread over her body as fear threatened to rob her of all thought. She fought the tears brimming on her lids.

"Craig?" She prayed he was somewhere near.

Nothing but the wind whipping around her small cave answered her. She shivered and drew in a breath. The stench of fertilizer made her cough. Was she in a shed? Or in a dumpster?

What did it matter? Wherever she was, freedom was her goal.

Reality pressed in on her. If she didn't get out soon, she'd die of exposure.

A wave of nausea blasted her, and her body swayed as her mind clouded. *Move.* She struggled to rise to her knees, but as she tried to press her hands on the ground, she failed. Someone had bound her hands and feet. Shit. Not again. She twisted her body right and left to loosen the ropes, but the jerky movement tore at her wrists and ankles. Blood dripped down her palms.

This bastard was not going to win.

Determined to do whatever it took to escape, Susan worked to undo her bindings, but after what seemed like half an hour, she had made no progress to free herself.

Instead of trying to undo the bindings, she tucked her legs under her butt and rocked to stand. Dizzy. Weary. And oh so cold. If she could reach a door handle, she could reach freedom. To what though, she didn't know.

Kneeling, Susan leaned against the side of the small building and swayed back and forth until she landed on her feet. Using all her energy, she half stood. Splinters sliced through her skin as she slid up the side wall. While she couldn't see her body, from the scraping on her shoulder and back, she was naked. Dear God. Had she been sexually assaulted?

It was too cold to tell, but she pushed her thoughts away from the atrocity and focused on finding some way to escape.

With her back to the wall, she edged around the confinement. Her knees buckled and she slammed back into the hard floor. Shit. Determined not to let the bastard get his way, she tried again. Standing took so much effort, but what choice did she have?

Her eyes had finally adjusted to the darkness. Thin slits of light eked their way through the wooden slats, allowing her to tell where a door might be. As she reached her destination, her hand brushed against cold metal. Yes, but when she pushed down on the latch and leaned against the door, the damn thing wouldn't budge. Locked or blocked, she couldn't get out. She slowly sank to the floor and let the pity take over.

She shivered and sobbed, but the warm tears nearly froze on her cheeks.

A creak outside caught her attention, and her muscles tensed. Was the killer coming for her? She debated beating against the wall to attract attention, but what if he was coming to see if she had died?

She stilled, and as she forced her breaths to slow, her mind lost focus. When the door didn't open, she decided the noise was only from a car going by in the distance.

"Help!"

She slammed her feet against the opposite wall to make a racket. Her frozen feet had no sensation. She pounded and yelled until her throat turned hoarse.

Out of energy, she slumped against the wall. Her toes were numb, her body no longer shivered, and each breath came out slower and slower. Susan tried to count backwards from one hundred, but couldn't remember anything below ninety-two. Her mind clouded, and she closed her eyes, too tired to struggle.

Her last thought was that she'd never see Jake again.

CHAPTER TWENTY-SEVEN

As soon as Peter opened his front door, Jake stepped inside without a word, and snow flurries followed him in. He stomped into the living room and turned around.

His friend planted a hand on his shoulder. "Susan was kidnapped? What happened?"

He jerked out of Peter's grasp. He couldn't handle pity right now. "Yes. She just disappeared."

"Disappeared? Or was kidnapped?"

"Both."

Peter stepped back. "When?"

"This morning."

A lithe, pixyish girl rushed in from the kitchen. She wiped her hands on her apron. "You must be Jake. I've heard a lot about you. Nice to finally see you in person."

Peter pulled the woman to his side. "Jake, this is Maria Francisco."

"Maria." He wasn't in the mood for socializing even though he was curious about Joseph Francisco's daughter.

Peter led Maria back to the sofa. "How did they get to Susan with you hovering over her all the time?"

Guilt crashed down on him. He told Peter and Maria about Susan's phone call to her mom, and the phone call she'd made to the perpetrator. "She voluntarily went into this warehouse at eight this morning to save her brother."

Veins bulged in Peter's neck. "You let her go in by herself? Are you fuckin' crazy?"

Jake held up his hands. "She wouldn't listen to reason." God only knew he should have stopped her and thought of some other way to free her brother without her jeopardizing her life. "Stanton and about five other agents came up with a plan that sounded foolproof."

"Stanton was part of this insanity? The FBI never substitutes one hostage for another. Why'd he let her go in alone? I hope she was armed or at least wired."

Jake stabbed a hand over his bald head. "She's stubborn. No to the weapons or the wire. She had a cell phone with a GPS, but they left the phone behind."

"I didn't think a prosecuting attorney would be so stupid—or careless. Didn't she care about her life?"

Jake winced. He was the one who understood the danger but had done nothing to stop her. Her passion for her brother had swayed him. If Peter had been kidnapped, he'd have done the same thing.

"We had snipers at every window and had the place surrounded. There was no way anyone could have snuck out of the warehouse. Every exit was covered." His rationalization sounded lame even to him.

His lips curled. "But apparently they did. I'm sorry. Do you want a drink?"

"Scotch. On the rocks." Beer wouldn't help quell the fury that burned through him.

Had the situation not been so serious, he would have smiled, picturing Susan's disdainful face when he first asked for a beer in the townhouse. What he wouldn't give to see her frown again.

Peter strode over to the wet bar, made a tall drink, and handed him the glass. "Sit down and start talking."

Jake wanted to pace, to think, but he might drive them crazy. He reigned in his panic and did as Peter asked.

Maria spoke up. "Do the FBI have any suspects?"

"Nothing solid." In fact, they had zip. He wasn't ready to propose his number one suspect.

Peter stabbed a glance at Maria then back at Jake. "Start from the top and tell us everything—in detail. Maybe there are similarities to what happened to me." Peter always was the straight shooting kind, though when had he been kidnapped? Jake didn't have time to ask.

"Craig, that's Susan's brother, said two men came to his house trying to sell him insurance. They were dressed in nice suits even. When he told them he wasn't interested, they barged in anyway and sedated him. When he came to, he was in the warehouse, tied down, blindfolded, and gagged."

Maria's mouth gaped open, and she leaned back into the sofa, her mind obviously searching for some reasonable explanation. "I'm so sorry that happened to Susan, and to her brother. With the death of her best friend, I'm sure she's still reeling."

"Yes, she is." He guessed Peter hadn't told her about the fire or being chased in the woods.

Peter waved his nearly empty glass. "You're the goddamn FBI. There had to be tracks of some kind outside the building leading somewhere. Did you check the whole warehouse?"

"Of course. We even have Tom searching the plans now for some kind of escape tunnel."

Peter spun around and took a seat next to Maria. "I'm sorry. I know your team has done everything possible to find Susan."

Jake stood, his legs needing to rid his body of the agitation clawing at him. He paced while the other two stared off into space. He needed suggestions, needed support. The tension in the room was nearly choking him.

Jake stopped in front of Maria. "Did your father tell you how Dominick died?" He held his breath, fearing she didn't know about the circumstances of his death.

Her eyes widened briefly, and then she looked down at her fingers before entwining her hand through Peter's. "Yes, he said Dom was at a liquor store when a robber came in. When my brother tried to take the guy down, the man shot and killed him before escaping."

Jesus. "Did you believe your dad?"

She glanced at Peter before returning her gaze to Jake. "What are you trying to say? That my brother was involved in something unethical and was murdered as a result?"

Jake planted his feet wide apart. "Close." He wasn't sure how much she needed to know, but the only way Peter wouldn't hate him for life was if he gave her the needed background. "I'm not sure if you want to know what really happened. I was there when Dom died."

Even Peter's eyes widened.

Her lips thinned, but her back straightened slightly. "I am aware my brother was no saint, but maybe it's time I take my head out of the sand. Tell me what he did. Father never would discuss his business or Dom's part in it."

She leaned forward, her jaw clenched.

"Your brother was responsible for at least one of the deaths of the jurors who presided over Peter's father's trial."

Her eyes lost their focus, and her cheeks sagged before a wistful smile lifted. "You know when he was home, he was a wonderful person." She lifted her face to him. "I always knew he had a cruel streak, but do I believe he'd kill in cold blood? No. I don't believe you."

Sad. Bursting someone's bubble hurt him almost as much as it would hurt her. Jake needed to better understand her relationship with Dominick. "And when your brother was not home? Did you know anything about where he went, what he did?" Or was she left totally in the dark?

"Not really." She bit her bottom lip. "I never wanted to know. Oh, I asked, but I might as well have tried to steal the gold out of Fort Knox." She locked her gaze with his. "Tell me straight. It's time I learn the truth about my family. I've heard stories, but Dad said they were lies."

Jake decided it best to leave out the part about her father bringing in women from Russia and Eastern Europe to sell them into prostitution. "A man by the name of Ronnie Stenoff tried to kill me when we were hiding out in my friend's cabin in West Virginia." He tapped his leg. "He stabbed me, but I managed to escape through an underground tunnel that led us into the woods. Your brother caught up with us and held Susan at gunpoint. I was off talking with Ronnie when he took her. She screamed, and when I came up behind him, he swung around, shot at me and missed, thank God. That's when I took him down."

He expected her to scream or toss out some accusations. Instead she nodded. "He would have killed her?"

She believed him. His relief weakened his legs. "Yes."

"Then he deserved to die." Her voice came out flat, distant, and empty.

"I agree."

Discussing Dom's death wouldn't get him any closer to finding Susan. He squatted in front of Maria to get her attention. "How angry was your father when he learned Dom had died?"

She wiped a tear from her face. "I never saw him cry, if that's what you're asking."

"Did he call the police to find out what happened? Demand retribution for the person who killed his son?" *Did he want to come after me?*

"I don't think so. He said he received a call late at night. I was working the late shift and didn't find out about Dom until early the next morning. He must have come to grips with the death by then."

"Or knew something bad could happen to his son at any moment and had expected the call for years," Jake mumbled.

"Maybe."

She dropped her face into her hands, and Peter rubbed circles on her back. When she looked up, red streaked her cheeks. "When he told me about Dom, he seemed more angry than distraught. But I saw hope in his eyes too. I can't explain it."

Hope? "And your sister-in-law? How did she take her husband's death?"

"Helena?" Maria wiped her cheeks dry. "Upset, of course, but I think she was a little bit relieved, though she'd never tell me that. From my prospective, Dom mentally abused her, and had since the day they were married. She did whatever he told her to do. The only time she was happy was when he was out of town."

Not surprising, killers weren't able to live double lives very well. Someone had to pay the price. "I kind of figured your father would be out for my head." His fists tightened.

Peter took a long drink. "Why? Because you killed his only son? The person he'd groomed to take over the business?"

To the point Peter. "Yeah, something like that."

Peter squeezed Maria's hand. "Sweetheart, we've got to get inside the Francisco compound and look for Susan."

Relief nearly drained him. Peter understood where he was heading with his line of questions.

She jerked her hand out of his grasp, and Jake backed out of the way.

"You think my father had something to do with kidnapping the man in the wheelchair and taking Susan?"

"Think about it," Peter said. "Someone framed me for that juror's death. Maybe your father knows about us."

Her gaze shifted right, then left. "No way. I've been really careful. He couldn't know."

Jake didn't need to get in the middle of a debate. "If he is innocent, Maria, then he shouldn't mind us taking a quick look around the place. Not Peter, of course. Just me and a few of my men."

She jumped off the sofa and raced over to the wet bar, her trembling back to them. She picked up a glass and twirled it around before placing it back down. She faced them. "Okay, but if I let you in, Dad will want to know how you even knew me. I can't exactly introduce you as Peter's friend."

Jake tapped his injured thigh and tossed her an easy smile. "We'll say you were my nurse in the hospital when my stab wound became infected. Do you think your father knows about Ronnie Stenoff's arrest?"

When she quirked a brow, he explained again. "Dom's partner?" Had she even understood his explanation?

"Right. Partner." She glanced over at Peter. "How about if I bring Jake home as my new boyfriend?"

"No. If he's been following this mess, he'll know who I am."

She pressed her lips together. "I'll give you the code to the gate. You can come at night when Dad's asleep and look around. I'll draw you a sketch of the rooms. He doesn't even have to know you've been inside." She picked up her purse, took out a large set of keys, and unhooked one of them. "This gets you into the back door, but please be quiet."

Her action was more than he'd expected. He took the key. "Thank you. You nor your father will know we've been there."

"If I thought you'd find anything, I wouldn't let you in. I'm sure my father didn't take Susan. I've been all over the house."

While he'd never been to the Francisco household, he'd seen online photos of the estate. There was more than one building on the premise. "Are the other buildings locked?"

"The storage shed might be, but I don't have a key. I know the large garage that houses the antique cars is locked and only Dad has the combination."

Entry into the house was more than he'd hoped, but the possibility he'd keep Susan hostage in the main building where his grandchildren or daughter could find her was slim. Still, he had to try.

He waved the key. "I'll leave this outside the back door when I leave."

"Dad stays up late. I'll turn off the alarm at two a.m., and I'll reset the system at four. Will that give you and your team enough time to search?"

"Plenty."

***

Susan woke up, groggy and disoriented. Her teeth had stopped chattering and her shoulders weren't shivering. The full realization hit her. Her body wasn't able to keep her warm anymore, which meant she was going to die soon.

If she didn't attempt to get out of this hellhole, she'd never see Jake again—or her mother or brother. Her father always praised her ability never to quit, and she wouldn't let him down now.

Only nothing would move. She squeezed her eyes shut and imagined lifting her feet and wiggling her fingers. Straining to move the dead limbs, she twisted her head back and forth.

That's it. Move the head, then work my way down my body.

Little by little, circulation returned here and there, but the pain burned through her blood. She was able to rock a little. Eventually, she managed to shrug her shoulders. Better, much better. Her toes wouldn't respond, but she kept active the parts that would move.

She bent her knees and almost cried out from the effort. In what seemed like hours, she put each body part in motion, except for her toes.

The handle above her head jangled, and her breath stopped in her throat. The door opened and silhouetted against the house light stood a man. She blinked to see his face, but the shadow obscured his features. The cold air stabbed at her body, and she bucked to roll over.

"What the hell?" he said.

CHAPTER TWENTY-EIGHT

Stanton motioned for Pritchard to check Francisco's shed and for Dalton to search the barn with the antique cars. Stanton and he would look through the main house.

Once Jake unlocked the back door, they slipped on gloves and surgical booties. They didn't need to leave traces of dirt and snow throughout the house, announcing someone had been there. He didn't think Maria was leading them into a trap, but to be sure, they withdrew their weapons. One never knew when Joseph Francisco would decide to come down for a midnight snack.

They'd already figured out who would search where. With strong-beamed lights in hand, they combed both floors. Jake took the second floor. He'd memorized which rooms belonged to Joseph, Helena, the two kids, and Maria. While the mansion was large, there wasn't much to search up there, other than a few hall closets.

Maria had told him the attic entrance was through the master bedroom—in Joseph's room. He'd wake Francisco for sure if went past his bed and pulled down the attic door. Until they found proof Susan had been there, they wouldn't be able to get a warrant to search all of the premises. While they had two hours, Jake didn't need more than fifteen minutes to be convinced she wasn't upstairs. He joined Stanton downstairs in the den.

"Anything?" Jake kept his voice low.

"Desk's locked, but no."

They'd already looked through the kitchen when they arrived. "I didn't expect he'd keep her here. Let's see what the other two are up to."

Stanton led the way. Jake locked the back door and placed the key next to the mat, as promised.

He stuffed the surgical boots in his pocket, and as he took off toward the back of the property, the cold air raced down his throat and nearly stole his breath. If Susan were outside in this mess, she wouldn't last long. He guessed the temp was nearing twenty degrees.

A garden shed, the large garage, a pool house, and accompanying cabana, were the only other buildings on the property.

"You take the pool house," Jake said, and Stanton took off toward the garden shed.

Jake met up with the other two agents. The moonlight was enough to show neither had found her. Damn it. Desperation clawed at him. Joseph Francisco was guilty. He knew it. Only where was he keeping her?

The pool house was unlocked, lessening the chance he'd find her there. But if the purpose of the kidnapping had been to lure him out in the open, Susan would be kept unharmed, and that fact kept him sane.

Maria had shut off the alarms for two hours, but did one system go for all buildings? Damn. He should have thought to ask.

Jake was as quiet as possible when he searched the closets as well as any piece of furniture large enough to hold a person captive.

"Anything?"

Jake swiveled around, his pulse racing. Stanton. "No."

"Let's regroup."

Shit. Where had he taken her?

*****

Joseph stood at his bedroom window with a smile on his face. Jake Yarnell was smart, but he'd never find Susan. Oh, he'd see her all right, but only when he wanted her to be seen. He wanted Yarnell tormented, knowing he was helpless to help her. Ripping someone out of your arms was akin to death. He knew that when Dom had been taken from him. He wasn't even sure he wanted to live anymore.

But he did have a replacement—his own flesh and blood to take Dominick's place. Maybe he'd even let James help decide how long to keep Yarnell on the edge. When Yarnell reached that certain level of desperation, he'd give the man a call and tell him how to find the girl. He never would come out and say if he'd kept her alive.

Speaking of calls, he needed to make one. It was time to move Susan. Then he'd decide how he would punish Maria for turning against him.

***

Remaining still, Susan let her senses react to the surroundings that were fresh, perfumed, and wonderfully warm. She remembered someone picking her up from that horrible place and carrying her into a house, but she couldn't visualize what the man looked like other than he had strong arms. It hadn't been Jake, she'd been sure of that, but who was he?

Had the kidnapper dumped her in some random shed and her banging had alerted the owner? That explanation seemed to be the only logical one, but why hadn't her rescuer called 9-1-1. He had to have noticed she was naked and possibly assaulted. She hadn't been raped, if the lack of burning between her thighs was any indication, but from the stitches on her face and her exposure to the freezing cold, he had to understand she needed help.

She was inside now, and that's all that mattered. Or had she had been checked out by a paramedic and declared okay without her knowledge? If so, wouldn't they keep her overnight at a hospital for observation? Since she didn't have any identification on her, the hospital should notify the police. The FBI surely would have put some kind of alert on her disappearance, and once Jake learned where she was, he'd come running. Her breath slowed and her stomach calmed.

But only for a moment. What if there had been no medic, no police to ask her questions, and most importantly, no Jake?

She wiggled her butt. A soft mattress was underneath her and lots of blankets on top. With her bonds cut, her muscles slowly relaxed. She rubbed her wrists and met bandages. Her savor must have doctored her. She wiggled her feet, but the circulation still hadn't returned. Despite the added comfort, cold was deeply imbedded in her pours. She doubted she'd ever be warm again.

She scanned the rather large room. Dawn was streaming in through luxurious sheer curtains. This might not be heaven, but she was sure the mysterious place was nearby.

There were two twin beds, a desk and a comfortable seating area. Given the personal pictures on the walls, she wasn't in a hotel room, so where was she?

She took one more sweep of the room, hoping there'd be a phone. No luck. Damn it. She needed to let Jake know she was safe. Crap. She didn't even know his number. If she ever got the chance, she'd call 9-1-1 and have them patch her through to the FBI.

Using her elbows to push up, Susan dragged her body to a sitting position. The sheet fell down, exposing her chest. She glanced down. Someone had draped her in a men's shirt, starched and smelling of lemons. Her fingers shot to her hips and met soft flannel. She lifted the covers. Men's pajama bottoms. Glory be.

Who was this man? And why hadn't he come in to see how she was doing? The room's light was growing stronger, so surely, he'd be in soon.

Susan dragged her legs off the side of the bed and placed her feet on the floor but couldn't sense the thick carpet. Once she warmed up, she'd get feeling back in her legs. Right? Her belly soured at the thought she might lose some appendage from exposure. Using her thumb and forefinger, she squeezed her thigh and yelped at the sharp sensation. As she worked her way down her leg, the numbness increased. At least her knees had blood flow.

Move. Check out the place.

Given the height of the trees outside the window, she was at least on the second floor. Escape out the window was not an option. Then again, why escape until after she had spoken with the owner to find out his intent?

Not sure if she could stand, she held onto the bedpost as she lifted up. Her knees buckled and one knee smacked the floor. Shit. Her hand loosened from the post, and she caught herself before she did a face plant. Not good.

She decided crawling was her safest option. The door wasn't more than twelve feet away. She could make it that far.

Susan crawled across the room, reached up, and twisted the knob.

It was locked. Why? She didn't like the implication, but she wanted to believe the worst was over, and that she just didn't have enough facts to draw the right conclusion.

Given she had little to lose, she pounded on the door, not caring if she woke up the whole household. She needed answers, but no one showed up to answer her please. She placed her ear to the door but heard no sounds—no clanking of coffee cups or feet stirring.

Okay. She'd at least use the bathroom before waiting until the household awoke. Her knees stung, but she managed to work her way across the room. Once in the bathroom, she locked the door and sat on her butt, her knees near her chest. The cold tiles did little to help her thaw, but the added layer of safety of the locked door between her and the outside world did a lot for her mental well-being.

Back up on her knees, she reached the faucet and gulped down handfuls of water.

Feet pounded down the hallway and into the bedroom. Her muscles stiffened.

Someone stood outside the bathroom and knocked. "Susan? Are you in there?"

Her breath caught in her throat. How did he know her name? She'd been naked and had no identification on her. Oh, shit.

***

Jake's cell roused him from a deep sleep. His hand patted the side table for the phone. Would Susan's kidnapper call this early?

A quick burst of adrenaline woke him, and he pressed the On button, recognizing the familiar number.

"Hi, Peter, what's up?"

"Listen, Maria and I are going out of town for a while. I have to stay in the state because of the ongoing investigation, but I can't take any chances something will happen to her."

He didn't need to add, like Susan.

"Sure, that's a good idea." Why was there such desperation in his voice?

"I just wanted you to know."

The dial tone rang in his ear before he had a chance to respond.

That was odd. His friend was obviously in a hurry. Jake wet his lips and eased out of bed. His head pounded from stress and lack of deep sleep.

The clock told him it was only six thirty in the morning. What had possessed Peter to call him at this hour? Why not wait to call until he reached his destination?

His muscles tensed. Was his friend being threatened? If so, by whom? Nothing would make sense until he took a shower since he needed time to sort things through.

The pulsating water marginally eased the pain thudding through his body. At this point, Susan had been gone close to twenty-four hours. He wished he could steal her pain from her or at least share the burden she was experiencing. She'd already been through too much.

He refused to believe she wasn't alive. She had to be.

Whoever was behind all this mess wanted him, not Susan, and he'd gladly exchange places with her if he could.

His mind raced too fast, and his shower lasted only three minutes, much shorter than his usual morning ritual. He towel dried, changed, and headed into his small office. He booted up the computer, in need of more research on Joseph Francisco.

He clicked on his email and fifteen messages loaded. The one from Peter caught his eye. The subject read: James.

The time was late last night, and he read the contents. Then he read it out loud, hoping he'd missed something.

Jake. Got off the phone with James. I know, I'm surprised too that he called. When was the last time we communicated? I forgot to tell you the bombshell Maria and I were told a few days ago. Apparently, my mother had an affair with Joseph Francisco. She became pregnant and spawned James. I confronted my brother about this a few days ago. He said Dad had told him about the affair the night before he was executed.

Here's the strange part. James was asked by Joseph to kidnap Susan. He refused and decided then and there he wanted nothing to do with any of the Franciscos. Can't say I blame him.

Jake's gaze latched onto Susan's name. He wasn't sure if he should be happy at the clue or panicked at the confirmation Joseph Francisco had her.

He read further.

James said he wants to "make up." Can you believe that shit? Maria and I decided to get the hell out of dodge for a few days. I need time to sort through things. I know you'll understand.

Stay safe.

Peter

Jake wasn't sure what it was about the letter that didn't ring true. He read it once more, looking for some clue why he wrote instead of calling. Sure, he was in a hurry this morning, but they'd often called each other in the middle of the night if something important came up.

Regardless, the news about James being Francisco's son stunned Jake. James must have gone crazy when he found out. Was all this killing and kidnapping some kind of revenge scheme? Against who though? If he'd been James, he would have been angry with Joseph Caravello for not telling him sooner.

If James had been responsible for some of these deaths, had he embraced Dominick as his brother and was willing to work with him? Or had he washed his hands of the Franciscos the day he found out he was his son?

No facts to back up any of the idle speculation, Jake went in search of coffee.

While the cup heated, he printed out the email, hoping a fresh eye could spot something he missed.

The coffee did little to settle his turbulent mind though. He bundled up against the driving snow and headed outside to his car. If he didn't find Susan soon, she might not live long enough for him to tell her he loved her.

***

Susan scooted backwards as the door bowed inward from the pounding.

"Unlock the door." At first, his voice was pleading. Now he sounded royally pissed.

"Who are you?"

"The person who saved you, God dammit. Don't make me break down my own door."

He would. "Okay."

The man could always shoot his way in, and the bathroom wasn't big enough for her to safely hide.

Rolling onto her sore knees, Susan flipped the lock upward, and then pulled open the door. Her heart stuck in her throat when she recognized him. "You?"

He held out his hand, his face softening. "Look, I'm sorry. It's a long story, so why don't you come down for breakfast and I'll tell you what happened."

The food part sounded good, as did the more information part. Could she eat the food? If he wanted her dead, he'd have already poisoned her. "Okay, but I can't walk. My feet are too numb."

"Do you think a bath would help?"

Was he kidding? "A bath sounds wonderful." Maybe he was on the up-and-up. According to Jake, Peter was innocent. Maybe his brother was too.

"Can you run the water yourself?"

Maybe she'd totally misjudged this man. Hell, she'd thought Jake was a killer at one time. Susan definitely needed to work on her people skills. "Yes."

His gaze slipped to the right. "Take a bath, and I'll have food ready when you're done."

He spun around and left before she had a chance to say thank you.

She wasn't sure she could get into the tub without help, but she sure as hell would try. She ran her hands over her feet to massage them. The skin was cold but not so dead that she didn't feel anything.

Filling the tub with warm, not hot water, might help ease the transition from frozen to normal. Not wanting him to come in, Susan locked the door again. Not that James Caravello hadn't seen her naked, but why tempt fate? She couldn't remember if he was married, but if he had a wife, he bet she would have provided something more feminine for Susan to wear.

With effort, she eased into the sudsy water. Her feet stung as the blood raced through her veins, but she welcomed the pain as the rewarming meant one step closer to recovery. Not wanting to piss off James by keeping him waiting, she stayed in long enough to stop shivering before she eased out. This time when she stood, her legs held her, and relief washed over her. She'd have breakfast, and then she'd ask to borrow James' phone to contact Jake.

Once dressed in her pajamas, she inched her way across the room, but her toes were still not responding well. Noise from the kitchen and the aroma of strong coffee made the direction evident.

James was at the kitchen counter with a pile of scrambled eggs and English muffins beside him. He looked up and smiled.

"You're looking much better."

"Yes, thank you. The bath helped." She scooted onto the stool next to him. Her chest and face wound needed some bandages, but she'd cover her injuries once she returned home.

Home. The next time she saw Jake, she'd tell him how she felt, and once Joseph Francisco was behind bars, maybe she and Jake could actually go on a date without having to look over their shoulders.

He slid a cup of coffee toward her. "Sugar and cream over there."

She took a sip. "Mmm." She'd eat, and then find out how he'd found her. "The eggs are delicious, thank you."

He merely nodded as she filled her belly. It was time to learn how she'd come to his house.

"Did you hear my banging on the shed door? Is that how you found me?"

"Actually the dog found you. As if on cue, the pup trotted back inside and barked up a storm. I'm surprised you don't remember him."

A half-filled dog dish sat in the corner, confirming his story. "How did I end up on your property?"

"Peter, my brother, I found out, has been in cahoots with Joseph Francisco. In fact, he plans on marrying his daughter."

Maria. This was not the story Jake said Peter told him. "Are you saying he kidnapped me and tossed me into your shed?"

"Yes, hoping to frame me. He always wanted to take over Dad's business and was jealous of me." He drained the rest of his coffee. "Only you were supposed to die. He figured that when the gardener discovered your body the next day and called the police, I would be accused of the murder."

The news overwhelmed her. Here, she'd thought Peter was the good son and James the bad. Where did Jake fit into this scheme? "Did Peter tell you all of this?"

A noise sounded behind her. She turned around and gasped. A man wearing a ski mask, dressed all in black, came at her.

"I see she didn't die after all."

Peter?

James jumped up from the stool and lunged at the intruder. The masked man punched James in the gut, who then stumbled backwards and hit his back against the refrigerator. Before she could get even get off the stool to escape, the masked man took two steps toward her and stabbed a needle in her neck.

Not again. The airflow stopped, and her eyes rolled back into her head.

CHAPTER TWENTY-NINE

The team didn't have squat. After they met with a dead end at the Francisco house, they weren't sure which way to turn. Stanton sat at the head of the large conference table. Tom, William Burroughs and Nancy Darden faced Jake. The missing seat, usually occupied by Richard Thomason remained empty. Jake wasn't ready to address his anger toward the man who started all this mess, nor was he wasn't ready to say he was glad Richard was dead, but the person in charge of finding safe houses for witnesses should have found help the moment his wife and children were threatened.

Twelve people died because of him. Twelve people who were doing their civic duty, who had families who loved them. Life might not be fair, but the deaths could have been avoided.

"You said Peter emailed you this morning?" T-Squared interrupted his internal rant.

His friend was the only one who'd met Peter and understood the childhood connection between them.

"Yes."

Jake passed out a copy of the email to the team and studied their reactions. Tom's eyes widened, whereas Stanton adjusted his tie, a sure sign of agitation and frustration. Nancy clasped a hand to her chest. William sat stone-faced as if he'd known the information all along.

Stanton looked up. "Any suggestions on how we should proceed? Jake, according to Richard's research, you've been friends with the Caravellos for years. How do you interpret this email?"

Shit. He hadn't wanted his background exposed in this manner. Now they'd reconsider his involvement with the jurors' deaths. The TV commercial where the guy wanted a Twix to stall for time flashed in his mind.

"I knew Peter well, but James wasn't around much when I was at the Caravello's."

"Can you give us a personality sketch of James?"

What to say, what to say. Jake's phone vibrated at his hip. This was his disposable phone and only Peter and Tom had the number. He pulled his cell from his pocket and checked the number. All it said was Out of Area.

"If you'll excuse me."

He pushed back his chair and raced out. As the door to the room swung close, William mumbled something that was probably derogatory.

Was this the kidnapper asking for a ransom? "Hello?"

The voice came out distorted. "You have ten minutes to get to Peter's house if you want to see Susan and Peter alive. Bring even one FBI agent and I swear, I'll kill them both. My men are scouting the whole area and will know if you try to pull any tricks."

He was sure his heart had stopped beating, and no air went into his lungs. Even if Jake had wanted to answer, he'd lost his voice. Then the dial tone rang loud and clear.

A hand clasped on his shoulder. "You okay?"

Stanton. Shit. If he did as the killer asked, he'd be breaking all Bureau protocol. He'd lose his job and be thrown out of the only home he'd ever known—the FBI. Being jobless would suck, but his actions might save Susan. And Peter.

Oh, shit. Would he end up like the chicken-shit Richard, thinking if he just did what the killer asked, all would be okay?

Jake pulled up every ounce of control he had and faced his boss. "It's my aunt. She was in a car accident. I have to go to the hospital."

Stanton watched him for a long minute. Nine minutes left. Even if he raced out of the building and into his car right now, he might not make it to Peter's in time—especially in this storm.

"I didn't know you had an aunt."

"She's old. She was the one who refused to take me in when Mom died." That part of the story was true.

Stanton stepped back. "Hurry back. We need you. And give me the damn number of your new cell." His gaze shot to the phone in his hand.

"Sure. 555-2385."

Stanton rushed over to an empty desk, ripped off a piece of paper from the pad and wrote down the number. "2395?"

Stay cool. Ten seconds won't matter. "2385."

"Keep in touch."

"Will do."

Once he ducked into his office to grab his coat, the urge to run nearly toppled him. Jake strode, guessing that if his aunt were in the hospital, his rushing made sense.

The moment he pushed open the front door, his heart sank. White blanketed the ground. Not that Virginia didn't have snow, but blizzards weren't all that common. How could he get to Peter's in less than seven minutes? It was impossible. But that wasn't going to stop him from trying.

His car needed new tires, but they should hold up for the eight-mile drive. Considering the crappy conditions, he prayed the morning commuters would stay home today. Jake slid in and cranked up the engine. Nothing. He slammed his hand against the wheel and worked the key again, and the engine caught on the third try. Breath back into his body, he drove off.

The roads around Quantico were clear, but when he hit the first road that wasn't heavily traveled, the snow was a good inch deep. Jake hit an ice patch, turned toward the skid, and slowed down. He wished his heart would do the same.

Racing to Peter's would only cause him to get in an accident. Jake needed to call the bastard back, to tell him he was on his way—alone.

He punched the redial number while keeping his gaze on the road. The windshield wipers barely kept up with clearing the driving snow.

The phone rang and rang. "Pick up, dammit."

The ringing stopped. No one had answered. Jake tossed the phone on the seat. Useless piece of crap.

Two cars had skidded off the side of the road, but instead of slowing, he sped up, his grip tight on the wheel. He had to make it; had to save the people who meant the most to him, and then put an end to the killer's life.

With the voice distortion, he couldn't identify the caller. Was it Joseph Francisco? Only why would he be at Peters? To frame him, again?

Had James found out about Maria and Peter as a couple? Is so, why involve Susan? Or himself?

Jake's tired, tumbled brain wasn't connecting the dots. One street away from Peter's house, he checked the time. Nine minutes had passed since the phone call, and is heart rattled in his chest. Would the killer hold him to the minute?

He needed to think, to plan. If he called Stanton now, the FBI could back him up. But if they showed their faces too soon, the killer might harm Susan and his friend.

He'd already lied to his boss, and that alone might get him canned. He loved his job. It was all he had, but Susan meant more to him than work.

Jake needed to see the killer's face, to help him decide what to do. After exiting the car, he raced toward Peter's house. With his head down, he ducked in between the houses, dodging right then left in case he was caught in a sniper's scope.

He wasn't sure what he'd do once he arrived, but he didn't want the killer to know when he arrived.

Jake patted his pocket for his secret weapon. He'd purchased mace to give to Susan, but she'd refused to take anything into the warehouse that could be construed as hostile.

He'd been a fool not to insist she go in protected, but Stanton had agreed with Susan. No weapons.

While he carried two guns, he figured whoever was after them would be clever enough to find both. The mace might be his only form of defense. With his bad leg, his ability to do hand-to-hand combat was limited, especially if more than one man was inside with her.

Jake stopped at the house next to Peter's, his heart pounding solidly against his ribs. Either he could knock on the front door and shoot the bastard the moment he opened up, or hope to surprise him at the back. He did, after all, have a key to Peter's house, which he bet the killer didn't know.

The back it was. The wind swirled around his feet and the snow fell in silent prayer. Lights blazed inside, but with the shades closed, he couldn't tell who was where. Damn.

Jake took one step at a time, stopping and scouting the area to locate the extra men who were supposedly surrounding the area, but he spotted no one. Had the killer been bluffing? It wouldn't be the first time a criminal lied.

With gun in hand, Jake slipped the key from his pocket with his other. As slowly as he could, he inserted the key into the lock. Muted voices sounded from inside. Good, they weren't expecting him.

The knob twisted, but when he pulled on the door, the wood didn't move. Shit. The deadbolt was on. Now what was he to do?

Jake stepped back, glanced up and studied the large, snow-covered tree next to the house that was taller than one of the bedroom windows. If he managed to climb up without falling, he'd have to break the window to get in, and the killer would hear him, which would defeat the purpose of the surprise attack.

Tick, tock. Time had run out. He prayed he could negotiate with the man to turn himself in. Maybe even have him rat out Joseph Caravello for some kind of deal—such as no death penalty. That wasn't likely though. If this man had killed several of the jurors, why would he be willing to surrender? For the notoriety? For the fame? If the caller had been Joseph, he'd never give himself up. James maybe, but never Joseph.

Time's up.

Jake raced to the front of the house, committing what his FBI manual would be called a very stupid act and rang the doorbell. Before the door opened, he tossed his gun in the bushes. The weapon might come in handy later.

As he waited for the killer to open the door, he held his hands up in surrender.

The door eased open. Jake kept his gaze straight ahead, and when James smiled and pointed a 9mm at his face, Jake's heart sank. That was not who he wanted to answer the door and not what he wanted to be staring down.

"Welcome." James' motioned he step past. "Gun, please."

So civilized. "Came without one and without backup, just as you requested. See? I can follow instructions."

His gaze raced around the room. Jake debated twisting around and trying to take him down, but with his bad leg, he might lose. James was stocky and strong. Jake was in pain and off balance. Not to mention, James held the weapon.

Jake halted once in the living room. Peter was gagged and tied to the chair. Shit. He'd be no help. Even though his right eye was swollen shut, and he had several cuts on his face, his friend was at least alive —barely.

He wondered where Maria was. Jake turned around. The gun remained raised. "Where's Susan?"

"In due time. In due time. Now sit on the sofa. We have things to discuss." So cool, detached, and sociopathic.

He never did like James. "What is there to discuss?"

"My immunity."

Jake had learned to act as if what a criminal told him was a reasonable demand. "From what? What have you done?" The words stung his throat.

"So far, nothing."

He didn't believe that lie. "Then why do you need immunity?" Jake wasn't sure why he was playing this game. Yes, he did—for Susan.

He should have called Stanton and told him to follow him. Christ. He didn't deserve to be an agent. Fear should be punching him in the face, but some kind of strange calm had taken over his body. He bet the composure would shatter if he learned Susan was dead.

"I need immunity because of what I'll need to do to get out of here. Okay, I might have assisted Dominick Francisco in finding some of the jurors, but that's all. I never killed anyone."

Sure, and the earth is flat. He could hear Susan saying all criminals claim they were innocent. "Why call me? Why not just leave Peter and Susan to fend for themselves? You knew I was on my way. You could have been long gone before I arrived."

James tilted his head to the side and shook it. "I have plans for you. Or rather Joseph Francisco has plans for you."

Francisco. He knew it. This was about revenge. That meant James planned on killing him. No surprise there.

"Mind if I see Susan before you carry out those plans?"

"Of course. I like to cooperate with the FBI."

"If you walk out right now, I'll make sure the FBI doesn't come after you, though you'll have to get your brother to buy into the deal. You've roughed him up pretty badly."

James didn't have to know he wasn't a member of any FBI team any more.

James leaned against the wall, all relaxed and confident. "Oh, he'll agree to anything I want. I have Maria."

Jake stole a glance at Peter fighting against his bonds, the fear pouring out of his eyes confirming what James had said was true. Jake fought to keep his hands unclenched and swallowed the urge to attack.

"Show me Susan. Alive. Then I'll do whatever you want." Or not.

"She's in there. Through the door. But don't expect her to greet you with open arms."

Jake launched off the sofa. The urge to strangle James overtook him. Two strides took him halfway to James, but then the cocking of the gun stopped him cold.

"See your woman first and we'll talk."

He took two deep breaths, thinking about his pistol in the ankle holster. Should he go for the weapon? Not yet. The best way to get the drop on James was from the other room.

"And keep the door open. Try anything, and I mean anything, and I'll kill her."

Jake believed him, though he was surprised he didn't add that Jake would be next in line to receive a bullet.

His palms sweated as he twisted the knob on the door to the den. He steeled his body for what he would see. When he pushed open the door, he froze.

CHAPTER THIRTY

Jake wasn't sure if Susan was still alive. She was bundled in a blanket on the sofa, either asleep or dead. He raced over to her, listening for James' footsteps to approach from behind for a rear attack.

As he knelt in front of her, he choked back a sob. "Susan?"

When she didn't move, he fumbled for a pulse, but his heartbeat drowned out hers—if she even had one. James chuckled from the doorway. "Is she alive?"

Asshole. If it was the last thing he did, Jake would take the man down. "I can't tell."

"A pity. I didn't do this to her, by the way."

Jake looked back over his shoulder. "Who did? Jack the Ripper?"

"I don't kiss and tell."

Smug bastard. Jake had to understand if she was alive in order to figure out his next move. He dipped a hand under the blanket and placed his palm over her heart. At the faint beating and warm skin, elation sped through him. He wanted to kiss her, hug her, and hold her, but giving away his feelings for Susan in front of James would add to the list of dumb moves. Indifference was the only emotion Peter's brother understood.

If he'd had his FBI issue phone, he could have pressed pound one on the keypad to call his boss without James even knowing. Too bad the throwaway didn't come with a GPS system. If the cell had one, someone could locate him, assuming they knew he was in trouble.

Jake stood and eased his way toward James. "You stuck to your word. She's here." He shrugged, praying his act of indifference was believable, despite his outcry of Susan's name. "Now what?"

Jake jabbed his hand in his pocket and kept his gaze lasered on James in an attempt to act casual. His fingers itched to pull out the mace.

"Hmm. I'm tempted to just leave and let you care for your woman and my brother, but then I'd disappoint my father."

Jake didn't react to the obvious attempt to get into a debate. "But the problem is that Mr. Caravello won't stop until his son's killer is destroyed, right?"

"You are perceptive. I really would like to leave, but your buddies will come after me for kidnapping, even though I didn't take Susan in the first place. You can ask her when she comes to. Did you know I found her naked?" His lips curled. "In the shed in my back yard. Tied up. Nearly frozen." He tapped is chest. "I saved her."

Likely story. "Why not call the police right away?" Through the doorway, Jake could see Peter wiggling, trying to get out of his bonds. Maybe he'd succeed if Jake could stall James long enough.

"And end my fun? Besides, I saw her as the perfect lure to get you here."

What a sick bastard. "So now what?"

James arm rose, the gun pointed right at Jake. The twitch in his cheek told it all. The fun stopped here. "Come with me."

That wasn't going to happen. Without hesitation, Jake dove halfway between the two of them and did a tuck and roll. As he righted himself, he shielded his eyes and sprayed mace upward.

James let out a yelp and stumbled backwards.

Go. Now.

He charged at James who was wiping his eyes. Jake too reeled from the spray in the air. Ramming his shoulder into James' gut, the two tumbled to the ground. His leg rebelled, stealing his breath, but he tucked away the pain. James let out a grunt. Using both hands, Jake grabbed for James' gun. Before he was able to wrest the weapon from his opponent's grasp, James swung his leg upward and smashed Jake's side. The impact pushed him off, forcing Jake to let go of the weapon. Damn. He'd been so close.

James swung the gun toward Jake. With a swift sidekick, Jake's foot met metal and bone, and James let out a yelp but kept his aim steady. He pulled the trigger just as Jake rolled to his left, the bullet splintering the glass window behind him.

That was a close call.

Before James had a chance to fire again, Jake vaulted toward James and landed on him. The force caused the gun to fly out of his hands and skitter across the floor. James pushed up on Jake's chest with one hand and slammed a fist into his face with the other, temporarily stunning him.

With Jake disoriented, James scrambled to his feet and raced toward the weapon. If he lost this fight, more than his life was as stake. Using every Academy lesson he'd used to good use, Jake managed to a stand and then kicked James's butt, which sent him sprawling. The sound of James' knee cracking on the floor sped up Jake's resolve and boosted his energy.

As James reached under an end table for his gun, Jake snatched the spare pistol from his ankle holster and shot—once, twice.

A splotch of blood colored James' shoulder. Then a second patch appeared on his side. Two for two, but neither wound appeared lethal. Damn it.

James turned and fired, the bullet hitting the mark. In Jake's arm. Shit. That burned bad.

James pulled the trigger once more. Jake expected the second hit to hurt, but he felt nothing. Had James missed?

Jake raised his arm to finish off James, but the target ducked just in time and raced out the room. Another shot rang out. Jake looked before he dashed out of the room to make sure James' wasn't waiting for him around the corner.

Footsteps pounded through the kitchen, and Jake went after him. He got off another shot, but the doorframe splintered instead of the man's body. Crap.

James was getting away, and with one hand clasped over the hole in his arm to stem the blood, Jake charged after him. As he reached the open door, he stilled.

If he went after James, who would get help for Susan? If James did have backup outside, Jake would be running into an ambush. Then where would Susan be?

A loud crash came from the living room. Peter.

He needed to help his friend first. He slammed and locked the back door to prevent James from returning with his small army. When he reached the living room, Peter's chair had toppled over with his head now on the floor. A large, bloody stain spread out on his chest.

"Hold on." James had shot his own brother. Christ.

He whipped out his cell and called 9-1-1, asking for two ambulances. Jake raced into the den to make sure Susan's condition hadn't deteriorated. She remained still as death on the sofa, but didn't seem any worse.

He needed to stop the bleeding in Peter's chest, and then attend to Susan. His own wound, he'd take care of later. Jake raced to the bathroom and grabbed two towels, and then charged into the kitchen for a knife to free his friend. In less than two minutes, he had Peter on the sofa, holding the towel firmly to the wound, his eyes glassy. He was going into shock.

"Hold on, buddy. Help is on the way."

Jake wanted to hold Susan, but he needed to watch Peter to make sure he didn't bleed out.

Jake dashed between the two people. Fearing he'd drop Susan if he moved her to the living room, he stroked her red cheek and kissed her nose.

"You're going to make it, I promise."

***

Stanton and Tom both charged into Susan's hospital room, and Jake jerked upright, his shoulder sending out a piercing stab.

"What the hell were you thinking?" Stanton shouted.

"I wasn't."

Jake hadn't sleep in God knows how long and his mind wasn't thinking clearly. His wound had been superficial, or so the paramedics had claimed. The hole sure hurt like hell for something to be called superficial. The fact the doctor had order an arm sling confirmed the bullet hadn't just grazed him. The through and through had taken some muscle with it. The doctor had checked his leg, which was healing, put a few stitches in his arm, and insisted he stay the night.

"You walked into a hostage situation without backup." Stanton got in his face. From the red blotches on his boss' cheeks, the man's blood pressure had hit two hundred. "Did you forget everything you learned at the Academy?"

Maybe. "I had exactly ten minutes to get to Susan and Peter before the bastard planned to kill them both. If I'd told you right after my phone call that I knew where she was, what would you have done in that time?"

"Told you to go, but we'd have had your back."

He scratched his bristly scalp. "I'm sorry. I let my heart take over my brain."

"No shit."

Tom pulled up a chair across from him. "I checked on Peter. He's still in surgery."

"Still?" How long did it take to remove a bullet?

Jake looked over at Susan. Her face was pale, but she was breathing on her own. The doctors were still unsure when she'd wake up—or if she'd wake up—but right now, Jake couldn't think about her dying. That option was unacceptable. He'd never forgive himself if she didn't make it.

"You do know this could cost you your job?" Stanton asked.

He wasn't up for doing battle with his boss. He'd gone against the rules. Fucked up. Almost cost the lives of two people he cared most about. "I know."

Wait a minute. *Could* cost him his job? He assumed he'd been booted out of the Bureau already for lying and breaching protocol.

"You'll get an Internal Affairs investigation for your actions."

"I expected as much." Not really. He assumed he'd walk away without a chance to explain. His job wasn't the big concern. Susan was.

Crap. He gripped the chair arms and raised his gaze to Stanton. "Maria Francisco. Has anyone found her? Or James?"

Stanton's red face stilled. "We didn't know she was missing."

"James said Peter would do whatever he asked of him because he *had* Maria."

Stanton's lip curled. "Aren't they half brother and sister? Why would he take her?"

"They are related via Joseph Caravello, but Maria and Peter want to get married. I'm guessing James didn't think much of the idea—nor did Joseph."

"Sure as shit the old man wouldn't be throwing the couple an engagement party anytime soon."

"No kidding."

Stanton's brows burrowed. "You said Joseph asked James to kill you for revenge of his son's death, and he wanted to do away with Peter because of his daughter's physical attraction to the enemy family?"

"Yes to the first part, if we can believe James. I'm only filling in the blanks on the second part."

The two said nothing more. Jake picked up Susan's hand and rubbed his thumb along her palm. In an even tone, he asked again about James.

"We have nothing." Stanton's cold response told him all he needed to know. The man had gone undercover.

A nurse poked her head into the room. "Sir?"

All three of them looked up. Jake knew why she was there. "How is he?"

"Mr. Caravello is out of surgery and in the ICU. I'll let you know when you can see him."

"Thank you."

Stanton placed a hand on Jake's shoulder. "I hope he makes it." All rancor was gone from his tone.

Jake nodded.

"When he's strong enough, see what he knows about this mess."

So much for the true sympathy. "Of course."

Stanton's phone rang. "Excuse me." He stepped into the hall.

Tom leaned over. "So what did the docs say about Susan? Was she injured in other way?"

"Besides the obvious few bruises, there was no assault. They're running a tox screen on her now. If I can believe James, she was exposed to the cold for some time. She might have some permanent damage as a result, but we can't tell until she comes to."

He didn't want to talk about Susan being naked and tied up. His blood pressure jumped thinking about the person who'd harmed her.

Stanton strode in. "Some good news. We received a warrant for James' house. When the team arrived, the housekeeper was taking care of two children. They were Thomason's kids. No Maria though."

Tom leaned back in the chair. "I'm happy they are safe. Now we need to find the bastard who took them."

"We're looking." Stanton motioned with his hand for Tom to come with him. "We've got some investigating to do, and I'll need your help, Tom, to check out a few things on the computer."

Tom squeezed Jake's shoulder on the way out who then closed his eyes and gave into the exhaustion.

Jake awoke with a start when his stomach grumbled. His mouth dry, he pushed back his chair. He needed food and a drink.

Jake had shuffled halfway to the door when he thought heard a groan and spun around. Susan's fingers were moving like she was typing, and the rapid eye movement under her lids made him believe she was coming too. He'd seen the signs before. Adrenaline pumping, he jetted back to the chair.

Visions of how they met returned. "Squeeze my hand, Susan."

He swore she did. Faint, quick, but there.

"That's good. Now open your eyes."

He wanted to pry them open, wanted her to see him, talk to him. She emitted small guttural sounds but couldn't seem to rouse herself.

"Susan."

He leaned over and kissed her forehead, her cheek, and then her soft lips. When her lids fluttered, his heart nearly stilled.

Her tongue peeked out of her lips. He sat up, grabbed the cup of half melted ice and pushed the button to elevate her bed. He held the cup to her lips as he squeezed her hand for reassurance. "Open up, please."

Her mouth opened and a sliver slipped into her mouth. She coughed and her eyes flew open.

He'd never been so happy to see anyone wake up. "Hi."

She blinked several times. "Jake?"

"That's me."

He grinned, and then laughed. He would have danced, but he didn't want to let go of her hand.

She licked her lips, not to tempt him he was sure, but to wet her mouth enough to talk. "How did I get... here?"

"That's a question I'm going to find the answer to."

"What happened to James? He saved me."

His fingers tightened their hold. "What do you mean? The bastard kidnapped you."

"Not him. He was so nice. He found me in the shed. I was so cold. The next thing I remember, I was in a warm, comfy bed. Then over breakfast, he told me Peter took me." She licked her lips again and took a sip of water.

A bed? Over breakfast? How had she come to be into her current state then? "Peter didn't take you. Did you see actually him?"

She closed her eyes and he thought he'd lost her for a moment. Her lids half opened. "No. That's what James told me happened. But wait. There's more. Before I finished eating, a masked man came into James' house. He struck him, then jabbed me in the neck with a needle before I could even get off the stool." Her gaze traced the ceiling. "Next thing I remember was waking up and seeing you." Her trembling lips quivered.

The pain and torment Susan had gone through was enough to send the sanest person over the edge. Jake wanted to protect her for life, but his actions never seemed to be enough.

God, he wanted get this bastard, or bastards. There was no doubt in his mind that James had orchestrated the whole masked man thing. The needle to the neck was too coincidental. The action smacked of Joseph Caravello.

He kissed her hand. "I'm sorry. I should have done more. If I'd just winged Dominick, you might not have been kidnapped in the first place."

"Shh. This is not your fault. I insisted on going into the warehouse alone."

True. "Remind me not to let you out of my sight. James is still out there."

"You really think James is behind this?"

He told he what happened at Peter's house.

"I wonder why he was so nice to me then."

"To make you believe Peter was guilty. To add to the frame."

"I can't believe I fell for it."

"You'd been traumatized. It's not your fault."

"I guess." Her eyes fluttered. "I'm so tired."

"Rest. We can talk later."

She squeezed his hand hard. "What about Craig? Is he okay?"

Jake smiled. "He's fine and back home with your mom. He too remembers little."

"Thank goodness." Her mouth opened for a second then closed. She'd fallen asleep and he hadn't told her how much he loved her.

"Agent Yarnell?"

He turned. Peter's nurse held up a hand.

"Yes?"

"You wanted to know when Mr. Caravello awoke."

"Thank you."

He took another glance at Susan. She needed the rest. He wouldn't be long.

***

About time Agent Yarnell left Susan's room. The cop standing guard wouldn't be a problem. The officer never asked for any identification from any nurse or doctor who'd stepped in her room.

What was the FBI thinking allowing a hospital cop to stand watch? This would be way too easy. He walked past Susan's room for the third time and peered in. Her eyes were closed, but he had no idea if she'd come out of her stupor. The amount of drugs pumped in her system might have killed her or merely put her in a coma for a while. Either way, she didn't have long to live. The needle in his pocket would see to that.

CHAPTER THIRTY-ONE

Susan opened her eyes and was disappointed Jake was not yet back from wherever he'd gone. She missed his calm, his encouragement, and his safety.

Her head drooped. She fought falling asleep again and needed something to prop open her eyes.

It didn't work. Whatever pain meds they'd given her was causing fatigue to grab hold. She gave in and closed her lids. That was better. To test her body's rate of healing, she wiggled her toes. They were still cold, but the rest of her body had warmed, or so said the nurse. Maybe she'd recover after all.

Footsteps sounded on the tile floor. She lifted her lids part way and spotted a white doctor's coat. Dr. Dalton? Had he heard she'd come to? She raised her gaze to meet the face of the man who'd saved her life. Again.

Oh, shit! Panic prickled up her arms and legs. It was James. She closed her eyes in order to think and to keep from letting him know she recognized him. She let her mouth drag open a little to make him believe she was asleep. Forcing her muscles to relax took all her concentration, but she would be no match for him if he tried something.

The footsteps stopped. His raspy breath barely sounded above her heart monitor. He must be looking down at her, trying to judge if she was alert or out of it. Would he see her heart beating frantically in her chest?

"Goodbye, Susan." His voice came out a whisper.

The deadly words nearly burst her heart. She couldn't die. Wouldn't die. Not without holding Jake one more time.

Summoning up every ounce of reserve energy, she forced open her eyes. Blood beat against her skull. James' back was turned. In his hand was a syringe that he was trying to put into her IV.

Dear God, no.

She sucked in a large breath, lifted both legs and swung them sideways. While she met with resistance from the tucked sheet, she was able to knock against his hard body, and the blow was enough to make him drop the needle.

He spun around. "You bitch."

From the quick widening of his eyes, he hadn't expected her to rouse. As he stooped to pick up the fallen needle, she tried to scream, but all that came out was a weak eek.

She had to move, had to get to the closed door. Jake said an officer was stationed outside, so where the hell was he?

She ripped the IV needle out of her arm and grimaced from the sharp stabbing. The light sheet was easy to slip off, but by the time she maneuvered her legs to the side of the bed, James was on top of her. His hand was wrapped around her throat, his thumb cutting off her air. She couldn't breathe.

He pinned her legs with his knees while he grabbed one arm over her head with his free hand. She punched his hard shoulder with the arm he hadn't secured. As much as she'd wanted to scratch his face and claw at his eyes, she couldn't quite reach. Damn it. She drew her arm back for another attack, but he tilted him head back, causing her swipe to miss.

Air. She needed air. Black dots floated across her eyes. Light headed, she couldn't fight him much longer. She flexed her leg to lift it, but his heavy weight held her down. She wanted to yell, wanted to live, wanted to tell Jake she loved him. Her brain fogged and her eyes rolled back into her head.

**

Peter was too groggy from the anesthesia to be of much help. All he remembered was that James had forced him to make the phone call to Jake that morning. He told him how two men had beaten him uncon-scious while James watched.

Jake's patience was nearing the end. James had stepped over the line. He leaned forward in the seat. "I knew something was off. You never would have called that early."

"You're right. James has Maria."

"I know."

"We have... to...find her." Each word seemed to exhaust his friend further.

He didn't need to give Peter any more stress. "We're trying to find her now. Rest. I'll be back."

"Find Ma..." And then he was out, blowing puffs in air into the room.

Good. Peter needed the time to recover.

Jake took the elevator down two floors. He slipped his arm out of the sling and tested the movement. It was stiff, but not bad.

He exited the elevator and glanced down the hall. His pulse raced. What the hell? No cop was in front of Susan's door—just an empty chair. Shit. Where the hell was he? Jake sprinted down the hall, narrowly missing an elderly woman holding onto her portable IV stand.

"Excuse me," he yelled over his shoulder after he nearly collided with her.

A nurse shouted from the desk. "Sir?"

Susan's door was closed. His throat turned dry and the blood beat against the back of his head. He moved his legs as fast as they would take him, but he needed to limp to reach her.

He twisted the knob. Thank God the door wasn't locked. When he burst into the room, his breath became more ragged, and fear nearly crippled him.

Had it not been for the bed bouncing and the man's shoulders moving up and down, he would have stilled. Given the fact the man was wearing a white coat, his first instinct was the man was giving Susan CPR, but the moment he moved to the side, Jake knew he was wrong. Dead wrong.

"Hey."

The man spun around, his eyes wide.

James faced Jake. "I see we meet again."

Jake's weapon was in his room. Shit. James let go of Susan, whipped back his coat and pulled his semiautomatic from his side holster.

Susan made some terrible choking sounds, and his gut nearly exploded. Adrenaline fueled his hate.

The small room provided little room to maneuver. Jake was within three feet of James, so he kicked his leg outward and smashed against James' arm. Too bad the man held onto the gun.

James laughed as he swung the gun back at Jake. "You don't have any mace now, do you?"

Instead of answering, Jake launched himself at James. In the tight confines of the room, there was no place for James to fall but on Susan. The bed screeched backwards, crashed into the IV stand and sent the metal monster plummeting to the ground.

Susan screamed. Jake wrestled for the gun as James tugged his arms downward. The weapon wedged between them. Jake's left arm lost strength, but he managed to get his knee between them.

The semiautomatic went off, and both he and James didn't move, his heart catching in mid beat. Footsteps rushed behind them, and then someone pulled him off James. Blood shot out near James' groin.

"Let me through," a male shouted from behind.

Stunned, Jake moved aside. He gaze shot to Susan who was rubbing her throat. Her face was blotchy and her breaths were too rapid. He wanted to comfort her, but the man's grip prevented him.

"Get her some help, dammit." Jake pointed at Susan.

The next few minutes were a blur. Two nurses insisted he come with them as a young woman wheeled in a gurney.

"I need to stay with Susan."

The nurses didn't seem to care what he wanted. "You're bleeding, sir. We need to patch you up."

Had he been shot?

A wheelchair appeared under his butt a moment later. Whoever pushed him must have driven at the Indy 500 for he arrived at a small room moments later, where the nurse instructed him to wait until the doctor arrived. So he waited. And waited. The air conditioning clicked on and chills crawled up and down his spine. Blood trickled down his arm where he'd been shot.

He debated racing out of there to check on Susan, but the warden outside the door would probably object.

He found some gauze pads on one of the counters and held the cloth over his wound to stem the flow. Fighting had not been on the list of acceptable activities in his condition, but he had no choice. James was killing Susan.

Needing to find out about how she was doing, he stood to tell the nurse outside he was fine, and that the injury was on the mend. Halfway to the door, he staggered and saw white. Damn. He was leaning against the padded examination table when the door opened.

"Please lie down, Agent Yarnell." A doctor, dressed in a green surgical uniform, frowned.

The kid didn't look older than twenty, but Jake obliged. He let the man clean and suture his wound again. Even though the doc had given him a topical anesthetic, the pricking irritated him.

Jake tapped the fingers of the uninjured arm. "Do you know how Ms. Chapman is?"

"No. Now don't move."

Come on, come on. This wasn't brain surgery.

Instead of issuing a complaint, he followed orders, but the man took forever.

"All done. Don't get in any more fights."

Jake sat up and winced. "I don't plan on taking up wrestling any time soon."

"The nurse will be in shortly to give you instructions."

He'd been through this routine once already. As soon as the doctor left the room, Jake snuck out. He had to find Susan.

The first stop was the registration desk. The woman sent him to the wrong place, but after a few more inquiries he eventually found Susan. The policeman who'd abandoned his position at Susan's room was back.

The guard stopped him as Jake tried to get past. "You can't go in, sir. Only doctors and nurses allowed."

"Then how did that killer get to her before? He wasn't any doctor."

The man's eyes widened. "I'm sorry about that, but I checked his ID and all seemed in order."

"Well, check this ID. Jake pulled his badge from his pocket."

He didn't wait for the man to answer and strode in.

Susan looked up and smiled. "Jake."

A sweeter sound he couldn't imagine. His heart beat fast against his chest. He loved her, pure and simple.

Jake stepped toward her. The nurses attending her blocked his path. One turned around. "Sir, can you come back later?"

From the way her upper lip rose, Susan didn't need him to watch. "Sure. I'll be in room 304."

"I'll call you," Susan said.

As he stepped outside, he faced the cop. "Don't let anyone but Dr. Dalton in there. Okay? Especially an Italian man with gray hair, in his early sixties. He'll be dressed in a very expensive suit. He wants to kill her."

The cop's mouth dropped open. "Yes, sir."

Jake went to his room to retrieve his phone and then dialed Stanton's number.

"Lowry."

"It's Jake. Anything on Maria?"

"Tom identified Francisco's real estate holdings as well as those owned by Caravello. I've sent my men to all three locations. I'll let you know what we find."

"And Joseph Francisco? Has he shown up?"

"Nothing yet."

"Thanks." Jake clipped the phone on his waistband and headed back to Peter's room.

His friend was still asleep when he arrived. Needles and tubes were attached to his arms and nose, and the monitors showing his vitals were stable.

As he turned to leave, he came face-to-face with Joseph Francisco.

CHAPTER THIRTY-TWO

Jake's pulse shot up, and every expletive he'd ever uttered came to mind. He had no gun, no mace, and a bum arm. Francisco would have come armed. All Jake had was surprise on his side. The glint of a knife clutched in Francisco's hand caught his attention. He wouldn't get in the way of the blade this time.

Go.

Attack.

Now.

With Francisco's back to the open door, Jake used his shoulder to plow into the man, sending both of them sprawling onto the hallway floor. Francisco's head slammed against the tile floor, and he let out a curse.

Fury unleashed every ounce of Jake's energy. He pummeled his fist into the man's face for Susan, for Peter, and for orchestrating the jurors' deaths.

Blood spurted from Francisco's nose. The old man didn't fight back, couldn't fight back. One arm was pinned beneath his body, the other flayed against Jake's good arm. Jake wouldn't let up until Francisco passed out.

Two sets of strong arms dragged him off the killer.

"Sir, stop fighting us."

When Jake saw the old man wasn't going to do battle, he relaxed. "Okay. I'm good." He shrugged off their hold and stepped back.

Francisco's eyes went wild, darting right and then left. He expected the old man to jump up and come at him again, but he lay there, still as death. Jake hadn't hit him that hard.

The two orderlies called for a gurney. In his humble opinion, the bastard didn't deserve to be patched up.

Jake faced one of the orderly. "Don't let him out of your sight. He's wanted by the FBI for the murder of several people."

The man's shoulders tensed, his eyes registering fear.

Joseph grunted something about not killing anyone. Right. Instructing his son to do the actual deed was the same as putting the knife in their chests himself.

Jake fumbled in his pocket for his phone. It wasn't there. Crap, he must have lost his cell in the fight. He didn't have time to search for it, so he stumbled over to the nurses' station where all eyes were on him.

"I need a phone."

The nurse's wide eyes told him he must look bad, but he didn't remember Caravello hitting him.

"Here you go, sir." She handed him the phone.

He called Stanton.

"Yeah?"

"Joseph Caravello came to the hospital with a knife to Peter's room. I happen to be there."

"Are you shitting me?"

"I wish I were. I gave him a bloody nose though. That's all. Come pick up the scum."

"On my way. And Jake?"

He leaned against the counter. The adrenaline rush was losing steam and the aches and pains were getting to him. "What?"

"Burroughs just called. They found Maria."

Jake's knees almost gave way. "How is she?"

"Dehydrated, but otherwise fine."

"Thank God." Peter would need Maria to help him heal.

He handed the phone back to the nurse and headed to Susan's

room, his head swimming. Was this nightmare really over? Could she get on with her life now?

He stopped in the hall and leaned against the wall to catch his breath. She could get on with her life. Would she thank him for saving her life, and then go back to work as if nothing had happened? Would she even think about the two of them—the amazing love making and the sharing of intimate details of their lives? Or their narrow brushes with death?

An ache, more severe than any bullet or blow, nearly crushed his body. What did he really want? He'd never had anyone who believed in him, so he'd built a shell around his heart so thick, he wasn't sure even he liked himself. Could Susan love someone like him?

Only one way to find out. Ask her. But first, he needed to tell her that he loved her.

Wow. Love. Was that what this desperation and need coursing through every cell in his body was called?

Yes.

He rushed down the hall to the elevator. This time when he reached her room, the cop was on duty in front. This time, he didn't give Jake any grief when he showed up. He'd been about to tell the cop his services weren't needed, that all of the threats to Susan's life were over, but given he hadn't eaten in who knows how long, he wasn't about to trust his decision making skills.

Could there be anyone else out there? With James in surgery, Dominick and Richard Thomason dead, and Papa Francisco in custody, had all the pieces fallen?

At the moment, he'd leave that piece of the puzzle to Stanton and the gang.

Susan's eyes were closed when he walked in, and from the even rise and fall of her chest, she was asleep. He slid into the chair next to her bed and took hold of her hand. Her skin was porcelain white. The stitches in her cheek were gone, leaving a long, red welt. He thought she looked beautiful, all relaxed and peaceful. The bruises that covered her neck would heal, but the fact they even existed jacked up his temperature once more.

His fists stung from ramming into Francisco's face, but the pain was the good kind of pain, all full of satisfaction and built up disgust. The throbbing reminded him he'd hurt the bastard who maybe had started this mess.

Her lids fluttered.

"Jake?" Her brows pinched, as did her pretty mouth.

"It's okay, sweetheart. It's really over."

"Over?"

"Yeah."

He told her about Joseph Francisco and how he was now in custody, or would be soon.

"And James?"

"I haven't heard if he's out of surgery. I don't think the staff is willing to tell me much of anything, given my recent outburst."

"I would have liked to have seen that fight."

"It wasn't much of a battle." He held up a finger. "I almost forgot. Stanton called."

She squeezed his hand. "Did something bad happen?"

He chuckled. "No. He's not always the messenger of bad news. They found Maria. She's fine."

Susan let go of his hand and relaxed back into the bed. "And Peter? How's he?"

"He'll mend."

Now came for the hard conversation. "I guess you'll be getting out of here soon and returning to your old life." His mouth turned dry. This was worse than being in front of his ninth grade class to give a required two-minute speech.

He leaned forward, expecting her to be excited at the prospect of entering into another trial. Instead, she turned her head to the side. Her eyes glistened and her mouth pinched.

"What's wrong?"

She turned back to him. "I've been doing a lot of thinking. When I was a little girl, I always wanted to please my father. He was my world. My dad was an attorney as I've mentioned before. Ergo, I wanted to be an attorney."

"I think many kids want to do what their parents do."

Not him. He'd wondered about the identify of his biological father, but the futile exercise always left him angry.

She wet her lips and his mind darted off in a different direction.

"I always like getting up in front of people and trying to persuade them that my ideas were right. I never planned on doing criminal law. When my father was shot by someone he'd put in prison, my world changed. Then some drunk driver plowed into Craig, ruining his life. I wanted justice and figured the best way to get it was to follow in my dad's footsteps." Her eyes turned all dreamy.

"And now?"

Her lips pulled back. "I have to rise above my frustrations and fears and do what I really wanted to do in the first place and not what would please others."

He had no idea where this was headed. "I need to buy a clue here."

"I want to teach. I want to stay away from the criminals, from the threats."

A smile tugged on his lips. "That's the first sensible thing I think you've said."

Her mouth dropped. "First sensible thing?"

He laughed. The sensation of joy creeping up his body was foreign, but a damn good one. "I mean about being safe."

Now she smiled. "What do you know about safety? You put your life in danger every day, protecting people."

He leaned back in his chair. "About that. I'm thinking of giving up the bodyguard business."

"You?"

"If the Bureau still wants me, I'd like to do homicide or something that would keep me in one place."

Her skin lost all color. "What are you saying?"

Damn. He'd blown it. His heart thudded in his chest. He'd never told anyone he loved them—at least not since after he'd turned six. *Spit it out.*

"That I love you and want to be by your side, not some stranger's."

Her mouth opened. Susan pushed up from the bed and surprised the hell out of him by throwing her arms around his neck. She leaned back and kissed him. "You do? You really, really do? Love me, that is?"

Isn't that what he'd said? Repeating those words would be hard—at least at first. "Yes."

"Me too."

He hadn't expected her to return his feelings. "You do?"

She ran a hand over his head. "Yes, silly. You are an amazing person; one who is principled, driven, caring, and loving. I want to be with you."

Before he had a chance to absorb everything she said, someone cleared a throat. Susan glanced up. The light in her eyes didn't dim, but the smile evaporated. She moved away from him, and he twisted around.

"Stanton." How much had he heard? If the upturn of his lips were any indication, quite a lot.

"I just checked with the doctor. James didn't make it."

He probably shouldn't be happy, but he was. Scum sucker didn't deserve to live. "And our other resident killer?"

"He won't be going anywhere soon."

Shit. "Surely, we have evidence tying him to the killings."

"You misunderstand. He won't be going anywhere because when you landed on Francisco, the knife he was holding cut his spine. He's paralyzed from the waist down."

Jake shut off the sympathy part of his brain. He didn't want to think about what he'd done to the man. "Pity. We'll prosecute him, won't we?"

"Oh, yeah. Tom's a genius. Or maybe I should give credit to Richard."

"Richard? How?"

"When Richard received the threatening phone calls, he recorded them. Tom was able to match Joseph's voice to the recording."

That wasn't enough. "We can't get him for killing the jurors?"

"That's the sweet part. Yes, we can. With the help of the forest rangers, we combed the area where you shot Dominick. We found his body—and his cell phone."

"And I bet by that smirk on your face that Tom was able to locate the call logs, which proved Dominick spoke to his dad."

"Yes. The timing of the deaths is too perfect. But the best one is the picture of you holding up Cho, along with one of Cho alive. I have no doubt Dominick Francisco stood outside the window to frame you."

He was truly exonerated. "That's great."

"We still have a little more work to do before we can bring Francisco to court, but we'll get him. Perhaps Maria knows something."

"Is she talking?"

"Oh, yeah."

Jake wasn't sure what else there was to say. He wanted to get back to the conversation with Susan. Stanton took the hint and eased out of the room.

"So, where do we go from here?" he asked her.

"I say let's get out of here. I'm sure once I get you home, I'll figure something out."

The glint in her eye brought him amazing peace and closure to his life. She'd been what he'd needed his whole life.

"Let's make it quick."

***

EXCERPT—FROM DANGER TO DESIRE

Don't forget to sign up for my newsletter to receive three free books, as well as up-to-date information on my stories. If you prefer to only receive notices regarding my releases, follow me on BookBub.

I hope you enjoyed Susan and Jake's story. Up next is FROM DANGER TO DESIRE.

Second chances are great until a killer comes between them.

Homicide detective, Derek Benally, thought his day couldn't get any worse after he spent all night processing a murder, but he couldn't have been more wrong. The phone call from his nephew telling him Derek's sister is dead unravels him.

Dr. Kelly Rutland is on the verge of a cancer breakthrough when she receives the horrifying news that her sister was in a fatal car accident. The cops ruled it accidental, but Kelly refuses to believe it was anything other than murder. She's determined to do whatever it takes to find the killer.

When Derek learns the woman he had never stopped loving has moved back to town, and that both of their sisters died on the same night, he reconnects with her. Little does he realize that seeing her again will send the killer in Kelly's direction.

Here is the first chapter.

Tampa Florida Homicide detective Derek Benally slammed his cruiser's door and scanned the crime scene. Streetlights along the I-275 entrance ramp flooded the main street. He ducked under the tape, his gray police issue, t-shirt plastered against his back. Damned humidity.

Cars honked on the busy thoroughfare and gas fumes mingled with the fishy smell of the bay, adding a measure of unpleasantness to what had already become an unpleasant night.

He halted at the scene and flashed his badge. The two officers guarding the body stepped back. The jumper lay broken on the concrete in front of the thirty-story Waters Edge Condominium. Derek looked up at the surrounding balconies, and his gut soured at the man's violent death.

Loosely covered by a bloodstained sheet, a hand and a foot stuck out at odd angles. Derek knelt next to the victim and studied the blood spatter that extended a good two feet to the street side of the body. Another nine inches and the victim would have soiled the stone fountain. Wouldn't the rich condo owners have had a fit over that desecration?

He shoved his hand in his pocket, squeezed his sage packet, and closed his eyes to center himself, to separate his logical mind from his emotions. He waited to learn if his spiritual guides would send down a hint about what had happened.

A low rumble grumbled in the sky. Could it be them? Anticipation sped up his pulse.

Flashes from the crowd broke his concentration—or had his guides cut the connection? Damn curiosity seekers. He needed help from above.

Did these gawkers actually think a photo of a covered body would satisfy them? Brain matter had oozed out from under than dead man's head, and from the bloody protrusion of the right femur, the victim's leg had been crushed in the fall. If they ever had an up-close look at a real dead body, they'd be sorry. They only looked good on TV.

He swatted away the bugs that landed around his eyes and nose. When one little bugger began feasting on his arm, he flicked the insect away.

Derek lifted the sheet covering the white male, careful not to touch the body. What a waste. Even after nine years on the force, he didn't like seeing the gruesome effect blunt force trauma had on someone.

He studied the building's balconies, trying to figure out why the body had come to rest so far from the condo? Assuming the man stepped off the balcony and hadn't leaped off the railing like a cliff diver, the victim should have landed closer to the entrance, not out by the road.

Given the body's location, suicide didn't seem to be cause of his death. Perhaps the man had been pushed. His pulse sped up at the emotional pain this victim must have experienced, and the implication of a possible murder prickled his skin.

Cars honked at the slowdown clogging the Interstate onramp in front of the condo. Damn rubberneckers.

Before Derek could make more mental calculations, Gonzalez, a new recruit, who had been the first on the scene, hovered over him.

Derek stood and looked down at the short, stocky officer. The young cop looked like a puppy dog—eager to please and happy to have a job. Ah, to be twenty-one again.

"The doorman ID'd him as Carl Vanderwall of condo 2104," the puppy cop said. "Given the location, I called the Captain." He puffed out his chest.

"And?"

The officer's baby-browns shot down to the sidewalk. "The Captain told me to tell you not to hassle the tenants too much." His voice faded at the last few words.

Derek bristled. He wanted to stop any speculation, especially since Gonzalez was new to the force. "I've never strong-armed anyone into talking."

The officer looked up with eyes wide and held up two hands. "Hey, don't shoot the messenger. He also said to remind you the Mayor lives in this high rise."

Like he gave a rat's ass. Derek nodded toward the balcony. "Anyone see him jump?"

Gonzalez motioned toward two teenaged girls sitting in the police car at the side of the building, away from the crowd. "They were leaving the library across the street when they saw him fall, but they couldn't say whether he was pushed or not. They remained calm at first, but then rushed to tell the doorman. They're pretty shaken up."

"Damn." Kids shouldn't be exposed to such horror. "Did the doorman see anything?"

"No, sir. He was attending to something at the desk when the man jumped. The moment he returned to his post, the girls raced up to him."

"Okay. I'll have a word with them. Did you call the medical examiner yet?"

"Sure did. He's on his way."

"Good work." He half expected Gonzalez's tongue to roll out and pant, but instead the new recruit shot Derek a toothy grin.

"And you notified the crime scene unit, right?" He couldn't be sure if procedure was cemented in his brain yet.

"Yes, sir."

Derek nodded, and then made his way to the witnesses. He whipped out his phone and called the precinct a few blocks away. Thinking the girls would feel more comfortable if a woman escorted them home, he asked for a female officer. He'd never been any good at handling females in a time of need.

A cool puff of rotten egg smelling wind pushed through the humid air, relieving the oppressive heat. The bay sure was in a bad mood tonight, belching algae bloom like a smokestack.

Derek stepped over to the cruiser where a beat cop stood watch. The two witnesses were huddled in the backseat—a blonde girl consoling a sobbing brunette. He couldn't be sure under the glare of the streetlights, but he guessed they were no more than sixteen or seventeen.

Derek dropped to his haunches and pulled out his notepad and pen. His pants bunched at his thighs, and he tugged on the fabric to ease the constraint.

The air conditioning poured out from the opened door, providing brief relief.

"Hi, I'm Detective Benally."

The blonde pulled out her iPod earplugs as the brunette sat up and froze, her eyes wide. He knew his six foot seven frame and bald head scared a lot of people, but he didn't know how to make himself look less intimidating other than to crouch down.

"Can you tell me your names?" He used as soft a tone as he could muster.

"I'm Carrie Wilman," the blonde answered.

"I'm Jennifer Mendez," the brunette said wiping the back of her hand under her nose and sniffling.

Derek pulled out a clean handkerchief and handed it to her.

"Thanks. He's really dead, isn't he?" the brunette asked.

"I'm afraid so. Can you girls tell me what you saw?"

The brunette spoke up. "We were crossing the street from the library to go to our car when I happened to look across the street. He was...in midair." She hiccuped a sob. "It was terrible. His arms were flapping and his feet were kicking." She squeezed her eyes shut. "I can't get the sight of him out of my head. When he hit the ground, he made such a loud thunk. Oh, God." She dropped her face into her hands and sobbed once more.

His heart lurched at her pain. She'd never forget the man's shattered body. He could still remember the first time he'd seen a fatal car wreck, and the horrific image had never faded.

Derek turned toward the more composed girl. "Did you happen to look up and see anyone on a balcony?" As in someone who pushed the victim?

"No," the blonde said.

It had been worth asking. "I've called for a policewoman to follow you home.

"Thanks," the brunette said, holding out his handkerchief.

Derek stuffed it in his back pocket, not knowing how else to comfort them. He glanced back at the street. The CSU team had arrived, their flashes lighting up the sidewalk in short bursts.

It was going to be a long, grueling night.

***

Seven frigging days of non-stop work and Derek still hadn't made any headway in the Vanderwall case. He had yet to figure out whether Carl had jumped from the high rise or had been pushed. The neighbors had offered no insight into the man's apparent suicide. His coworkers had claimed there was no way he'd take his life. They said he'd only invested a small portion of his money in market, and when it tanked, he'd remained calm, unlike so many of his clients.

Before Derek had a chance to decide his next investigative lead, the phone next to his bed rang. He dropped the dumbbells he'd been hefting and answered, slightly out of breath. "Benally."

"Uncle Derek," his nephew whimpered. "Mom's...Mom's dead. She's really dead. I don't know what to do." Billy's breath hitched. "She...she shot herself in the head."

The fear lacing his voice ripped at Derek's soul. His mind screamed a panic alert as his blood pressure skyrocketed. *Think. I'm a First Responder, dammit.* His nephew was fifteen. He could handle this. "Are you sure she isn't breathing?"

Good. *ABC.* Airway, breathing, circulation. A bullet to the head wasn't an automatic death sentence.

"She's not moving or anything."

His heart nearly jumped out of his chest. Rayne couldn't be gone.

"Call 9-1-1 and hold a towel to the wound, okay? I'll be there as fast as I can."

Anger clenched his gut. Derek grabbed his sage packet and squeezed hard, but his talisman failed to give him any solace.

"Hurry!" Billy cried.

Heart racing, he snatched his wallet, badge, gun, and keys. Once in the car, Derek dialed Billy needing to hear that maybe his nephew had overreacted; that his sister might be only slightly wounded, but the line was busy. Shit, that's right. 9-1-1 kept the caller on the line until help arrived.

Derek tossed his cell on the passenger's seat and sped down the tree-lined street. His fingers gripped the wheel too tight, and he over-corrected on the first bend, nearly clipping an oncoming car. A horn blared.

His sister couldn't be dead. There had to be a mistake. Billy was wrong. He had to be.

Derek turned the truck's AC on high, hoping the cool air would clear his head. After what seemed like an endless drive, he pulled in front of Rayne's house, hoping Billy might be playing a sick joke on him, something he'd done many times before. Unfortunately, the flashing ambulance lights confirmed the worst.

The call was real.

His muscles tightened as adrenaline shot to his heart, and a metallic taste tinged his tongue.

He cut the engine a second before another police car came to a stop behind him. A few neighbors stood outside their doors gawking, apparently not willing to miss out on the chaos.

Derek jumped out of his truck and raced up the drive. Oh, man. There was the pile of lumber he'd placed at the side of her house that he'd promised Rayne he'd build a new porch with. She'd bugged him for weeks to begin the project. This weekend he'd planned to start.

A lump caught in his throat as he swiped a hand across his eyes. She couldn't be gone.

Before he reached the front door, Officer Juan Sosa escorted Derek's nephew outside.

"Billy?" Derek scanned the boy from head to toe to make sure he too hadn't been injured.

His nephew looked up at him, his eyes red, his shoulders slumped. "Mom's d...dead." He hiccuped and his whole body shook, tearing Derek up inside.

Derek rushed forward and drew Billy to his chest, but his nephew didn't hug back, as giant sobs erupted from Billy's thin body.

Darkness clouded his brain as tears trickled down his own cheeks, and Derek grasped onto Billy for support.

His nephew pushed away and wiped the tears from his face. "Why did she do it? Why did she have to kill herself?" His lower lip trembled.

"I-I don't know." Derek's voice faded with the last word. "I need to see her." To make sure there wasn't something he could do.

Officer Sosa placed a hand on Billy's back. "Come on, son. Let's sit in the car. I'd like to ask you some more questions." He nodded to Derek as he escorted Billy to the patrol car.

Derek rushed inside Rayne's house and froze. His sister's lifeless body was on the floor in a pool of blood, and his gaze went to the gun in her hand.

His gun. *His* Glock. Suicide: the worse crime he could imagine.

Guilt swamped him. He shouldn't have lent the weapon to her, but she'd insisted.

A paramedic kneeling beside Rayne looked up and shook his head.

Derek nearly lost his morning bagel as a wave of depression, dark and heavy, nearly drowned him. He reached out to grab the table near the entrance to keep from losing his balance, and then fumbled for his sage packet.

"The child is his mother's son."

Derek spun around to see who'd spoken, but no one was there. Had his spiritual guides reached out to him? Or had he imagined the unearthly sounding words?

"Sir, are you all right?" the paramedic asked.

Derek turned back to the man kneeling on the floor. "I'm fine." Like hell he was. It took all he had to keep his voice even. He swallowed hard. "Have you determined time of death?"

"You'll have to wait for the medical examiner."

He knew that.

As if by magic, his long-time friend and Assistant ME, John Ayo, came in with his gear, followed by the CSU team, headed by Carson Stepping. The team, all dressed in white, looked like angels coming to claim their victim.

When both men offered their condolences, all Derek could do was nod at their offered sympathy.

He studied the position of Rayne's body. Despite the evidence before him, no way would she have taken her own life.

Ayo knelt down beside her and examined Rayne with a gentleness and thoroughness Derek appreciated. The doctor wrote detailed notes and took scrapings from her scalp and under her nails. He then helped direct one of the CSU techs taking photos of the body.

Minutes seemed like hours. Wanting to ask him to hurry, Derek nearly bit his tongue. The large black man didn't seem to notice his need to know.

Derek scanned the dining room. Nothing was broken. Nothing had been disturbed. There hadn't been an apparent attack, and his body nearly caved at the lack of foul play.

After what must have been at least half an hour, Derek's impatience got the best of him. "Do you have a fix on the time of death yet?"

Ayo let out a long breath and sat back on his haunches. "If I had to guess from the rigor, I'd say about twelve hours ago. Look here." John pulled Rayne's body toward him and pointed to the back of her neck. "See the lividity pattern? The bruising shows she died here."

Had he expected she'd been killed elsewhere, and then dumped back at her house? He could only hope. Suicide and Rayne were incomprehensible together.

Stepping's team continued to photograph the scene, while another woman he'd never met pulled out her tape measure and took careful measurements of the body's position in relation to the room.

When a hand grabbed his arm, Derek jerked.

"You can't stay here any longer, Derek." It was Sosa. "This is a crime scene."

He was well aware of the rules. He wanted to stay; wanted to make sure the team did everything they could to prove someone had killed his sister.

His friend tugged on his arm again. *Time's up*. Derek took one final look at the tragedy, turned, and followed his fellow cop outside. The sun's rays beat down on his face, and the air was unusually calm, as if nothing sinister had happened inside.

Miraculously, the neighbors had disappeared, almost as if the President has issued a nuclear bomb warning. Billy's face was pressed against the cruiser's window looking lost, and Derek's heart broke. Again.

He wanted to shut his eyes and pretend when he opened them, the nightmare would be over, that Rayne would drive in and laugh at the practical joke, and Billy would race by on his skateboard doing dumb-ass tricks like Derek used to do when he was Billy's age.

But he knew this horror was all too real.

Convinced Billy held the key to Rayne's death, Derek approached the squad car. Before he reached his nephew, the front door opened behind him.

"Benally," the familiar voice called.

Derek turned. Detective Seinkievitz, the primary on the case, motioned him inside. Glancing back at Billy, he held up his hand to indicate he'd be right back and followed the detective inside.

"Did you find something?" Derek clenched his fists at his side.

"Yup."

***

Kelly Rutland frowned when her door chimed out the first few beats of *Send My Regards to Broadway*. She'd just arrived home from having breakfast with a friend and wanted nothing more than to get out of her sticky clothes and take a shower.

With one hand on the doorknob, she looked through the peephole and forgot about the shower.

Two policemen stood back from the entrance. Heart pounding, she unlocked the door, and as soon as opened it, warm moist air smacked her in the face.

"Doctor Kelly Rutland?" a female officer asked.

Their cruiser sat in her drive. The officer's rigid stance made her muscles tighten. "Yes?" She swallowed hard.

"I'm Officer Carranza and this is my partner, Officer Oxtal. May we come in?" Both officers showed their badges. The male cop reminded her of Ichabod Crane while the female looked like a much younger version of the cop on that 80's TV show, *Cagney and Lacy*.

"Sure." This must be bad. Really, really bad.

They followed her to the living room. "I think you'd better sit down," Officer Oxtal said, sounding like the funeral director who'd buried her dad.

Kelly's legs nearly buckled. "What's happened?" Ugly, sludgy dread moved through her veins as she dropped into the nearest chair.

The two officers remained standing, backs ramrod straight, and for one hysterical moment, she wondered if they were getting ready for inspection or a firing squad. They said nothing. Jesus, why didn't they answer her? "Tell me what happened."

Finally, the Cagney look-alike took a step forward and twisted her fingers into a knot, her eyes full of sympathy. "I'm really sorry to have to tell you, but your sister, Stefanie –"

Kelly's vision blurred, and her breath caught in her throat. Not Stefanie. No!

"Was in a fatal car wreck last night," the cop finished.

"That can't be!" Kelly shot out of the chair as a giant sob caught in her throat. "I don't believe you. St-Stef can't be—" She couldn't say the word. Couldn't even think it.

These people were lying. Stef would walk through the door any minute now and—

"I'm sorry," Officer Oxtal said.

Kelly grabbed her stomach to calm the sharp jabbing in her abdomen. "How? When?" A gush of tears poured down her cheeks as a low keening sound came out of her mouth. "Nooo. It can't be." Kelly swiped a hand under her eyes, but the flow of tears wouldn't stop.

"The roads were pretty slick last night. From the length of the skid marks on the pavement, she was going close to ninety when her car flipped over a guardrail on the Crosstown Expressway. I'm very sorry."

His eyes spoke the truth—a truth that clawed at her heart. Kelly wanted Stef next to her, warm, happy, alive.

Another piercing stab shot straight to her belly. God, this couldn't be true. She sniffled, but her crying wouldn't cease. "Was she run...run off the road? Was another car involved?" The eyes of the officers never changed. She hadn't misunderstood. "There's no way she'd be speeding unless someone was chasing her." An evil darkness slid down her spine, taking her breath away.

"We're still investigating."

Kelly raced to the kitchen counter and grabbed a handful of tissues. She blew her nose and swiped her cheeks clean, but the ache continued to gnaw at her. With her arms wrapped tightly around her waist, she headed back to the sofa. She stopped short, and then spun toward them. "What time was the accident?" She needed facts. Needed the focus. Needed anything except for this awful biting pain.

She reached up and whipped off her ponytail holder, the band's constraint oppressive.

"The medical examiner put time of death at approximately eight thirty last night."

"Last *night*? Why didn't you notify me earlier?"

His gaze dropped to the floor for a split second. "We couldn't find any ID on her. At least at first. Her cell had wedged under the front seat. Once we located it, we called the last number, but it went to voicemail."

Her mind ceased to function for a moment, the horror too much to bear. Voicemail? Oh, God. She'd turned off her cell right after she spoke with Stef. "I... I did speak with her on the phone around eight. I asked her to go see a movie with me, but she...she said she was on her way to visit a friend who wasn't feeling well." Kelly swallowed the lump in her throat.

The policeman pulled out his pad, and her gaze followed his movements. His fingernails needed cleaning, and his right thumbnail was jagged.

"Do you know the name of this friend?" he asked in a robotic monotone.

Agony squeezed her heart as Kelly shot her gaze to his expressionless face. "No. Yes. I —" God, she couldn't think. Her mind refused to focus. She rubbed her forehead with her palm. Then the name came to her, as it had from Stef's mouth many times. "Rayne Anderson. She's a trial attorney in town."

"Rain? As in R-A-I-N?" His pen hovered above his pad—a gnarly, tooth bitten pen. His brows pointed southward.

"No." She was losing her mind. She never noticed quirky details like dirty, chipped fingernails or chomped-on pens. Maybe she'd entered some alternate reality and Stef wasn't really dead. Maybe all of this was an illusion caused by heat exhaustion.

"Ma'am?"

She looked up at his expectant face. Reality slammed into her again. "No. That's not right."

"Excuse me?" he asked.

Stick to the facts. "I think she spells it, R-A-Y-N-E."

He jotted down the information before glancing up. "Perhaps your sister was running late and driving too fast for the wet conditions."

"That's bullshit! My sister would never drive that fast."

"Ma'am—"

"Oh, no." Bile raced up her throat as she fumbled for the chair for support and slid down.

"What is it?" The cop took a slight step forward. This time he sounded less like a robot and more like a human who cared.

The End

ABOUT THE AUTHOR

Love it HOT and STEAMY? Sign up for my newsletter and receive MONTANA DESIRE for FREE. Click here

OR Are you a fan of quirky PARANORMAL COZY MYSTERIES? Sign up for this newsletter. Click Here

Not only do I love to read, write, and dream, I'm an extrovert. I enjoy being around people and am always trying to understand what makes them tick. Not only must my romance books have a happily ever after, I need characters I can relate to. My men are wonderful, dynamic, smart, strong, and the best lovers in the world (of course).

My Paranormal Cozy Mysteries are where I let my imagination run wild with witches and a talking pink iguana who believes he's a real sleuth.

I believe I am the luckiest woman. I do what I love and I have a wonderful, supportive husband, who happens to be hot!

Fun facts about me
(1) I'm a math nerd who loves spreadsheets. Give me numbers and I'll find a pattern.
(2) I live on a Costa Rica beach!
(3) I also like to exercise. Yes, I know I'm odd.

I love hearing from readers either on FB or via email (hint, hint).

Social Media Sites

Website: www.velladay.com
FB: www.facebook.com/vella.day.90
Twitter: velladay4
Gmail: velladayauthor@gmail.com
Tiktok: Velladayauthor1

ALSO BY VELLA DAY

SILVER LAKE SERIES (3 OF THEM)

(1). <u>HIDDEN REALMS OF SILVER LAKE</u> (Paranormal Romance)

Awakened By Flames (book 1)

Seduced By Flames (book 2)

Kissed By Flames (book 3)

Destiny In Flames (book 4)

Box Set (books 1-4)

Passionate Flames (book 5)

Ignited By Flames (book 6)

Touched By Flames (book 7)

Box Set (books 5-7)

Bound By Flames (book 8)

Fueled By Flames (book 9)

Scorched By Flames (book 10)

(2). <u>GODDESSES OF DESTINY</u> Paranormal Romance)

Slade (book 1)

Rafe (book 2)

Will (book 3)

Josh (book 4)

Box Set (books 1-4)

Jace (book 5)

Tanner (book 6)

(3). <u>WERES AND WITCHES OF SILVER LAKE</u> (Paranormal Romance)

A Magical Shift (book 1)

Catching Her Bear (book 2)

Surge of Magic (book 3)

The Bear's Forbidden Wolf (book 4)

Her Reluctant Bear (book 5)

Freeing His Tiger (book 6)

Protecting His Wolf (book 7)

Waking His Bear (book 8)

Melting Her Wolf's Heart (book 9)

Her Wolf's Guarded Heart (book 10)

His Rogue Bear (book 11)

Box Set (books 1-4)

Box Set (books 5-8)

Reawakening Their Bears (book 12)

OTHER PARANORMAL SERIES

PACK WARS (Paranormal Romance)

Training Their Mate (book 1)

Claiming Their Mate (book 2)

Rescuing Their Virgin Mate (book 3)

Box Set (books 1-3)

Loving Their Vixen Mate (book 4)

Fighting For Their Mate (book 5)

Enticing Their Mate (book 6)

Box Set (books 1-4)

Their Huntress Mate (book 7)

Craving Their Mate (book 8)

PACK WARS-THE GRANGERS

Meant for them (book 1)

Meant for wolves (book 2)

Meant for forever (book 3)

Meant for her (book 4)

HIDDEN HILLS SHIFTERS (Paranormal Romance)

An Unexpected Diversion (book 1)

Bare Instincts (book 2)

Shifting Destinies (book 3)

Embracing Fate (book 4)

Promises Unbroken (book 5)

Bare 'N Dirty (book 6)

Hidden Hills Shifters Complete Box Set (books 1-6)

CONTEMPORARY SERIES

MONTANA PROMISES (Full length contemporary Romance)

Promises of Mercy (book 1)

Foundations For Three (book 2)

Montana Fire (book 3)

Montana Promises Box Set (books 1-3)

Hart To Hart (Book 4)

Burning Seduction (Book 5)

Montana Promises Complete Box Set (books 1-5)

Novellas:

Montana Desire (book 1)

Awakening Passions (book 2)

PLEDGED TO PROTECT (contemporary romantic suspense)

From Panic To Passion (book 1)

From Danger To Desire (book 2)

From Terror To Temptation (book 3)

BURIED SERIES (contemporary romantic suspense)

Buried Alive (book 1)

Buried Secrets (book 2)

Buried Deep (book 3)

The Buried Series Complete Box Set (books 1-3)

A NASH MYSTERY (Contemporary Romance)

Sidearms and Silk(book 1)

Black Ops and Lingerie(book 2)

A Nash Mystery Box Set (books 1-2)

STARTER SETS (Romance)

Contemporary

Paranormal

www.ingramcontent.com/pod-product-compliance
Lightning Source LLC
Chambersburg PA
CBHW020254200626
46816CB00001BA/289